Sign up for our newsletter to hear
about new and upcoming releases.

www.ylva-publishing.com

OTHER BOOKS FROM LEE WINTER

The Red Files

BOOKS IN THE SERIES THE LAW GAME

Requiem for Immortals by Lee Winter
Archer Securities by Jove Belle
Daughter of Baal by Gill McKnight
Evolution of an Art Thief by Jessie Chandler
If Looks Could Kill by Andi Marquette

THE LAW GAME - BOOK ONE

Ylva

REQUIEM FOR IMMORTALS

BY LEE WINTER

ACKNOWLEDGEMENT

It takes a huge leap of faith to green-light a novel about a lesbian assassin cellist. Astrid at Ylva Publishing miraculously said yes, and allowed me to breathe life into Requiem. Thanks from the bottom of my heart for that decision, which changed so much for me.

My novel would not exist without my South African violinist mate, Milena, whose tales from the dark side of orchestras greatly enriched this book. She also helped find the key compositions that defined my cellist's musical soul perfectly.

I would not have stayed sane without my beta reader Charlotte filling me with encouragement at every turn.

Thanks, finally, to the wordsmiths Sheri and Blythe, who poked at and massaged my words until even the perfectionist Requiem would be impressed. And that's saying something.

DEDICATION

To Milena, a music immortal whose dark genius inspired every word.

Prologue

To say Requiem felt nothing was incorrect. A common misconception about those in her line of work.

Disdain was not nothing.

She adjusted her black leather gloves, ensuring they sat snugly in each indent between her fingers.

Requiem circled the barren room. The concrete floor was lit by a dust-filtered arc of moonlight streaming through the cracked window. With a measured step, she moved to the centre and studied the timber walls, which were as wet as the floor. She crouched and placed a large box on the ground. From it, she removed a Chinese paper lantern. Some people called them wish lanterns. Her father had bought one for Requiem when she was a little girl. Together they had made a wish and watched it sail into the night sky, propelled by its naked flame until it disintegrated and fell back to earth in pieces.

This lantern was made of light white paper that encased a bamboo ring with a tiny fuel cell in the centre. A teepee of six long-burning incense sticks had been stuck to the bamboo frame, pointing toward the fuel cell.

Requiem lit the flame and checked that each incense stick was also ablaze. They contained a resin that gave off a unique aroma. As the lantern rose, she stepped back. It was beautiful. Like the perfect stillness of a lake at dawn or the soft curve of a woman's bare breast.

It bobbed against the dusty ceiling, casting an ominous glow over the room. After watching it for a moment, she turned and left, closing the door firmly behind her.

Requiem slid onto her motorcycle, a Kawasaki Ninja H2, and pulled her small, silver MP3 player from her vest pocket. She pressed play, verified on the screen that the volume was at exactly the level she desired, and then put the earbuds in. After she zipped up her leather jacket and slid on her helmet, she revved the engine and roared away.

The soul-cleansing strains of Arvo Pärt's *Fratres (String and Percussion)* played on.

Three days later, Melbourne's *Herald Sun* reported that a man, found in the hogtied position, had been burnt to death in a small room in an abandoned building. Squatters had stumbled upon his remains and alerted police.

The newspaper noted that, over the past seven weeks, the derelict industrial estate had been targeted by an arsonist who had set small, contained fires. So, on the night of the blaze, fire units had not responded to reports of another incident. They were unusually busy, and it was deemed a waste of resources.

Dental records determined that the deceased was a career criminal wanted for the torture and assault of the daughter of a Melbourne crime family boss, Carlo Trioli.

The Victorian Arson and Explosives Squad told the media they were initially baffled after discovering a small, melted, plastic substance in a room that had been doused in petrol. In addition to the petrol fumes, there was also a distinct smell they couldn't place.

Herald Sun police sources later identified the plastic as being from a fuel cell commonly used in wish lanterns.

"Someone clearly got their wish for this individual," a source said. "Investigations are continuing."

CHAPTER 1

Natalya Tsvetnenko glanced around the packed concert hall, seeking one face among many. The July mid-year launch of the Victorian Philharmonic Orchestra's program was taking place on an unseasonably warm night and had attracted the who's who of Melbourne's cultural elite. And, much to her satisfaction, it had lured in a particular reclusive chemical entrepreneur.

Uli Busch was an enormous man. The CEO of a German corporation, BioChem Farming Solutions, used a polished silver cane to walk and wheezed with every step. His sway was exaggerated owing to two knee replacements and, so rumour had it, a once badly broken back.

Natalya drew her gaze back to her sheet music, listening intently for the end of the movement. She lifted her bow, placing it precisely, and drew a deep, guttural growl from her cello.

Four minutes, twelve seconds later, she paused as the lead violinist began her solo.

Her gaze drifted back to Busch's ruddy face.

One might think he would be an exceptionally easy target to erase from the mortal coil. Natalya knew better.

It wasn't that he rarely left his luxury yacht, which was moored in a different location each day. Natalya had a well-placed insider within Victoria's close-knit yachting fraternity. She already knew what he had for breakfast (nine sausages, four buttered Brötchen, and a black coffee), how often he washed his 4XL Y-fronts (not often enough), and which high-class escorts he preferred (Sasha on Fridays, random redheads on weekends).

No, it was his bodyguards—a quartet of mean-eyed ex-Mossad agents who had been so ruthlessly trained that everyone in her business gave them a wide berth. Facing just one of these vicious rottweilers would be testing. But four?

Well. She did enjoy a challenge. At least, her lethal alter ego certainly did.

Natalya had seen a lot of Busch over the years. The billionaire happened to be a devoted classical music fan. His collection of official live recordings was reputed to be the finest anywhere. Every major orchestra in the world had been graced with his imposing presence at least once every season.

His need for bodyguards had a lot to do with how Busch made his money. He liked to bulk-buy any pesticide outlawed by a country for next to nothing. Sometimes, instead of purchasing it, they would pay him to destroy it. Instead, he would on-sell it to Western countries which hadn't yet implemented the bans Europe had, or poorer nations susceptible to bribery.

When things got too hot, such as BioChem being linked to too many birth defects or farm worker deaths, he'd move on to the next unwitting nation, rinse, and repeat.

At the moment, Busch's obnoxiously named yacht, *Breakin' Wind*, was moored off Victoria, which meant he was busy selling his toxic wares to Australians. And that, in turn, explained why Requiem now had a wealthy Australian client with a farmer brother who was on life support after he'd tested BioChem's newest pesticide.

The client needed Busch to know exactly what his brother had endured. He had sought out Requiem because two previous assassins had met ends too grisly to be explained to their loved ones. The client had learned a valuable lesson about settling for less than the best.

She had already anticipated this and prepared accordingly.

Busch, Natalya knew, had a special fondness for Tchaikovsky, which was the Victorian Philharmonic's theme for its new season. A theme Natalya had casually suggested four months ago when she'd heard of the second assassin's failure.

If she'd been wrong about the client likely approaching her, it hardly mattered. She liked Tchaikovsky well enough to play him all season.

Natalya snatched glimpses of Busch in the VIP box throughout the rest of the concert, his beefy hand mopping his brow with a white handkerchief.

She rose with the rest of the orchestra as they duly marked their respect for the composer, taking in the ecstatic applause. Normally, Natalya would be on a

4

high from performing. Tonight, though, she was in a rare and uncomfortable position: she was mixing business with pleasure for the first time.

The question remained, which was the business, and which the pleasure?

In her twenty-four years of dual careers, she had never found an answer for that. Each had highs that were unmatched.

She packed up her cello, nodded to her colleagues who were buzzing about the after-party, and then asked the VPO's security guard to lock her instrument away for a few hours. She reached for a glossy, black handbag she'd prepared for the occasion. Natalya removed from it her MP3 player, pressed play, inserted the earpieces, and slowly walked the two blocks to the VIP after-party.

With each step, as Arvo Pärt emptied her mind, she shed Natalya Tsvetnenko and became Requiem. Her eyes focused. Her expression flattened out to neutral. Her mind replayed over and over what she had to do, sharpening, homing in on the most dangerous aspect—the last thirty seconds before Uli Busch would take his final breath.

She would kill one of the most protected men on earth in front of his vicious lapdogs, and no one would say a word. Busch would probably smile at her, never knowing he'd heard his last Tchaikovsky.

Pedestrians stepped away from Requiem as they neared her. She was peripherally aware of them but did not make eye contact. No better than cattle. Slow. Blinkered. Weak. Telegraphing their every move.

She did not even consider herself to be a member of the same species.

Calmness settled over her, and her movements became liquid as she smoothed out any errant thoughts.

A block from the venue, she stopped at a bench, removed her earphones, and sifted through her bag. She pulled out a small pearl ring from a protective box, and positioned it on her left, middle finger. Sliding the bag back over her shoulder, she resumed walking.

The after-party was taking place at Nova, a spacious, modern, inner-city nightclub, supposedly the hottest "it" spot in town this month. It was the closest place to the VPO that could easily handle the swell of 400 dignitaries expected tonight.

Nova was wedged between a kebab shop and an Italian restaurant and had a rabbit's warren of rarely used back alleys behind it. Only the street cleaners knew where this tight tangle of back streets went, and few people ever had a need to use them.

At night, the darkened area was silent, save only for the faint rumble of traffic from the main road. Not so at Nova.

The theme inside the club was *Phantom of the Opera*, and Requiem had to admire the work that had gone into the decorations, even though it seemed a baffling choice for a Tchaikovsky season. She supposed the party planner's limited imagination on musical themes could only extend to the populist. Either that or a long-dead Russian composer was considered too uncool.

Ghostly white masks hung from fishing wire at different heights from the ceiling. Waitresses swished by with smoking cocktails as the music thumped around them. The venue's corners were as dark as tar, giving ready hiding places to those who might need them. She would have to be exceptionally careful.

Busch stuck to drinks supplied by his bodyguards. Wise. Especially given several assassins over the years had attempted to get to him through his food or drink. She sneered. How unoriginal. Far too easy to anticipate.

The German usually stayed at these things for four or five drinks, no more. Requiem picked her position and never took her gaze off his face. Waiting.

"Why, Natalya!" a perky voice said beside her. "What a lovely ring. I've never seen it before. Wherever did you get it?"

Requiem snapped her head around, schooling her features into a pleasant mask. Amanda Marks. First Violinist. High priestess of the social media crowd and adoring arts luvvies.

She glanced at her ring and back at Marks. "An associate," Requiem answered honestly. "Who wished me well." She shot her a thin smile.

"Oh." Amanda pouted. She probably hoped the story came with a salacious romance. The irritant opened her mouth to ask more, but Requiem had at last spotted her cue.

Busch grunted, muttered something to his closest bodyguard, and eased his thick jacket off his shoulders. Behind him stood a man with sharp eyes who took it.

Show time.

"Do you…" Amanda began.

Requiem waved towards her ear, feigning being unable to hear over the music, which had turned into some not-even-slightly-music techno mess.

She stalked away, letting the violinist get back to her adoring groupies who were far too old and immaculately dressed to be asking for selfies. Not that it stopped them. As she left them, her gaze fell on one woman in her early to mid-thirties with brown hair and fine features.

This one was watching everything with an awed expression, as though she didn't get out much. Since she was within the periphery of Marks's posse, the woman's judgment was clearly flawed. Suddenly, the mousy creature turned, and their eyes met. Then, equally suddenly, she smiled at Requiem. For no reason whatsoever.

Requiem paused in surprise. What had possessed the woman? Did she just randomly smile at strangers? Was this another of those maddening, socially expected female things?

Requiem dismissed her and strode onwards to her goal. She forced herself not to quicken her pace. She headed into a darkened area, lit only by a green fire escape "exit" sign.

Requiem looked around again. Nothing but a deserted, dead-end corridor vibrating faintly with the background bass thump of the (non) music from three rooms over.

Still in the filmy, long, black evening dress she had performed in, she dropped easily to a crouch. She turned her hand face up, rotated her "pearl" ring, and gently unscrewed the hollow bauble, leaving only a flat, round base with a tiny, threaded ridge.

In the centre, jutting up from this base, was the thinnest needle that money could buy—almost invisible to the human eye and no longer than two grains of rice. Such needle nibs were remarkably easy to acquire—one only needed to find a pharmacy selling diabetic supplies.

Taking a deep breath, she reached into her bag, opened a small vacuum-sealed container, and gently rolled a gel capsule onto the floor. It was the size of a pill, but its contents—a small amount of liquid—were anything but medicinal.

Requiem flipped her hand and lowered the tiny spike until it pierced the capsule's thin skin. She wiggled her hand slightly, ensuring the tip was liberally coated by the liquid within. She reached for the tweezers in her bag and with painful slowness pulled the gel pill from the wet needle tip. She dropped the tweezers and pearl bauble back into her bag.

Requiem rose, cautiously keeping her hand face down as though she were about to pat a dog. She kicked the gel pill into a gap in the old timber floorboards.

As she walked back to the party and made her way to her conductor, Anthony Lyman, she was careful to avoid any jostles. At least it looked like she was headed towards Lyman. As it happened, he was talking to Busch.

The sharp scent of the German's perspiration filled her senses. Four suspicious ex-Mossad agents snapped their gazes toward her to assess the possibility of threat. They relaxed when the conductor waved her over and introduced her as *his* "prodigiously talented cellist." He did this condescending routine over the VPO's women every time he had a VIP to impress.

For once, she didn't mind. It suited her purposes.

"Now, Natalya," Lyman continued, "have you met Mr Busch yet? Mr Busch, Natalya Tsvetnenko." The hopeful look in his eye told her he was desperate to bail on the man. Her nostrils twitched at his steep body odour, and she understood only too well Lyman's eagerness.

"No, we haven't met." She smiled and held out her hand to shake Busch's. "It's an honour."

"Well, I must mingle," Lyman said hastily and scuttled away. Requiem ignored him, focusing her entire being on this moment. Blood rushed in her ears, her heart thumped faster. She controlled her breathing, and a soothing coolness settled over her.

Busch shook her hand firmly, his sweating, meaty grip engulfing her fingers.

She smiled again, hiding her revulsion, and casually brought her left hand up under the fleshy forearm of the hand shaking hers, presidential style, and then pressed firmly.

The needle pushing into his flesh from her ring was so fine it was highly unlikely he felt it. She exhaled slowly as Busch merely smiled benevolently at her and started to talk.

"Your favourite composer," Busch asked, pinning her with a stare. "Who is this? Why is he this?"

She carefully lowered both hands, acutely aware of the position of the lethal needle nib, and studied his white sleeve. There was about a thirty percent chance of a tell-tale pinprick of blood being left behind as the needle withdrew.

No red spot appeared.

"Arvo Pärt," Requiem replied, satisfied. "A modern composer who fills the soul that is empty, and empties the soul that is full."

He looked at her, clearly startled by her answer. She gave him another smile, mentally ticking away how many seconds the toxin had been pumping around his system, doing its damage. It was the most fast-acting poison known to man. It was completely natural, but unlike a snake or spider bite, there was no cure. A single drop could kill ten men.

Very soon, Uli Busch's breathing would become impaired. A little after that, the mere act of inhaling would start to feel impossible.

By the time he fell to the floor, twitching in what might look like a seizure, his entire diaphragm would stop rising and falling with a paralysis that forced a person to hold his breath forever.

That's when the terror would strike—and, if she calculated correctly, it would be exactly what a young farmer on a wheat station felt when he, too, discovered he could no longer draw breath. The panic at not knowing what was happening. The horror of wondering if this was his last moment. BioChem's CEO was moments away from becoming intimately acquainted with his victims' pain.

Busch turned, barking for his men to provide him more wine. He turned back, mouth opening, most likely to offer her a drink, but Requiem was already slipping away. Steadily she walked, ignoring the greetings of other orchestra members as she disappeared into the remote fire exit passage.

Requiem gingerly reattached the pearl bauble over the deadly needle, then slid the ring off, put it in the container, and sealed it. Under the light of the neon green exit sign, she dropped it in her bag, and then rapidly dressed herself in leathers, boots, and gloves.

She had tested the fire exit two nights ago for an alarm. There wasn't one. She eased the door open, slung her bag over her shoulder, and slipped out into the darkness.

Halfway down the fire escape, she heard the first shout for an ambulance. Good luck. Busch would be dead before it arrived; possibly before they even placed the call.

When they examined his body, they would see no entry wounds.

She navigated the twists and turns of the back alley to find her Ninja H2 waiting for her, crouched beneath a lone security light. The moths darting all around provided a mottled lighting effect to the area—nature's own mirror ball.

She'd planned ahead with her Ninja. If Busch's rottweilers actually got a clue, she would need a demon of a machine which topped 400 km/h. Even if they didn't catch on, Requiem, unlike Natalya, travelled no other way.

She stowed her bag in a small custom compartment at the rear of the motorbike, slid onto the seat, and settled. By rote, she reached for her MP3 player. Her maestro would strip any mess from her mind, tucking away unschooled thoughts like errant hairs behind an ear, and ground her.

As she lifted her helmet, she saw it. The faintest movement glinted in the shine of the helmet's glossy black paint. Requiem reacted instantly, diving from her bike and rolling away just as a figure in freefall dropped from a drainpipe and landed lightly a foot away.

How the hell had the rottweilers worked it out? This particular quartet's skills lay in torture and knife-work, not in grasping the complexities of a brilliantly conceived plan. Requiem was irritated that somehow she'd given herself away. She must have made a mistake somewhere. That did *not* happen.

At least there was only one of them to contend with. The other three were likely still trying to save their dying master.

She twisted away from the shadowy form just as it lunged at her, and Requiem kicked out blindly. Her foot connected, and she pushed back, the force of her powerful thigh flipping the attacker's body over. There was a startled "oomph" as he landed on his back and the air whooshed from his lungs.

Requiem threw herself onto the figure, and flipped her wrist up, positioning the base of her hand to break the attacker's nose and ram the bone fragments up into the brain. Just as she was about to strike, her attacker's head rolled to one side and light fell on the face. Short black hair, dark, narrow eyes, a flat nose, and curling, mean lips greeted her.

She stopped.

Mean, *sensuous* lips.

Her hand froze. Sonja bloody Kim. The best bodyguard of Ken Lee's gang, not to mention his enforcer and occasional assassin.

The Korean was lethal at close range and slippery as hell to pin down. She was a champion wrestler who had an ability to twist men's bones like pipe cleaners. And that was before you got to her skills with concealed weapons. She loved to play with kunai throwing knives.

"You!" Requiem spat. "Tell me you're not freelancing for Busch now?" She grabbed a fistful of Sonja's shirt, wrenched it up, and then slammed her head into the ground. "You do pick the bottom feeders."

"Says the great Requiem who has no loyalty to any family," Sonja shot back.

She bucked beneath Requiem who, despite being almost twice her size, struggled to contain her. In the middle of it all, Sonja inched her left hand toward her waistband.

"Why the hell can't the families stay in-house?" Sonja complained, scowling. Her hand suddenly flew to her waist but Requiem snatched it and pinned it by Sonja's ear.

As though her sneaky move hadn't just been interrupted, Sonja continued, "But no, they choose *you* for the dirtiest work. A freelancer! You, who'd kill any of them for the highest price. It's so stupid. They are weak!"

"They like my creative touch." Requiem smashed Sonja's head into the road again. "I send a message. Sometimes *all* they want is the message. But you? You're about as subtle as a two-by-four, with the brains to match."

She slipped her hand under Sonja's T-shirt, searching for whatever Sonja's fingers had been creeping towards, and pulled out the knife tucked in her waistband.

Requiem held it up to the light and examined it.

"How many others?" she asked, indicating the weapon.

Sonja shook her head, refusing to answer.

Requiem placed it at her throat. "How many others?"

"*Shi bai kepu seck yi!*"

"Even if I had an Oedipal complex, my mother is dead," Requiem said coolly. "So no, I can't."

"You speak Korean?" Sonja started.

"Just the essentials," Requiem said. "Last chance." She scraped the edge of the knife lightly down Sonja's jaw. The fine hairs on her cheek bent under the blade and then sprang up again. "How many more of these are you hiding? Or shall I strip you naked to find them?"

"Bite me."

"You'd probably like that," Requiem said. She offered a dangerous smile. She took the blade and slashed from the top of the T-shirt to the hem.

Pale brown skin, criss-crossed with scars, greeted her. She moved the knife to Sonja's white sports bra and sliced it in one motion. Each half fell to the side.

Sonja stared up at her pugnaciously, but there was something odd about her expression.

Requiem considered Sonja for a moment, and then her gaze dropped. She took in the muscled, flat stomach, and slid her attention higher to soft mounds tipped with brown nipples, hardening in the night air.

"Like what you see?" Sonja asked, her voice teasing and provocative. Requiem didn't bother to respond. Pleased as she was with the view, this was just business.

She returned the knife to Sonja's throat and slid her other hand around and then shoved it under Sonja's shredded T-shirt between her body and the road. Skidding her fingers over the imperfections of scars and softness in the spaces between, Requiem checked her back. She found nothing taped or hidden there. Then, she brought her hand around, slid it up to her skull, and expertly ran it through Sonja's hair. Clean. Behind the ears was also nothing.

Requiem shifted her knife hand down to the jeans. The change in Requiem's centre of gravity was all it took. No longer properly pinned down, despite

Requiem's weight across her hips, Sonja's hand shot out, grabbed Requiem's wrist, and jerked it back—hard. The knife flew into the distance and clattered against the road when it landed.

Sonja's left leg flew straight up behind Requiem, and the steel toe of her boot impacted the back of Requiem's head. Pain lanced through her. She fell forward, collapsing onto Sonja's chest, dazed. Sonja wrapped her legs around Requiem's waist, then moved her knees higher to her ribcage, and locked them in place. With a malicious glint in her eyes, she clapped her hands around Requiem's throat and squeezed.

"How smart are you now, huh?" Her breath dusted across Requiem's lips. "Stupid gae saeki."

Requiem, her brain still jangling, tried to shake off the vice-like grip around her ribs, but it only tightened. *Christ.* She should have known better. You *never* let Sonja Kim within wrestling distance. She'd simply been biding her time to strike.

Requiem's entire body creaked with the pressure, her breath shortening. It was like going up against an anaconda.

"Mr Lee heard there's a hit out for him," Sonja said, pulsing her thighs in crushing squeezes. "He knows they'll hire you to come for him. Consider this a pre-emptive strike."

The hands at her throat tightened. Requiem's consciousness flirted with the darkness, and she couldn't believe the power Sonja held in her compact body. Poor judgment on her part, clearly, as she knew Kim had once snapped a man's shin bone in two when he'd laughed at her diminutive stature.

Requiem wasn't laughing.

She tried shifting her arms, but they were firmly locked against her sides by Sonja's thighs. Requiem stared down into Sonja's eyes, black and piercing.

She was reminded of a vision from years ago. A man in a workshop, a wide-eyed little girl at his side.

She smiled at the memory, and Sonja blinked uncertainly.

"What the fuck are you smiling at? You'll be dead in seconds. The Great Requiem dead. The end!"

"Nabi," she said with dawning recognition.

The fingers at her throat slackened. "What?"

"I was just remembering the day we met. You as a girl. So adorable."

The hands unclasped and fell to Requiem's shoulders.

"At your father's workshop," Requiem continued, sucking in a lungful of air. "Carrying his tools while he maintained the Lee family's equipment. Years ago. Before the Lees got into the flesh trade."

Requiem smiled. "If I recall, Nabi means butterfly. Or kitten or something?"

Sonja flushed. "Fuck you."

"You wish," Requiem purred softly. "Don't you?"

She recalled the young girl, barely in her teens, following her around for weeks when she'd first returned from Vienna after completing her cello scholarship at a top conservatorium. Natalya had been what? Nineteen? Twenty?

Some of Lee's associates had sponsored her after one of their ambitious wives had taken an interest in the young Natalya—in both her prodigious talent and the possibilities she presented.

Natalya had been doing the rounds, thanking the appropriate men. They, in turn, expected her to fulfil her end of the bargain. Shortly afterwards, she resumed her secret tutelage for an apprenticeship of a most unusual kind.

Requiem's weapons training over the next few years had been unmatched, which wasn't surprising because Lee's weapons expert, Dimitri, was the best there had ever been.

This had been before the crime family wars, before Dimitri had left to create a rival house and everything had gone to hell. And in this relatively peaceful window of her life, a Korean girl, eyes wide with adoration, had followed Requiem everywhere.

"My shadow," Requiem said, slowly. "I called you my shadow."

"I'm not her anymore." Sonja's eyes flared.

"Aren't you?" Requiem taunted. She leaned closer. "You did what you said you would do. Do you remember?"

"No." Sonja's face turned darker. The lie was obvious. Her legs, finally, began to loosen around Requiem's ribs.

"You said you wanted to be just like me." Requiem chuckled. "And look at you now. A killer, a lethal body for hire."

Sonja looked at her, clearly confused by this turn of conversation.

"I'm curious, Nabi, why you chose to jump me here. There are much more private places. My own home, for instance. Your boss knows exactly where I live. But no—here we are, in a dark alley, in public. How *curious*."

"Not curious. Convenient." Sonja looked away.

"I have never seen anyone better at knives than you, Nabi, not in all my life. Not even Popov," she continued conversationally, "and that man was a master of the blade." Requiem leaned forward. "So, my question is, why am I not lying in that gutter with your gleaming little ninja knives poking out of my back already?"

"In the back? That's such bullshit. I'm no coward."

"Or my front, then?"

Sonja glared at her but had no answer.

"Anyone would think you, or at least a part of you, are desperately hoping to be interrupted by choosing a city street. The problem is, you don't know what I do. You don't know how deserted this particular area is."

"You're making no sense."

"No? Because I think, deep down, you don't actually want to kill me at all. After all, it's hard to kill a woman you're in love with."

The slap came lightning fast, but Requiem had slithered an arm free and was prepared. She caught Sonja's hand and then forced the arm back to the ground.

She leaned forward until her lips were in line with Sonja's, inches apart. "Am I really wrong?"

She noted dispassionately the quickening rise and fall in Sonja's breathing. She smiled. Oh, Requiem knew arousal when she saw it. Her own pulse picked up at the promise of what lay ahead. Of showing Sonja that she didn't rule the game, that the game was Requiem's, balanced eternally in her favour.

A part of her was vastly irritated at how close she'd come to being throttled at the hands of this slip of a woman. She grabbed Sonja's other hand and angrily slapped that into the ground, too, and shot her a glare.

For Requiem, the sex act itself held little appeal. It was hot and sweaty and chaotic and left a mess. Worse, she lost control at one pivotal moment, no matter how hard she tried to maintain it. But power? Requiem was addicted to its sweet taste. It was a high that had no peer, so she would tolerate one to indulge in the other. Even if it involved a public alley and— she wrinkled her nose in distaste—*dirt*.

"A fucking lie!" Sonja spat in protest. "Kuh-juh!"

Requiem lowered her head until it was just inches above Sonja's. "Is it a lie?" she goaded. She released one wrist and ran a fingertip over a nipple, circling it until it puckered into a hard knot.

A blush rose on Sonja's cheeks, and her eyes narrowed into a glower. Requiem gave a low laugh.

"So conflicted. You want to tell me to fuck off, but you're so aroused at the thought that I might finally give you what you've always wanted—what poor little *Nabi* wanted—that you can barely see straight."

Requiem rolled her hips against her, and Sonja's crushing grip fell away completely. Requiem's diaphragm gratefully expanded properly for the first time in seven minutes. Her relief was enormous.

She should probably kill Sonja now. Or flee. Or both. But she wasn't going to miss this opportunity. No, no. It comes along so rarely, the chance to show another person who really holds the power. The chance to crush the pitiful idea that Sonja had any control at all when playing in Requiem's arena was truly delicious. Teach this lesson right the first time, and it would last a lifetime.

Sonja was about to become an apt pupil. She would walk away tonight and never again doubt who was in charge.

"You've wanted me for how long?" Requiem demanded, lips curling.

Sonja gritted her teeth.

"No need to be shy. Tell me, and I might even let you have a taste." She gave her a lingering, dark look filled with every illicit promise.

A tremor ran through Sonja's body, and Requiem offered a knowing smile. Then she struck, her teeth latching onto Sonja's neck, biting hard. To her satisfaction, Sonja actually mewed. Requiem pulled back and laughed that Sonja looked appalled by her own response.

"Oh my dear, little Nabi, you liked that. Didn't you?" Requiem taunted.

Sonja scowled and shook her head.

"I don't believe you," Requiem said. "Last chance—nod for me if you want this, or I'll just stop right now and leave you all hot and bothered."

Sonja glared at her, but there was hunger in her eyes. Slowly, with a reluctant jerking motion as if it physically pained her, Sonja gave the smallest of nods. A heady rush of power surged through Requiem, and she smiled triumphantly.

She bent over Sonja and latched onto a plump brown nipple, viciously attacking it. Sonja squirmed beneath her. Knowing her strength when it was unleashed excited Requiem all the more.

Something clawed at Requiem's pants. She looked down to discover Sonja's hand worming its way up her leathers, towards her centre. She growled, snatched it back, and flattened Sonja's wrist to the ground. "You want to play with me, you want *me* to allow this, then you play my way."

Sonja tossed her an irritated look but complied. Moments later, Requiem unbuttoned Sonja's jeans, shoved her gloved hand inside, and pushed past the flimsy cotton to find a slickness. She rubbed fiercely as Sonja wriggled and gasped.

Requiem paused, looked her directly in the eye, and positioned her gloved fingers at Sonja's entrance. In the strange, dappled light, she wondered what this looked like, this frantic coupling of a towering woman engulfing her smaller, willing prey.

She entered her with two fingers and no preamble, and Sonja issued a low moan, followed by a string of Korean too fast for Requiem to decipher. It didn't need much translation. Sonja's heat warmed her sleek black gloves, and the sticky, obscene sounds of their meeting filled the night air.

Sonja's gasps were choked but loud enough to draw attention. Requiem slammed her hand over her mouth. "Shut up," she demanded.

Sonja viciously bit her glove, and Requiem snarled, jerking her hand away. She grabbed a handful of hair, tugging her head back roughly. That exposed Sonja's neck, and she couldn't resist. Requiem made short work of claiming it with her teeth, scraping, then licking to ease the pain, and then nipping and biting once more. Sonja cried out as she undulated against her.

Requiem pulled her hand out of the pants, rolled back onto her haunches, and in one powerful move, yanked down Sonja's jeans and underwear until they were at her knees.

This was exactly where she wanted her. Unable to move, unable to attack, bare and exposed to Requiem's gaze.

Requiem studied her as one might consider a specimen under glass. Sonja's hairless lower lips, delicate, pink, and swollen, were wet with arousal. Sonja shivered before her. In anticipation or cold, Requiem couldn't say.

"Such a lovely body, little Nabi," she purred. She traced several scrapes and nicks on her torso and thighs with her fingers. "Love bites from our colleagues, I see," she said. "How thoughtful of them to leave souvenirs."

Sonja smirked. "I left worse on them. Those still walking, anyway."

"I have no doubt," Requiem agreed with an amused smile and continued her slow journey south, her finger slipping lower until it found her slit once more. She dipped into the wetness, running up and down, then lifted her slippery leather-clad finger higher. She rolled the protruding clit in a circle. Sonja made an excited gasp, so Requiem focused on the exposed little protrusion, teasing, twirling, rolling.

"You want this, don't you," Requiem said with a purr. "Me, fucking you? How long have you thought about it? How long have you wanted me? Tell me."

Sonja moaned. Requiem flicked her clit hard. Sonja gave a small, startled grunt of pain, so Requiem did it again and was satisfied to achieve the same result.

"You get off on this," Requiem said in a low voice. "The danger. The killing's just incidental for you, isn't it? The excitement comes from everything else. The build-up..." She pulled her fingers away from her clit, slid them down her swollen lips, pleased at Sonja's soft whimper of regret at the loss of sensation. She rammed her fingers deep inside her, three this time.

"The build-up beforehand and the high after the pay-off," Requiem pumped again, "that's what turns you on. Danger and thrills. Not the kills."

She listened to the noise, the slippery, sucking noise of leather pushing in and out of soaked flesh. "But what you love is *this*, with me," she continued, slamming her fingers in harder, "most of all."

A whimper was her answer.

"No comment?" Requiem lifted her eyebrow and looked up to study Sonja's upturned face, flushed red, eyes blinking into the night. "If I sat on your face, if I made you lick me, would you like that? Little Nabi finally gets her tongue on the great Requiem's *cunt.*"

Sonja whimpered at the deliberately provocative word, and her head rolled listlessly to one side, her breath coming in pants. Requiem withdrew her sopping fingers and gave her clit another powerful flick. "Well?"

"Screw you." Sonja gasped. The words seemed wrenched from her.

"Not unless I allow it." Requiem sneered. A siren wailed in the distance. "Not long now."

She thumbed Sonja's clit in circles, smirking as it twitched, begging for more. Sonja made a low keening noise.

"Say it," Requiem ordered. "You've wanted me since?"

"Fuck off." Then came another stream of Korean. This time, she recognised more than a few words, each worse than the last.

"No need to be crass. I might just leave you like this if you don't choose your words better."

She pulled her hand away, wiping her essence down Sonja's bare thighs. Then she leaned forward, mouth just over her prey's. "You want me," she told Sonja cockily, looking her in the eye. "Desperately. You always have. And that is not a lie."

Sonja reared up until her lips brushed against Requiem's mouth. Requiem snapped her head away in distaste. "No kissing," she snapped. "I'm not your fucking girlfriend."

"Requiem," Sonja moaned. "I...please."

"Better." Requiem rewarded her by moving back to hip level and watching her closely. She bent just above Sonja's clit. "How long have you wanted me? Mmm?" she murmured over the heated skin.

Sonja hesitated. Requiem tapped her clit with her tongue. "Since before Dimitri left Lee's crew?"

Sonja nodded, and Requiem rewarded her with another quick flick of her tongue over her clit. Sonja's thighs trembled, and she reached for Requiem's hair.

Requiem slapped her hands away. "No."

The ambulance's wail grew louder.

"Answer me! Since when?"

"The day you started training at Mr Lee's."

Requiem looked at her triumphantly. "So—it turns out I didn't lie, then."

"No," Sonja said, her voice defeated. Ragged. She didn't even bother to curse her existence this time.

"No," Requiem agreed and covered her cunt with the flat of her tongue, luxuriating in the creamy, piquant taste, lavishing the skin with her warmth and leaving shining wet trails. Her tongue's rough flesh slipped over the clit, swirling and jabbing.

Sonja squeezed her eyes shut, started to speak, then gasped, shrieked and came. Hard. Requiem lapped up her essence, then pulsed her tongue inside her. Sonja's thighs trembled anew.

Requiem rose up on her haunches.

Sonja looked at her. "My turn," she said quickly, almost fearfully. And there was so much desire in those eyes that Requiem had to glance away. First loves were a powerful thing. Hell, she knew all about that.

"You promised," Sonja added. She seemed ashamed of her neediness and bit her lip. Requiem experienced the same surge of power she'd felt the moment she realised she could teach this one a lesson about the game.

Requiem stood fluidly, walked over Sonja to plant a boot on either side of her ribs, and stared down at her. "Eager, are we?" she said. "Well, it's true; I did promise."

She paused there for a moment, cocking her head as she listened to the wail of the ambulance growing incrementally louder. Then she glanced back down again, to take in the eagerness in Sonja's glazed eyes as she watched her.

She unbuckled the belt on her leather pants and, achingly slowly, slid them down her muscled legs. Sonja stared, unblinking, as though memorising every detail.

When Requiem reached just above her ankles, she ran her hands back up her legs. They were mainly smooth with only two scars—one from a stray bullet; the other a knife that missed its mark. Her thighs were powerful, and she was aware enough to know she was a remarkable specimen of her gender. It wasn't vanity. Simply a fact to be exploited when necessary.

Sonja's irises grew wide with desire, and pride welled within Natalya.

"Impatient?" she teased her as she trailed a finger over her own mound, over her underwear. She smiled at the frustrated growl.

Requiem hooked her thumbs in black cotton—tight, practical, boy-cut panties—and slid them down her legs. And then she stood, hands on hips, like a goddess. Sonja absorbed her so intently that she seemed to have forgotten how to breathe.

Sonja's nipples had grown erect again, and her breathing had begun to deepen.

"Oh god," Sonja whispered so softly that Requiem almost missed it. "*Neh...*"

Slowly, Requiem knelt, one knee to either side of Sonja's head, one ankle over each shoulder, and the straining stretch of her leather pants now pressed into Sonja's chest. Requiem bent forward, scooped the back of Sonja's head in one hand, and without a word, pushed her mouth into her folds.

"As promised," she said. "You have five minutes. I need to be gone before that ambulance arrives. Impress me."

She leaned back slightly and watched as Sonja eagerly went to work, sliding her tongue over her slit, slipping in and out, scraping the clit. She had some talent; Requiem had to give her that. Her muscles turned to liquid, and then came the tell-tale twitch in her cunt that said someone was doing something very right to it.

Requiem held her firmly against her neatly trimmed mound, not giving an inch. She knew her face would appear the picture of control. She reminded herself who she was. Who was receiving the lessons. Whose game this was. Who always won.

Her nostrils twitched, though, when that tongue tapped her in *exactly* the right place. Her thighs quivered with the effort of holding her position, and her bare knees drilled painfully into the dirt.

Sonja found her wellspring. Requiem was completely soaked from this display of submission from the second-best assassin she'd ever known.

"Clean it up," she ordered, her voice strained as the tongue stroked and plundered her. "That's it." She tugged Sonja's head tighter to her and, much to her chagrin, groaned when Sonja's tongue performed a sublime little pirouette that made her want to fuck her properly. In a bed. For a week.

But that wasn't who Requiem was. Or Natalya, for that matter.

The siren's wail was much closer now. It had to be only a couple of blocks away.

"Time's up," she ground out. The frenzied lashing increased, and her clit ached to come. *So close.* The power and adrenalin surged through her. Sonja was trembling, too. Requiem realised the other woman was close to coming again.

Well, Requiem smirked, Sonja was tasting an immortal. Who could blame her?

Sonja's tongue froze mid-stroke, her body shaking, and she made a strangled noise at the back of her throat. Requiem exhaled, lowered Sonja's head to the ground, and rose, unsated physically, but emotionally feeling like a god.

She looked down at herself. Her sex dripped in the faint light, moisture from her arousal clinging to the tiny hairs. She stood stock still for a second, allowing the night air to hit her. The coolness washing over her furnace was heady. She gave herself a brief rub over her clit, enjoying the sensation as it sat up in delight, purring. Had she been alone, she might have allowed herself to come right then.

Instead she cleared her throat. "Close but no cigar," she told Sonja. She pulled her underwear and leathers back up her thighs quickly, watching the disappointment on Sonja's face.

"Was it everything you dreamed of?" Requiem taunted as she rebelted her pants. She walked languidly over to her Ninja, found her discarded MP3 player and helmet, then slid onto its seat, unable to resist rubbing herself against the smooth, hard surface. An electric frisson shot straight to her centre.

Christ, she was close.

"Did I live up to your teenage fantasies? Was it the same as when you fucked yourself under the sheets every school night?"

Sonja's chest rose and fell swiftly. Even from this distance, her embarrassed flush was visible in the low light.

"I'll take your two orgasms as a yes. I, however, remain less impressed." She slid her helmet on, flicked up the visor, and studied her. "Oh, but you can tell your boss that he's right. Ken Lee is on my dance card in the near future. I have a very special exit planned for the man who sells the bodies of innocent young girls."

She gave her a cool, twisted smile. "It's quite shocking really."

Sonja scowled, sitting up. She couldn't go anywhere with her pants in a twisted mess and she'd apparently just remembered her main mission.

"Fuck!" she said, scrabbling at her jeans.

Requiem watched, revving her bike as a pointed reminder that she was now too far away for Sonja to stop her.

"I believe I already did." Requiem let her gaze linger over the half-naked form. "You're welcome," she said with a cruel smile. "Oh, my little Nabi, look what you let me do to you when you should have been killing me. You're a *terrible* assassin."

Requiem gave her bike another rev and pulled away with a roar of the engine. She didn't look back.

She passed an ambulance screeching to a stop outside the nightclub. A crowd of onlookers stood on the footpath, including many of her colleagues and several agitated bodyguards who were gesturing frantically to the emergency vehicle.

She focused on the cleansing sounds of Arvo Pärt as it filtered into her brain, drowning out the chaos. The thrum of her black beast vibrated between her legs.

Well, she'd had worse nights. A lot worse.

Requiem smiled.

CHAPTER 2

Three months later

Natalya woke precisely at 5:15am. She carried out her morning routine efficiently, made her bed with military corners and then dressed in black leggings and a form-fitting sports T-shirt.

She made a quick tour of her home, checking positions of locks as she went. Then she turned on her computer's security bot program and set it to run through overnight camera footage and look for anomalies. It would beep if anything was amiss.

From the street, her residence might be dismissed as an old warehouse, hidden behind twelve-foot high brick walls. Only the roofline was visible to passersby.

Natalya padded down to her indoor gym and stepped onto the treadmill. For a moment she stopped and stared out of the floor-to-ceiling window at the strip of dismal grey sky above the riot of vines scribbling across the wall that encircled her property. She gave her head a shake and began her usual seven kilometre run.

She increased her pace quickly and began her mental exercise of tuning out distractions. She was a rock. Powerful. Solid. She controlled her world. The world didn't control her. Her feet pounded like a metronome, ticking away in her brain: *One-four, two-four, three-four, four-four, inhale, exhale. Repeat.*

Precisely thirty minutes later, she stepped off the machine, breathing more heavily but not hard. She shook out a neatly folded towel from the stack next to her equipment and mopped up her perspiration. She began to stretch her arms and shoulders in preparation for her weight-training session, which would be followed by an hour of yoga. A faint beep sounded in the distance. She paused to listen. A rapid series of beeps followed.

Her alarm. Her home's security system included cameras and movement sensors to go with the coiled barbed-wire and the poisonous, prickly climbers running along the top of her walls. No intruder could get far without detection—or pain. Because, if they made it over the wall, an array of thorned plants and a tight row of *Hippomane mancinella* trees would cause a most painful reaction.

She jogged to the lounge, opened the sliding glass door, and stared out over her property. Sergei Duggan was attempting to cross her lawn. *Attempting* being the operative word. She lowered herself onto her travertine bench, crossed her legs at the ankle, and watched as the renowned killer's skin reacted violently to her aptly named "little apple of death" trees.

It was pathetic, really, a big strong man like this reduced to his knees by flora. It was almost educational. She flicked invisible lint off her leggings as he floundered before her, a fleshy sack of human failings.

He grimaced in pain, rubbed anxiously at his blistering skin, and cursed furiously. He looked at her, his dark eyes filled with an anguished plea he was too proud to utter.

It would be pointless anyway. What did he expect her to do? Save his slimy neck?

As he convulsed, his hidden garrotte slithered from his sleeve. Natalya watched impassively as the life faded from his eyes.

This had been one of the world's top assassins? Natalya sniffed. Please. He hadn't even gotten as far as her water feature.

This so-called professional hadn't done his homework and had met a predictable end. Research was everything.

She sighed in irritation. Now she'd have to organise a clean-up. She could do it herself, of course, but the benefits of being the best in her field meant she could delegate any wet work—and the risks of being caught during body disposal—to one of her associate's underlings.

Flicking the towel over her shoulder, Natalya gave Duggan a parting look, aggrieved that he'd thrown her off her routine and ruined her workout. She headed for the shower.

Natalya turned the music player on just outside the bathroom and flicked through the selections until she came to *Lacrimosa* from Mozart's *Requiem*.

She shifted the volume precisely four turns, waiting for the strains to begin. Then she entered the polished granite bathroom.

Natalya shed her workout clothes, filed them neatly in her laundry hamper, and turned the cold tap on full. She stepped into the biting spray and counted to thirty. The mark of discipline was to withstand that which the body said it could not. Like making a cello weep, it was necessary to hold the trembling notes a little past what made the listener comfortable. But if one held it, quivering until the limits were reached, then exceeded…the payoff was always worth it.

At thirty seconds, she flicked the water to hot and reached for her liquid soap. She took careful stock of her pale body where wounds were apt to stand out. It wasn't vanity. Too often, injuries were overlooked in the rush of adrenalin.

With her fingers lathered with suds, she started at her collarbone, skidded past a bruise, and then sank lower, to her breasts. A faint white line ran perpendicular down the left breast—courtesy of a close call with a Serbian who had Mafia ties. He was as mad as a heat-stroked poodle, but by god, the man was skilled with his knives. He should be—he was a Michelin star restaurant chef.

She dropped her fingers to her ribs and methodically counted nine imperfections with her fingers. She sought out every pockmarked scar and automatically catalogued the details of each—days, places, faces. Cool men. Insane men. Cunning men. Angry men.

And one woman.

The large purple bruise on her hip was still healing from that vicious encounter. She pushed her fingers into it and hissed at the resulting jolt of pain.

Three months back, she'd promised Sonja she'd take down her boss, Ken Lee. He was a hard man to gain access to, but nine days ago she'd finally made good on her vow and caught him with his pants down. Literally.

The demise of the man who ran the world's largest prostitution ring and trafficked pre-teen girls from South-East Asia was about as fitting as it got. Natalya had quite enjoyed electrifying the small metal grid she'd connected to the base of Lee's private urinal at his favourite gentleman's club. The crack of lethal energy shot up the first natural conductor it found—which, in this case, was salt. From Lee's urine.

Sonja had been less inclined to appreciate the artistic merit of her boss's shocking exit. Everyone's a critic.

It wasn't like Natalya hadn't expected some retaliation, so she hadn't been too startled when Sonja had jumped her yesterday and left her mark.

Natalya's hip twinged again as she rubbed her soapy hand across the bruise. Of course, Sonja had more reasons to be furious with her, thanks to their little tryst all those months ago, but that wasn't what this was about. As a professional, Sonja had an obligation to extract payback on behalf of her crime family. She'd severely lost face over Lee's humiliating assassination.

It was an occupational hazard, dodging her own kind. The professionals who came for her—usually hired by clients who might have lost a favoured associate in one of her hits—were especially dedicated to seeing that she was "punished."

Good luck with that.

She had lived longer than most in her profession. She had done so by demanding perfection of herself. Taking pride in her work. Being disciplined. Faultless in her planning. Meticulous in her attention to detail. It served her in both her careers. And so, at age forty-one, the assassin known as Requiem continued to live, while others twitched and drooled on her manicured lawn, making her motion sensors light up like a Christmas tree.

Natalya drew herself out of her reverie and shampooed her hair. It was long and glossy, sitting well below her shoulder blades. It was her only indulgence, her sole vanity.

She slid on her silk robe and slippers and padded out into the lounge, still drying her hair with a fluffy white towel. She headed for her fish tanks. One held a dozen small goldfish. The second, a cone snail—a beautifully coloured orange and white-shelled *Conus geographus*. She had carefully harvested it specifically for its unique properties during a dive off Ningaloo Reef.

Beside the tank, perfectly aligned, lay a pair of forceps and a row of test tubes. She slung her towel over her shoulder and used a small fish net to scoop up a goldfish and plop it into the cone snail's tank. With a detached fascination, she watched as the lethal marine creature's sting shocked its prey into paralysis. Within seconds the goldfish was dead.

Satisfied, she headed over to her pride and joy.

In a small pot by the lounge window, sat a single, vivid purple flower—her favourite. An African violet, *Saintapaulia ionantha*. Preferring no moisture on the leaves, African violets had to be watered from the bottom. They did not enjoy anything on the surface at all, including dust, water, and grime. With such pristine requirements, it was little wonder Natalya's African violet always thrived.

She gave it sixty millilitres of tepid, filtered water, dusted the leaves, and then moved over to her phone. She had a situation to remedy on her front lawn.

She pressed a speed-dial number, listened to an odd assortment of computerised clicks and beeps, and then heard a male voice say: "Yes?"

"I have a package that needs urgent collection."

"Where?"

"Home."

"Just the one?"

"Yes."

"One hour."

She hung up and then pressed play on her phone messages.

Voice message received, 11:38pm, Friday. Ms Tsvetnenko, it's Mesut Schulz, from the Berliner Philharmoniker. Our cellist Milena Lomas is ill. We understand you are already going to be in Europe next month. So we wanted to know if you're available for depping on the French leg of our world tour? Moscow Symphony Orchestra gives you an excellent reference from their 2013 tour. You'd be needed in Paris in a little over three weeks for rehearsals. My assistant will make all the visa arrangements and so forth. Please call her.

Voice message received, today, 9:03am. Hello, ah, Ms Tsveetnarcko, it's Kylie Payne from Classical Notes. We have managed to source that rare sheet music for Carl Reinecke's Cello Concerto in D minor, Opus Eighty-two. *Took some doing, but it's in. We're open 'til five.*

There was a clunk and a mechanical whirr that went along with accessing her second, encoded line. She'd hired a man who used to be employed by the KGB for hacking dissidents' telecommunications. He had secured her phones from every conceivable law-enforcement agency surveillance tap. Even he couldn't crack her devices now, he'd told her with enormous pride before dropping a bill the size of a third-world country's debt in her lap.

Voice message received, today, 6:13am. Well, well, Req, you picked it. Mr S came crawling back and rolled over. He's paying full tote. Check your secured email for the new packet for his job. Oh, and we've had a reply from that mystery client. I explained the protocol, that we need to know who we're working for, but instead of answers they paid double on the condition we don't ask questions and don't dig into it. Still can't trace their origins, but it came through the usual gang of four's contacts, so I've approved it.

The gang of four were Requiem's main source of business. This destructive quartet of Melbourne clans and their allies had divvied up most of Victoria's criminal enterprises between them. The Trioli family, for instance, ran all the fixed racing games in town.

The late Ken Lee had run Moonlight Crew, which was formerly an armaments importation ring and now brought in underage girls from poor rural areas in South-East Asia and sold them to illegal brothels.

Fleet Crew was formed when weapons expert Dimitri Kozlovsky left Ken Lee to set up his own empire. No one outside of the gang knew who Fleet's kingpin was since Kozlovsky's death in 2002. The crew worked illegal guns and ammo, and ran professional armed robberies.

The High Street boys, headed by Mr S—aka Santos—specialised in the manufacture and Australian-wide distribution of ice, or crystal meth.

The various gangs did not play well together and, since 1998, had a nasty habit of killing key members of other families. These murders ran almost unchecked because the police were more interested in focusing on crimes the public cared about. Criminals eating their own was a low priority.

It was a mystery how the feud between the families had started, and each side blamed the other. No one knew what the trigger had been except Requiem. And one other.

Natalya folded her towel and tuned back into her associate's conversation.

I've sent you that mystery client's packet, too. The individual you'll be visiting is… *uh…unusual. You'll see. I know that curious brain of yours will love profiling her.*

Anyway, that job comes with a couple of stipulations. Make the visit up close *and personal so they know what's what. Don't do the job at their home or that of* *their family. And you have to wait three weeks before you do the work and not a* *second sooner. Oh and—*

The message ended abruptly as it ran out of allocated space. Her associate always did ramble on.

Three weeks? Natalya's eyebrow lifted. Why the delay? Life insurance papers? Pushing for a new will?

Natalya reached for her mobile phone and flicked to her email. A decrypted document appeared, and she tapped in a 10-digit password as her landline kicked in again.

Voice message received, today, 6:16am. I just wanted to say good job on Ken *Lee. That can't have been easy,* her associate continued as though there had been no interruption. *Oh and I've finally seen the paper. You did take that earlier brief* *literally, didn't you? That client is so happy with your particular brand of wish* *fulfilment for his little girl that he wants to name his next kid after you. How does* *that grab you?*

Natalya pressed her lips together in a disapproving line. *Requiem Trioli?* No, it did not grab her in the slightest.

The phone message ended, and her gaze fell on the document she'd downloaded. Natalya studied the brief, then tapped the candid photo accompanying the packet to enlarge it.

Wide blue eyes stared back at her. Pale skin, brown, shoulder-length hair. Small, compact frame. Something about that face niggled at the back of her brain.

The photo had been taken as the woman walked in a city park, juggling a handbag, water bottle, and sandwich bag. She broadcasted helplessness.

This was the woman someone needed a professional to eradicate?

She frowned and scoured the rest of the document. No information on who ordered the hit. No clue as to what this tiny mouse of a creature had done to merit a hired killer.

Blackmailer, maybe? Informant?

She scrolled back to the photo. The woman's body language set her teeth on edge. Why did women persist in trying to take up less space than they needed? She should take what was hers, not shrink from her own shadow.

Natalya's father, a military man, had taught her to claim her space. He'd taught her how to stand tall, shake hands firmly, look people in the eye, and stake her place in the world, unflinching and unapologetic. Women, like men, had to demand to be counted.

This woman's shoulders were hunched, arms pressed against her sides even as she tried to juggle her various possessions. She was far too fragile to be a target that required a professional hit. A stiff breeze would blow her over.

Something really didn't smell right. The job was too easy. She didn't like easy any more than she liked a mystery her clever mind could not solve.

She scanned the data once more.

```
Name: Alison Ryan
Age: 34
Employment: Government worker, Solomon Lewis Building.
    Consult Addendum A for map.
Hobbies: Classical music.
Spouse/Partner: None.
Pets: None.
Living arrangements: 9 Benong Court, Frankston.
    Cohabits with elderly mother who has health and
    mobility issues.
```

Natalya considered the address. Frankston was an outer Melbourne suburb with a working-class reputation. It was also a world beneath the wealth of her usual clientele.

She returned her attention to the photo and studied the woman's face again.

What had she done? And who had she done it to?

The client who had paid double for the kill could be a jealous lover, she supposed, although Requiem's specialty and six-figure fee should have automatically precluded such a low-brow client. Her expertise was in gangland killings, and anybody with the connections to hire her knew that.

As for a clause demanding no questions? Double payment or not, she didn't operate that way. She tapped in a number she knew by heart and waited for it to ring twice. Then she hung up and repeated the process.

Her phone rang five seconds later, and tell-tale electronic pops and beeps sounded at the other end.

"Req?" The Hacker's voice was more mechanical than human, thanks to all the filters and security he'd put in place.

"I need a new look-up," she replied without preamble. "Name's Alison Ryan. She works in the Solomon Lewis building in the CBD. I need to know exactly what she does for a living. Career highlights."

"Solomon Lewis? Okay, could be anything—you know how many departments are wedged in there right now?"

"I know. Can you do it quickly?"

The Hacker's tinny laughter was his only response.

"Okay," Natalya said, pleased. "And be discreet. I don't want her to know she has a shadow."

"Always." The phone went dead.

The Hacker was most famous for his industrial espionage, and there wasn't a database he hadn't been able to infiltrate. She pictured her associate's furious glare given this was supposed to be a don't-ask, don't-tell job—but then again, her associate's neck wasn't the one on the damn line.

Natalya consulted her phone's calendar. She could take care of this job and the Paris leg of the Berlin orchestra tour. And she could probably even throw in the Santos target before she left as well.

Viktor Raven. She sneered. Well that was the name he was going by these days. She'd known him when he was Joe Hastings from Dandenong. The cowardly slug of an informant had finally done something to upset Santos to the point of homicide, and he was well aware he had a mark on his head. Rumour had it, he'd hired a top-drawer private bodyguard, someone very hard to kill.

Well, that should make life interesting.

She tapped open her work calendar and entered a few coded notes: Watch the little mouse, find and eradicate the slug, roast said mouse, then head to Paris.

Sorted, she strode to her timber-floored rehearsal room and opened her cello case. She eased into the seat, rubbing the ridges on the thumb of her left hand. No matter how much she practised easing her grip, still they remained.

She closed her eyes, positioned the rare Charles Adolphe Maucotel instrument, and began to play. Music washed away everything. It was her greatest love. Her soul ripped itself apart and restitched itself anew. Becoming immortal, she called it. Her ability to die and be reborn every time she touched her cello.

Hunger drove her, four hours later, to lift her gaze from the possession she loved most. She eased her instrument regretfully away from her, wondering at the mere mortals who never felt what she did. Those who experienced music on the periphery, who heard it as pleasant sounds rather than felt it resonate with every fibre of their being.

She froze, the bow sagging in her hand. *That's* where she knew her latest target from. She'd seen this woman at a Victorian Philharmonic Orchestra season launch party three months ago. The night of the Uli Busch hit, if she wasn't mistaken.

Natalya never forgot a face. The little mouse had been among the fawning groupies for Amanda Marks. Marks, in her flowing white gown, with perky, elfin features, had an ego almost as sizeable as her adoring fan base.

Violinists, Natalya snorted. Always the rock stars.

Not that Natalya particularly cared. She was more interested in fading into the background and not being bothered by the unwashed masses with their cloying demands for autographs and photos.

She packed away her cello and began her mental list of how to proceed next. She had three weeks. Plenty of time to learn all she needed to about Alison Ryan and the most optimum method for doing what had to be done.

Even so, her mind kept darting back to the woman's face. She realised, as she visualised it, that one word above all others kept rising to the fore— Innocent.

How unusual. She generally dealt with the guilty—and some were *very* guilty indeed. Her mind drifted to a certain despicable German chemicals entrepreneur who had become her favourite hit of all time—for reasons not entirely due to the manner of his untimely demise.

CHAPTER 3

Requiem tapped her thumb impatiently against her phone. Alison Ryan would be leaving work shortly. She studied the pugnacious, chunky lines of the Solomon Lewis building which rose nine floors. It was a typically grotesque monument to brutalist architecture. Odd that it never went to ten storeys. It was as though even the builders couldn't contain their revulsion and walked away at number nine.

This concrete eyesore had been pressed into work when four of the city's major buildings had been shut down for asbestos removal last year. So, crammed within its confines now were the Supreme Court of Victoria on Ground Level, Police Headquarters above that, the Australian Taxation Department, higher still, and assorted government offices on the top floors. It meant that literally anyone in Victoria having a bad day involving crime or punishment would wind up here.

She glanced at her watch. Ryan should exit her building at 5:03pm. Requiem admired her punctuality.

Her phone rang, and she answered, still keeping an eye on the building.

"Req? I have answers," a tinny voice said.

"I'm all ears."

"That party works on the second floor of Solomon Lewis."

Level two? "She's a cop?" Requiem asked incredulously.

"Nah," came an amused reply. "Administrative assistant. A lifer. Wanna hear her job descrip? 'Develop and maintain computerised records and systems. Liaise with, and provide information to, members of the Department, Victoria Police, and external contacts on behalf of the office. Perform courier and coffee-making duties as required.'

"She makes a spit over forty-six gees per annum plus super. She's been doing it for decades. I swear my blind, deaf Great Aunt Edith has more fun in a day. Your girl has no dirt of any kind on her personnel file. Okay, so that all?"

"Yes."

The phone went dead.

She glanced back at the building. Still no sign of her quarry. Requiem was seated on a park bench facing a small public lawn across from the entrance. From her perch, where she feigned reading her phone, she had already recognised seven faces in ten minutes—two high-profile lawyers, an article clerk whose father was in one of Victoria's most prominent underworld families, three career criminals, and one noxious detective. The latter was Detective Senior Sergeant Barry Moore, head of the Homicide Squad.

She lowered her phone slightly. The heavy man had a buzz-cut and was all swagger and rolling beer gut. He slapped on his mirrored sunglasses, loosened the cheap tie on his even cheaper charcoal suit, and headed towards the local pub. With this imbecile in charge, it was little wonder Victoria's crime lords were, literally, getting away with murder.

Moore's threat level was low to nil. If the intel from various sources was anything to go by, he was not immune to accepting bribes.

One of her best informants also swore Moore had stomped a pair of homeless men to death in a fit of rage and had covered it up. It had acquired the cop the nickname of Zebra: An ass with stripes. That was too kind for the festering boil. The underworld was far too unimaginative. No wonder Requiem was always in work.

Requiem had nothing but contempt for men like this who could not control themselves. And wearing the badge that he did meant Moore was a hypocrite to boot. His mother must be so proud.

He strode off as if he was god's gift to policing, and she wondered, not for the first time, how such an individual with so many anger issues had been put in charge of an entire police unit.

As Moore passed, he tilted his bulbous face in Requiem's direction, giving her a view of a spider's web of broken capillaries. He was a walking advertisement on the merits of sobriety. Moore spat on the footpath and plodded off down a side street. Requiem's lip curled in disgust.

She glanced at her watch again and wondered what was keeping her target. After a week of following her, Requiem now knew Ryan was a creature of habit. Exceedingly dull habit.

Leave home at 8am. Reach her government office at 8:52am. Emerge from the tower at 12:03pm, buy the same salad on whole-wheat sandwich, bottled water or coffee (white, two sugars)—depending on the weather—and apple (Granny Smith) each day at the same sandwich bar, Toast Amazeballs. Return to work at 12:27pm. Exit the building at 5:03pm. Home by 5:55pm.

The only variation was whether she took a train or drove. That decision seemed random. Though Requiem was sure, given enough time, she would figure that pattern out, too.

She appeared to have no friends. She also never left the building with anyone, as others often did.

Ryan's home life, Requiem had discovered, was as uninspiring as her work existence. Ryan cracked the door to her seventies suburban home at 5:30am, peered up at the weather pensively, and crept outside in old house shoes and a robe— worn over her pyjamas—to collect her newspaper.

It usually rolled into the agave patch, which the neighbour's feral cat liberally fertilised during the night. Ryan always frowned and gingerly pulled the paper out and wiped it down on the dewy, half-dead grass eking out an existence on the tiny front lawn. Then she'd sigh, look resigned, and pad back inside.

Like clockwork, every single day.

Half an hour later, her mother, Elsie, bellowed for her tea and her meds and complained loudly about everything else.

Ryan's family appeared, so far, to be comprised of just this abusive, acid-tongued mother, and Requiem's surreptitious poking through the letterbox contents over a week had confirmed it. All mail went to Elsie/E. Ryan, and it was as though her daughter had been rendered invisible.

Elsie was by turns furious, bitter, or, when a visitor called during the day, sweet as a peach. After a week, Requiem knew precisely how the elder Ryan liked her tea, food, meds, and life—the polar opposite of however her daughter did it.

Not that Alison ever complained. God forbid. The tortured woman never said much of anything to her mother. She just took it. Requiem was starting to wonder if killing her would be a mercy.

At 5:09pm the reason for the target's delay was clear. Requiem edged forward to the office building, her phone now pocketed, and watched the security guard attempting to hit on Ryan.

The muscled ape seemed to be making an artform out of stroking her arm while trying to simultaneously flex his biceps. This was not an achievable feat as it turned out. She edged closer. For god's sake, the woman wasn't in a petting zoo.

Ryan shook her head at him, her mouth pulled down in a grimace. As Ryan firmly and politely yanked her arm back, she said sorry repeatedly. Requiem didn't even need her lip-reading skills to follow what was happening.

Requiem's nostrils flared. *Sorry?* If it had been her, the man would be the one apologising. And then probably pissing his pants.

Finally free, Ryan exited the building with a tight expression and surprising speed.

Requiem forced herself back into the zone, watching which direction the quarry was headed, noting her body language, pace, and turn of her head.

This was Requiem's forte.

The art of surveillance was to know the nature of man. All humans, from cleaners to CEOs, from spies to drug couriers, were creatures of routine and habit, making them hopelessly flawed. Even the most formidable opponent, skilled in the art of defence, would still have cracks.

So, the key to getting close to this prey was all about knowing her rhythms, profiling her well, and walking in her shoes until you virtually share the same blisters.

All Requiem needed to know was *who* she was at a cellular level, not her lists of crimes or infractions. And, of course, she had to stay unseen while gathering this information.

Requiem had once tailed a legendary former agent for a week without him knowing. He was an ASIO asset turned underworld figure so skilled in the spy game he'd been dubbed The Master. So, when she finally cornered him, it was immensely gratifying to see the man staring at her from the doorstep of his safe house, one hand still frozen on the key in the lock he'd been turning.

"How?" was all he asked, his voice cracking.

She merely smiled. How? He was arrogant and flawed. He had looked right at her dozens of times in the previous week and never seen her. She'd just been some housewife out shopping that he'd dismissed as a no one.

This was the art, and at this particular game of cat and mouse, Requiem was unmatched. She quickened her pace behind her target and mused at how galling it was to use her gift on a quarry so far beneath Requiem's skillset.

Ryan was clearly clueless to the point of oblivious. Requiem suspected she could walk right beside the woman for ten blocks and she wouldn't even notice.

There was a faint leakage from Ryan's headphones, and she tried to stitch together the musical strains she could hear to work out the composition's name.

She identified the piece after a few more blocks of trailing her. Arvo Pärt's *Spiegel im Spiegel*. So the little mouse had a decent musical palate, Requiem would give her that. They neared the parking building entrance Ryan used when she wasn't catching the train. But instead of going inside, the woman kept walking.

This was new. A few quick lefts, then rights, and a left again and the unthinkable happened.

Alison Ryan disappeared.

Requiem stopped cold, eyeing the inner-city alley in front of her. Her neck snapped around. She should have been *right here*. What the hell? She was about to retrace her steps when her prey stepped out from behind a large green industrial bin and folded her arms, glaring.

"Are you following me?" she asked furiously. She plucked her ear buds out and shoved them and her MP3 player into her bag.

Requiem started and glanced over her shoulder.

"Yes, you. Lady with the fuck-'em-all attitude. Are. You. Following. Me?"

Requiem scowled. So the mouse had teeth. "Why would I be following you?"

Ryan tilted her head. "That's what I was asking myself. You've been following me since I left work."

"Or going in the same direction." Requiem gave a slow smile. "You really should see someone about that paranoia."

Ryan glared at her. "I notice you didn't answer my question. So here's an easier one—if you aren't following me, where are you going? There's nothing much of anything around here."

Requiem didn't respond. *She* didn't answer to anyone and certainly not to her quarry. She pushed aside the small part of her brain impressed at having been spotted at all, let alone so quickly. She'd never had the tables turned like this. And by an amateur?

Requiem stared her down, unmoving, unflinching, and damned sure she wasn't about to start answering questions.

Ryan's expression became more suspicious. "Who *are* you?" She shifted her weight from foot to foot, as if deciding whether to run.

Up this close, it became apparent that Ryan wore no make-up at all. The woman appeared fit and fine-boned. In her own way, she had an arresting, sincere look, veering towards pleasing. But it was obvious she wasn't aware of that.

Her hair had been pulled back from her face in a short, brown ponytail highlighting her high cheekbones and pale skin. No freckles. No lines. She was unblemished, which made her highly unusual in the circles Requiem moved in.

Ryan suddenly plunged her hand into her bag and wrenched it out again. She held a small canister in her fist.

Requiem was startled. Irritation for her slow reaction flared. Stopping to admire a prey's flawless skin-care regime could get her ass in a hole in the ground.

"I have capsicum spray, in case you think I'm worth robbing," Ryan warned. "Trust me, it's not worth it. Your eyes will feel like they're on fire." She pointed the canister menacingly at Requiem.

She looked so earnest, so ferocious—like a puppy that thinks it's a pitbull—that for a moment, Requiem was derailed. She stared at her in surprise before she regained her equilibrium.

Then she suddenly laughed. It was absurd. All of it. Requiem took a step forward, daring the little mouse to react. "Well go on then," she goaded her. "I'd mace me, too, if you really think I'm some threat."

Ryan's hand twitched as though she really was contemplating a pre-emptive strike.

Honestly, it was adorable. Requiem had to chuckle at her ballsiness. She shook her head and ambled over, closing her hand around the small fist and its cargo.

Requiem lowered her voice.

"I really don't think though your fresh mint breath spray will have quite the same impact as capsicum. Do you?"

She prised it from her hand, studied the label to confirm her guess, and then gave her a knowing smile as she handed it back.

"Oh," Ryan said. "I didn't think you could read the label from that far away."

"I have excellent vision."

Ryan rammed the small canister back in her handbag and studied her. "I really don't have any cash on me."

"I'm not robbing you," Requiem sighed. "Do I *look* like some two-bit, back-alley thug? She pushed her dark sunglasses to the top of her head and gave her an exasperated eye roll.

Ryan suddenly blinked in surprise as she met her eyes.

"Oh," she said, snapping her fingers. "I know who you are!"

Requiem's eyebrow cocked. "How exciting for you."

"You...you're that cellist. With the VPO. Right?"

"I'm well aware of who I play for." That came out more annoyed than she'd intended so Requiem smiled her best public smile, the reassuring one that contained a few teeth but didn't look as terrifying as it usually did.

"Guilty," she added in her most charming tone.

"And now I know why you're here, too. God, why didn't you just say?"

Ryan seemed so cross, Requiem wanted to laugh again. She resisted the urge as Ryan continued.

"Okay, well, since we're both almost here, we may as well see what the fuss is about, right?"

Requiem nodded, unwilling to ask the obvious. Ryan grinned suddenly.

"I only got emailed the new password an hour ago. I hope it's worth it. Been looking forward to this all month."

She took off down the alley.

In spite of every howl of protest her brain shouted at her—she was supposed to be following her target, not engaging with her—her legs were propelled along in the slipstream of this diminutive woman, completely without Requiem's permission.

After a block more, Ryan stopped outside a worn red door. She glanced up at Requiem, excitement in her eyes. "I'll do the honours."

She rapped three times and, when a small window was shoved open, said: "Yo-Yo Ma."

The window closed again. A few seconds later the door opened.

Beyond it was the interior of a small, dark club. The smell of spirits and the thick, dull clang of ice bouncing into glasses hit Requiem at the same time. To the right of the bar, which ran down the left wall, was a spot-lit stage, with instruments being set up. She was too far away to determine much more.

"Coming?" Ryan asked, cocking an eyebrow. "I'll even buy the first round to make up for accusing you of being a 'two-bit, back-alley thief.' Fair?"

She headed into the dark bowels of the musical club, leaving Requiem standing on the threshold.

She should just go. Disappear back home. Feed her goldfish…to her cone snail. Put her frozen lasagne on to heat. Work out how to kill Viktor Raven without his new bodyguard blowing her head off.

Besides, it's not like she could continue watching Ryan any more. Incognito was no longer possible. She still wasn't sure how the other woman had noticed her. That spelled danger in its own way.

So, really, the safest and most logical course of action would be to just disappear back into the alley. Leave her prey to her night out. She started to pivot away from the club.

Ryan, now at the bar, shot her wide, guileless smile and waved her over.

So innocent. Requiem contemplated her. Innocence was like catnip to assassins, she was sure of it. Against all her better judgment, she took a step forward. Then another. And a third.

Natalya left Requiem outside, cooling her heels, while she stepped forward, drawn into the warmth.

CHAPTER 4

They were seated at a small round table to the side of the stage. Ryan was nursing some sparkling concoction that smelled like lemon, lime, and bitters. Natalya had acquired a sealed bottle of water—the closest thing to a biosecure drink she could find.

On stage were eight musicians, to use the term loosely, banging away at an array of experimental instruments she'd not seen since she first studied music in Vienna. String Theory, they called themselves.

Their cult leader was, clearly, the revolutionary American composer Harry Partch. He was revolutionary because he wanted a classical music revolution, not because Natalya actually liked the caterwauling of the quadrangularis reversum, eucal blossom, and lord knows what other of Partch's invented instruments had been squeezed onto the stage. The players appeared to be posed, trance-like, as their implements produced sounds the human ear was never meant to be exposed to.

Ryan sipped her sugar-rush drink, and her bright, excited eyes took their fill.

"Well?" she asked enthusiastically, when the musicians paused to wheel in a new creation of musical torture.

"Cats in heat are only slightly less atonal," Natalya noted. "Although the gourd tree and cone gongs are very pleasing. To look at."

Ryan's expression fell. "Oh. I thought you'd really like it. It's like rebel music. Breaks all the rules."

"You think I break the rules?" Natalya asked, wondering what the hell had given her away.

"No," Ryan grinned and slurped her drink again. "I think you believe the rules don't apply to you."

"Based on?"

Ryan shrugged. "I'm not sure. It's the way your eyes weigh up everything around you and dismiss it as inferior."

Natalya started. That was an eerily accurate assessment. Her lips twitched in amusement.

"So, based on this theory, you thought I'd like a wailing wall of sound that disregards the golden rules of twelve notes per octave and squeezes in forty-three?" she asked.

"Yes. I thought you'd believe arbitrary rules are meant to be broken." Ryan ran her finger down the condensation of her glass, drawing abstract patterns.

"Some rules should never be broken," Natalya said with certainty, leaning back, regarding her with hooded eyes. "Some rules are so perfect, they should never be challenged. Twelve notes per octave gives us a purity of sound that is so balanced, it's like the building blocks of life. It's as clean as pure mathematics. Would you argue that zero should not exist?"

"Zero?" Ryan shook her head, looking baffled. "What on earth has zero got to do with anything?"

"Maths didn't make sense without it," Natalya said, and took another sip from her bottle of water. She was starting to wish she'd gone for vodka now she'd heard the on-stage entertainment. "Even so, its invention led to raging philosophical and even religious debates. But its inherent beauty could not be denied in the end."

"So you're saying that 'nothing' is beautiful?" Ryan laughed. "Right."

"Adding silence to a song can be important. It can empower the notes around it. So yes, zero can be beautiful."

Ryan paused. "Okay, sure, I'll give you that."

"And once something is accepted as so perfect, so logical, so pure that it makes such universal sense, why would you ever go back and try and change it? This xylophones-on-acid cacophony," she waved at the stage, "is an insult to every purist."

"You're a purist?" Ryan considered her. "I guess I just assumed most musicians would like to be daring and try new things."

Natalya gave her a small smile. "I can be very creative when I wish. But the rules, the building blocks of music, are immutable. The foundation should not be shaken."

"Or else?"

Natalya pointed at the stage. "Chaos."

"You really don't think anything that plays with the basics of music is worth a listen?"

"No," Natalya said, no doubt at all in her mind. "*Never.*"

Ryan said nothing, and Natalya studied her. She was clearly trying *not* to say something.

"Well?" Natalya taunted. "Don't hold back now. You're on a roll."

"You're wrong. You're rigid and you're wrong," Ryan said defiantly. "I bet I could find you some experimental music that you'd like without your purist world ending."

"That's a bet you would lose."

"I don't think so. In fact, I know I could do it."

A challenge. Natalya's eyebrows lifted in surprise. This was new.

"Tell you what—send me a traditional piece of music you think is so perfect that it can't be improved upon," Ryan said, rifling through her handbag, pulling out a notepad and pen, "and I'll send you music that breaks every rule—and yet *you* will love it."

She wrote down a mobile number, then passed her pen and pad to Natalya, looking at her expectantly. "Sorry, I left my phone at home or I'd just, you know…"

Natalya stared at the page and then slid her gaze back to the waiting blue eyes.

She never gave out her particulars. Not to strangers. Or colleagues. Employers perhaps, if absolutely required. This? This was unprecedented. She paused a beat too long, and Ryan suddenly seemed to realise what she'd asked of her.

"Oh," she said. Shame filled her eyes. "I'm sorry. That was so forward." She retracted the pad and pen.

Natalya sighed and reached forward, hesitated, then put a stilling hand on Ryan's. She then extracted the pad and slid it to her own side of the table.

"For the record," Natalya said as she wrote out her mobile number, "there is no such thing as perfection in music because the musician is always human. Therefore the piece will always be flawed."

She shot her a Cheshire cat smile and slowly ripped off the part of the page with Ryan's number on it. She pushed the notepad and pen back.

"Hmm," Ryan mused. She returned the items to her bag. "I get that it's hard for you, but please try," she said with a grin. "To the very best of your flawed, human soul, find me perfection in purity. And I will find you perfection in *im*purity."

She rose. "This has been really interesting, but I have to go. I look forward to your text message." She leaned forward. "Don't forget, okay?"

After a wave, she was gone.

Natalya stared at the scrap of paper and wondered what the hell had just happened. Had she inadvertently just made a friend? With a woman she was supposed to kill in two weeks' time?

Before she could think too hard on that, the ear drum-destroying wailings of mutilated xylophones began again.

CHAPTER 5

The text messages, delivered with Ryan's trademark, burbling enthusiasm, had been arriving regularly ever since that night. Natalya dispassionately noted she had not (yet) switched off her own phone.

Did you know Karlheinz Stockhausen composed a piece that had to be performed in three helicopters! No, that's not my final answer. If you hated Partch, you'll hate this, too. But doesn't that blow your mind? Oh, right, I forgot, minds can't be blown by musical rule breakers! Sacrilege!!!

Natalya shuddered. Yes, she'd heard the god-awful *Helicopter String Quartet*. It would have been marginally improved if the musicians had been ejected from said helicopters. Shrieks did have a certain musicality to them, as she well knew. She briefly contemplated sharing that factoid with Alison.

Instead, she wrote: *A publicity stunt does not music make. Are you even trying?*

Alison replied. *Just warming up. Don't make me send you John Cage's amplified cacti and feathers.*

The hitting of random objects doesn't count as a composition, either, Natalya texted back. *If it did, every toddler would be hailed a musical genius.*

She hit send, briefly wondering what Alison would reply. Then she froze. With irritation, she tossed her phone aside and stalked into her rehearsal room, slid onto the stool, and reached for her bow. Her thumb ran along its smooth back, and focused on her breathing.

Her name was *Ryan*. Not *Alison*. She was a *target*, for god's sake.

Christ. Natalya shook her head and began to play.

Within moments she was lost.

The next day a flurry of text messages arrived once more.

Have you ever been to Russia? With a surname like Tsvetnenko, I figured the odds are good.

Many times. Natalya texted back. *My father was from St Petersburg. I have depped with the Moscow Symphony Orchestra.*

Depped? Alison asked.

Filled in for an unavailable orchestra member. I have toured most of Europe depping with various orchestras.

That sounds amazing. But you didn't answer my question. What's Russia like?

What sort of a vague question was that? Natalya frowned at her phone and tapped out a reply.

Politically, socioeconomically, or personally?

Personally.

Natalya smiled and answered. *Very beautiful. It's lovely to visit. And St Petersburg in winter is like standing still in time. History is etched in every crevice of every building.*

You write as well as you play, I see.

Almost as well as Amanda Marks plays, you mean?

Well, she couldn't resist. Natalya had seen her with the woman's gawping groupies, after all.

Hey, give me some credit. Did you HEAR her at the Tchaikovsky season opener? I felt like slipping her a stimulant. Her fingers were slow. Her timing was sloppy.

Natalya stared at her screen in surprise. Was she not actually a fan of Marks?

How did you see that? Most people think professional musicians are machines. Nuance and flaws are never noticed.

Ryan took an eternity to answer. Finally Natalya's phone beeped and the answer was nothing she'd expected.

I don't like to talk about it, but I used to play violin. Not at concert level, of course. But I had a scholarship at the Sydney Conservatorium of Music for two terms.

Why only two? Natalya asked in surprise.

My mother became unwell. I came home to be her carer.

Natalya could feel a lot of pain behind the reply. To give up such a renowned scholarship? Her stomach knotted at the very thought of it. And the selflessness involved? She hissed in a breath and typed back.

Do you still play?

Never.

Natalya winced. She couldn't imagine a day without her music in it.

Why not? she asked.

It reminds me of what I've lost. And please don't ask me about it anymore. Makes me so sad. Can't we talk about you? Where's the best place on earth you've ever played?

Natalya very much wanted to push for more. Instead she considered the unexpected question.

I did an outdoor concert under some white blossoms in Okayama in Japan. It was like it was snowing along the canals. We all got covered in blossom. I was plucking it out of my cello for days. It was worth it. It was so quiet and surreal; I could almost hear people breathing. I thought I was in Narnia.

Natalya peered at her message the moment she'd sent it, wishing she could recall it. She sounded ridiculous mentioning Narnia.

Sounds heavenly. I'd have given every cent to see that.

Natalya snorted and wrote back. *That would have been a bargain.*

You saying you think I'm poor? :)

Natalya laughed aloud at that. Hell, she'd seen where she lived and knew exactly how much she earned. Doubtlessly the sick mother didn't help her bottom line.

She typed back: *I'm saying the moment was priceless.*

Ah. So is there anywhere you really want to play?

No. I have played them all. It wasn't boasting if it was true, Natalya decided, as she hit send.

Well that's depressing.

Why?

You always have to have something to look forward to. What about on top of Uluru?

Natalya blinked. The woman could not be serious! She typed furiously. *Given the wind gusts known to sweep people to their deaths, how would you propose I get my cello up there?*

Helicopter with a winch?

Natalya stared at her phone incredulously. *Are you insane?*

No imagination, lady.

If only she knew. Natalya decided it was time to dig into the little mouse's psyche. *So if everyone has to have something to look forward to, what is it you dream about?*

The reply took a few moments to arrive. *To be noticed.*

Natalya paused at the agony buried in those three stark words. She wasn't sure how she was supposed to answer that. She stared at the message for a good two minutes, when her phone lit up again.

I know that sounds weird. You'd never get it. You're not the invisible woman. You're the opposite of me. You're powerful, confident and I'm just…not. I'm the woman living with her mother who her colleagues treat as a joke. I'm great at my job but they don't see it. They don't see me at all. No one does.

The phone beeped almost immediately afterwards. *OK, have to go. I've embarrassed myself enough for one day. Thanks for the chat.*

Natalya considered Ryan's words. It was true, she didn't understand how women like her even existed. How could they not confront the world boldly, with confidence, head on? And how could she ever give up her music?
She glanced at her watch.

I have to go as well. I'm prepping for the 6th. We're playing it Friday.

Her phone beeped quickly. *Wish I could be there. That's my fave Tchaikovsky. I have to work back late at the office Friday. I'm getting close to tying up some loose ends.*

What do you do exactly? Natalya was curious as to how she'd answer. Would she talk herself up? Lie to impress her?

Officially? Or in reality?

Titles meant nothing, so Natalya wrote: *Reality.*

OK—I check the veracity of reports written by people from years ago. If there are errors I make them right. So many reports are incomplete or just plain wrong. It's crazy!

Natalya frowned. That sounded like much more than admin assistant work. Although the Victorian Government had been merging public servant jobs of late to save money. She wondered just how many jobs Ryan was stuck doing. No wonder she seemed so tired.

You're a fact checker? she asked.

Sort of. Either way it's a mountain of work. Let's just say an office grunt's inbox is never empty! But you'd never know about that.

Sounds like hell. Natalya had never meant anything more in her life.

It can be. But I'm good at it, despite my colleagues' views. It was sort of an accidental career when I had to give up music. And it suits my detail-oriented brain. So…here I am. One foot after the other.

Natalya shook her head. This was absurd. *It can't possibly be better than the career you almost had, though. Not even close to the dream you gave up.*

There was no question in Natalya's message, just the bald statement. She truly couldn't understand this career move. Not in the slightest. To go from musician to paper pusher was unthinkable.

The phone didn't beep again. No usual farewells, nothing.

Natalya gave the device the evil eye. Had she somehow offended her little mouse? Natalya's opinion was entirely right, of course, and she was simply pointing that out, nothing more, nothing less.

She threw her phone down. Well. She didn't have time to psychoanalyse Ryan. She had a concert to prepare for.

CHAPTER 6

Natalya was disgruntled. It was two days later, Friday morning, and still nothing from Ryan. She decided she was not pleased. It's not that the woman had anything to offer her, per se. Not like she was enriching Natalya's life in the least. Natalya needed no one for that. Well, to be exact, she needed no one for anything. She was the most self-sufficient person she'd ever known.

However, she mused, the little mouse probably felt judged and found lacking over her career choices.

Natalya sniffed. So what? A songbird caging itself? Such self-destruction shouldn't be overlooked or, worse, endorsed by her. Natalya was doing her a favour, pointing out the error in her thinking.

Why couldn't she see that?

Her lips thinned. This was getting absurd. Natalya should not care in the slightest about any of this. She certainly shouldn't be picturing big, sad eyes hurt over a throwaway text that stated a fact. And it was a fact. She returned to her sheet music with an angry slap.

By eleven that morning, still unable to properly practise, Natalya became irritated to find Ryan could invade her thoughts in this way. What was she to her? Nothing but a helpless target who wouldn't make old bones.

Natalya's nostrils flared as a stab of regret hit her again. She was starting to feel it a little more each day—a curling tendril of doubt about agreeing to do this job. She hadn't agreed to a "double the money, no questions asked" job in many years. For good reason. Although not essential, Natalya preferred to have all the answers. If one knows why and by whom someone is being targeted, one could anticipate complications.

She tapped her bow absentmindedly, thinking. Perhaps she could ask her associate to reduce the fee in exchange for further information? She paused. But that would make her seem weak. Her associate would seize on that, she had no doubt. Questions would follow, and Natalya had no answers for this situation. She didn't understand it herself.

Indecision was not something Natalya generally indulged in. Her path was usually so simple. Music was clear-cut like that. Clean. A note was either being played or it wasn't. Even if *some people* liked to pretend the musical wheel could be reinvented in more aurally destructive ways and rebadged as "creativity."

She tapped her bow again. She loathed indecision even more than she hated the flesh traders such as Ken Lee. People who robbed others of choice.

She was aware of the irony. She robbed others of their life. But this was different.

It just was.

A thought flitted back into her mind—Ryan didn't think she had any choice but to give up music. And instead of understanding her position, which Natalya didn't and never would, she had criticised her choice. It was always so easy to fix other people's lives. And the little mouse, who didn't walk the tallest among her peers to begin with, had felt Natalya's judgment keenly.

She sighed, laid down her bow, picked up her phone, and did something she hadn't done in years. Against all her internal protests, she apologised.

In her own way. Which was to say, she didn't actually say the exact words.

Forget work tonight, she tapped out to Ryan. *I'll have a ticket for the 6th left for you at the door. You will come. Be transported. We will confer afterwards at the café across from the VPO, and you can tell me all the ways experimental ear-bleeding wailing is somehow impressive compared to such perfection. I will, of course, offer a contrary—and superior—opinion. N."*

She waited. She waited for twenty minutes, her attention divided between the swaying trees outside her window and the phone in her lap.

Annoyed at hearing nothing but silence, she dropped the device to the floor and began to play. And this time, come hell or high water, she *would* focus.

That evening, as Natalya's performance was about to start, she reached for her phone to turn it off. She had one missed text. Her heart rate picked up for no damned reason, a condition she found odd and unsettling.

She flicked to the new message.

Well, who can refuse such a request? Expect to have your elitist opinions whumped, though. A.

Natalya stared at the message in relief.

"Why, Natalya," came a sultry, goading voice beside her that made her want to seriously rethink her unwritten rule of not killing colleagues. "Smiling before a performance? Smiling at all? Is it end times, dear?" Amanda Marks leaned over to pat her arm, laughing shrilly.

"Amanda." Natalya greeted the lead violinist coolly and glared at the invading arm. She *did* know how to rip that appendage off. "It's *always* end times. Most people just don't notice."

She gave her a cat-like grin and took pleasure in the confusion on Marks's face. Marks gave her a supercilious laugh, obviously aimed at disguising how confounded she felt, and walked off.

People were so shallow. Some were more insular and lacking in mental acuity than others. And others, such as Amanda Marks, were so utterly devoid of substance one could hold them up to the light and see right through them. It was a sad indictment of the human race that Natalya generally found most people duller than an Amish fashion show.

When was the last time anyone caught her attention and held it? Or properly challenged her? Held her interest for longer than a minute? She pushed away an image that immediately came to mind.

For God's sake, anyone but *her*. Alison Ryan made vanilla look edgy.

Despite her internal protestations, Natalya found herself looking forward to the concert's end so she could pick apart the other woman's arguments with gusto. She knew Ryan's claims would be illogical, maddening, eccentric, and heartily expressed.

Something akin to anticipation shot through her, and Natalya couldn't resist smiling again.

She stopped herself immediately. *Dear God.* This was getting habit forming.

CHAPTER 7

Maestros café was intimate and small, and soft classical music murmured in the background. At least it no longer played the elevator version of masterpieces. Natalya had retrained the management about the correct classical repertoire to pipe through a cafe when you're frequented by musicians.

On the walls, pinned like unfortunate insects, were old violins and other musical instruments. It was a sad end for them.

Natalya glanced around at the candles in red glass jars on tables and realised, with a sinking feeling, that she hadn't actually thought this through. The setting could be construed as intimate.

Alison's eyebrow had risen as she took in the surroundings. Clearly the same thought had crossed her mind.

"Oh," she whispered. "This place is really nice. Is this, um, I mean—"

"It's the closest café," Natalya said quickly, summoning the waiter with a wave. "All the orchestra members come here sooner or later to deconstruct."

"Oh, right." Alison nodded once and shot her a shy look. "So that's what we're doing? Deconstructing?"

"Of course," Natalya said as the waiter neared. "What else?"

"Ahh, Ms Tsvetnenko. A pleasure to see you again. it's been too long. How was your performance this evening?"

"Acceptable," she replied. Anton, while more familiar with her than she would prefer, had served her for years. He also made an adequate Russian Roulette which enabled her to tolerate his intrusions.

Anton's eyes flicked curiously to Alison. "And you have a guest this evening," he said brightly. "Ms Tsvetnenko usually graces us with her presence alone. I am Anton."

"Hey," she said. "I'm Alison. And her performance wasn't just acceptable, it was amazing."

He rocked back onto his heels and regarded them both for a moment, as though trying to figure them out against the backdrop of such a cosy setting.

Natalya found the scrutiny presumptuous. "I'll have my usual," she said, interrupting his reverie, "with extra vodka." She glanced over to Alison, silently asking.

"Ah, coffee, please. Just plain."

"Would you care to see the menu? Or the sweets tray? Chef has a delicious fruit of the forest tart tonight. Perfect for an after-show nibble. You could share, perhaps," he added boldly.

Alison was growing pink, and Natalya was nearing her wit's end. This was not a date. This would never be a date. She did not date. Ever. This was a mistake; that's what it was.

"No," Natalya said curtly. If looks could kill, she was damn sure Anton would be a smouldering ash pile right now.

The waiter got a clue and scurried away, and she exhaled, then realised her oversight. "You didn't want dessert, did you?"

Alison fiddled with a napkin. "I shouldn't. Have to be careful." She patted her stomach regretfully.

Natalya studied her with curiosity. "Careful of what? You *are* in proportion, aren't you? Not a diabetic? Or is this one of those things where women say they shouldn't and mustn't and so on and then sneak some anyway? I'd rather you just have what you really want than worry about what I'd think. Life's too short. Trust me."

Alison studied her pensively. "I wasn't worried about what you'd think. I was more concerned with what my mother would think if I porked out." She laughed sheepishly. "She really worries about image. I'd never hear the end of it."

Natalya wasn't fooled by the lightness of her tone.

"What do you care what she thinks you should eat?" she asked, baffled. "You're an adult."

"She's my mother! Of course what she thinks matters."

Natalya shook her head. "That's ludicrous. A parent's job is to raise you to fend for yourself in adulthood. Not to make you too traumatised to have a treat on a night out."

Alison's jaw clamped shut.

Natalya regarded her stormy expression and wondered what she'd said now. Women were the most frustrating, maddening creatures on earth to deal with. She rubbed her forehead. Why had she ever thought tonight was a good idea? Give her an assassin any day over whatever was happening here.

Anton returned and put down their drinks. He gave them both a friendly wink. "Enjoy, ladies."

"What did you think of the concert?" Natalya asked when he left, unimpressed by the innuendo dripping from his voice.

"Oh," Alison said, her eyes brightening. "It was like a religious experience." She looked at her nervously. "I know that probably sounds so silly."

"Not at all," Natalya said, firmly. "It's like being transported to the heavens."

"Yes!" Alison said. "I cried at the end. I always do."

Natalya considered her next words carefully. She'd never admitted this to a soul.

"So do I. Every time. *Pathétique* is the embodiment of human pain. It picks mankind apart. And it articulates death. Tchaikovsky touches on everything—sorrow, pleading, love, longing, despair, and hope. If you don't hear his ache, then you're not alive. By the time I finish the 6*th* Symphony, I'm always feeling raw, and I can never stop the prick of tears."

"Why would you even try?"

Natalya pursed her lips. "It's not good to have distractions. Even so, I leave a part of myself on stage every time I play that. It reminds me of what we really are. Fallen. Flawed. Tchaikovsky points to our conceit and how meaningless it all is. It's the most honest work I've ever played."

Alison fiddled with her coffee. "That's a bleak outlook. I see the 6*th* more as a cry for what we lose when we die. Not a mockery of dreams that can't be."

"Please. He was a tortured Russian gay man forced to hide who he really was his whole life. Trust me; he was doing plenty of mocking of humanity's unfulfilled dreams and losses. It's almost entirely pathos; little else."

"Well, that's depressing. He could have just been imaginative."

"And that's insanely optimistic. Besides, I'm being kind. Some historians called the piece a portentous suicide note—even if he did die of cholera. It was a requiem of sorts."

"A requiem?" Alison repeated.

Natalya studied her cautiously. "Yes. Why?"

"It's just…It's not a common word."

"You need to associate with more musicians."

Alison sighed. "I need to associate with *anyone* more."

"Oh?"

"I don't get out much. Well not for the past fifteen years." She shot her an embarrassed grin. "It's currently kind of sad. My life."

"Why don't you get out?"

"I have to look after Mum. She's not mobile. She likes having me nearby."

"They do have nursing services. Carers who do this sort of thing professionally. Even part-time."

"She doesn't want to use one. My sister and I offered to pool our resources and get her someone, and help find her a better house, too. But it would mean using our inheritance from Dad and his late second wife.

"Problem is, Mum would rather stew in her juices and be enraged at him long after he's dead, cursing his 'whore money,' than have a good life. Why be happy when you can wallow in your own bitterness?"

"Yet, she's fine with *you* having no life? Are you fine with that, too?" Natalya kept her tone deceptively polite. Inside she was roiling at the old woman's selfishness.

Alison folded her arms. "You're doing it again."

"What?"

"Judging me for choices that are out of my hands. You don't know what it's like to be me."

"Nothing is ever out of our hands. Women, especially, too often believe it to be so, because that's what the world wants us to believe."

Alison shook her head. "What about people in really hard situations, who might be trapped by circumstance?"

"If someone wants something more than anything else, they will inevitably achieve it," Natalya said flatly. "People say they can't do things far too often. It's weak. More often than not, they haven't even tested their limits."

"That's too simplistic. You strip all the emotion out of how difficult these things are for some people. How wrenching it can be."

"Then they should look at the larger picture and do what needs to be done. If that means putting aside the emotional consequences until they can deal with them later—so be it."

"But they're emotions! You can't just park them till later. They're unavoidable. You're a musician who gets moved to tears you can't control. So how can you even believe that?"

Natalya regarded her seriously. "A momentary loss of control is not the same as allowing myself to *be* controlled. There is a reason I had played at every major concert hall with all the world's leading orchestras before I was twenty-eight. Do you think that just happened? Yet I began with nothing and had to fight for it with just my wits and skill. I was prepared to do what it took to get what I wanted."

She paused and remembered the men in expensive suits at Ken Lee's warehouse who had first laughed when she'd made her proposal as an earnest seventeen-year-old.

The only one who hadn't laughed had been Dimitri's ambitious new wife, Lola, who'd seen her potential. The mob wife had her own reputation to prove.

She'd taken Natalya aside, looked her over and done a deal so breathtakingly far-reaching and diabolical that two and a half decades later Melbourne's crime families were still paying the price for it.

Natalya had to grow up fast in those early days because several patrons felt their sponsorship of her should include certain entitlements in return. The first man to make that mistake bled out within minutes, his manhood stapled to his office door.

The others had taken careful note of that rebuttal. Natalya's reputation had been cemented. No one laid so much as a fingernail on her after that.

"I also had to ensure I was not seen by my sponsors as some weak pushover," Natalya continued. "Strength doesn't lie in emotions. Strength lies in knowing how to reign in your emotions to get the end result. You control them, you win."

Alison looked at her incredulously. "That's just…that's…so sad. Emotions aren't a weakness! How can you think like that? I feel everything and it's just who I am. It doesn't make me weak.

"I get weepy over sappy TV commercials. I cry when an old couple falls in love. I turn to mush when my niece sends me silly home-made birthday cards. I cling to the dog I adopted in Sydney like I'm losing a child every time I say goodbye to her because I can't stand not being with her, but Mum's allergies mean she lives with my sister instead.

"I still hurt over what I left behind in Sydney. It was more than just a scholarship and a musical career. I left Melissa. She was funny and kind. She played flute and sang bad falsettos out car windows and she had my heart. I had to give her up to come home. I still get this pain, this deep ache, when I think of what could have been.

"But I wouldn't swap all that emotional turmoil for feeling nothing. It's *living*, Natalya. It's being *human*. You can't just shove that aside. That's like me telling you that you should stop feeling anything during Tchaikovsky's 6*th*.

"God, what will happen if you ever face an emotional storm you can't handle, that's too big for you to suppress through sheer force of will?"

"Well, that will never happen. It's all about discipline." Natalya finished her drink and placed the glass neatly on the table. She found it interesting that Alison preferred the company of women. But the rest—well, she could barely relate. Who embraces chaos? Why would anyone willingly do that? It made little sense. Natalya rotated her glass 15 degrees to straighten it, before flicking her gaze up. "You really are like no one I have ever met before."

"Is that a good thing?"

Natalya gave her a sideways look. "I'm not sure. Probably good. I have met some appalling people. Classical musicians can be the worst. They all think they're gods. Me included."

Alison grinned. "Well, you're not like anyone I've ever met, either."

"No," Natalya agreed with complete certainty. "I'm not."

"Why are you?" Alison asked, seemingly unaware she hadn't even uttered a complete sentence.

"Why am I what?"

"Sitting here? With me? In your gorgeous black evening gown, with posh jewellery, all regal and perfect. Like some European countess. And here's me: Unimportant, with my best Target necklace on. A no one."

Natalya wished she knew the answer. This evening had crossed every line. Every rule drilled into her. Instead she replied lightly: "You're here because I wished to hear your views on the 6*th* *Symphony*."

"Why do you care what *I* think?" Alison peered at her and waited.

"I suppose you have an earnest, if backward, view about what constitutes music." Natalya offered her a hint of a smile. "It's unusual. And you cry at puppies and sunshine or some such thing, and are both modest and amusing, so that makes you about as unique as a unicorn in my world."

"Oh, I get it," Alison laughed. "I'm like some weird circus bearded lady. And, hello? 'Backward view'? Did you just insult me?"

"Quite possibly," Natalya said agreeably. "Don't expect an apology."

"Let me guess: it's a sign of weakness?"

"Something like that. Or I may be out of practice. Who would I ever have to apologise to? Everyone else is always the one in the wrong."

"God," Alison muttered. "How do you even exist? I mean, seriously. You're so high maintenance. I'd need an instruction manual to understand you."

"Yet you're the one who insists on the entire world processing its emotions without filters. That's how wars get started."

"Or ended. Love is an emotion, too."

Natalya noted the triumphant gleam. She arched an eyebrow. "I swear if you break into *Age of Aquarius*, we are done."

"We? What, um…" Alison faded out.

Natalya's expression faltered. She had not meant to say that. She began to pray for her mythical assassin to appear. *That* she could deal with.

"It's not a…" Natalya tried to order her thoughts. "I didn't mean to imply that we…" she waggled her fingers between herself and Alison. "I don't…" She stopped again, frowning.

Alison leaned over and patted her hand. "Hey, don't worry. Don't overthink it."

Natalya felt the pulse in the other woman's wrist. The warmth under her skin. She resisted the urge to curl her fingers into Alison's and retracted her hand swiftly.

"Well, I think it's time you tell me: how are you coming along with your cacophony of experimental music you claim that I'll like?"

"It's coming. Just keep your phone handy this week while I narrow down the field. What about you? How goes the hunt for a pure piece of perfection?"

Natalya leaned back in her chair. "Purity is actually easy to find in music. It's narrowing it down to *perfection* that's difficult. It's an impossible task you've set."

"I thought you said people gave up too easily? Although, you know there *is* such a thing as being too perfect."

"Heresy," Natalya said sharply. "Next you'll say musicians aren't at the top of the social food chain."

"I wouldn't dare." Alison laughed.

"Glad that's settled. Now, dessert." She eyed her expectantly and offered an encouraging smile. "Yes?"

Alison twisted her napkin into a knot. Then untwisted it and folded it, patting it flat as Natalya waited. She suddenly looked up and smiled and it was like sun breaking through clouds. It was unsettling.

"You know, I think that's a great idea," Alison said.

Natalya nodded once, feeling a mix of triumph and approval, and summoned Anton.

They walked together back to the VPO's open-air parking lot. It was an incongruous sight, Natalya thought, with her formidable height, and Alison's tiny features. Like an oak tree swaying next to a daffodil.

The heavens opened up and a fine rain began. It was too light to worry about. Alison suddenly stopped and smiled up at the skies, startling Natalya. She then opened her arms as she gazed up at the blackness.

A streetlight a block away illuminated the fine drops in its halo. It was too far away to see the details, so from where she stood it looked like a sphere of mist engulfing the light.

Alison turned full circle, her face up, and grinned even wider.

"God," she whispered. "How amazing is this?" She glanced over to Natalya, who had remained stock still, feeling vaguely astonished.

"Don't you love rain?" Alison asked her. "It's so renewing."

"Apparently so," she said dryly and Alison laughed. She stopped twirling. "Sorry. I just realised that probably looks cooler if you're an Austrian nun."

Alison slicked back her hair with her hand, wrenching out the elastic band corralling her ponytail and shoving it in her pocket. She combed her fingers through her wet hair.

"Never apologise for being who you are," Natalya said, quietly. "If you have the urge to dance in the rain, dance in the rain."

"And have you stand there and laugh at me? Please, I know your game now," Alison joked. "I'm your cheap entertainment. Like some weird interactive art installation: *Insane Woman In Rain.*"

Natalya fell silent, her gaze dropping to Alison's chest. The rain had now rendered her pale cotton shirt translucent. Her white bra was clearly outlined. The sight was…pleasing.

Alison followed her gaze and flushed.

"I'm not laughing," Natalya replied softly and, after a beat, her gaze drifted back up again. She lifted her eyebrow, wondering what Alison's next unorthodox move would be.

Alison cleared her throat and looked embarrassed. She waved towards a Datsun 120Y in the parking lot. Mustard yellow, about 500 years old. Rust was creeping up its undercarriage. It took everything in Natalya's arsenal not to show her distaste.

"Well, this is me," Alison said. "Where are you?"

Natalya inclined her head towards her silver Jaguar. "Not far. Although I still have to pick up my cello."

"Oh," Alison said, sounding interested. "A Jag?"

"Yes. Why?"

"I think I half expected you to ride a motorcycle. Something fast and high-powered. That'd be cool."

"Impractical for a cellist, don't you think?" she countered. "And my evening gown would get caught in the spokes. That'd be quite a statement."

"You don't ride even recreationally?" Alison asked. "Off road or something?"

"Off road? You mean in the bush? Why would anyone do that? One fall and a glorious musical career would be over, and I'm rather fond of my glorious musical career."

"Lots of musicians ride bikes. They're like chefs," Alison said. "Or so I hear. I guess they like to blow off steam. High-powered job and all that."

Natalya kept her face a mask. "If you say so."

Alison leaned back against her car. "How do you then? Blow off steam, I mean? Come down from the heavens as you call it. What do *you* do?"

"I could tell you, but then I'd have to kill you."

Alison blinked at her, startled.

"It's a saying," Natalya said, laughing at her expression. She rolled her eyes. "You're right: you really need to get out more."

"Yeah, yeah, I know. I forgot to thank you, by the way. I appreciate you leaving me a ticket at the door. This was fun." She straightened and leaned closer to Natalya. Her eyes slid to Natalya's lips.

To her complete surprise, Natalya's own body betrayed her, swaying closer. That apparently was all the invitation Alison needed as she tilted her head up. Natalya's hands immediately shot out, catching Alison by the biceps, holding her within breath-sipping distance from her.

"No," Natalya said, but realised she hadn't exactly pulled back.

Alison's face reddened. "God, I'm so sorry. I thought…"

"I know what you thought. And that's not something I'm interested in. With anyone."

They were still inches apart. Natalya should have pushed her away and stepped back by now. Alison's warm breath feathered across her skin and Natalya's gaze traced the perfect bow-shape of her lips. As she admired them analytically for their geometric perfection and the way the edges turned up pleasantly, something stirred inside, and her breath quickened.

Oh good grief, no. Not over the little mouse! That was insane.

Alison obviously decided to be bold and try again. She pushed closer to Natalya and lifted her chin again.

Natalya sighed, which halted the movement, doubt once more flashing across Alison's features, along with embarrassment. Natalya's exhalation dusted the fine hairs on the soft face upturned before hers.

So trusting. It would be so easy. She could almost taste the most alluring essence there ever was, the thing she so rarely encountered, and it drew her like a siren's song.

Innocence.

Natalya's gaze traced Alison's mouth. So tempting. Did virtue and goodness have an actual taste? What it would be like, taking her right here, against this sorry excuse of a car, that perfectly proper skirt of hers rucked up? She hissed in a breath at the thought. She briefly closed her eyes, stilling her breath, calling on her well of discipline.

"Are you curious, at least?" Alison asked with a thick voice. "About what you and I would be like?"

"We're such opposites," Natalya said. "We'd only cancel each other out. We'd self-destruct."

Alison gave a tiny laugh. "What a way to go. And that wasn't a no."

She pressed herself against Natalya, a plea for more. "You're so beautiful," Alison said, her hands dropping to Natalya's hips.

Alison's fingers pulled their bodies closer until all Natalya felt was a wall of soft heat.

"Natalya. Please?"

Please. She'd heard the word "please" many times over the years. Begging. Begging her not to kill them. The timbre was even the same. An edge of desperation, with the faintest sliver of hope. She had ignored them all. Because that was what she did. She was Requiem. And Requiem killed.

This would never be right. This was her *target*, for god's sake. She abruptly pushed Ryan away.

"I can't," Natalya said coolly. "No…just, no."

"Damn," Alison said quietly. "I've made a fool of myself."

She moved away, to the driver's side of her car. "I get it," she added. "It's okay. I mean, look at you and look at me." She gave a strangled laugh and shook her head.

"Alison."

"No, it's fine. You probably have your pick of people. Anyone in the world would want you. And I'm just Alison, the idiot who amuses you with her bizarre musical tastes."

She got inside and slammed her car door.

Natalya stared after her, robbed of words, as the little yellow car pulled away. If only she knew who the real target of derision should be.

She was still standing there minutes later, unmoving, as the rain continued to fall.

CHAPTER 8

Natalya had never hated herself more as she headed home. She threw her keys onto the side table instead of hanging them up. She kicked her heels off and slammed her cello case against the wall, then bit her lip regretfully, tracing her fingers over the instrument. She'd never done that before. Never.

Nor had she made this call before. Not once in twenty-four years. She paced her home, stared at her fish tanks, then paced some more, waiting for her mobile phone's security mechanism to kick in and leapfrog the call halfway around the world and back.

Her associate picked up on the first ring. "Req? This is a surprise," she said. "You've taken care of Viktor already?"

"No," Natalya said. "It's the other job. I need to know why."

"Ryan? They paid big money for no questions."

"Then refund some. I want answers."

"Why? You've never cared before. Why now?"

"She's unusual."

"I'm well aware. I told you that, if you recall. But even so, asking questions is not in your job description. You were trained better than that. Now unless you need more information to do your job, there's nothing more I can tell you."

Natalya stalked over to her freezer and pulled out her vodka bottle and a chilled glass. "In order to do this job I have to know what she did and who she did it to."

There was a long pause.

"They were specific," her associate said. "Don't ask, don't tell. If it helps, I know the job was external to the families but it still came via them. It was one of Santos's men who passed it along to me on behalf of the client. That's all I know."

"That's not good enough." Natalya gave the liquid in her glass an agitated swirl. "Not this time."

"And again, Req, I have to ask: Why? What's different?"

"*She* is," Natalya said and lifted the drink to her lips. The bite was sharp and she immediately relaxed into it, enjoying the burn. She swallowed. "She's an innocent. I've been following her. She looks after her sick mother, for God's sake. Gave up her dream career and her dog to do the noble thing. The woman pushes paperwork around all day and actually thinks she's daring for loving Harry fucking Partch."

"Is that her boyfriend? I thought she was single?"

Natalya snorted derisively. "You are a complete Philistine."

"Is that any way to talk to your mother?"

Natalya rolled her eyes at the thick sarcasm. "*Step* mother. And even then only for two years before you decided the heady life of a crime boss's wife suited you far more than mundane suburbia with us."

"Oh *please*. Remember who you're talking to. We both know you don't have a mundane bone in your body and never did. Your father, on the other hand, with all his tiresome adherence to Russian military precision–"

"Lola," Natalya warned. "Don't start. Now get me *more*."

"Just tell me why. Are you going soft now? Is that what this is? *Ah*. I just looked up Mr Partch. So you like that she's into music? That it?"

"Harry Partch is the absence of music."

"Req, this is business. You're better than this. I never thought we'd *ever* have to have this talk. Your reputation is all about supreme efficiency and ruthlessness. You get cold feet on even one job, and everyone will assume you're unreliable. How many times have I heard you rant about the rest? 'Unprofessional, flawed sacks of humanity', you called them. Don't let this target get under your skin. The deal was a *no-questions-asked* hit. That won't change. So get focused. Stay focused. Then do your damned job."

The phone went dead.

Natalya stared morosely at it. She angrily slammed her glass onto the table.

Lola was right. She wondered how she'd let a little mouse make her question everything. She never felt much of anything when she dispatched the others. She made sure she didn't. It was all business. So why did she care now? Who was Alison Ryan in the scheme of things? No one. Even Ryan herself believed it.

She was *no one.*

Natalya sipped her vodka and finally faced what she had been avoiding all night: It *would* be different, looking into this one's eyes as the light died from them.

Her guts tightened at the thought and she resented the sickening sensation. Resented the hell out of the fact that she gave Ryan a second thought at all.

Lola hadn't lied about how her reputation would suffer, bailing on a job. Natalya *was* better than this. She was a professional. She would do her damn job. And she wouldn't think of inviting lips and trusting blue eyes. Wouldn't recall how tempting that innocence had been, coming at her in waves, daring her to slam Ryan's back against that ugly car bonnet, hike up her skirt, slide her fingers up those soft white thighs, and fuck her into next week.

She definitely wouldn't think about how it would feel to make her moan. Make her sigh. Make her whisper Natalya's name. How good it could be to show her the art of pleasuring the human body. She'd watch her as she came, as she trembled and cried out. As she kissed her.

Natalya's breath caught.

Kissed her?

Shit.

She slammed down the rest of her drink and then, with shaking hands, washed the glass and dried it over and over until it shone. Her hands were aching and red. Still she continued, drying and drying. It was a comforting motion and it blocked out the other thing.

Part of her was furious that she even had to block it out at all.

She finally exhaled and slapped the glass down on the counter, then headed for her rehearsal room, angry and dismayed. There would be no more of this… fraternisation. Talking to Ryan…to the prey. None of that. Never again.

This was business. All business.

CHAPTER 9

Requiem crossed the Railway Parade railway line and turned into Seaford North Reserve, a small suburban oval just north of Frankston. She parked her Ninja out of sight, under a row of trees, and locked her helmet on the bike's side clip. She had dressed for her environment. Fitted jeans, brown boots, a white T-shirt with a long-sleeve, pale blue shirt over the top. Suburban mum, with just a hint of assassin.

Well, she was dressed as close as she could manage to the stereotype without throwing up a bit in her mouth. Her hair was in a long no-nonsense plait.

She stealthily scouted the edges of the area. It was now Saturday. She had gone two days without replying to Ryan's messages. Those texts hadn't alluded to their near kiss nor their not-date at all. They'd been funny and light, and had included four more links for her to try—experimental music from Ryan's short list.

She hadn't clicked on any of them.

One of her best-paid informants told her that Viktor Raven was dedicated to his daughter, who, it turned out, was a soccer player for a team here today. Her informant had failed to produce a name for the girl because Raven protected her identity too well. So far all her source could supply was a blurry, black-and-white, long-distance photo from behind the unnamed child leaving a soccer game. That was fine, though—it wasn't the girl she was after.

Of course, if Raven had any brains at all, logic dictated he'd remain far, far away from here right now. But, human nature being what it was, she suspected the man, like most flawed humans, would be weak when it came to his offspring.

And so, here Requiem sat, watching the Dandenong Rampagers take on the Frankston Fillies. Frankston was killing them. And, as the Under-14 teams pelted down the ground, it quickly became clear why.

"Chandra! Front pocket, shadow No. 31."

A woman in shorts and a white T-shirt, the word "COACH" emblazoned on the back in enormous letters, was at the far end of the ground. She faced away from Requiem for most of the game, hunched over a small whiteboard. The woman missed nothing. Every quarter, she stood in the middle of a huddle of teens with her blue cap and large, wide sunglasses as she explained their next moves. The girls nodded along, their heads bobbing earnestly.

The coach's plays were like a chess game and behind every play was a clever tactic that had been well thought out ahead of time. She frowned each time she heard her shout. It seemed familiar—which was absurd. Who did she know who coached junior soccer?

A girl with a brown ponytail shot another goal, her third, and the coach clapped. "Good girl!"

The game was over at noon—to the Dandenong players' relief. The star of the Frankston team ran over and hugged the coach with more than passing familiarity. The coach nodded, pointed towards the car park, and then began heading towards it herself. Halfway across the pitch, she glanced towards Requiem's position.

And that's when she inhaled sharply. Great. So now her target was a kids' soccer coach? Her eyes flicked around for an escape route, hoping to slip away unseen.

Ryan had stopped walking and was staring in her direction in surprise. She lifted her hand and waved furiously, a smile splitting her face.

Requiem inwardly groaned.

Oh joy. The woman thought she was here for her.

Requiem debated leaving anyway. But that wouldn't solve her pressing Viktor situation. Shrugging off her alter-ego with some effort, Natalya affixed a neutral expression and sauntered over.

Ryan continued walking until she reached a station wagon. She began squeezing sporting gear into the back. Given the car's array of macho Melbourne Storm rugby league stickers plastered along the rear window, Natalya guessed it was borrowed.

"How did you know I'd be here?" Ryan asked when Natalya reached her, as she crammed the gear in. "Well, however you figured it out, I'm really glad you are."

"Need a hand?" Natalya said, sidestepping the question as Ryan pushed a washing basket full of soccer balls into the rear. One escaped and bounced towards Natalya.

She stopped it with her foot and then flicked it with her toe back towards the car. In one bounce it landed inside.

Ryan gave her an impressed look. "Wow. I could use you on my wing."

"Somehow, I don't think you need any help. How long have you coached?"

"I just do it occasionally, when the Fillies' coach can't. He's on his honeymoon right now."

"I'd think he'd be feeling a bit threatened by that score line. Five nil?"

Ryan shrugged modestly. "Score is irrelevant. They're just little girls. I'm teaching them teamwork. That matters more than anything else."

"Does it?" Natalya asked. "I'd have thought individuality would be a more important lesson. Especially at this age, when they're facing peer pressure."

Ryan shook her head. "Please. Society's already too me-me-me. What they pick up here is stuff they can't learn easily elsewhere."

She paused and looked at Natalya. "You look really nice," she said. "Although I don't think I'll ever get used to the sight of you in jeans."

"Oh?" Natalya said, glancing down at herself. Surely she didn't stand out too much?

"Yeah. You're so naturally elegant, and yet this is so casual. It's like seeing Aphrodite in her gym clothes or something."

"I'm no goddess. Not even close."

"No," Ryan agreed, with a small smile, "but you create music like one. And you could pass for one if you could be bothered. On the flip side, goddesses have all those annoying fan girls, don't they? How irritating for them," she said lightly, lips twisting. "Hey, hand me that bag?"

Natalya passed over a sports bag, which was duly wedged into the boot, as she processed Ryan's self-deprecation.

So, she had decided Natalya thought Ryan was just some fan who had been swatted aside as irritating?

Actually, the masses desperate for selfies and autographs were the true irritation for artists, because they sought a slice of one's fame and made no true effort to understand that their object of devotion was real. The celebrity was seen as little more than a commodity to be collected, traded, and ultimately discarded when they disappointed. Their heroes were not even human, just "perfect" or "flawless."

Until they weren't.

The little mouse had never done that with her. She seemed to have no interest in Natalya's fame at all. She was entirely focused on knowing Natalya herself. So, no, she was not irritating. Quite the opposite.

And that was the problem.

Natalya could tell her that, of course, but what was the point? Ryan was still her target. Natalya was supposed to be keeping her distance from her, not worrying about boosting her self-confidence.

The car boot was slammed shut. Ryan glanced around, her star player catching her eye in the distance. She waved to the girl who was talking to her friends. The teenager began to trot over.

"Want a bite to eat?" Ryan asked. "Almost lunch time. I've worked up an appetite. You can explain why you've been ignoring my musical masterpieces."

Natalya couldn't read her expression through the dark sunglasses.

"I've been busy practising music that sounds actually musical," Natalya said. "Not the sound a mechanic makes when he drops his wrench."

Her gaze darted back to the clusters of parents and children on the sidelines. It looked like her primary target was a no-show. So much for family ties. She wondered whether Ryan knew which girl playing today had a father with such a distinctive name as Viktor Raven? As a coach, she well might. Her racing mind perked up at the thought. Perhaps this wasn't a bust after all.

"But yes," Natalya said with forced brightness. "Lunch."

"Great!" Alison smiled at her and sounded relieved. "Right, hang on, I have to talk to Hailey."

She walked off and was soon in conversation with the girl she'd waved over.

Natalya contemplated their surroundings. They were miles from anywhere, in a part of town not exactly known for its fine eateries. Lord only knew where lunch would be.

"Okay, I'm ready," Ryan said after jogging back to her. "Hope you don't mind but I have to babysit Hailey today as her dad couldn't make it. But I can assure you she's pretty amusing company. Thirteen years old and absolutely no censor button."

Natalya paused. A girl with a missing father? And Natalya was looking for one? It could just be a coincidence but still…

"No problem at all," she said and smiled. "Kids and I get on just fine." Well, almost true. She had talked to a child once. It had not run away.

Alison shot her a sceptical look. "Um, okay. After that, well, I'm all yours." Her smile was hesitant and guarded. Natalya couldn't blame her given how they'd left things.

"Burgers all right?" Ryan asked. "They're gourmet if that helps. There's a Hamburger Heaven over the road and up a bit on Station St. We can walk across from here."

Natalya quashed her initial response and nodded tightly again. Dear God. *Hamburger Heaven?* What insanity was this?

Ryan laughed, and Natalya chose not to dignify it with a response.

CHAPTER 10

Natalya was in suburban hell. It was possible she was in actual hell, too. Primary colours pummelled her eyeballs. A number of girls from both teams, along with their parents, had decided Hamburger Heaven was the ideal post-match lunch location and had converged on this family-friendly satanic hell pit, too.

Adding a touch of class, every so often the room would be drowned out by the clanging sound of the boom gates on the nearby railway line. Glasses of drinks trembled on the tables as the train roared by.

"Any allergies, ladies?" Alison asked, eyes gleaming with amusement at the appalled expression Natalya no doubt was wearing. The tables were covered with plastic, red and white checked tablecloths and cheap napkin dispensers.

Hailey rolled her eyes in an exact mirror of Natalya at the question.

"Okay then, I'll be right back. Trust me!" Alison said.

Because, of course, table service would be too much to ask for.

"So," Hailey said, considering Natalya for a beat. "You and my aunt, huh? How long have you two been dating?"

Natalya blinked. "She's your aunt?"

"That's what you took from my comment? Okay, so that proves it. You two are on like Donkey Kong. Hey, do you have any pets? You have to like dogs if you date her. Like—*have* to. I have one dog, Charlotte, but she's really old. Actually it's my aunt's dog but she lives with us. The dog, not my aunt." She giggled.

"What?" Natalya peered at the little upstart, wondering what Donkey Kong had to do with anything. As for pets, did a cone snail count?

"You look sooo confused. Was it the Donkey Kong thing? Don't you know what that is? It's a computer game from, like, a century ago." She studied her closely. "How old are you anyway? You look wayyy older than my aunt."

"Charming. Do you kiss your mother with that mouth?"

Hailey gave a bark of laughter. "Oooh, super snark. You remind me of my best friend Petey. He's gay, too."

"It's rude to announce people's sexualities to them. What if you're wrong?"

"Am I? And why's it rude unless you think being gay's a bad thing? Oh, I get it: Are you one of those self-loathing homophobes? I saw a daytime special about that once." The kid gave Natalya a shit-eating smirk.

"I'm not a homophobe," Natalya bit back, snarling, "and anything else is none of your damn business."

"Ooh! No swearing!"

Natalya gave her an evil sneer which just made the little shit laugh harder. Natalya was losing her touch. Her sneer fell away as she suddenly considered the implications. If Hailey was Viktor Raven's kid, did that mean Ryan was the weasel's sister?

She tried to recall the image of the pasty-faced slug with his narrow, watchful eyes. They didn't appear to be in the same gene pool, but stranger things had happened. And it might explain how Ryan had ended up on someone's kill list. Did she know something? Or had she witnessed something?

Hailey played with the salt shaker. "You're funny. And that evil glare is totally awesome. It'd melt the paint off a car. But I was totally just trying to be friendly. Seriously, Mum will be really pleased. She says her big sister got stuck with Grandma and it's, like, killing her social life."

"Did your aunt have much of a social life before your grandmother got sick?" Natalya asked curiously.

Hailey shrugged. "Nope. Well, I don't think so. But I wasn't alive then."

"So what makes you so sure she's gay?"

"I overheard Mum talking to Dad once. Like a few years ago. She was asking him to treat her better at work. And he said he couldn't or it'd look like nepalism and besides no way the rest of the team wanted some dyke getting all the good jobs. And she was too pathetic to do anything but paperwork anyway. No one would take her seriously."

"Nepotism," Natalya corrected quietly and flicked her gaze to the counter, where Alison was now queuing to place their order. "Your father is Alison's boss? What do they do exactly?"

"How can you not know that? Come on, you're dating her!" Hailey said, eyeing her suspiciously. She gave a savage huff of breath and leaned forward. "No offence, but you sound like a really crap girlfriend. You should get her chocolates. A box of Whitestars. With fudge centres. She loves those even though she says she can't have too many."

"Fudge centres," Natalya repeated. "Well that's a dentist's visit just waiting to happen."

"I take it back, you're not funny, you're mean." Hailey folded her arms and studied her. "How did you two even meet?"

"At an orchestral event," Natalya replied archly. "I'm a cellist."

"Oh." Hailey sat back abruptly and nodded as though that explained everything. "Okay then. Fine."

"Fine?"

"Yep. I get it. My aunt loves all that old boring music. How long have you been dating anyway?"

Natalya glanced at her watch by way of answer. The kid didn't seem to be taking her denials as truth anyway.

"Oh!" Hailey looked shocked. "Did I just crash your first date? I didn't know, swear!"

Natalya was faintly amused. "Well, I daresay at least it's been entertaining."

Hailey grinned back. "See? I *knew* it was a date."

Natalya shook her head in amusement. She saw a leaf sticking out of Hailey's hair, and her hand shot out to pluck it from the strands.

Hailey flinched, bringing her elbow up to protect the side of her face. Natalya's hand immediately retracted showing her the leaf.

"It was a leaf," she murmured as a red tint spread over the girl's cheeks.

Who hits you?, she wondered darkly. *Viktor?* The slug had the eyes for it. She opened her mouth to ask.

"Don't," Hailey said quietly.

Natalya looked at her, startled by the world of pain in her tone.

"Don't ask. You can't help. You don't know my family. You don't know Dad. What he can do. No one does."

Her voice was chilling, and nothing like that of the carefree teen she'd first sat down with. Natalya flicked her eyes over to the counter to see Alison turning towards them with a tray of food.

"Don't say anything," Hailey hissed.

"Your aunt doesn't know?"

"He'd hurt her if she did. Please don't tell her."

Natalya studied her. "Suit yourself."

Hailey shot her a shaky smile. "You're okay. I guess." She plucked her knife from the cutlery bundle rolled up in a serviette and waved it playfully. "But don't you hurt my aunt. I might be little but I would track you down and cut you one."

Natalya was impressed at Hailey's loyalty and ferocity. She laced her fingers together. "You know, I'm not *actually* romancing her."

"Well, then, success! Because you suck at romance," Hailey said brightly, but Natalya saw the attempt at distraction for what it was.

"Hailey," Natalya said in a low voice as Ryan neared. "There are people who can help."

"I know you like her," Hailey interrupted, ignoring the topic shift. "Can't lie to me."

Natalya gave her a mock glare and Hailey shot her a grin in retaliation.

Definitely losing her touch. She really wished she didn't know this much about the kid. Life was so much easier without knowing people's pain.

Ryan was suddenly at their side and slid the tray of food down. "Did you behave?" she asked.

Hailey shot her an askance look.

"Oh, I wasn't asking about you, missy. I'm seeing whether Natalya was on her best behaviour or whether she grew weary of having to converse with someone who lives for flouting the rules."

Natalya eyed her. "You're so sure I live by the rules? I thought you said I don't think the rules apply to me."

"Paradoxically both can be true. It all depends on which rules. Did you even click any of the links I sent?"

"I was waiting for you to send me something sensible before wasting my time," Natalya retorted. She studied the enormous carb-laden feast before her and slid her gaze back up to Ryan. "Is this really a meal for one?"

Hailey giggled. "Hells, yeah!"

"Language," Ryan corrected automatically before giving them a bright smile. "Hamburger Heaven has no regard for portion control. They must think we're all front rowers for the Wallabies."

Natalya stared at her blankly.

"Rugby," Hailey groaned and turned to her aunt. "Geez, what do you see in her?"

"See in her?" Ryan repeated, puzzled. Her eyes darted back and forth between the two. "What have you told my niece?" she asked, spearing a fry on a fork.

Natalya pursed her lips. "Your niece appears to have convinced herself of a great many things with no help from me."

"You two are totally dating," Hailey announced. "And you," she told her aunt, "think she's hot."

Ryan looked pointedly at her food. "I think you're imagining things, young lady."

"So you don't think she's hot?" Hailey tilted her head, stymied by the denial. "*Really?*"

Her scepticism was written so clearly on her face and Ryan looked so awkward that Natalya wanted to laugh—if it didn't also involve her.

That kid was trouble.

Ryan shook her head. "I'm quite sure one of the most renowned cellists in Australia can do better than an occasional soccer coach." Her accompanying laugh was forced.

"Why not?" Hailey asked. "Soccer coaches are cool. Even you!"

"Thanks for the vote," Ryan said and reached for the salt.

Natalya's gaze drifted to the windows, wondering how she'd gotten caught up in this domestic quagmire. She didn't do *this*. She *never* did this. She should remove herself immediately. Her stomach rumbled faintly.

Well, maybe after the burger.

And then her gaze met a shocked one in the window.

Viktor Raven! His hand was casually resting on the shoulder of young girl wearing a Dandenong Rampagers uniform and he was frozen, as though he'd been about to enter the restaurant when he'd seen her. Beside him, also clocking her with a measuring look, stood his new lethal bodyguard.

Sonja Kim.

Oh hell.

Natalya was instantly in Requiem mode as she studied the woman for weaknesses. She looked far better than the mess she'd left her in a few weeks ago, when Sonja had attacked her for electrocuting her boss. The slippery little shit was lucky to be alive, and only the fact that Sonja had leapt out a two-storey window and rolled down the awning had saved her from being killed.

Sonja looked a whole new level of pissed off right now, though. The murderous expression was startlingly familiar—and their sordid, sexual power play in a back alley almost four months ago came to mind. She gave Sonja her most confident, slow-curling smile, noting with satisfaction the Korean's answering enraged look.

Requiem placed the expression: A woman scorned with nothing to lose. The most dangerous kind there was.

Raven placed his hands protectively on his daughter's head and then pushed her behind him, murmuring something to her, and never taking his eyes off Requiem. Sonja, meanwhile, had positioned herself in front of them both, hand reaching under her jacket. She then shouldered her two charges out of sight of the windows, before glancing back. Her dark gaze slid to who Requiem was sitting beside, her brow arching in surprise. She smiled menacingly, and stalked away.

Requiem stood immediately.

"I have to go," she said curtly, eyes fixed on the door, half expecting her nemesis to burst in and begin tossing knives around.

"I'm sorry," Hailey said, worry lacing her voice. "I was just kidding around. I didn't mean to ruin your date."

"It wasn't a date," Ryan snapped, her voice tight.

Requiem glanced at them. A matching pair of wide, hurt eyes. Christ. She didn't have time to offer the reassuring platitudes they wanted. They were going to be far worse than embarrassed if she didn't take this outside immediately.

"I have something I have to do," she said and exited the booth. "I just remembered. Goodbye."

She left swiftly, her mind blocking out their dismayed words, urgings for her to stay, and tried to focus. She should have been outside the moment she'd seen the rat's face. She'd had the briefest window of opportunity before she'd been seen. Had she been alone, she would have ended him already.

Requiem strode out the restaurant, furious with herself. A true assassin never hesitates. Never loses focus. What the hell had she been thinking playing happy families?

The moment she was through the restaurant door, the cold steel of a knife was biting into her throat. She was yanked around the corner, out of sight, into a side alley containing rubbish bins and empty food cartons.

"Lookee here, the great Requiem in her natural setting. Who was that you were with? Your sweetheart? You have a brat, too? People'll be so shocked when I tell them."

Requiem forced herself not to react to the words and began a mental checklist. She calculated where Kim's body was in relation to her own. There was a telltale strip of warmth down her back where their bodies touched, and a bump against her left leg. Kneecap. Useful.

She heard a squeal of rubber and knew it was Viktor escaping.

"I think you just lost your ride," Requiem taunted. A faint breathy exhalation fluttered against her ear as Sonja relaxed. Well, that wouldn't do at all. A tightly wound Sonja was the best option for her survival. Stressed people make mistakes and lower their guards.

"I booby-trapped his car," Requiem lied calmly. "He'll be dead in five."

"Bullshit! You don't even know which car he's in!"

Despite the words, Sonja's body went rigid and in that split second Requiem simultaneously grabbed her knife arm with both hands, pulling it off her throat, while leaning forward and stomping backwards on the knee behind her with her boot.

Sonja went down in a hissing heap. At that exact moment she heard the restaurant door open. Ryan stuck her head around the corner.

"Natalya? Are you okay? You left so fas…" Her eyes went to Sonja, lying on the ground, clutching her knee.

"Aww. She's so worried about you!" Kim laughed through gritted teeth.

Requiem spoke evenly. "Everything's fine. Go back inside."

Ryan stared at Sonja. "Why's she on the ground?"

"She tripped," Requiem said coolly. "I was helping her."

Sonja laughed again. "Ow," she added melodramatically. "Big fall."

Ryan looked between the two women. "You two know each other?"

"Might say that," Sonja said and her voice almost purred. "She's a *special* ladyfriend. Ask her what we did together."

"*Sonja*," Requiem warned, eyes flashing her a furious warning.

Triumph lit Sonja's eyes, clearly smelling blood in the water, and Requiem's own cold focus slowly dissolved.

"What's the matter?" Sonja taunted. "Afraid she might not like you anymore?"

"What do you mean?" Ryan whispered faintly. Her hand came up to rest on her stomach, as though bracing herself.

"She fucked me," Sonja announced gleefully, pointing at Requiem. "In some alley, like a horny tomcat. Want me to tell you how? The things she di–"

A rage Requiem had never experienced before flared, hot, white and lethal. "Shut up!" she snarled.

Savage delight crossed Sonja's face.

Requiem's hands formed fists that clenched and unclenched. She wanted to pound in that smug, goading face. Ordinarily she disliked punching people. One ill-timed hit could mess up her hands. Right now she'd gladly throw that rule out a plate-glass window, along with Sonja Kim.

Ryan's tiny, soft hiss made her glance over. Shock, humiliation, and betrayal were plainly displayed on her stricken face. A blush was spidering up her neck.

"I see I was right," she murmured. "It *was* me you didn't want. I didn't mean to intrude. I'll leave you to catch up with your…friend."

Ryan left and Requiem wanted to unleash her rage with a howl. Instead she hauled Sonja up by the scruff of her shirt and threw her at a nearby dumpster.

The Korean let out a pained cry, and fell onto her back. Natalya stood over her and laid into her with her boots.

"That was…" she kicked her in the ribs while Sonja snickered and cradled her knee, "*fucked up.*"

Requiem next smashed her knee.

Sonja grunted painfully, then laughed again.

"Screw you. It was fun," she spat at her, unable to contain her glee. "You started this. You treat people like shit, you get it back. Oh fuck—your faces! I think your honey's not your honey for much longer."

Requiem suddenly realised a new danger. The cruel and brutal things her many enemies could do to Alison and Hailey if they thought the pair meant something to her. She should kill Sonja on the spot but the place was brimming with people and dozens of witnesses had seen her walk outside and turn toward the alley.

She forced herself to still her features, to let the rage ebb away and to think carefully about her next move. It was a mental exercise Dimitri had drilled into her. She would become flat like a rock. Powerful. Solid. Impossible to hurt. She was almost there, in her serene place, when she recalled Ryan's betrayed expression.

Without another thought, she cocked a fist and smashed it into Sonja's taunting face.

"We're not dating," she told her with menace. "She's my *target*, you crazy bitch." She slammed her fist into her face again as she said the word.

"Sure, she means nothing," Sonja said, unmoved, blood rushing from her nose. She wiped it away with the back of her hand, then glanced back at her. "That's why you're busy hitting me instead of chasing Viktor."

Hell!

Requiem scrambled off her immediately. What was she even doing? She should have realised what was going on when the wrestling champion had actually stayed still long enough to let Requiem mess with her. The devious bitch had been stalling to help Viktor's escape.

Christ, she had to get her head in the game.

"It's too late now," Sonja called after her, as Requiem bolted toward the soccer oval, streets away, where her Ninja was parked, praying no trains were about to roar by and hold her up. "He knows his escape route, you won't find him now."

She heard more laughter in the distance, then some Korean swearing which Requiem deciphered as "gone fucking soft."

A large part of her would have happily stayed to hit her some more, or do worse, but she had work to do. Santos's little Judas would never be this exposed again. Sonja was too good and she would make sure of that.

Requiem fired up her Ninja and roared away. She mentally calculated distance. He had to be about two kilometres away by now. And, Sonja was right, Requiem didn't have the first clue what he was driving. It would be sheer luck if she found him, and only then if he stayed on the main road. Her only advantage was speed, and at least she had plenty of that.

She gunned her bike and speared down the dead-straight Railway Parade, hoping she'd gambled right and he was heading north. She slowed at a three-way roundabout, where Eel Race Road sliced through on the left and right.

She glanced at the thick bushes on the other side of the road and blinked.

How had a car missed the bend and wound up *there*? It had clearly hit the tangle of trees and bushes at an awkward angle, as the plume of black smoke spewing from its engine attested. She could make out at least one shape still trapped inside the mutilated metal. It seemed an unlikely coincidence, given she'd been pursuing a man driving at high speed. She pulled over and picked her way carefully over to the wreck.

Helmet still on, she flicked up her visor and peered inside. Viktor's helpless, shocked eyes stared back. The unnatural angle of his body told her that her job was close to done. He probably had minutes left.

What a mess he'd made of himself. The idiot had actually gotten away and still managed to wreck his car on the only bend on this stretch of road for miles.

"Help," he croaked. "P-please?"

She recoiled at the word. *Seriously?* Of course an assassin would spare someone who said "please."

"Help? That's not what I do, Viktor, you know that," Requiem said and began to lean back out of the car.

"I sent you work," he gasped out. "A hit. On a woman. That has to be worth something."

Requiem froze. Then leaned back in. "Who was the client? Who wanted her dead?"

"Kelly," he cried out. "Where's Kelly?"

Natalya glanced at the girl in the passenger seat. Beyond her shattered window she could see what was left of a stray dog. The angle of the car meant Viktor had probably swerved to avoid it, and then tried to protect his daughter when the car spun, taking full impact with the tree himself.

He might be a slug of an informant but he clearly loved his kid.

She reached for the girl's pulse. Strong and steady. Kelly moved and began to moan.

"The girl will live. The client. Tell me: Who. Was. It?"

Viktor's eyes glazed over in relief. She grabbed him by the collar and tugged him nearer to her. "Who wanted me to kill the woman?"

"Help Kelly first," he gasped. "Get her help, then I'll–"

He slumped, lifeless, his eyes empty.

"Help?" the girl called out. Her eyes were swollen shut. Blood covered her face and ran down into her sports uniform.

"Is there someone here? I think my dad's hurt! Please."

Please.

Natalya stepped back and flicked her visor down. She firmed her jaw and returned to her Ninja, revving it so she couldn't hear the girl's cries. She couldn't do this.

She roared away, going faster and faster until she was well past the bloodied scene. Even then she didn't slow. She drove on, refusing to look back.

The little girl's voice remained, looping through her head. Requiem had *actually* thought about helping someone irrelevant to her. Even though it would have enormously increased the odds of her being caught, of questions being raised. Even though it was a busy road and there would be cars passing the scene soon enough.

And yet she'd seriously thought about it.

She ground her jaw. Her business associate had been right. She *was* getting soft. She would not let it happen again.

At the next red light, she pulled her phone out and flicked to Ryan's number, blocking it. The little mouse probably wouldn't want to look at her again anyway. Well, that would suit them both, wouldn't it?

She pocketed her phone and zipped up her jacket viciously. Because Natalya Tsvetnenko did not do soft. And Requiem sure as hell didn't.

CHAPTER 11

Two days later, Natalya padded through her house, face tight, lips pulled into a grim line. It was barely four in the morning. She started with her bathroom, pulling out a steam cleaner and beginning with the floor, then the shower walls, sterilising every inch until it gleamed.

She heard a beep, as the alarm on the phone in her pocket went off. She ignored it and strode off to get her ladder. She attacked the ducted air-conditioning vents next. Dust could gather in the small slats if you weren't careful. She wiped them down with gusto, all twelve outlets, and then put the ladder away in her utility room.

She took one look at that storage room and shook her head. She began to reorganise it. By the time she was done alphabetising her paints, tools and grouting supplies, her phone had beeped three more times.

Her eye fell to an oilcan. It had been at least two months since her Ninja's last oil change. She was about to head for the garage when her phone beeped a fifth time. The sound was starting to grate on her so, with a grimace, she finally turned it on, her heart thudding.

She already knew exactly what it would say. She stared at it anyway.

The reminder message lit up: *Monday, November 1, All Day Event. Project due: Roast Mouse.*

She slammed her phone on the shelf, and headed for her bedroom. Natalya couldn't believe how fast the three weeks had passed. She stared at her wardrobe and the suitcases on the top shelf. She could always start packing. Europe beckoned. That would take at least another hour.

But instead of packing, she stood there, considering the alternative.

How hard could it be, anyway? Ryan was just another target. Not a particularly difficult one, come to that. She knew where she'd be and when. Simple.

Do it up close and personal so the target knows what's coming. Don't do it at their home or that of their family.

Lola's voice on her answering machine three weeks ago came back to her. It had been so detached as she'd described the death of a woman who, as far as Natalya could tell, had no enemies in the world.

She could knock the job off before Ryan went to work. She knew what time she passed a particular small alley not far from work. She could even make it look like a mugging to the outside world. So that took care of the where. She just had to choose the how.

Up close and personal.

Requiem could simply close her fingers around that soft throat and squeeze. In moments it would be done, before the surprised look on Ryan's face had even crossed to betrayal. She would drop limply to the ground.

The rest was easy: Dress her in old rags, smear her face with a little dirt, put her under a newspaper reeking of urine and she'd be ignored for days. It was one of the simplest methods to dispose of another human being: using society's loathing of its underclasses against itself.

Simple. Easy. Perfect.

Or...Natalya could stay home and wash her doormats.

Four hours later, by the time Natalya was up to vacuuming the curtains in her bedroom, she realised why killing Ryan in the way she'd mapped out was unthinkable.

The mouse deserved better than to be cast aside like trash, left to rot in some alley. Ignored by all as a worthless, disposable person. It was bad enough that society did it to its homeless population, but to deliberately subject Alison Ryan to that? Her mouth twisted in distaste. No, a woman such as Ryan needed respect. Something subtle and dignified.

She considered her alternatives. A sip of poison? Except poison rarely acted as quickly or painlessly as it did in the movies. In fact it caused suffering and attracted attention.

She switched off her vacuum cleaner and stormed over to her rehearsal room. Music would solve everything. It would soothe her and all would be right with the world.

As she seated herself and picked up her cello, she tried once again to push from her mind the hurt, horrified look she knew would be in big, blue eyes, as Ryan clutched at her poisoned throat and fell to her knees.

It twisted Natalya's stomach, the idea that those sad eyes might accuse her silently in Ryan's last moments, knowing what she'd done to her.

Unbidden, Natalya pictured Hailey being told the news. An inhuman, young howl filled her mind as she slashed her bow viciously across her cello trying to block it out.

She played faster and faster, willing the notes to stuff her ears, her mind, and stop the images mocking her.

Natalya played like a woman creating her own electrical storm, fury and fear whipping her arm to and fro, fingers a blur, strings creaking and breaking until finally she could no longer play. She flung the bow savagely to the floor, its deformed, snapped strings hanging loose, mocking her.

Screw this. She couldn't do it. She could not kill Ryan. Natalya stared at her fingers, which she now realised were bleeding from her exertions. Red dripped slowly onto the floor as she looked at it sightlessly.

She had no clue what to do next. Natalya had absolutely no contingency plan for this whatsoever. It had never happened before.

Chest heaving, she rose, kicked her seat across the room with a furious crash and headed outside. Her Ninja still needed an oil and filter change, after all.

CHAPTER 12

The Melbourne Cup, Australia's famous horserace that stops a nation, was chaos as usual. The VIP area, known as the Birdcage, was packed full of marquees from major sponsors that had spared no expense in glamming up their individual spaces—including hanging chandeliers, cramming in a jungle of greenery, and spotlighting the wide windows facing the track—all to show off their star-pulling cachet.

Everyone wanted "in" at the Birdcage. And everyone thronging to the invitation-only hot spot—from world-famous models and washed-up actors, to pouting, Instagramming reality TV stars—was dressed to the eyeballs with absurd hats, plunging cleavages, and fancy plumage that would put a peacock to shame.

The mega sponsors willing to slap down a cool million for these exclusive marquees would each choose an exotic theme and try and outdo their chief rival. Emirates was always the one to beat, and this year the airliner's luxury "tent" had chosen its theme to be the beauty of Russia. Given the VPO's new season was Tchaikovsky focused, some bright spark had decided to combine the two.

Which was how the renowned Australian cellist, Natalya Tsvetnenko, found herself squeezed into a corner with five other string players, attempting to craft perfection over the cacophony of laughter, clinks of champagne glasses, raucous conversation, drunken bellows, and roar of the race caller on the loud speakers outside.

She could see the horses flash by occasionally as she flicked her gaze towards the line of windows.

This was intolerable. Times like these she'd wished she'd taken up offers for orchestras in Europe. She would have agreed if she hadn't had her other career—and Melbourne did have so many interesting opportunities for an assassin with a gangland specialty.

She eyed Amanda Marks who had a similarly pinched expression and almost felt a tug of solidarity. A rotund, bosomy woman squeezed into cream taffeta came shrieking by, waving a presumably winning ticket, wobbling on her heels. It took every ounce of energy not to shoot her an evil glare.

The mingling crowd thronged closer, and half a dozen people actually seemed to be listening to the music.

Natalya's fingers flew and she gritted her teeth, determined to get through this. Of course the VPO thought this was a brilliant idea—get more classical out to the masses. Right now though, the masses seemed too preoccupied by whether the spotted pink or striped blue jockey was winning.

Her mind wandered. Viktor Raven was dead. She had to laugh—she got paid for it regardless of the method of his exit. Santos had assumed she'd messed with his car. He even enquired what 'message' she'd sent. She'd been half tempted to text back: "Don't swerve to avoid stray animals."

Sonja had disappeared, presumably to lick her wounds, boasting a likely shattered kneecap and broken nose. How careless of her. It wasn't a good look losing Ken Lee and Viktor Raven on her watch in consecutive jobs. She imagined her nemesis would be pretty furious at her right now—and that was before she factored in their little sexual skirmish.

She couldn't blame Sonja for her rage over that entertaining event. But then she had been teaching Sonja a valuable lesson in the futility of loving those you admire the most. They will never be what you want them to be. People like her and Sonja didn't get their happy endings. Frankly, Sonja should be thanking her for the free life advice.

As the movement ended and Marks launched into her solo, Natalya lifted her eyes and noted that the milling crowd had thickened—well, for those who were actually listening to them, rather than treating the performance as live elevator music.

The hats and so-called "fascinators"—barely there bits of wire and flowers and inventive fluff and nonsense affixed to women's hair—had somehow become even more outrageous since she'd last glanced up. Everyone was in their absolute best outfits.

Well, almost everyone.

Her eyes were drawn to a partly obscured couple off to one side, in far plainer outfits, studying the programme, their heads bent. A mother and kid? Probably scored a VIP pass in a radio giveaway or knew someone who couldn't go. They were definitely out of place amidst the Emirates crowd's finery.

When they looked up, Natalya started. She instantly clamped her lips together to prevent any untoward displays.

Hailey and Ryan. A cacophony of emotions rocketed through her, before she shoved them aside, building her mental walls and pushing away anything else.

She could do this. She was a rock. Powerful. Solid. Unmoving. Through sheer force of will she achieved the desired result, emptying her mind once more, but never had it been so difficult to even want to do this.

People began shifting again, some coming inside, some leaving the marquee for fresh air, to get snapped by paparazzi, or to place a bet. She righted her cello to continue, just as Marks finished her solo, ready to throw herself back into her music.

Her eye caught something that almost made her snap her bow. Standing directly behind the pair now appeared a man in a starched white button-up shirt and cheap black pants. She'd seen his face all over the world, in many sizes and shapes. She studied his blank eyes and recognised him as one of a thousand men who all looked the same. Hired thugs. Trained to administer a beating, a killing, or just intimidate the weak.

He watched her for a beat, then lifted his hand, straightening his fingers into the shape of a gun and mimed shooting the backs of Ryan's and Hailey's heads. He blew across the top of his finger for good measure and smiled at her.

It was an ugly, cold smile.

She was reminded of Sonja's threat—to tell everyone the pair meant something to Requiem. Her eyes narrowed, but she also heard her musical cue and dragged her gaze back to her sheet music.

She had another four more minutes of playing, she knew, before she could lift her eyes again. Her heart thundered as she considered the possibilities— was the thug just messing with her? How had he worked out who she was?

Four minutes before she could look again.

Requiem ground her teeth. She tried to focus on the music, but not glancing over was agony.

When she snapped her head up again, exactly four minutes later, Ryan and Hailey were gone.

And so was the man.

Her string ensemble was supposed to launch straight into the next piece but Natalya touched the lead violinist on the arm and shook her head.

"I'm done. As in right now."

Marks lifted her pale eyebrows. Of course Natalya knew how that sounded. She knew she was infamous for her punishing schedule and never needing a break.

Marks instead nodded. "Go," she said. "We'll cover."

She didn't listen as the remaining five players bent their heads together and worked out which piece to move onto without a cellist in the mix. Natalya placed her cello in its case with sharp, abrupt movements. She knew without asking that the other players would keep it safe. She would have done the same for them.

Requiem dispensed with Natalya as she stood at the marquee's exit, and looked around. Odd—there was no security guard checking VIP passes. Yet, there had been one when she'd arrived.

She decided not to think too hard as to why that might be. A downpour earlier in the day had made the ground soft and muddy, and she could see a set of small footprints to her left, leading away. People jostled her as they tried to get inside and she bit back some choice insults.

She just had to be sure she was about to follow the right kid.

Her gaze fell to a deeper mark to the left of the footprints and she saw a man's wide heel. Deep, and distorted—smeared from side to side, as though he was twisting as he moved. Perhaps trying to keep a hold of a wriggling teenage girl?

Direction chosen, Requiem took off, walking as quickly as she could, following the trail. Within metres, she was half running, hands lifting her black dress above the ankles to evade the mud, as she tried not to draw attention to herself.

She pressed on past the contractors' compound, where the crowds started thinning out rapidly, and saw three sets of footprints going into a grassy area where all the horse floats had been parked. The sea of silver rounded trailers stretched far as she could see.

Her heels kept sinking into the mud as she hurried forward and several times she almost slipped out of them. Requiem hissed in frustration. A man leaning against his float, smoking, laughed at her ungainly efforts.

"What's yer hurry, love?" he called out.

She threw him a poisonous look, which made him laugh harder, and struggled by. It was slow going and she finally gave up, kicking her heels off with an annoyed grunt. The area in front of her was empty of people so she began to run. Fast.

In the distance she could hear the thunder of hooves and the cries over the loudspeaker of a race caller, along with the whoops of the crowd. Smells of rubbish, turf, and manure made her nose itch.

One thought raced through her mind: *Was she too late?*

Followed by a harder one: *Why did she even care if she was?*

The footprints led her to a large, gleaming motorhome. She glanced around suspiciously. This should not be parked here and the fact it had neither been towed nor ticketed was a warning someone of great importance owned it.

Requiem shook out her arms, feeling adrenalin shoot through her body as she carefully tested the door.

It opened.

Inside was the most lavishly fitted out motorhome she had ever seen. The ceiling, with recessed lighting, glowed warmly against the luxurious creams and golds of the interior. Classical music played softly in the background but for once Requiem was too distracted to figure out which piece. Because there, arranged artfully in the padded booth in the centre of the room, sat Lola.

Her yellow, silk dress, pearl necklace, and earrings were impeccable and showed off her slim frame to stunning effect. She had draped herself over the booth seat as though she was a fifties film goddess, and waved her champagne glass at Requiem.

Requiem had seen her practise this effect more than once in front of a mirror. She was going for her otherworldly Cate Blanchett meets Greta Garbo look—and succeeding.

"Finally," Lola purred. "I was starting to think you weren't as good a tracker as we trained you to be."

Requiem glanced around. As opulent as this vehicle was, it was not exactly to Lola's refined tastes.

"Planning a road trip?" she asked. Her ears sought out the sounds of other people, but she heard nothing.

"No, dear." Lola tapped the table lightly in front of her. "This is actually yours. A little keepsake from Carlo Trioli."

"What?"

"A special thanks for immolating his daughter's kidnapper. His little girl still talks about wish lanterns."

"Why would he think I'd want this pretentious thing?"

"You know Trioli owns all the races and games. He had this one just lying around Flemington."

Requiem lifted a sceptical eyebrow.

"Well sort of," Lola amended. "He's only just relieved it off some recently deceased Saudi billionaire who won't be needing it anymore. He asked if you'd have a use for it, what with Cup day coming up. I imagine he pictured you partying merrily with all your assassin friends or some such thing. Well, I thought since I'd planned to attend this year and watch you perform, why not make use of it myself?"

"Except you didn't watch me perform." Requiem's mind flicked through the faces of attendees. As if she'd have missed seeing Lola sweep into the marquee and cause all the men's tongues to unfurl.

"No, as it turns out. Something came up." She thrummed her manicured fingernails on the smooth table. "Or someone."

Lola patted the seat beside her. "Join me for champagne?"

"I have to get back. I have a concert." Requiem remained standing.

"Yes. You do, don't you?" Lola raked her gaze across her outfit and settled on Requiem's face. "So it's curious as to why you're here, not there. It's unlike you. This must surely be the first concert you've ever missed."

Requiem could hear the clever, subtle way she'd worded the probing statement. Little escaped Lola.

"Perhaps I could spare a few minutes. A water?"

Lola clapped her hands and the thug she'd seen at the Birdcage materialised from a rear compartment. He shut the door firmly behind him and strode up to them.

"Water," Lola ordered. "A sealed bottle. Just the way our Req likes it."

He nodded and shuffled ten feet away to a kitchenette area. He turned and opened the compact fridge, studying the contents. It looked ridiculous, this giant of a man hunched over the small white unit.

"Who's your Igor?" Requiem asked.

"That's Gunther, my newest acquisition. I won him in a poker game, if you can believe it. He's skilled in many things you wouldn't want to test him on."

"Not too bright, though." Requiem observed.

"Oh?" Lola's pale eyebrows lifted.

Requiem was in the kitchenette in three strides and clapped her arms around a startled Gunther, as though giving him the Heimlich manoeuvre. She crossed both her arms over the front of his chest, grasping each side of his shirt tightly, then with vicious force, scissored the fabric in opposing directions across his throat. He gasped for air and clawed at her hands before passing out in seconds with a shuddering thud.

"He turned his back on me," Requiem said as she returned to where an unflappable Lola sat, watching her with hooded eyes. "Like I said: Not too smart."

"Req," Lola tsked, with a frown. "Was that *really* necessary?"

"I prefer to delete the third wheel where possible. One less variable."

"Delete?" Lola peered over at the torso on the kitchen floor, paying him closer attention. "Tell me you didn't kill him?"

"Would you care if I had?"

"Not especially, but Santos was fond of him. He might enquire after his man next time. And Gunther is a somewhat adequate lay whenever I get bored."

Requiem sighed. "Why did you summon me?"

"Is that what this is?" Lola asked innocently.

"Your man inhaling carpet over there made an overt threat against my target. My presence was requested here as loudly as if you'd made the announcement over the racetrack speakers."

"Can't you work out why?" Lola asked. "Put that much-vaunted intellect of yours to use?"

"Let me guess," Requiem said, finally dropping into the seat opposite. "Sonja Kim has been telling tall tales."

"Are they so tall, though? Stories like that do real damage. Falling for your target? Getting domesticated? It's hard enough in a man's world without those sorts of stories confirming what every misogynist underworld middleman thinks of us already. That women are not cut out for this business. That we're too emotional and prone to outbreaks of hysteria. Or worse. Love."

"It would only be damaging if it were true. You taught me better. Trained me rigidly. Drilled every errant emotion out of me. Or did you forget about making me your little monster?"

"So melodramatic, dear." Lola swirled her glass of champagne. She smiled but it did not reach her eyes. "I seized an opportunity when you came along. Nothing more. You might have said no."

"And miss a scholarship of a lifetime?"

"Now, now. We both know that was not the only reason you agreed to be my lethal pet, don't we?"

Requiem glared at her. "Don't you dare go there."

Lola smiled, her perfect crocodile smile. She waved her hand and an array of elegant silver bangles jangled. "So touchy today."

"Where are they?" Requiem asked, twisting in her seat. "Your abductees? What are your plans?"

"That depends on you. And whether Sonja Kim's 'tall tales' have any grain of truth to them."

"So," Requiem said, with an aggrieved look, "you're just checking that I haven't gone to the light side? I can save you the effort: It's business. And Sonja's lashing out. Do you remember Nabi? Following me around? Guess who?"

"Oh, I'm well aware who Nabi became. But her bitter little piece of gossip wasn't what swayed me. It did, however, bring to mind all your teeth gnashing the other week about how you couldn't do the Ryan job. 'Give me more, Lola.' I've never heard you wail and carry on like that before."

Requiem grimaced. "I don't wail."

"Could have fooled me, dear. So—she means nothing to you? That's what you're sticking with?"

"No she does not." Requiem glared at her, letting her frustration leak out. "Nothing."

Lola leaned back on the seat and studied her coolly. "Then why haven't you done the hit? Your three weeks were up a day ago. I kept waiting for a call that never came."

"The brief said 'no sooner' than three weeks."

"Technically, I suppose. But you're late, Req. The job should have happened yesterday. You are never late."

"I've been busy."

"Doing what?"

"Packing for Europe. Cleaning. Concerts. Rehearsals."

"Requiem, I've seen your target. I saw her by accident today, actually, when I was heading over to watch you play. Never has an easier kill existed on God's green earth. I am fairly sure you could do her while blindfolded and strung upside-down in a strait jacket. So—I have to wonder: Why is Alison Ryan, this mother-tending saint of yours, still drawing breath?"

Requiem stared at those sharp blue eyes and wished she had an answer.

"Well?"

"I don't answer to you," Requiem said in a warning voice. "In case you've forgotten, I'm the talent, and you're nothing but the booking agent in this arrangement. I will do Ryan when I'm ready. Not before."

"I see," Lola said pleasantly, and clasped her hands. "Then, as your so-called booking agent, it behoves me to tell you that the fastest way to wash Sonja's rumour away is to kill Ryan. Immediately."

"You want me to kill her now? In *this* shoe box? There are too many people around. It's *Melbourne Cup Day*, for god's sake. This is insane. I need preparation time and an exit strategy."

"This lovely little vehicle is sound-proofed thanks to its former Sheikh owner, who insisted upon it. The crime scene is mobile—you just drive away with the evidence. And I have a silenced weapon for you. Really, now you're just making excuses. Tell me," she said leaning forward, "why is that?"

"I'm not," Requiem said. "I like to know all my options."

"Well then, I have already considered them. Option one: You kill the two now.

"Option two: I find someone else to kill them if you are unable. This will have some consequences, and the rumours that you've gone soft will persist. I can repair your reputation, after a fashion. But people *will* remember.

"Option three: Nobody kills anyone. But that one comes with a very harsh price. So—choose."

"What is this price?"

The silence was long and pained, disappointment washing across Lola's face. Finally she downed her champagne, reached for the bottle, and poured more. Only the sound of fizz hitting the cut-crystal glass could be heard. When Lola finally spoke, it was quiet.

"So it's true. You care for her."

"I only asked the price."

"Yes. You did, didn't you?"

Oh. Requiem cursed herself. Such a simple trap.

"I just like to know all the details," she bluffed. "It makes me organised, nothing more."

Lola snorted. "Is that so? Well then, tell me: Where are your shoes?"

For the second time in mere moments, Requiem cursed her mistake and Lola's observant eyes. "They were sticking in the mud. I removed them."

Lola gave her a pitying look. "What you mean is that you kicked them off and ran like a frightened poodle to reach your lover and her niece."

"No! It's *business*! For God's sake, are you deaf?"

"I think we're done," Lola said, and her face lost any veneer of politeness. There was dismissiveness and anger beneath the surface that Requiem had never seen before. At least, never directed at her.

"We need a relationship based on trust and you just keep lying to my face," Lola said. "This will no longer continue."

Requiem stared at her in disbelief. "Just like that? I've been your star killing machine for twenty-four years, and you toss me aside like this? Over *this*? Some paper pusher and her niece?"

"I do. After all, dear, as you say: it's only business. A diseased limb gets amputated when it no longer is capable of functioning. I will find and train another. In fact, in light of Lee's unfortunate demise, I was thinking of reaching out to his enforcer. I believe Sonja Kim is the only one of your kind who you keep fighting but aren't able to kill. She must have talent. Hmm?

"Or you're subconsciously avoiding killing someone who reminds you so much of your younger self. Either way, I'd rather enjoy moulding the new you."

Requiem stared at her, robbed of speech. Just like that. Lola would find it so easy. Her jaw worked, and still no words came out.

After everything, after how it had all begun, she meant nothing to this woman who had governed her entire world.

Requiem was merely disposable.

Her shocked mind shifted to the day she'd met the woman who'd upended her life. How could she ever forget it? Lola Sweetman, all perfume, perfection, charm, and coquettishness, had stood on her doorstep, curious blue eyes scanning her as her father introduced his new, young bride. It was a moment that defined her new world. Or shattered it. It depended on how one looked at it.

The most vivid day of her life, however, was not that one. It came three weeks later. Natalya was fourteen, and her new stepmother had been summoned to her school over a playground infraction.

"Fighting," they'd called it.

How little they'd understood. Natalya had actually been showing the school bully, repeatedly, by applying his face to the mud, that she was no one's chew toy. And if he persisted on picking on anyone else smaller than him, she'd explained earnestly while inserting her elbow into his groin, she would repeat the lesson. Daily, if need be.

Lola had swept into the school principal's office in a swirl of lilac chiffon and expensive perfume, looking like some exotic European screen idol. All that had been missing was the long-handled cigarette holder and aloof accent, although Lola had perfected the latter in the years that followed.

She gave the principal a disdainful sneer and Natalya stared in wonder as the normally stern man quailed before her.

Lola expressed outrage over Natalya's "disgraceful behaviour" and promised "severe punishments." She didn't wait for his approval or even his input, but she snatched Natalya by the wrist, then turned on her immaculate heel, and hauled the mulish fourteen-year-old out of the office.

It had been the most blatant demonstration of the power of sheer charisma and confidence an awestruck Natalya had ever seen.

In the car Lola had turned to her. "I'm disappointed in you. I thought you were smarter than this." She slammed her seatbelt into its clasp.

A teenage Natalya had glowered and impudently folded her arms, toned from the hours of military-style workouts her father had drilled into her since her mother had died. He had thought it was bonding.

Maybe it was.

She ignored Lola and stared out the window.

"I mean if you want to teach some little prick a lesson, the secret is never, ever to get caught," Lola added waspishly. "Better yet, find a way to pin it on someone else."

Natalya's head snapped back in shock as her new stepmother smiled. She continued.

"You can't always rely on those broad shoulders and fine muscles of yours—you need your brain, too. Boys are all hormones and ego. They will get you back unless you can hide. You can do that in plain sight if you're clever about it. So, we need to teach you subtlety."

Natalya had stared at her, slack jawed, senses overloading.

Lola smirked, leaned over, placed an elegant finger under her chin, and snapped Natalya's mouth shut. "And a poker face."

She started the car. "Now come on, dear. Kicking some little turd into the dirt at your age deserves an ice cream."

As the years went by, Natalya earned many, many ice creams.

By the time she was sixteen, Natalya had learned a great many things from Lola Sweetman. And felt a few things she knew she shouldn't have.

Lola eventually had grown bored of tormenting Natalya's authoritarian father, Vadim, for his rigid ways, despite them being what had drawn her to him in the first place.

Lola, who was addicted to the taste of power in all its forms, had suddenly scored a place at the table with some Asian crime family Natalya had never heard of. She'd acquired a multi-million-dollar apartment thanks to her new criminal mastermind boyfriend.

She spared no expense in furnishing it. The only reminder of her old life was the slobbering old Doberman with a nervous tic that she'd somehow won off Natalya's father.

The day the divorce came through, Natalya turned up with a bottle of champagne. She stepped over the familiar pet, slumbering on the timber floorboards in the modern apartment. Natalya dropped her school bag beside her dad's former animal and considered the twitching dog. The battle to win him had been so hard fought. More for the mutt than for the money.

"I didn't think you even liked Alexi."

Lola gave a small snort. "Please. You should know the rules by now. Crush your enemy's heart and they'll be too enraged to think straight. And he's called Brutus these days."

She took the champagne. "I won't ask how you got this. I suppose you want some?" she sniffed. "What are you now? Sixteen? Seventeen? Think you're old enough for the boys and the booze?"

"No," Natalya said. She worked her jaw and rammed her hands in the pockets of her navy blue school blazer. "I don't want some stupid boy."

Something telling must have flickered in Natalya's eyes. She knew it by the way Lola had sat up straighter, studying her with a suddenly wary expression. Natalya gave her an impassive look and shook out her long hair.

She was growing it. She liked how people underestimated her because of it. They never underestimated her for long, though.

They'd stared at each other and Lola hadn't said a word. But Lola *knew*. It had taught Natalya a painful lesson about not wanting. Not being obvious. And understanding your target as well as you know yourself. A rookie mistake, she told herself later, as she cried useless tears that night. Assuming your own wishes and hopes count for anything.

They never spoke of Natalya's crush on her mentor again and Natalya became a master in the art of never wanting someone so badly that it would hurt not to get her.

She threw herself into music and tried to forget the stunning Lola Sweetman. It was only when she needed help her father couldn't afford that she found herself in a strange warehouse in West Melbourne, staring at a scribbled address Lola had sent her.

She'd made her pitch for a sponsor to a room full of men who had laughed at the stupid cello-playing kid. They laughed at her hopes. Her dreams.

And then Lola had stepped up next to her new husband, Dimitri, and smiled. "Oh, don't be so dismissive, dears," she told them all, flirting furiously. "I think she has potential. Let me talk to her, see who she is, and find out what we can get out of this. Yes?"

Lola had returned an hour later to tell the men that she saw in Natalya the perfect vessel to create an invisible enforcer. Ken Lee needed someone more discreet than his current hatchet man who every criminal and his dog knew on sight.

What if, she asked them, Natalya got skilled up from the best there was? She'd be untouchable. Powerful. Strong. Like a ghost. After all, who would expect such a sweet young face with a talent at strings to hide so lethal an ability?

In exchange, Lee's right-hand man, Dimitri, and a few other associates, would finance the parts of her studies abroad not covered by her scholarship. Five years in their service. Five years of murder in exchange for music. At the end of her tenure she would be free to leave. Live her life as she saw fit—on the condition she kept her mouth shut.

It had been chicken feed to them, and few wanted to rile Dimitri who seemed so enamoured of his wife, that they agreed. But that had not been the full plan.

In that hour with Lola in the strange warehouse, Natalya heard the rest of it. It seemed that after only a month into her marriage to Dimitri, she'd realised her new husband was brutal and cruel. Oh, Lola didn't mind when he was that way with others; in fact she didn't care about other people at all. But doing it to *her* was simply out of the question.

Divorces initiated by women in gangland families were rarely tolerated—consequences could be fatal for making the crime bosses' egos suffer. Running never got you far, either. So Lola had been at a loss as to what to do about her situation until the day Natalya had written an earnest letter to ask if she had any contacts to help her financially while she was studying in Vienna.

Lola Sweetman was a woman who seized opportunities as she saw them. And she seized Natalya with both hands. To this day, few people in their world knew how much of a scorpion Lola was. She'd often been dismissed as Dimitri's empty-headed trophy wife.

But Natalya knew.

That day the men of the Moonlight Society had sat around laughing at her, Lola whispered to her an incredible plan. The other, audacious part of it that no one knew about.

Lola wanted a permanent divorce but ordering a hit on Dimitri would be too obvious. The wife was always suspected. So she would set up a conflict—convincing Dimitri, who had an enormous ego, that he'd be better off going it alone, away from Ken Lee.

She explained to Natalya that it would be easy to start picking off crime gang members in ways that looked like paid hits. They would be random targets from all sides with no rhyme or reason, designed to make the bosses go mad trying to work out the pattern. They would blame each other, get lost in the feud, and no one would fixate too hard on figuring out how it began.

Lola had decreed that after five years, it would be safe for Natalya to kill Dimitri. By then everyone would assume it was another family behind the hit. And Lola, ever ambitious, would have had the time to position herself to become the matriarch of the new crime family. The mistress of all she surveyed.

Natalya could go back to focusing solely on her cello playing once the plan came to fruition. A small chunk of her life surrendered for a future in the world of music.

That had been the plan. The reality turned out a little differently. No one had anticipated how enthusiastically Melbourne's crime bosses would take to killing their own or how long their rage would drag on for. How well Dimitri's new gang, Fleet Crew, would do at carving out a place in the crime world, causing even more tensions. How the two-decade-long gang wars would be left to run almost entirely unchecked, thanks to police indifference.

And no one anticipated how perfectly well-suited Natalya Tsvetnenko would be to a career that was to have been only temporary.

People generally assumed she'd stayed on for the money. She didn't do it for so tawdry an outcome. She did it because she was an artisan. Because she was brilliant at it. She also did it for Lola, who smiled at her a special smile whenever she'd done a hit everyone had deemed impossible.

And she did it because the moment of watching a soul leave a body was the same sensation she experienced when she was lost in her music. She was leant wings to soar. Immortal. Bruising her skin against the sun. At any moment she could fall, but she hadn't.

She did it for the rush that had no equal.

She did it because she could.

And now it could all be over. Her partnership with Lola. All because of a curious little mouse she couldn't bring herself to kill.

"What of *them*?" Requiem asked, her throat dry.

Lola laughed savagely. "Even now, still you ask? Well, fine. You asked for the price? The price to let them both walk is your music. Your talent."

"My music?" Requiem gaped at her. "You can't stop me from playing."

"Is that so?" Lola reached into her Chanel handbag, and withdrew a gun. Requiem recognised it immediately. Dimitri's. Inherited when he'd died in the gang wars. When Requiem had looked into his trusting eyes and shot him dead. The last time she'd ever touched a firearm.

Lola had apparently kept the chilling weapon for sentimental reasons. Even the sight of it still made Requiem's stomach turn.

"I will put a bullet in each of your hands," Lola said calmly. "Shatter the fine bones until they are a pulped mess of muscle, ligament and fragments. You will be on your knees in pain and horror.

"But if you subject yourself to this, then you can walk away cleanly, no strings attached. And so can they. It will send a certain message about people who defy me. And you, more than anyone, know the power of sending messages. That's why they all queue up for your services, even though you've killed some of their own. Messages have power."

"I could disable you ten different ways before you even pulled that trigger," Requiem ground out.

"I know," Lola said simply. "It is purely voluntary."

"I could rescue those two myself, and walk away right now."

"Yes." Lola looked at her. "Of course you could, but then you'd never be free. My syndicate now runs to thousands of members. The armaments industry is a hungry one and it's growing, worldwide. If I let it be known an associate would be amply rewarded for your death, there would be nowhere to hide. And you'd lose your career anyway, because you'd be on the run, unable to be visible even for a concert."

"Lola," Requiem stared at her in disbelief. "We were *family*."

"And this is just business—important and necessary business. You understood that when you stapled Yeo Han's prick to a door. It's not personal. You knew the rules and you broke them. For God's sake, I taught you the rules. How many times have I told you? How many times did I drill it into you?"

"Emotion is weak," Requiem muttered.

"You should have listened. Now be a dear and put your hands on the table. I'd hate to have a wonky aim. Imagine that: Trying to disfigure you and I end up killing you."

"I despise you," Requiem said, sliding her hands to the table, and hating how compliant she was even now. She, a killer of men. Destroyer of the pitiful.

Her hands trembled.

Lola smiled. "You despise me? Oh I'm sure that's not true. Is it, dear?"

CHAPTER 13

Requiem stared at her hands, trying to imagine not being able to play. It was the same panic she felt at the thought of killing Lola. She loved her music. And she had loved Lola. Somehow in her mind, years ago, the two had become one. Lola and her music, interwoven. Both beautiful. Dangerous. Capable of breaching her walls and making her cry.

Even when she knew Lola was pure scorpion, she still couldn't stop this connection. And now it was as though her hands were frozen, so trained were they to dutifully follow Lola's whims. It was shocking. She had no precedent, no training as to how to overcome this.

The little mouse's impassioned words came back to her suddenly from their evening at the café: "What will happen if you ever face an emotional storm you can't handle, that's too big for you to suppress through sheer force of will?"

And now she knew the answer to a question she'd dismissed so cockily: She would freeze. No one had ever told her there was a third option to fight or flight.

She couldn't even consciously twitch her fingers, she noted from a far-off part of her consciousness. She stared at them on the table, willing them to move, willing herself to fight back against the woman who had haunted her dreams for good and ill for more than twenty years.

The cold muzzle stroked along the veins of the skin of her left hand.

"That's a good girl," Lola purred. "So compliant. Oh my dear, how adorable."

Requiem's brain raged and swirled even as she watched in stony silence as the metal dragged across her skin.

Lola didn't care about her, Requiem's brain whispered. She *never* had. Requiem knew that. She did. She'd thought it often enough, so this wasn't a surprise. And yet there was a sickening difference between suspecting a thing and seeing it.

Lola's hand holding the pistol was so soft. White, unblemished. Her fingertips, with a pale pink lacquer on the nails, were perfection. She could be a model. Yet she had such cruelty in those hands, capable of the vilest of acts. She'd seen those fingers run down the cheek of a man about to die, tracing the wet path his tears took. She mocked him for breaking down. He'd just seen his wife die. And she mocked him.

Requiem shouldn't be in her thrall. She should be able to look at this ugliness in Lola's soul and turn away in revulsion.

And yet…Lola had such charisma. Her eyes would watch you as though you were the only person who mattered in the world. She *knew* people. All facets of them. All their little secrets. She could just glance at a man and know which things would most likely bring him to his knees with shame or terror. And she would press into the scar, the weakness, with the precision of a surgeon wielding a scalpel.

Even knowing this, knowing her cold, vicious heart, Requiem still found she couldn't move her hands from the table where they sat in matching sweaty puddles.

Not against Lola's orders.

Requiem wasn't afraid of reprisals, nor was she weak from the fear that afflicted others. Those pathetic targets who'd look at her and say *"Please"* were nothing like her.

It was just…*Lola.*

"Oh my poor, poor dear. You would love to hurt me right now, wouldn't you? But you can't. Because it goes against all your training. And those secret, dirty feelings you have for me."

There it was. Lola's gift for homing in on weakness remained unparalleled. Requiem tried not to care. Tried not to mind Lola scouring a pain so poorly healed, she'd never moved on. Or, more depressingly, had never wanted to.

"Had for you," she corrected, her voice sounding rough and dry to her own ears.

Lola ignored her.

"I loved how obedient you were," she said conversationally. "Like a little puppy. So eager to please. You even took care of Dimitri for me, even though he did so much for you. He was your master who you worshipped and you killed him. Stared him right in the eyes, said sorry, and shot him dead. Because I asked.

"It's interesting, isn't it. You never used a gun on anyone ever again, did you?"

The gun muzzle against her flattened hands inched forward. It was so cold. Requiem shivered.

Her finger twitched. She stared at it. Well, that was progress, of sorts.

"If you're trying to find out whether I would have done anything for you, you know damned well you owned my soul," Requiem said coolly. "A fact you took advantage of time and again."

"Yes, well," Lola said, flippantly. "I found it amusing. So, tell me: What are you going to do with yourself when you can no longer play your music? I am quite curious. You can hardly continue killing, either. Will you try to romance the trembling leaf in the other room?"

Requiem snarled. "Fuck you."

Lola smiled at her agitation and stood closer to her. "Not my type—much to your everlasting agony."

"You really *don't* care, do you?" Requiem muttered in a flat voice. "Dr Frankenstein, taking her monster apart. First you assemble me. Then you disassemble me."

"One has to love the symmetry." Lola's voice dropped to a confessional whisper. "And no, I really don't care. You're just like your father. Useful and amusing—until you're not."

Lola's eyes went cold as her finger moved to the trigger. Instantly, Requiem came alive and lashed out, kicking the other woman's legs out from under her. The gun clattered to the floor, skidding out of both their reaches.

Requiem stood and leaned over Lola's prostrate form, balling her hands into white-knuckled fists. "Leave Papa out of this."

Lola sat up and blinked in surprise. "Good god, you still love the old fool. Even though he's been wasting away in some nursing home for, what, ten years? Drooling? Can't even remember his own name?

"Do you know he begs me to visit? Of course I took great pleasure in explaining to the nurses that watching two diseased dogs rutting would be more entertaining. But *him* you love more than me? We've carved up the universe together! Remade the underworld! But *that* snivelling sack of dribble you love the most?"

"You're right," Requiem said, biting back her rage. "We *are* done. You have no hold over me anymore."

"Really, dear?" Lola teased. "Could have fooled me. What would you do if I offered myself to you? You'd come crawling back in an instant." She snapped her fingers.

Requiem's throat went dry.

"What if I said, you could have me, willingly, if only you killed *them*," Lola taunted.

"You wouldn't. You don't even like women."

"No. But I love power." Lola laughed, clearly enjoying herself. "You know how I love that. Just imagine how much you'd enjoy finally having me."

Requiem stared at her. She didn't have to imagine how that would end. She'd already lived this scenario with Sonja Kim from the other side.

Bile rose up as she realised the depths of her cruelty to Nabi. How much it was like having your heart ripped open being on the receiving end of that vicious power play.

Her jaw tightened. "If you made me that offer, I would say you're not worthy," Requiem said. "And I have more self-respect than to touch someone like you."

"Someone like *me*?" All playfulness instantly fell from Lola's voice. It became hard and cold and Requiem wondered if *this* was the real woman at last, the one behind the games, the tricks and manipulations. The one no one ever got to see.

"Yes. Someone so ugly."

"Oh and you're so perfect," Lola scoffed. "Look in the mirror. You're damaged goods. No one will want you. Not the trembling leaf you've thrown everything away for. We both know she can't have any sort of good or happy life if it includes you in it."

"No," Requiem said. "I already know my life doesn't include her. But it doesn't include you, either. You're grotesque, Lola. That's who you really are.

No one would want to be near you if they knew you as I do. If they could see your soul, no one would want you at all. You would be alone. No one around to admire you but yourself. An empty soul you fill with mirrors."

Lola looked as though someone had sucked all the air out of the room. "Well done, dear." She gave her a slow clap. "You *are* a monster."

"If I am it's who you made me. But you know what's scariest about monsters? It's our knowledge that they're just human beings, like everyone else, one twist away from normal. Not even a full twist."

"You'll never be normal. You're kidding yourself."

"You don't think I know that? I'm not part of the rest of the world."

Lola's smile positively glittered. "At least you know your place."

"Oh I do. And I thank you for teaching me it." She suddenly snatched Lola's arm and twisted the wrist with both hands until it snapped. "Your education has had its uses. Have this reminder that I passed with top marks."

Lola screamed in pain. "You're still *my* monster, you rotten child. Behave!"

"Those days are over."

"I used to laugh at you, you know," Lola sneered at her, cradling her broken arm, "the teenage you, wearing your heart on your sleeve. It was embarrassing how much you wanted me."

"At least I had the courage of my convictions. Shall I do your other arm? I know how well you like to co-ordinate your looks."

"I *made* you! You will obey me!" Lola hissed sharply.

Requiem leaned over her, concentrated and then viciously snapped her other wrist. "Matching," she observed. "How lovely."

Tears of pain slid down Lola's cheeks, causing her ordinarily perfect mascara to run. Her eyes looked like a grime ring around a cracked sink as her expression contorted into agony.

"Whatever you do, wherever you go, you *can't* let them live," Lola ground out, changing tack. "This will all get tied back to you when Ryan goes to the police."

"I'd think you'd have a bit more to worry about than my future." Requiem edged closer and gave her a menacing look.

"You wouldn't dare kill me! I *made* you. After everything I've done for you! The life I introduced you to, a life you love! Besides, you worship me!"

"Past tense," Requiem drawled. "Now I just see the ugly."

"Well *she'll* never want you. Do you know who her niece is? Do you? The girl was shouting it loud enough when Gunther dragged her through here."

Requiem crossed the room, picked up the pistol off the floor, checked its safety was off, and pointed.

"Sound-proof, you say?" she asked, ignoring the baiting.

"They will arrest you! You, the Great Requiem, in jail with the filthy, unwashed masses. All that grime and dirt! Pissing and showering shoulder to shoulder with them. And they will deny you your music. You will be powerless! Small."

"They will have no proof I was ever involved. And if they even come close, or if you're tempted to talk, I will destroy you. I could pick your organisation apart with ease. Because the only person I was ever loyal to in your precious Fleet Crew is dead to me. If she even existed in the first place."

She corrected her aim, adjusting it.

"You're broken," Lola hissed. "Do you even get that? You're *nothing*. No one will ever want you. No one will ever find anything loveable about you."

"If I'm broken it's still better than having no heart at all. Of us both, it's you who's the real monster. Enough. I'm not even sure I can say that it's been a pleasure."

She squeezed the trigger.

Nothing happened. The damned thing had jammed, probably damaged when it had been violently tossed across the room.

There was a movement behind them, as the once unconscious thug groggily got to his knees. Requiem turned.

"Gunther!" Lola cried out. "Kill them. In the back room. Now!"

He rose to his feet and stumbled obediently, but barely conscious, for the rear door.

"Decisions, decisions," Lola laughed in her face. "Run and save them or stay and kill me. I assure you by the time you return I'll be gone. And if you kill me first, Gunther will have killed them. So—what are you going to do?"

Requiem shoved Lola aside, tossed the gun to the floor and ran for the back room.

She could not prepare herself for what she found. The giant of a man was wrestling with Ryan who somehow appeared to be holding her own. Her mouth fell open. The little mouse was fending him off remarkably well, finding and using pressure points to make the man squeal like a stuck pig.

Suddenly he turned, grabbed Hailey by the throat with one meaty hand, and squeezed.

The teenager's face grew bright red and her eyes rolled back in her head. Ryan's lack of bulk was now a huge disadvantage and he shrugged her off him, flinging Ryan against the far wall.

Their gazes intersected. Ryan's silent, desperate plea met Requiem's disgust at his actions.

Who strangles a child?

A fury flashed so deep inside her that she had no words. Taking one step forward, Requiem grabbed Gunther's other arm, twisted it at an obscene angle behind his back until it broke in one loud snap. He dropped Hailey instantly, cried out, and spun around to face his attacker.

Requiem used his turning momentum to hurl his bulk from the room and into the main area. In three strides she was on him, kicking him savagely in the groin. She crouched over him and with a well-aimed, pointed elbow, broke his nose.

The crunching of cartilage was masked by the sound of Gunther's primal howl. Requiem silenced him by giving him an uppercut so powerful he lost consciousness again, his body arcing upwards from the power behind it before slumping back to floor.

Hailey screamed in fear at his howls and Requiem heard Ryan consoling her. She heard faint laughter and glanced back to the vehicle's door.

Lola was leaving. And, hell, if she didn't look like some vaunted queen when she did. Two broken wrists, a tear-stained face, and still she had attitude. A part of Requiem, the part of her that was still sixteen and in awe, was highly impressed.

"Well," Lola said, as she stood next to the open door, wincing from the pain of moving, "I have to admit: You, dear, were my favourite monster."

"Lola," Requiem ground out. Not quite sure what to say to her.

Lola laughed. "Heavens, look at you! Even now, you can't bring yourself to stop me. You're useless, aren't you? Cowering before me. How priceless! What a final image."

She exited and the door closed with a slap. Requiem turned to see Alison standing there, an odd look on her face. She'd witnessed the scene along with Requiem's entire sickening weakness.

Before she could move, a blur of teenager was upon her.

"You saved us!" Hailey squealed and flung her arms around her.

Requiem froze, unsure what to do. No one ever thanked her. No one ever touched her. It was so strange, this cascade of emotions, churning inside. She wondered how long she had to wait before she could disengage herself.

She slowly shifted her gaze up to see Ryan who was watching her intently.

Alison Ryan—who had taken on a brute of a man without thinking. Who had held him off with a variety of effective holds that Requiem suddenly realised she recognised. Ryan who had been impressive, confident and unfazed. Professional even.

Requiem dropped to a crouch in front of Gunther. She checked his breathing knowing that if Ryan wasn't sitting there, she would have ended him. One less witness.

Even so, she still debated it. A sharp snap of the neck and...

"Don't," Ryan whispered, voice thick, next to her ear. "It'll only make everything much worse. And if you don't care about that, at least don't with Hailey here."

She took in Ryan's white face, which still looked more steady than it had a right to be.

Requiem's hands stilled and dropped to rest on her thighs.

"Who is Hailey's father?" she asked tightly.

"Barry Moore. Head of Homicide."

"So you're a cop," Requiem said flatly. Those chokeholds had been straight out of the police manual.

Alison looked back at her steadily. Her shoulders had slumped but her voice did not waver.

"And you're Requiem."

CHAPTER 14

Ryan stood in the centre of the room, appearing to contemplate what to do next. She turned and glanced back at the room she'd been held hostage in. She then took a few steps towards the next room down, a master suite, her gaze fixing on the phone on its wall.

Gunther would have taken hers.

"I should call the police," Ryan said. "Pick up that thug for abduction. And Lola for…whatever she was doing. Accessory? Or was she the mastermind?"

"If you think you should, then call," Natalya said. "Or you could walk away. This problem would disappear if I made a different call entirely."

They took each other's measure.

"I'm a homicide detective," Ryan said.

"I see no bodies."

"Thanks to me intervening." Ryan paused. "I swore to uphold the law."

It came out like a justification more than a plan of action.

Natalya arranged herself regally on the padded booth seat. *"Project confidence,"* Lola had told her often enough, *"and people will believe it."*

"What an interesting choice you have then." Natalya studied her nails casually.

"If I call the police, you'll be gone before I've even read out my badge number."

"Like I said, interesting choice."

Hailey, who'd seemingly been lost in her own world, suddenly looked between the two of them. "Wait, why wouldn't we call the cops? That man tried to strangle me! Like, to death!"

Ryan's lips pressed together at the reminder and she immediately walked into the bedroom to make the call.

"What's going on?" Hailey asked Natalya. "There's a weird vibe in here."

"What do you think is going on?"

Hailey frowned. "I think you pissed off my aunt. I just can't figure out how, especially since you saved us."

"Hmm."

"Why does she think you want to run off?"

"She knows I have to get back to my concert."

"So why aren't you?"

A good question. She should have retreated the second Ryan left the room. Instead a strange sense of calm settled over her. She recalled one of the first things Lola had ever taught her: When you run, people give chase. It's instinctual. When you stand still, they're not quite sure what to make of you. *You* set the tone.

"By the way I think it's kinda cute how you've got a pet name for my aunt," Hailey said suddenly.

"What?" Natalya started. She gave the teen her fullest attention.

"You know, you call her Alison. I know she goes by her middle name at work cos of all the mix-ups with that other old cop lady who's also Emily Ryan. She works in Traffic. That's where Aunty Emily first started work as a cop."

Natalya stared at her. "Alison's name is really Emily?"

"Emily Alison Ryan. You don't know much, do you?" Hailey peered at her. "I thought by now you'd be improving as a girlfriend." She shot her a cheeky grin. "But, hey, you did save us, so...I *totally* forgive you."

Natalya wanted to hit something. Why hadn't her supposed genius hacker thought to widen his search to middle names? So who the hell was Alison Ryan the admin assistant he'd pinged? It was her own damned fault for not briefing him more thoroughly.

She was slipping—and she never slipped. She'd been making careless mistakes from the moment she'd first taken Ryan's case. She considered the implications. She'd had a cop under her nose the entire time and had been too damned distracted to notice. Worse, a *homicide* detective. Jesus!

This was unacceptable. When Lola found out, the mockery would be...she paused. Wait. Had the sly scorpion known all along? Had Requiem been set up? She'd put nothing past Lola, especially after today.

Ryan chose that moment to return. Her eyes went to Hailey, as though reassuring herself her niece was still okay, and then shifted back to Natalya.

"You're still here," she said, surprise colouring her voice.

"Of course," Natalya said serenely. She gave her a shark-like grin. "I am a witness. I do like to help the authorities when I am able—good citizen that I am. Despite rumours to the contrary."

A dissatisfied expression washed over Ryan. Natalya wondered whether she was annoyed she couldn't prove who Requiem was. Because even after what had happened today, she would have nothing beyond circumstantial evidence, if that. Requiem had been too careful.

"How did you know?" Hailey suddenly piped up, tugging Natalya's sleeve. "To come and rescue us?"

"I saw the man take you," she replied, turning to her. "I have had training in several forms of martial arts. There weren't any police around so I decided to come and get you myself."

"Just like that," Ryan drawled, shooting her a dark look, "*you* decided to take on a kidnapper the size of a mountain."

Natalya's lips twitched, her gaze intersecting sceptical blue eyes. "Yes," she agreed, deadpan. "Just like that."

"Wow," Hailey said. "You're, like, a superhero."

Natalya's lips curled. "I just did what anyone would," she said, preening a little, just to piss off Ryan. She flashed them a magnanimous smile. "It's important to stand up for what's right."

Ryan rolled her eyes. "I'm going to see if there's any water in the fridge. For some reason I have indigestion."

Natalya called after her in faux concern: "How odd it should come on so suddenly."

"Yes. How odd," Ryan agreed. "Perhaps you could use your superhero skills to tie up the lump of asshole over there? I don't know how long he'll be unconscious for."

Natalya rose.

"I'll help," Hailey said, adoration shining in her eyes.

Natalya's head snapped around. "No," she said sharply. "This is not suitable for little girls."

"But I'm thirteen!" Hailey protested. "Not a little girl."

"Or teenagers," Natalya corrected, walking over to a set of venetian blinds above the kitchen sink. "Trust me."

A flash of memory of the first time she'd ever done anything like this came to mind, and the thought of Hailey doing the same filled her with loathing. Kids should be allowed to be kids.

"She's right," Ryan said. "Go into the bedroom. We'll call your mother in a minute. Close the door. I don't want you to watch."

With one firm yank, Natalya wrenched the blind off the wall and set about efficiently cannibalising it for its cord. Natalya heard both the fridge open and the bedroom door bang shut. She could feel Alison studying her.

"So you're Emily," Natalya stated coldly without looking up. "Not Alison."

"I see Hailey's been over-sharing again. But, yeah. Well, actually, I answer to either name. You try working in one department with two cops called Emily Ryan and see how much fun that is. Switchboard kept putting her kids through to me on a daily basis. I was starting to think they *were* mine.

"Oh and just for added confusion I found out after I started going by 'Alison' that there was also an 'Allison' Ryan working there, as a secretary, but that was much easier to deal with. Our jobs and ages were too different to cause any mix-ups. Besides, it's a different spelling." There was a rummaging noise and a pause. "I see your friends like a lot of champagne. I mean that's pretty much all there is in here."

"They're not my friends," Natalya said curtly. "They're not anyone's friends."

"Well, that Lola woman sure seemed to know you," Ryan said. "That was an unusual farewell: You're her favourite monster. What was that about?"

Natalya merely grunted, unwilling to be drawn.

"You know what I find so intriguing," Ryan continued, "is that you and Lola both sit in exactly the same way. Like queens surveying their dominions. In fact the similarities go right down to the fingers drumming on the back of the seat and the tilt of the head. Isn't that interesting?"

Natalya said nothing as she continued working on her knots.

"And the way she mocked you for not taking her on? That was personal. I think she's family. Your mother maybe? A bit young? Well, she *is* related though."

Natalya twitched. So Ryan wasn't entirely useless at her job. In fact, if today's events were anything to go by, far from it.

"I'm sorry she's that way," Ryan continued and her voice sounded genuine. "She was vicious to you. No one deserves that."

Natalya loathed the tone. *Sympathy*? From the *mouse*? That was rich.

"You'd know all about that," she said coolly. "Manipulative mothers."

"What's that supposed to mean? You don't know a thing about my mother!"

Natalya wondered if now was a good time to point out she knew what Mrs Elsie Ryan had for breakfast, right down to how she liked her tea with milk and two sugars. Instead she tugged on the knots binding Gunther extra hard.

"Okay," Ryan continued, undaunted by her silence, "so was there some reason she was cradling her arms when she left? And had tears running down her face?"

"She may have fallen and broken both her wrists." Natalya finally looked up.

Ryan turned abruptly from the fridge, her eyebrows shooting skywards as she met Natalya's gaze. "She...what?"

"She's very clumsy."

"Like that crazy ex of yours outside Hamburger Heaven?"

"Not my ex. A business associate."

"I'll bet. Why does everyone in your orbit end up clutching damaged body parts?" Ryan asked, closing the fridge door with her foot and walking over to her.

"It's a mystery." Natalya rose, stepping back to show Ryan the unconscious thug had been hogtied.

"Oh, very expertly done," Ryan said sarcastically. "Cellists are *so* well-rounded. I had no idea."

"No one does. It's always the violinists who get the glory," Natalya said dryly, flicking her eyes over Ryan, and heading back to the seating area.

She arranged herself artfully on the seat again as Ryan knelt to check that the man had been adequately bound. Such little faith. No one was breaking those bonds anytime soon.

"POLICE!" came a bellow from the door, followed by a banging that set the walls shuddering.

"Ah," Natalya noted, "showtime."

"I'll bet," Ryan muttered as she stood and walked to the door. "You're good at performing. Everything's just a façade to you, isn't it?"

"You can talk," Natalya said, relaxing her features. Her body language oozed confidence and control. Inside, anger surged at Ryan's hypocrisy. "Tell me, Alison, or Emily, or whoever you really are, was there any part of our acquaintance that wasn't a lie?"

The other woman paused. "What?"

"You know exactly what I mean," Natalya said, her gaze hooded. "Sneaky little mouse. Playing me the whole time."

Ryan's head snapped around to glare at her, just as four men in uniform surged into the motorhome.

CHAPTER 15

Natalya finally made it home, later than she'd expected. She'd picked up her cello from Marks who wanted to grill her about her sudden departure from their ensemble. Natalya had simply walked away, grinding her teeth, her tolerance levels for humanity, especially the shallow end of the gene pool, at their lowest ebb.

She fed her cone snail. Watered her African violet. Then she wandered around her home with a restlessness she'd not felt in years. Her mind drifted back to how the rest of the afternoon had played out. Her calculated gamble. The boldest of choices: To stay.

She flipped on the TV news, wondering whether the media had picked up the story.

Sure enough.

"Just repeating our top story. One man has been arrested, and a woman is in the hospital under police guard after the abduction of a Victoria Police homicide detective's daughter at the Melbourne Cup. The thirteen-year-old and her aunt, also a homicide detective, were kidnapped and held in a motorhome trackside for a brief period. A good Samaritan with martial arts skills reportedly assisted in raising the alarm. Further details on the hero and the names of those involved have not yet been released.

"The arrested woman was picked up attempting to get medical treatment. Police sources say she is alleging her controlling boyfriend broke both her wrists when she refused to help him, quote "kidnap a cop's brat." The pair will face court tomorrow.

"Meanwhile, Flemington saw plenty of drama of a different kind today at the race that stops a nation. Peppermint Dream's two-length win was overshadowed when an internationally renowned celebrity chef and a busty reality star had a drunken dust-up in the Birdcage. Punters' phone footage shows..."

Natalya snapped off the TV. Lola was as slippery as she was charming, so her escape from the hospital was inevitable. She texted a coded query to Lola's right-hand man asking for an update. For all she knew, her former stepmother might be out already.

Her phone beeped a reply a minute later.

Still visiting hogs. Pool is @ six.

So she was still under police custody. Six hours? That was how long most of Fleet Crew were betting it would take their boss to make her escape.

Idiots. She'd be out in three.

Natalya finally had enough of pacing her empty home. She grabbed her car keys.

Half an hour later she parked in her usual spot, and entered the Rose Gardens Nursing Home. She headed down the hallway at a fast clip. It was well lit, the walls painted hospital green. The skeleton staff would be on and they all knew her. And, most importantly, they knew to leave her undisturbed.

She came up to the third floor nurse's reception area. The desk was unmanned at this hour so she poked her head in a small side office.

"How is he today?" she demanded without preamble.

She had never bothered to learn the nurses' names, although she was quite sure every one of them knew hers. It was a bit hard to avoid since her name was gracing the assisted care wing built with her donated funds. A useful investment, as it turned out, because she could visit any time she pleased.

"Ma'am." The nurse bobbed her head up and down forcefully, as though checking it was still attached to her neck. She wore a non-regulation, vivid blue scarf and a nervous expression. The latter was satisfactory, at least.

"He's been quite lucid this afternoon. He had his dinner and has been resting quietly ever since. He remembered his name and where he was when I checked in on him an hour ago. He keeps asking for his wife. He drifts in and out of awareness."

"Ex-wife," Natalya corrected. "And to spare your people asking again, no, she will never visit him."

"Oh," Blue Scarf said. "That's a real shame. He really misses her."

Natalya ignored that and headed down the hallway. Her black, polished heels drilled into the creaking linoleum as she followed the path she knew so well.

As she entered, she took in Vadim's room with a critical eye. It was pristine, just as she'd demanded, larger than any others on the floor, and had a wide window that offered a panoramic view of the gardens during the day. The very best money could buy.

The only thing it couldn't buy was the man she knew.

She eased herself into the thinly padded chair beside the bed and studied the worn shape next to her. He had stubble, white and scraggly, which meant he'd fought the nurse again when she'd tried to shave him. His pyjamas were grey with white stripes. He seemed thinner. Loss of appetite was a side effect of his many medications.

She reached over and took his right hand, which was covered in stark blue veins and liver spots. It seemed lighter than the last time she'd held it, a week ago.

He didn't respond to the touch.

"Papa," she said quietly.

He turned his head then, and his ancient eyes studied her. They were empty.

She exhaled. It was always a crapshoot as to the mental state he'd be in.

"Who are you?" he asked. "You look like someone. Someone I know." He fidgeted. "You remind me of my daughter. My little sun—solnyshko." He frowned at her. "Except you're old."

Natalya squeezed his hand. "It *is* me, Papa."

He considered her words carefully, sifting through them as though weighing them up for truth. It was so achingly familiar; it was like he was still *him*.

"How can that be?" he asked suspiciously. "You and Natalya? Both my daughter?"

"A lot of time has passed."

"Where's Lola? She will visit, too, yes?"

"Not today, Papa."

His face fell.

"Tomorrow?" he asked, hopefully.

"Maybe," Natalya said, knowing he likely wouldn't remember this conversation in five minutes. And yet, she still couldn't not have it. "I have to tell you something."

"Yes?"

"I'm going away for a while. I've been asked to dep for an orchestra overseas. I'm leaving soon."

"Where are you going?"

"The tour's across Europe."

"Ahh," he said. "Europe. It is important you visit Vienna. My daughter played there, do you know? She was in papers over there. She won awards for cello playing."

"Yes," Natalya said softly. "She did."

"What do you do?" Vadim asked curiously. "Do you play the music, too?"

"I do."

"My solnyshko plays cello," he repeated and his eyes became distant. He stared at the silent, dead television on the far wall intensely, seeing something that wasn't there.

After a few beats he turned back to look at her.

"Natalya?" he asked, and this time pride coated his voice.

She smiled at his recognition. "Yes Papa."

"You're visiting early this week."

"I am."

"Have you seen Lola lately?"

She wanted to roll her eyes. *Always her*. His condition was in some ways a blessing, because he'd forgotten all the ways she'd tried to screw him over on the way out the door.

"I saw her today, actually."

"How is she?"

Brutal, cruel, mocking, her brain supplied. She would have robbed me of my soul without a second thought. She tried to steal my music.

"Same old Lola."

He nodded, and then studied her. "You are troubled."

"It's nothing. A friend…of sorts…turned out to be not what she presented."

"And who is this friend?"

"A...violinist."

"Ah." He nodded at her. "You and your music." He contemplated her. "You don't talk of friends often, Natalya. I have never heard it. It is important to have them. Remember that when you conquer the world. Don't isolate yourself too much, my solnyshko."

"It's fine, Papa. My friend, really, it's all over. She won't bother me again."

"Oh? You'll cut her off? Be cold to this one as you always are? A second chance never given? You always did this. Is it really the best way?"

"It's the only way," Natalya said darkly. "This is black and white, Papa. Betrayal and deception deserve only one response."

"It is *grey*, doch. Just let her explain first. Then you can bring down your cold war if that is your want."

"I fail to see why anyone should get the benefit of doubt," Natalya snapped, eyeing him in irritation. "She's lucky I still let her breathe in my existence."

He shook his head and closed his eyes for a moment.

"On this earth I have walked for eighty-four years, Natalya. Time, it goes so fast. Look at me: One day, ordering my men around the field, seen as the man to go to for wisdom. The next I am in this little room with nurses who bellow at me as though I am deaf and feed me the blue poison."

"It's jelly, Papa, not poison."

"Well, it's not food, even if it is safe." He gave a half laugh at his small joke, and she could see his teeth, yellowed by years of smoking. He smoked so much she had been sure the cigarettes would kill him. Instead, *this*. She wasn't entirely sure which was worse.

"I am Russian, solnyshko. A proud military man. I was raised the correct way to behave and, so, this I did. It was always hard for me to tell you things you needed to hear. Your mother died on the day of your birth. I did not know what to do with this child. How would I talk to her? What would I say? What did I know of little girls? It was not easy.

"Maybe it was wrong I treated you like a son and taught you the discipline of fighting men. I did not know what else to do. I did not know what to tell you. But I watched, so proud, when you grew: So tall, so strong. So much talent. However, I made one mistake: I never talked of love."

Tears filled his eyes, and Natalya tried to hide her shock. She'd never seen her father cry, ever. Not even after Lola had left him.

"It wasn't the way for men in my world to talk of feelings," Vadim continued. He ran a wizened finger down her cheek. It was warm and rough. "I worry I did not do right by you, Natalya. That I didn't do all of my duty. Just half. Expressing love, feelings—I never taught you how to do these."

"I'm fine, Papa," Natalya said uncomfortably. "Really. It was never you."

"But you are alone. This, I worry about. You never talk of finding someone to share life's burdens. Even as a girl, you never spoke of such dreams. This saddens an old man. And it is hard for me to see that you have no one even now."

"Some people don't need others to be content," she said. "Emotion is weakness, after all."

"Never," he said and his pale eyes flashed suddenly. He pointed a gnarled finger at her. "Whoever told you that is a fool. Emotion can be harnessed, Natalya. You cannot tell men to go into a battle and kill and feel *nothing*. It does not work that way. But if you tell them they must fight for family? Then they have a strength of twenty bears. My own eyes have seen it. Emotion, Natalya, is *strength*."

She stared at him.

"I see your face, doch. You think because I kept my own counsel all these years that I had no emotions? I promise you that my heart was brimming enough to fill a well."

"No," Natalya said. "I just don't think those rules apply to everyone."

He laughed, a low booming sound that came deep from his core. It was so familiar and yet sounded odd coming from so frail a body.

"Ah, so you mean humanity's rules do not apply to *you*," Vadim said. "The rules that say everyone needs someone. Even if they do not get this person, they still want; they still dream. Never have I met a soul on this earth who did not want someone, just once, to look with love in their eyes at them."

Natalya fidgeted, feeling well out of her depth. She didn't discuss emotions for this reason. There was no control with emotions. No order.

"Not everyone is like that, Papa. Some of us are different. Some set themselves apart. The chaos of emotional attachment is not desired."

"Mm," he said regretfully. "I wish…" he faded out.

"What?"

He patted her hand.

"Daughter, perhaps you should try the roosters," he said earnestly. "Hens are so fickle."

Natalya froze and stared at her father in shock.

He smiled at her expression. "You thought I didn't know? I may be old, solnyshko; I may be Russian and military. But when you get closer to grave than cradle, you find that the more time and age closes old eyes, the more it is you see.

"I just want you to have happiness. Rooster or hen, it is as it will be, but you need someone who brightens in spirit when they see you. Someone who challenges you and your stubborn ways. Stubborn ways you learnt from me. Most of all you need someone to look at you with love."

She opened her mouth to reply just as his expression drifted. His hand went limp in hers, as her mind reeled. How long had he known about her? He'd never given any indication.

"Who are you?" Vadim asked flatly.

Natalya leaned over and gave him a light farewell kiss, rubbing his stubbly cheek with her thumb. He pulled away uncertainly.

"I'm no one," she said.

"Mmph." He eyeballed her crossly. "Then go away," he said. "It is late. You do not belong here."

"No," she agreed softly. "I don't belong."

She rose, walked to the door, and turned. She studied Vadim for a moment as he rolled over to face the window. So small now, shrunken inside his pyjamas. They engulfed him, an apt metaphor for his life.

"Goodbye, Papa," she said in a low voice.

When she arrived back home, it was close to one in the morning. Natalya made three secured calls to the top associates in Fleet Crew. The trio of men would each rather be running Lola's enterprise themselves but had failed to wrest control of it upon Dimitri's death.

Oh, they had the skills, cunning and ambition, but they all lacked one vital thing: Requiem. No one had the courage to take on Lola while she owned a lethal, loyal pitbull.

Natalya stood at her windows, staring out at her darkened gardens, phone to her ear, as she casually informed each of the sleepy men that Requiem had, effective immediately, shifted her allegiance from Lola to neutral. They could do what they pleased now without Requiem's interference.

The message was clear: their power-hungry, fat asses would be safe if any of them grew a pair and tried to throw their boss over. The reign of Lola Sweetman was essentially over the moment the words were out of Requiem's mouth.

She stared at her reflection, backlit in the glass. She could see the cold detachment with which she announced the queen was dead.

The men had been extremely grateful for this information, with one, Sal, asking repeatedly if there was "anything, anything at all" he could do to assist her in her future plans.

She sneered inwardly at the toadying lickspittle, but she had to admire his shrewdness. Sal had worked out that he didn't want Fleet Crew's single most deadly (and secret) asset to side with a rival Fleet boss contender.

Natalya told him she would be in need of his cleaning services soon. With her alliance to Lola now ashes, Requiem's automatic access to Fleet's scrubbing crews and any other services had died with it.

Her possessions still needed to be packed away safely and her home wiped of incriminating traces of anything involving Requiem's life while she embarked on an extended trip overseas. Just in case she had unwelcome visitors while she was touring.

Fleet Crew had a reputation for being without peer at site scrubs. No prosecutions had ever resulted from police searching an establishment cleaned by Fleet's finest.

"Sure," Sal said enthusiastically. "No problem, Requiem. We'll have the A team there within the hour whenever you text us, day or night. Be in and out before any turd cutters get a chance to scratch their balls. Anything else?"

Natalya thought about that as a small white moth danced in front of her garden up-lights. She warred with herself for a moment before she spoke.

"Put two names on the permanent white list. They are *never* to be touched, no matter who gives the order or you'll have to answer to me. Emily Alison Ryan and her niece, Hailey Moore. I want them protected from future fallout in any coups."

"Ryan and Moore? Okay. Uh, wait, *Moore*…she's not related to Zebra is she? Christ, tell me she's not the boss hog's brat who got kidnapped today?"

"She is."

He inhaled sharply as he processed what she'd asked of him. Fleet Crew all knew the abduction was Lola's job gone sour. And now Natalya was asking Sal to go directly against his boss. Disloyalty like that could be fatal—unless you slithered over her head into the top job yourself.

"Is that a problem?" she asked in a challenging voice.

"No!" Sal said quickly. "It's done. Just wondering—you don't want your own name on the white list? Just in case? Lola's arms are fucking long and her vendettas are legend."

That was a kind way of looking at it. She would become Lola's personal target now for betraying her with this call.

Well, Lola had betrayed her first. The same sick sensation coiled in Natalya's stomach as she'd felt when she'd been a breath away from losing her music by Lola's hand. To not be able to play was barbarism—she had no other word for it. She could still see the casual expression on Lola's face as she outlined her plans. As though it was a matter of little consequence.

A cold fury flooded through her. Oh yes, the betrayal was all Lola's.

Natalya realised Sal was still waiting for a reply and forced out a bark of laughter.

"All right, Sal, sure. I don't need every two-bit thug gunning for me to make their name; I'd never get anything done. Although good luck finding anyone who could come close to hurting me."

"Yeah," Sal agreed reverently.

She hung up.

If only he knew. Two people *had* managed to get through her defences and hurt her in just the past eight hours.

Lola: Indifferent and cruel. Disloyal and brutal.

And Ryan, who wasn't the woman Natalya thought she was. She didn't know where the lies began and ended with that one.

How long had Ryan been laying her little traps for Requiem? She had played her with an innocent routine that had sucked Natalya in and she'd swallowed it whole. Her eyes hardened. She could count on one hand the number of people who had ever done that to her.

She drew in a sharp breath and leaned her forehead against the window. Her breath fogged up the glass and she recalled her impulsive decree to Sal: No one hurts Ryan. Because, despite it all, it didn't automatically follow that she wanted the woman dead—at least, not at some oafish stranger's hand who was trying to win Lola's favour. That would not befit the sneaky little mouse.

Ryan's life was Requiem's to play with, not theirs. She alone would decide whether Emily Alison Ryan lived to see another day.

CHAPTER 16

Natalya woke precisely at 5:15am. She carried out her morning routine efficiently, dressing in tight black pants and a white designer T-shirt. Her bed was made, as usual, with precise military corners, even though she knew it was pointless. All of it. She stopped, hands resting on the sheet.

She would have to leave this place today and was unsure whether she'd ever return. It would be a shame if she had to abandon her city, her home, forever. She was well-used to its pulse. It had a rhythm and it suited her. But her future was too uncertain and Natalya was nothing if not adaptable.

A beeping sounded from her security computer, and Natalya headed towards it, wondering what had set it off. It was far too early for police. For once she was grateful for the nation's absurd obsession with a horse race. She doubted even ASIO, Australia's top spy agency, could have managed to order a raid on such short notice the day after the Melbourne Cup. It went against the laws of physics and Australian culture.

In fact by the time Ryan managed to get her request high enough up the bureaucratic totem pole to be acted upon—a big ask, given a lack of evidence—Natalya would be halfway to Paris to connect with the Berlin Philharmonic. And Fleet's boys would be already unloading her possessions into a secured, secret storage facility, having cleansed her home of all traces of her existence.

She reached for her computer, and spun the mouse to see what had it fired up.

Natalya headed down the hallway in long strides, side-stepping her pile of packed luggage. Her roaming gaze drilled the lounge like machine gun fire, her mouth fixed in a firm line. There was an intruder *inside* her home. Someone was about to be very sorry, very soon.

Her furious movement came to an abrupt halt.

Alison Ryan was sitting on her couch, hands folded, serene as could be.

Natalya shifted to an aggressive pose, fingers flexing and unflexing, and she looked carefully around the room, half expecting someone to jump out at her. She eased onto the balls of her feet, the threat clear.

"Good morning," Ryan said evenly. "Sorry it's so early but I thought we should talk. Especially since we might not get the opportunity later." She waved in the direction of the luggage pile.

"How did you get in?" Natalya snapped. She pointed towards the windows to the exterior walls outside. "Those are twelve feet high!"

"Does it really matter?"

Natalya glared. "Don't be cute. Tell me."

"Arvo Pärt's birthday. I punched it in on the security gate. Remember you told me he was your favourite composer? Well I did try your birthday first. And then, um, '666', in case you had a dark sense of humour or something. But, no, Pärt was it."

Natalya sized up Ryan who gazed steadily back at her, cool and confident. Time to shake that up. She strode over and unceremoniously yanked her out of her seat by her shirt collar.

Ryan's surprised look was enjoyable. Natalya knew her display of strength was unexpected. Most people underestimated her, to their cost.

Ryan's pulse thudded at her neck as Natalya dragged her over to a wall and pushed her against it. Her gaze raked every inch of her quarry's face and Natalya allowed some of her anger over the past twelve hours to show.

"You have some nerve," she hissed. "Anyone else who'd tried this stunt would be regretting it all over my floor."

She began to roughly frisk her, efficiently and thoroughly, from her ankles, sliding into white socks, up the outside of her jean-clad calves, thighs, and hips.

Natalya then returned her hands to the ankles and ran her fingers up the inner calves and thighs this time. Ryan's thighs were clenching tensely as she got higher, but Natalya was in no mood to make a comment. This was business.

As her hand slid up to Ryan's crotch, the other woman flinched. Finding nothing, Requiem dropped her hand and rose to full height.

She threw Ryan a chilling look and then, without warning, ripped apart her white button-down shirt. Several buttons sprayed across the polished floorboards in a dancing clatter. Ryan gave a shocked gasp.

Natalya's fingers slid around and up her bare back, moving restlessly across the skin, dipping under her bra strap, ignoring the faint shiver of the skin beneath her. She returned around to Ryan's front and lifted the base of her bra, and gave it a shake, then ran quickly under the straps, probing just inside the tops of her cups.

Ryan turned pink.

Not so tough then.

Natalya's hands flew upwards and disappeared into the fine brown hair then checked behind Ryan's ears. Finished, she shook her head incredulously.

Unarmed, unbugged, and uninvited? Did she have a death wish?

Now no longer focused on her search, her eyes dropped to the exposed chest in front of her, Ryan's bra the only thing protecting her dignity. Arousal pleasantly twitched in her as she slowly studied the lace and the contained soft flesh rising and falling beneath it.

At her lingering scrutiny, Ryan scrabbled to do up the few remaining buttons with an indignant huff. "Are you quite done?" she snapped.

"You're either very foolish or very brave," Natalya said in a lazy voice, making eye contact once more. "So let's get some things straight: You broke into my property and are now trespassing. I could have *you* arrested for this illegal action. For the record: I do *not* give you permission to be here. I do not give you permission to interview me. I do *not* agree that any part of this conversation can be taken down and used against me. Everything I say is inadmissible in a court of law. Is that understood?"

Ryan finally gave up on the buttons and folded her arms across her chest. "Okay," she said. "But…"

"There are no buts. I am well aware of my rights. You have no legal leg to stand on and no way of pulling off whatever your cunning little brain has dreamed up. And even if you did find some way to wiggle around the law, who would a jury believe? A respected cellist who has no criminal record? Or an ambitious cop trying to slide up the greasy pole at work? I'll give you a hint: Everyone knows the Victorian Homicide Squad's appalling record on wrongful prosecutions."

"Arresting you is not why I'm here," Ryan said. "And be thankful I'm not anything like you just claimed."

"Oh really." Natalya let the sarcasm drip off her tongue.

"*Really*. This is an off-the-record visit. If anyone asks, I'm still in bed, fast asleep."

Natalya's hand suddenly forcefully slapped the wall right beside her ear so loudly that Ryan jumped.

"Just checking you're actually awake now, because sleep walking your way in here is about the only explanation that could make sense of this... *invasion*—especially given who you suspect me to be."

"Who I *know* you to be," Ryan said. "Unless there are any other classical musicians who can toss a two-hundred-kilogram man across a room, break his arm and deliver an uppercut so powerful his back left the floor the moment he passed out."

"Don't underestimate classical musicians," Natalya said darkly. "There are plenty of highly skilled martial artists among us. As I explained to those nice police officers yesterday."

Ryan eyed her. "Don't treat me as an idiot. Anything but that."

"You wish to be considered intelligent? Yet here you are alone with me. That was your first mistake. Your second was how exceptionally dim-witted you must be to play *me* for a fool. That has consequences."

She leaned closer, imposing herself inside Ryan's space. Her warm breath ruffled the hair next to Ryan's ear.

"What *was* your plan, anyway? Hmm? Stalk me, seduce me and get me to confess to my sins during pillow talk? Is this some cynical new undercover program they're trying out in Homicide? Serve up fake ingénues to lure suspects in? I suppose you'd like that aspect, though: the idea of sliding between my sheets."

Her tongue darted against Ryan's ear, and she was amused at the telling, harsh hiss of breath.

"Ahh. Not *all* work then was it?" Natalya said. She lifted her hand to Ryan's cleavage and ran a finger down the pale skin, pushing aside the barely held together shirt. "How did you know I'd even like you?" she asked, curiously, dropping whispered words into Ryan's ear. "Such a risky plan. You're not exactly a classic femme fatale, are you?"

She knew without looking she'd scored a direct hit. The first time she'd ever seen Ryan's photo she knew this woman didn't believe herself to be attractive. In fact there was none of the confidence or charm she might expect from one who had intended to lure her into a web.

Ryan was such a paradox: Cutthroat enough to use herself in the hunt for Requiem; soft enough to be maimed with a single barbed sentence. At that thought, she straightened. Time to remind the mouse whose arena this was and the consequences for playing in it uninvited. Natalya already knew her weakness. It would be so easy—but then it always was. Her selected candidates never said no.

Her fingertip skidded across a hard knot straining under Ryan's lacy white bra. "I'd say you must enjoy your undercover work a great deal if this is the reaction."

Ryan blushed hotly but her eyes flashed in annoyance. Natalya pressed her body firmly against her, feeling a wall of heat and softness. Her muscled thigh pushed Ryan's legs apart until the crotch of Ryan's jeans nestled at her thigh's apex. It was a most excellent position from which to conduct her lesson in futility and powerlessness.

"Maybe this is like a bonus for you?" Natalya suggested, dropping her fingers to Ryan's hips and pulling the smaller woman's centre harder against her thigh.

"Oh my, the perks," Natalya drawled, rolling her body against her once more. "The upside of playing with fire." She allowed her lips to trail the creamy neck before her. "Toying with me, with those big blue eyes and sad tales of lost love and shattered dreams. Tsk Alison. Or is it *Emily?*"

At the harsh reminder of her own carelessness, she slid her tongue more savagely down the vulnerable skin at Ryan's throat, followed by a threatening scrape of teeth.

Ryan trembled against her. "Stop that," she whispered, the hint of desperation laced with lust unmistakeable.

"Oh?" Natalya purred. "Too much truth spoils your appetite?"

Ryan's hands came up to Natalya's waist to steady herself, as the assassin rocked them.

"Even now you still want me. Even now, after I've pointed out you're a fraud who's using her body to get to me? Even knowing what you think I'm capable of?" Natalya asked. "Oh, how your weakness is showing." Her voice dropped to a dangerous hiss. "And you're *very* wrong about me: As bad as you think I am, I'm far, far worse."

Ryan turned her head away and for a moment Natalya could only hear ragged breathing.

"Let me guess," she continued, and pointedly traced Ryan's taut nipple, "you wanted me to finish what you'd started? Is that why you came here today?"

"No." The voice sounded tired.

"No? 'Oh, Natalya, do you think about us? I do,'" Natalya mocked, recalling Ryan's words from that night in the rain. "It *sounded* like you wanted more."

Ryan's head snapped up and her eyes were flashing with rage. "That's low." Hurt eyes glared at her.

"Oh, you wanted me to touch you that night," Natalya goaded, and her voice became like dripping molasses, "to feel what true power was. You thought I'd like a little bit of vanilla on the side, was that it? That *I* wanted you, too."

"I didn't think that," Ryan said crossly.

Natalya's fingers slid up to Ryan's chin, and tilted her head until their gazes were locked, mouths inches away. Her lips curved into a cruel smile. "No, you're right. You don't think anyone would find you desirable. But even so, you hoped," she whispered. "Deep down, in the parts of your soul that you share with no one."

"Natalya," Ryan said, "for God's sake!"

"Poor little mouse," she mocked, "just aching for a friend. Or a *special* friend. And here you were, trying so hard to act cocky a few minutes ago. You invite yourself into my sanctuary, so convinced you have some kind of power over me that I would never hurt you. You don't understand the game at all. And where did you ever get the idea I could never hurt you?"

"I never said you couldn't."

"But you *thought* I wouldn't. Because I saved your precious niece, you thought that meant something. I'll tell you a secret: It didn't. Sometimes I play god. Sometimes I let the fleas go, and sometimes I don't. It doesn't mean a thing. You see, that's human nature: Hurting things." Natalya paused.

"To hurt things *expertly*, see, that's the true skill," she mused. "You have to know what makes a person tick to cause true damage. And I learnt from the best there ever was."

"Lola," Ryan guessed.

Natalya had to admit she was sharp. Her expression grew cold. "We can't choose family, can we? But then you'd know," she said.

She placed her lips against Ryan's earlobe. "Tell me something: every day when you're at home, being told of your failings, being forced into a tiny box just to protect who you are, or even just to breathe, you must wonder what you did to deserve that.

"But your dirty little secret is that a part of you knows it *must* be your fault. You think you're not deserving of better treatment. That all you are is your sum worth to your mother. And when your usefulness is over, what are you then? Nothing. Nothing at all."

Ryan stared at her unflinching. Her lip curled in derision.

"You seem to be talking from experience," she bit back. "Lola really did a number on you, didn't she?"

Natalya drew her fingertips lightly down the woman's cheek and Ryan snapped her head away.

"Lashing out? I see I struck a nerve," Natalya said. "I'm not saying all this to be cruel but to show how, in trying to get to me, you have revealed your own weaknesses. You are so easy to read, so easy to exploit. How simply I could destroy you if I chose."

"Destroy me?" Ryan said. "And what would be your weapon this time? Not guns—it's never guns, is it? Ice? Ropes? Needles? Poison? Wish lanterns?"

"Words," Natalya said calmly. But it was disconcerting that Ryan appeared to know a great many of her kills, two of which went back decades. So, not some hapless wannabe then. Well, that made things easier. Time to finish her lesson.

She leaned closer, eyes glittering. "I will answer your question: I *have* thought about it. I have thought about you and me, like this. I don't do love, but, oh, little mouse, I know you do. And it would hurt you if I took you and made you beg for more and tossed you aside. It would crush you as though I'd squeezed the life right out of you.

"And even knowing that, I would bet there's a part of you right now that wants me anyway." Their lips were virtually touching. "*Isn't there?*"

She rolled her hips provocatively against Ryan to punctuate her point and heard a soft moan. She smirked and shifted her hand to Ryan's waistband.

To her shock, she found herself spun around and slammed against the wall with force.

"What the hell are you doing?" Ryan spat. "I mean *what in the hell*, Natalya? And don't give me that Requiem power-seduction routine, because I know underneath this little performance art that you're still just Natalya. Natalya who's terrified you might, oh I don't know, feel something. You know—have an honest-to-god emotion you haven't prepped for months in advance like one of your fancy concerts."

Natalya was disconcerted to find no witty retorts on the tip of her tongue. Alison pushed her away and stepped back.

"Yes, you're charming and charismatic and you know it. I know it, too. Big deal. Yes, I find you attractive and arousing," Ryan said and sounded aggrieved. "So what?"

Natalya turned to face her as Ryan fixed her with an intense glare and continued.

"I'm not from your world where you fuck crazy women in back alleys," she said. "I'm not some toy you get to tease and mess with and then laugh at for wanting you. I don't deserve that. Don't you know by now who I am? You say you do, but you really don't, do you?"

"You're a cop," Natalya snarled, her mouth dry. She was more thrown than she cared to admit. *Since when did her prey say no?*

"Yes, I am. But I don't believe that's all you see. Natalya, I'm the woman who cries at sappy ads and old people falling in love and my niece's birthday cards. You *know* that's who I am. You just wish it wasn't because it scares you shitless. I'm much easier to dismiss as a liar and a fake or just a cop than to admit I'm real."

"Oh really...*Emily*."

Ryan glared. "My name means nothing to me. I have *never* lied to you. As for me playing you? *You're* the one pretending you're just some innocent cellist. I had no idea you were Requiem until yesterday when you suddenly showed up at my kidnapping to lay my abductor out cold. Which, by the way, thanks."

"Liar," Natalya said softly. "How about 'Oh tell me Natalya, do you ride a motorcycle, you do look like the type.' That was *two weeks ago*."

Ryan gave an exasperated sigh. "And you answered that so truthfully didn't you?"

"I did not lie. Unlike you. You believed I was Requiem for weeks at least. Admit it."

Ryan laughed and sounded pained. "God, if only. Unfortunately I'd dismissed you as my main suspect and I actually thought you might be interested in me. Turns out you're a far better actress than I gave you credit for." She gave a second, more derisive laugh. "My other suspect, however, was far less convincing on that front."

"Who was it?" Natalya asked, her mind whirring through all the possibilities.

"Irrelevant," Ryan snapped. "I obviously made a terrible mistake in ruling you out. Not that it matters any more, but I didn't know and I wasn't playing you."

"I don't buy it. You're lying," Natalya said, testing her.

"Do you really believe I'd let my niece, who I love very much, sit at a table at Hamburger Heaven with someone I suspected of multiple killings?"

"I have *no* idea what you're capable of," Natalya retorted acidly. "Ambition warps the mind. This could have been your huge break. You want something badly enough, you'll do anything to get it. Oh and by the way, 'fact checker' and 'homicide detective' are not even in the same universe for professions. You *have* lied."

Ryan gave her a pitying stare. "I *am* a fact checker. All I do is *cold cases*. That's it. My entire working life is pushing paperwork around and testing the veracity of reports. It's how I discovered Requiem exists. But Jesus, Natalya, you don't get to play the wounded party here! You presented yourself as some humble classical musician. That trumps me hiding the fact I'm a cop from you just because I know my job title makes people act weird."

Natalya took a stilling breath as she digested that.

"I never presented myself as a humble anything," she finally said, smiling slowly. "That's a lie and you know it."

Ryan paused and suddenly burst into strangled laughter.

"Okay, I concede that point," she said, as her laughter petered out, replaced by irritation. "Goddamn you, Natalya. I just…why did you have to be *her?*"

CHAPTER 17

There was so much anguish in the question that Natalya was taken aback. The level of emotion, the tears pricking blue eyes…

She firmed her jaw. This was the problem with embracing feelings. *This*. Emotions made it hard to think, to strategise or manipulate. Instead they disoriented. The sensation was as unsettling as it was infuriating.

Or so she imagined, because she *absolutely* wasn't feeling a thing.

She stalked away and stopped at her wall-length windows to stare out at her gardens. She spoke grimly into the glass, seeing the reflection of Ryan in front of her. "You *really* didn't think I was Requiem? Until yesterday?"

"Of course not."

Ryan's shoulders slumped in frustration.

"Mm," Natalya said. A wasp lazily made its way into the garden bed, its stinger hanging from it like a threat. She admired the efficiency of it—the lack of subtlety. Advertising its lethal intentions.

Her mind whirred. It seemed a little too convenient to believe Ryan was as upfront as she claimed, even if she hadn't played her.

"So if you are so sure I'm this Requiem you're chasing, why didn't you arrest me yesterday?" she asked.

"Police don't arrest suspects without some evidence."

"The Victorian Homicide Squad does," Natalya countered, watching the bright flash of her own teeth in the glass. "Infamously so."

"True. Unfortunately. But I'm not like them." Ryan rubbed her temple. "And the truth is I really didn't want to have to explain to Hailey why I was arresting her newest and greatest hero right in front of her. She was already so shaken up. Right then she needed to believe she had this protector who had kept her safe. I figured I could wait a day or so to bring you in for questioning."

"Quite a gamble." Natalya thought of her pile of luggage in the hall. She would have skipped town yesterday ahead of schedule, but every Melbourne flight was booked thanks to that ridiculous race carnival. More frustrating, all the private airlines had been shut for the public holiday. She would have to travel on the ticket she'd already been sent by the Berlin orchestra.

"Not really a gamble," Ryan shrugged. "I simply bet that even you wouldn't have gotten too far on Cup Day."

"Well then, now I'm curious as to why you are here," Natalya said. "Alone, unprotected, invading the home of someone you think kills for a living."

"I wouldn't say I have *no* protection." Ryan turned and whistled sharply.

A red heeler trotted into the room, tail wagging excitedly as it took in the assortment of new smells, looking about avidly. Ryan made a 'down' gesture and her dog dutifully sat beside her.

"This is Charlotte," Ryan said, patting the dog affectionately. "She might live with my sister's family but she's mine. Very loyal."

Natalya looked at the canine, amused. The animal appeared to be ancient. She walked over to inspect her.

"If you make any threatening gesture to me, she will rip your throat out," Ryan warned. "Just be glad she wasn't in here a minute ago when you went all TSA airport security on me."

Charlotte gazed up at Natalya, tongue lolling, and thumped her tail happily.

Natalya squatted so she could look into the heeler's eyes. "Hello, Charlotte," she said reverently. "Aren't you beautiful?"

Charlotte nudged her nose under Natalya's hand. She patted her and gave her ears a thorough, affectionate scratch. The dog licked her hand and Natalya immediately rose and walked to the adjacent kitchen area.

"Oh yes," Natalya said as she washed and then dried her hands on a small hand towel. "I can see Charlotte is a real killer."

Ryan sighed and grumbled into her dog's ear. "Do you have to love everyone?"

Natalya walked back to them. "How old is she anyway?"

Ryan muttered under her breath and Natalya laughed, relaxing.

"*Fifteen*," she repeated, lips curling in mirth. "So *this* is your cavalry? Please. Where is your real cavalry? What *is* your plan of attack?"

"I didn't come here to attack."

"So you keep saying. Now why do I find all this so very hard to believe?" Natalya asked suspiciously. Her gaze fell to Charlotte and she paused, suddenly pursing her lips. "Perhaps because it *is*?"

She held out her hand to the dog who immediately padded over. "Aren't you a clever girl," Natalya said, and her gaze flicked to Ryan pointedly. She patted Charlotte then slid her fingers under the dog's neck, finding the buckle on its black leather collar.

She undid it and examined an odd-shaped bulge she found there. "A recording device," she noted, tapping the bulge. "I admire your creativity. No one ever would check the dog for a bug. Not that anything said would be legally admissible, but I don't like leaving a trail." She rose and began to walk away.

Ryan jumped to her feet. "Wait!" she cried out. "Don't! It's not what you think!"

Natalya came to a stop in front of her cone snail tank. She took her forceps and held the collar above the water. "Tropical salt water," she told Ryan. "Excellent for fritzing electronics."

She began to lower the collar carefully in and slapped away Ryan's darting hand as it attempted to intercept the device's watery descent.

"No," Natalya warned her sharply. "One drop of toxin from a cone snail could kill ten men. And probably twenty of you. If its harpoon injects you, you'd be convulsing on my floor in seconds."

Ryan's gaze darted to the forceps and then the side of the tank where Natalya kept her test tubes as part of the toxin-extraction process.

"Uli Busch," Ryan gasped, eyes widening. "I left that night just before he died. I found out later they never could work out why he suddenly had this weird seizure. His guards were screaming blue bloody murder but everyone thought they were just being paranoid. The cops who handled the case said none of it made sense. He had no medical history of seizures at all."

"*They* are imbeciles." Natalya tossed the now drowned collar into Ryan's hands in distaste. "*You*, there's hope for." She placed the forceps beside the tank, aligning them perfectly parallel. "You have imagination at least. Although I don't appreciate you using it to try and get me."

"Well, I'm glad you think I'm imaginative but you just killed my pet tracker."

"Your what?"

"It's called a Pod," Ryan sighed. "I bought it so I could keep track of Charlotte. Sometimes she wanders off. Shit. That was expensive, too." Her shoulders slumped.

Natalya, who had been staring at the drenched blob of plastic and collar, looked up in surprise. "So let me understand this: you really did come here with nothing but your fifteen-year-old dog that is more prone to lick someone to death than maul them?" she asked.

"Yeah."

"No gun, no bug, *nothing*?"

Ryan shrugged. "Nope."

Natalya retraced her steps, then washed her hands meticulously in the kitchen again, followed by drying them. She gave a disbelieving snort. "You really are from another planet."

She opened her fridge and returned, holding a T-bone in a pincer grip between a piece of folded paper towel. "Wagyu gourmet organic steak," she noted with a sigh of disappointment. "It was to have been dinner tonight, but it turns out I've had to make other plans."

Natalya waved it in front of Charlotte's nose and the excited dog bounded to her feet, following her to the sliding exterior door.

"Please don't," Ryan sighed.

Natalya snorted. "And if I said, 'Please don't tell anyone who you think I really am,' would you do that?"

Ryan's mouth clamped shut.

"That's what I thought."

Ryan followed them outside, as Natalya tossed the meat far into the rear of the garden. Ryan stared moodily as her first and last line of defence trembled in doggy delight then bounded off with a joyful bark.

"Nice dog," Natalya said, wiping her fingertips on the paper towel. "And I do like her or I would have tossed it into the part of the garden where my poisonous trees are."

Ryan frowned. "You wouldn't."

"I definitely would have. So, now I have stripped you of all your defences and shown you how vulnerable you are, can you explain to me what on earth you hope to accomplish here? Or is this some weird surrender?"

"It's not a surrender. I wanted to talk while we still can."

"Hmm," Natalya said, stalking back inside to the sink to wash her hands for a third time. Ryan's curious gaze watched her as she made her way to the couch.

Natalya finished up and sank into the armchair opposite. She studied her. "Well, you have my attention. I'm all ears about how you plan to make use of anything I say, given that it's inadmissible in court."

"I don't plan to," Ryan said. "Like I said, this is an off-the-books visit. I'm not really here, remember? I'm at home sleeping in."

Natalya's eyebrow rose.

"Yup, under my blanket, dreaming of fudge-centre chocolates."

"Well," Natalya said, at a loss. "How nice for you."

"Look, there's three things I came for: One, you saved Hailey's life, Natalya."

"So?"

"I *had* to thank you, and I had to do it now, before all of this…" she waved her hand between them, "becomes an 'us vs you' thing. Which it will, because after I leave here I will become a detective again, tracking down Australia's most feared gangland assassin. And you will be a suspect on the run wanted for questioning. But that's not right now. Right now I'm just an aunt—a very, *very* grateful aunt, telling her brave and incredible friend thank you. *Thank you.*"

Natalya was startled. *Friend?*

"Hailey's special," Ryan continued. "She's talented and funny and so smart, and she has her whole life ahead of her. And, in the blink of an eye, she almost died yesterday.

"Do you get what that was like for me? How my heart stopped when I couldn't do a thing to save her? How I felt helpless even though I'm a trained cop? I tried every technique I knew on that gorilla and nothing was enough. He was just too big. Too strong.

"And then, there *you* were, flinging open the door, storming in like something from the pits of Hell. You waded in like it was nothing, like *he* was nothing, and gave me Hailey back.

"You didn't have to do that. I know it would have been a lot easier for you not to put yourself in the frame, yet you did it anyway. What you did made things very personal for me. I won't forget what you did. Never *ever* will I forget that."

Ryan's expression was pure gratitude, her eyes shining with sincerity. Natalya shifted uncomfortably.

"Well, I find your niece amusing in her own annoying way," she said. "She's got spirit. I like that."

"Oh, yeah. She really does." Ryan nodded vehemently, grinning.

"Is that all? You could have texted me your undying thanks."

"It's not the same thing. I had to look you in the eye and thank you. I have no words for what you did. Besides, you've been ignoring my texts lately."

Natalya fidgeted, wishing they were discussing anything else. "And your second reason?" she asked. "You said you had three."

"Oh!" Ryan said. "Yeah. Deal's a deal."

She reached into her jeans pocket and pulled out an MP3 player and powered it up. "Track three. The experimental musical piece—celebrating the impurities, breaking all the rules. And you'll love it."

"Alison…"

"You haven't heard it yet. Do you need an earpiece?"

Natalya reached into a drawer under the coffee table and pulled out a set. She inserted them into the device and jumped to track three, hitting play. "It's unlikely I will enjoy anything experimental," she warned.

"You will," Ryan said.

Finally, after fiddling with the volume settings, she inserted the earbuds into her ears. A strange look crossed Ryan's face as she watched Natalya's ordered little ritual.

"What?" she asked Ryan.

"Nothing. Just listen."

Natalya listened to the beats, the clanging of Aboriginal music sticks, discordant sounding at first, and yet they still had a pattern of sorts. She closed her eyes.

The low, guttural sounds of a didgeridoo sounded and then, remarkably, cutting through the thrumming, earthy bass, came the clear tones of a violin, aching and sobbing as the rumble of ancient music played underneath as a counterpoint.

It broke every rule. Didgeridoos and violins? Aboriginal music sticks! It was a mess of shattered rules, but somehow it worked.

Natalya opened her eyes when it ended and stared directly at Ryan in bewilderment at what she'd just heard. "Who composed this?"

Ryan fidgeted. "I did. I went to one of the remote communities in the Outback during my holidays when I was still studying music and recorded some didgeridoo and basic beats with the Koori elders. I played the violin myself later and looped it in.

"It was a troubled place," she added with a frown. "So many social issues, like poverty and alcohol abuse. I think you can hear the sadness in the way the elders played. It's like, I don't know, their instruments cried. But they also have hope that things will get better one day. That's in there, too.

"So I know my piece is flawed and imperfect because it's about us: Humans. And, also, *I* was playing and I'm no professional violinist. But equally I happen to think it's perfect for its impurities. It reminds me of our place in the world."

"Which is?"

Ryan looked at her earnestly. "We're ants. Tiny. Insignificant. Our vast land lives on, timeless and untouchable, and will remain that way when we are long forgotten. So, this music? Well, it's a way to remember us. Our dreams."

"So this is a requiem? Honouring our deaths?"

"In a way. But it's also about hope. About life after we're dead."

"So it's a requiem for our immortality."

Ryan nodded and gave a widening smile. "I guess it is."

"How is it you can create something extraordinary like this and yet work in an office all day?"

"You liked it?" Ryan asked casually but Natalya could hear the prick of hope.

"It's exquisite," she said, unplugging her earpiece and handing the MP3 player back. "I have no idea why you gave up something you're brilliant at for something as mundane as police work."

"You forget, though," Ryan said, "I'm also brilliant at my current job."

"Is that so?"

"I found you, didn't I?"

"Technically, I found you. If you're so brilliant at being a detective, why were you even on cold cases to begin with? Why didn't they let you loose in the field?"

Ryan's face fell. "That's a long story. But the bottom line is my boss hates me. When we were teenagers, I told Barry he was a neckless loser who wasn't good enough to marry my sister. It might not have been the best idea to do it in front of his mates because they teased him relentlessly after that. He's been punishing me ever since."

"That doesn't explain why you even wanted to become a cop in the first place. In fact, you're the most un-coplike cop I have ever met, and I've seen a few. You have no edge, no attitude. How did the Academy even pass you?"

"Well, it would have been a bit hard to fail me since I aced all their damned tests except one." Alison glared at her. "And don't you dare call me soft! Or weak. Or 'too nice,'" she said putting air quotes around the words. "I'm sick of hearing it.

"I jumped through every damned hoop, listened to all the crap the other recruits threw at me. I'm tougher than I look and you don't need to swagger about like a jock to solve a crime. I got into Homicide to prove that. I knew I could do so much more than in Traffic. I was bored to tears there."

"Which test?"

"What?" Alison blinked at her in confusion.

"Which one didn't you ace?"

Alison looked mutinous. "Grip test. You have to be able to squeeze thirty kilograms. I did it eventually, but they gave me so much shit for it."

"Ah," Natalya said. "I thought it would be 'command presence.'"

"That's not a measurable test," Alison said shooting her a dark look.

"Lucky for you," Natalya said, only half joking.

"I take it back, you're not charming at all. But you'll notice that none of the 'cop-like cops' with all that presence and attitude you seem to admire so much actually tracked down Requiem," Alison said silkily. "*I did.*"

"Why policing at all?" Natalya asked, not biting. "You're a musician."

"The call for applicants came when I desperately needed a job to help look after Mum. Besides, police are all about justice. That's something I believe in. And as much as you pretend to be too cool for anything, I know there's a part of you who believes in it, too, in your own weird way. Actually, *you* should get why I do this more than most people."

"What *are* you talking about?"

"Well, I wouldn't have thought an assassin would make a call to emergency services reporting Viktor Raven's daughter was still alive in a wrecked car, but you did."

"That would be an unlikely thing for an assassin to do."

"Yes, it would," Ryan agreed. "Oh the voice was disguised, but I thought about it last night. The timing of when you left and where it happened, the voice being female; it *had* to be you."

"You're imagining a great deal." Natalya folded her arms and glared. "In fact, you're just making up things now."

"Can't you just be honest with me for one minute?" Ryan said with an annoyed frown. "Give me one minute of truth?"

"You're a *cop*, Alison," Natalya said. "And that's not changing any time soon."

"I'm not even here, though, remember? Nothing that happens here or is said here will see the light of day. I was *never* here."

Natalya shook her head. "I can't trust that. Trust leads to betrayal. I know that more than most."

The vision of Lola's gun stroking her hand slipped into her brain and she tried not to shudder.

"Oh? What's happened?" Ryan asked, sounding concerned. She leaned forward.

Natalya shook her head incredulously. "Seriously, do you really not understand? We're not *friends*. We could never be. Do you not get what this dynamic is?" she said, waving her fingers between them. "We're hunter and prey."

Ryan stared back at her evenly. "And which of us is which?" she asked coolly.

For the longest moment they just looked at each other. The silence grew awkward.

"Right, so, the third reason why I'm here," Ryan said, finally breaking the standoff, "is because you could have killed me on Monday when the three-week deadline was up. And you didn't. So that gets you my personal thanks. That's the other reason for you getting a free pass from me today."

Natalya's mind went into overdrive. How could she have known? How long had she?

"I know you were hired to kill me," Ryan clarified.

Another beat passed as they stared at each other.

"How?" Natalya eventually ground out, her brain reeling. *Who the hell had talked? Surely not Lola?*

Ryan gave her a coy smile and laced her fingers across her stomach. "I know because of who it was who put the hit out on me."

For once Natalya couldn't disguise her shock. "Who was it?"

"That's quite a story."

Natalya spoke with a deadly softness. "It turns out I've got the time."

CHAPTER 18

Alison ordered her thoughts, casting her mind back to the day her world upended itself. The day, two years ago, she'd been at work, minding her own business on her usual cold cases when the report came through that a drug runner had died. His body had been found in the middle of the dusty, red desert at Mundi Mundi. The preliminary report said he'd drowned.

Drowned.

She listened in on the conversations of the other detectives as they laughed about the strangest case that had ever crossed their desks.

When her colleagues had gone home that night, she'd shoved aside her cold case and called up the file. The man, Beattie, had been a drug runner for High Street. One of Santos's men. His body soon would be sent to Melbourne for an autopsy, but the Broken Hill police officer who'd attended the scene had jumped to a fairly obvious conclusion.

Stapled to the man's chest had been a four-kilogram, empty, plastic frozen-ice bag. Given Beattie was found clutching his throat, the officer had speculated its contents had been forced down it in such vast quantities that he'd either drowned or choked on it.

Alison stared at the report in disbelief. This wasn't a killing so much as a mockery. Someone was making a statement.

She flicked back to the first page to look up which drugs he ran. Crystal meth. Alison stared. He ran *ice*. And he'd been stuffed full of *ice*. A different sort, but still.

She printed out the report and sat at her desk, gazing at it. From that moment on, everything changed.

Her curiosity was piqued. She wondered if there'd ever been a similar case like this. A murder as pointed as this didn't happen in isolation, surely?

And the perpetrator seemed too assured and mocking not to have killed before.

She went back through her computer, looking at every murder in recent years. No other reports of a killer using ice came up. No other poetic justice-style killings, either.

What about the other files, though? The ones she never got to see? The gangland cases? Clearly the man was linked to one of the families. She glanced at her watch. It was still early. She had no one around to tell her no.

Alison changed the parameters of her search back to when the underworld killings started in 1998. Every gangland-associated murder, solved and unsolved, within Victoria, where the method of death was not by knife, gun, or choking.

After a few minutes her screen filled with the results. The list went for pages.

She groaned. She stretched her neck, cracked her knuckles, then hit enter on the first killing: January 4, 1998.

It's not like she didn't have plenty of time. Or a life.

Over the next year, Alison had become the department's secret resident expert on the gangland wars. She dug into them mainly in her own time, given Moore's insistence that she stick to cases the public and the politicians cared about. And the masses could not care less if the underworld's most vicious criminals cannibalised themselves.

She understood that. She did. But there was also something compelling about picking apart the structures of the warring crime families and piecing together the patterns no one else could see.

Like a beehive, she had come to see the order within the chaos. In the impersonal typed reports, in the photos of men with dull eyes and scarred faces, she found something to get out of bed for. It had taken a long time for her to be this interested in work again since her first dream had ended in tatters.

Now her fingers tingled with each new piece of the puzzle she fitted together. On the days she made a breakthrough, there was no other sensation like it in the world.

After years of feeling mired in tar, just going through the motions, she finally felt a sense of purpose. She was doing something important. It made her feel 100 feet tall and unstoppable. On those days she felt immortal.

Well, until she went home.

Chapter 19

After eighteen months, Alison had uncovered over a dozen underworld deaths that she was sure were linked to the same killer, and a further six that were not gangland hits but were possibly also the same person, where an unaligned criminal had died. With her research folder bulging, a colourful flowchart and a chronology mapped out, she decided it was time to present her facts to her boss.

She'd planned it carefully. She'd do it on the weekend, while on a visit to catch up with her sister Susan and Hailey. Away from the office, Barry Moore was less likely to make his disdain for her a team sport with the other detectives. She might even get a good hearing. And even if the asshole hated her, Moore might still keep an open mind about this. Business was business, after all.

She sat beside Moore on an outdoor chair in his grassed back yard and gave Charlotte a fond stroke behind the ears as her old dog sat at her side. Finally sucking up the courage, Alison passed her boss the folder. Then she nervously and painstakingly explained her theory.

"One person," she said as she finished, "I really believe one person did all of these."

"Serial killers don't change their MOs so much," he grunted at her, cracking the bottle top and passing her a beer. "And if it's an assassin, they'd never be hired by all four rival crime families. So I don't buy it."

Alison took the beer, listening politely. She hated beer—a fact her brother-in-law knew all too well. She sipped it. Nope, still as bad as she remembered. She placed it on the grass beside her. Moore leaned back in his canvas chair, his ample stomach stretching his purple Melbourne Storm T-shirt.

"Look," he continued, "these families are loyal to their own. They'd never use the same assassin that killed one of theirs. There's a code. No way in hell. It's tribal with them."

It was a good point. She'd already considered that. But the facts didn't lie.

"I understand that's the usual way," Alison said carefully. "But I also believe this is a rare circumstance, where one person has gained the business of all of them by being neutral, by being extremely good—able to kill even the hardest-to-get-to person—and critically, by doing it in a unique way, with a signature.

"I think half the reason the families like indulging in these revenge killings is for that reason. The 'screw-you' message. It's all about egos to them."

Susan came out and joined them, scooping up Alison's discarded beer and replacing it with a diet cola. Alison shot her a grateful smile.

"These assholes do like their revenge," Moore agreed with a grunt. "But I just can't see them crossing family lines to do it. It's unheard of."

"Until now."

"Says you."

"Says my dozens of cross-matched crime scene reports."

"Industrious little thing, aren't you? How do I know you didn't just make all this up to be the hero?"

"Barry," Susan admonished gently, "Em would never do that. You know that."

Moore scratched his gut, ignored the interruption, and took another swig of beer.

"I don't know anything," he said, but he wasn't sounding too disagreeable. Just arguing with his wife because he could. As usual. "That's quite a conspiracy theory you've cooked up there."

"It's not cooked," Alison said tightly. "I'd like to show you my work so you can see the patterns I've found. All the knots match on the seven hogtied victims. Here…" She reached for another folder but he held up a hand.

"No." He glanced at his watch. "My game's about to start. Is that it?"

"Well, I have one more theory. Um, I really think the killer's a woman."

The dismayed look on Susan's face told her everything she needed to know. Her brother-in-law was a knuckle dragger. But she hadn't been entirely sure how much his sexism was just for show at the boys' club at work. Susan's reaction was depressing.

"Ryan, is this some new feminazi crap of yours? Women need to be the greatest villains ever or something? What next? *Jackie* the Ripper did it all along?"

"No," Alison frowned. "I don't care which gender the killer is. I just want the truth."

"The truth? These killings are *cold blooded*. You can feel the testosterone dripping down the walls. Besides, you really can't see that they'd never, ever, allow some *girl* to do the deed for them? That's like cutting off their own dicks. And you have no proof."

"I have the vibe I get when I study all these crime scenes. The deaths are pointed and subtle, detail-oriented and clever. Sometimes they're even poetic. It *feels* female."

"Can you even hear yourself? Vibe? Poetic? Feels? I told you the sorry day you landed in my department that you weren't suited to this job. Soft as a day-old kitten. Anyway, enough of this shit. I think that's the last time I need to hear your conspiracy theories. Got it?"

He didn't wait for an answer. Just grabbed his beer, shot her a disgusted look, and went inside.

Alison exhaled. Well. So much for her powers of persuasion.

"Sorry, sis," Susan murmured. "You know what he's like when he thinks he's right."

Alison sipped her drink morosely.

"Maybe you should just let it go," Susan continued. "He's never going to change his mind."

"I'm not wrong about this," Alison said adamantly. "I'm not. I can feel it."

"He won't thank you even if you're right."

"I can find absolute proof. Then he'll have to acknowledge I'm right or miss getting the reflected glory."

"Or you won't find proof because maybe he is right: It's all in your head," Susan suggested quietly. "Same as Mum and her grand fantasies about how things should be."

"Don't compare me to her. We're nothing alike."

"No? You both think you're made for better. Well, guess what: Sometimes you just have to accept that life is what it is—crappy."

"Like you did?" Alison tilted her head.

Susan was not in a happy marriage, and Alison wished her sister could find some inner strength to take Hailey and leave the bastard. Raising the topic just led to angry denials from her sister about how bad the man really was. But Alison had heard the way he shouted at his wife. It could rattle the rafters.

Sometimes Alison wasn't sure which Susan was more afraid of: the truth, or that she'd then feel obligated to act on it. Denial was just easier.

"Can't you just drop it, Emily?" Susan asked. "For once in your life, stop being so damn stubborn! God, you want the other detectives to take you seriously so badly you'll clutch at straws."

She held up her hand at Alison's indignant squawk of protest. "Okay, sorry. Look, even if you are right, you know he'll take his bad mood out on me. He hates being one-upped by a woman. I'll hear about nothing else for weeks."

"That's not fair," Alison protested, feeling sick. "Don't make me choose between justice and you. This is my case of a lifetime. I haven't felt this good since…" She faded out.

"Since Sydney? And that roommate you don't like to talk about? And the career you almost had until we forced you home? Are you *still* mad about that? Look, Em, I'm sorry, but it was the only option. I'm sorry Mum had that spectacular freaking breakdown in the aisles of David Jones when Dad left her. But you know I'd just had Hailey and we were out of other options.

"And how were any of us to know Mum would have that fall just after she got herself back together? It's not like we knew she'd be immobile for *another fourteen damn years*. It was only supposed to be temporary. You *know* that. Don't blame us. Blame Mum for being stubborn like she always is and refusing home help."

Alison bit her lip to prevent herself from saying something they'd both regret. She'd heard it all before. Every single rationalisation that her sister gave for why they'd insisted Alison give up her scholarship and do the "right thing." Every single bullshit reason as to why Susan and Barry couldn't shoulder Elsie for a few years now so that she could have a break.

"Let it go," Susan said. "For your own good. It'll help you to move on. Find someone else. Something else."

"I've *already* found something else," Alison pointed out. "And Barry wants to crush that now, too. Well not this time."

She shot a warning look at her sister and was dismayed to see fear lacing her eyes. Fear of the unknown and of taking a risk. Alison couldn't become that. Wouldn't.

But she'd already been halfway there at one time. Alison had gone through a period of wondering what the point was of even having fresh dreams if she couldn't face the thought of having to stitch her heart back together again if she lost them.

She had only snatches of memories from back then, like small markers on the side of the road. Her sister's hysterical call about their mother's breakdown; taking Elsie to psych appointments, buying her pain meds. Her father's devastation at her stepmother's funeral a few years later.

But mainly what she remembered was her own pain. Crying, packing up, looking around an empty apartment bedroom and finding her girlfriend's sad eyes. Knowing that, for all Melissa's reassurances, she probably wouldn't see her again. Because Melissa was going to be a renowned flautist some day and her life was firmly in Sydney.

Alison could still remember the faint touch of Melissa's fingertips against her own as the taxi pulled away.

Loss was a devious little trap, Alison had often thought. It lay in wait to ambush you months or years later, when you thought you'd moved on and dealt with the sadness. She had been unprepared for how her father's death, a few years after his new wife's, had brought up everything else. It was like the emotional resonance for every past hurt had flooded her bloodstream in one sudden, shocking hit.

"Morbidity due to alcohol use," the coroner noted clinically, later. A fancy way of saying that living the champagne lifestyle of her father's dreams had been incompatible with his thoroughly sauced liver.

Alison's soul compressed itself into a frozen ball of pain the day he died, and stayed that way.

In the intervening years Elsie regularly punished Alison for not being the husband she wished was there instead of her. Alison's interest in life slowly faded away with each new cup of tea and reheated meal she ferried down the hall to her demanding mother. Every plumped pillow, every pill bottle handed over, was a reminder that nothing had moved on in her life since.

And then came the day she awoke. The day a body was found at Mundi Mundi.

She hadn't made the conscious decision to breathe again. It just happened gradually. But bit by bit, Alison noticed she no longer dreaded waking each day. Achingly slowly, she learned to exhale, to take risks, to reach beyond that which she thought she was capable of, and then to excel at it.

It seemed only fitting then, that one day, eighteen months after the Mundi Mundi drug runner met his unfortunate death, she realised she had well and truly found life again.

So, no, she wasn't going to stand by and let Barry Moore or anyone else take away her reason for living a second time.

Alison was just going to have to prove she was right.

CHAPTER 20

The breakthrough Alison was looking for came, like most things, when she was least expecting it, buried in the bottom of a file about the death of a meth lab cook called Collins.

The initial findings were inconclusive, which had kept the case open.

While the man had died after being overcome by toxic fumes—a by-product of what he was making—the coroner's report noted in bemusement the perfectly functioning ventilation system and the fact Collins appeared to have been well protected by full-body coveralls. The coroner, duly baffled, left an open verdict.

Alison was a sucker for a good mystery.

She dug a little deeper and found an informant's offhand comment on the death made to an undercover homicide detective, Stan Polaski. The canary in question, someone called Viktor Raven, had been singing for the price of a few beers at the Bear and Clover pub. He'd mainly been tossing around bull about how many underworld people he knew, but then he'd been asked about the drug cook's death.

"Oh, that one," Raven was reported as saying. "Yeah, a classic hit by Wreck. Sounds just like the sadistic asshole. Sneaky as fuck."

Alison performed every type of search she could think of, but that was all that had been recorded of that conversation.

Someone was convinced the drug cook was murdered?

Alison pored over the Collins file. The Forensic Services Department hadn't even been sent the man's clothing for testing, presumably because it had seemed such an open-and-shut case. Drug cook dies of chemical fumes.

She found Collins's clothes still bagged up in Evidence and sent them off for a full analysis. A few months later, due to the backlog of cases, the forensics report came back. A microscopic inspection found more than a thousand tiny pin pricks all over the coveralls, allowing the fumes to pass through the material and overcome Collins.

Death by a thousand cuts. *Literally?*

She really thought about that. *One thousand* pin pricks? Someone had sat down for hours and gone to the effort of pricking his outfit with that many holes?

The bastard had never stood a chance.

It was also clearly murder, and if the informant had been right about that, then he might have been right about the killer's identity. The problem she had, though, was she highly doubted any woman would ever go by the name Wreck and certainly not a killer so subtle as hers.

She found Detective Polaski chewing on a steak and salad sandwich, spraying lettuce and carrot across his desk, while reading the sport pages. She slid a page from his report across the desk.

"Hey, Stan, remember this drug cook case from four years ago? One of Santos's boys? How did you know how to spell this name? Did you ask?" She tapped the word "Wreck."

Detective Polaski swallowed his mouthful and leaned forward, eyeballing the page. He screwed up his face and thought for a minute.

"No, I didn't bloody get him to spell anything. That bastard was high as a kite. I just wrote down what he said so I could get my expenses back for the beers I bought him."

"You got a tip on a killer and ignored it?" Alison stared at him in disbelief.

"Higher than a kite," Polaski repeated. "You didn't see Raven. And don't forget that was an accidental death. There *was* no killer to be identified. Now can you chase your crap conspiracy theories on your own time? I'm busy." He resumed eating.

"Actually it was an open case," Alison corrected him. "Coroner didn't rule on it either way."

He grunted and dismissed her, returning to his sports results.

Alison took the page and returned to her desk, her mind buzzing. He'd just *guessed*. Her mind rolled over all the possible alternatives to spelling a word that sounded like "Wreck."

Rick. Rec. Req. If she was right and the killer was female…she ruled out the first one. It sounded like a shortening for something. That favourite Aussie pastime of shortening long names and lengthening short ones came to mind. She looked up a dictionary, took out her pen and paper and began to write.

Her list ran to a thousand words by the time it was finished and she sighed, staring at Recruit, Requirement and Requisition, among all the others. It was useless. How would she narrow it down? She had no clue. Besides, maybe it didn't mean anything at all and the name was just a code?

She flicked a look at her watch. Okay, she could make the orchestra tonight. The VPO had a new program and she wanted to hear what Amanda Marks would be playing in the solo. Alison still missed the beauty of hearing the violin, even though her fingers no longer twitched to play it.

Alison looked around the after-party for the VPO's new season with wide eyes. Masks hung from the ceiling in some weird *Phantom of the Opera* theme, although what that had to do with anything was a mystery. She'd been enraptured by Tchaikovsky—and, as always, was brought to tears by the *6ᵗʰ Symphony*.

She found herself on the periphery of Amanda Marks's fans. She couldn't quite see the appeal of the violinist, herself. Yes, Amanda was pretty in a pixie/ Disney princess way. But how did that qualify her for so much fan swooning? If you wanted to single out talent for adulation, her picks for the evening were the elderly oboe player and the dark-haired cellist.

She must have been staring too long because Amanda's gaze suddenly swung around and fell to her. "And what did you think?" she asked Alison.

Alison blinked out of her reverie and attempted to be diplomatic. By the time she'd waxed lyrical about tempo and the movements she had enjoyed (none of which involved Marks's playing), the diva's nearest groupies were looking alternately bored or ready to kill her.

The violinist, however, was not.

"You're a professional then?" Marks asked curiously. "Which orchestra? Who are you? I believe I've seen you around at a number of VPO events over recent years."

"Emily Ryan, although everyone calls me Alison, and no orchestra," Alison said, nervous about having so many eyes on her. "I trained in violin at the Sydney Conservatorium for a little while but it didn't happen. I'm actually a detective. Homicide Squad."

Amanda studied her for a moment, a strange expression crossing her face. "How fascinating," she said, and immediately turned back to her posse, and began to pose for photos.

Fascinating? Sure it was. Alison sighed. She got this reaction all the time from people leery of cops. Worse, she was in Homicide. To the general public, her job was only just one step up from abattoir head slaughterer.

She glanced around the room to discover the brown eyes of the cellist she'd been thinking about earlier looking right at her. Alison smiled automatically. The woman's gaze drilled into hers for a second, flicked to the groupies surrounding her, and cooled noticeably, her lips pressing together in disapproval.

The cellist moved away in long, confident strides, with a grace not often seen off a runway. She seemed European. She wasn't pretty or girly in the style of Marks but she was definitely striking. Alison couldn't help but be impressed.

Intrigued, she pulled out her phone and typed in "VPO cellist."

"Natalya Tsvetnenko" came up.

Alison studied the photo. She could see strength and charisma in her in a way that Marks could only dream of. And, there it was, in the set of the jaw and the steady, almost daring stare—power.

Marks was studying her again like a problem to be solved, so Alison ducked away behind a pillar, uncomfortable at being under so much scrutiny. She should probably head home anyway. She really wasn't cut out to be a social butterfly.

Alison was unlocking her front door a short time later, pleasantly buzzed by the rare chance to be out of the house. The lights were off, so her mother had, mercifully, already gone to bed. She'd obviously found the dinner she'd left for her, or there would have been biting lectures about how she could have "starved to death."

Honestly, Alison wasn't sure why she put up with the vitriol. Initially she'd been too checked out to care about anything much, let alone what her mother ranted at her. Now, though, she noticed it. There was a limit to her patience. Even so, a part of her knew how crushing it must have been for her mother to lose her independence, so she held her tongue.

Tchaikovsky was still running through her mind, and she found herself humming her favourite, his infamous, unofficial requiem. The 6th. It was a piece that captured the gravitas of death perfectly.

She almost dropped her keys at the connection. A song of *death*? The thought slammed into her so fast that she sagged against the doorframe.

Wreck was Req. Her killer's name was *Requiem*.

And if it wasn't, it damn well should be.

CHAPTER 21

Alison perched on the cream-coloured leather couch in Natalya's home and regarded the astonished look on the assassin's face as the question hung in the room.

Who had put the hit on her?

"I have been tracking Requiem for two years," Alison told her. "Two years of spending every waking hour on my theory. Once I worked out that Req was short for Requiem, everything pointed to her being a musician. And not just any musician. One of extraordinary discipline to carry out the killings. There was subtlety there. Restraint. Also, a mocking playfulness. She was delicate yet powerful. Poetic, almost artistic. She killed and made it a message, like a mockery of her victim's patheticness.

"A classical musician would perfectly match such a person. They have the drive and the discipline. They have the focus. They even have opportunity and access, mixing up close with many reclusive and powerful people. Many have god complexes. It fit."

Natalya eyed her. "Interesting theory. But not easily proved."

"It's not hard to cross-match every orchestra in Victoria with every death I thought Requiem had committed," Alison said. "It just takes time. In the end I was left with only one company's name that had been in Melbourne at the time of every killing: The Victorian Philharmonic Orchestra."

"Or, it was a coincidence," Natalya countered.

Alison laughed. "Right. Every time in twenty-four years that the VPO toured, no gangland member died a poetic-justice death? Some coincidence."

"Stranger things have happened," Natalya murmured. "But how did you get from an orchestra full of suspects to one?"

I didn't, Alison almost said, and the shame of her stupid mistake burned through her.

She thought back over the past three months. She'd pulled up biographies of all thirty female members of the VPO. She worked through the names methodically—dismissing as she went: Women too old. Too young. Too physically weak. Too pregnant.

She initially dismissed Amanda Marks as too sociable and outgoing to be involved in such a ruthless, bleak business. She was definitely not a loner. She loved attention and had to be the centre of any circle. But she was also undoubtedly a narcissist. And she clearly thought everyone who wasn't her was a lesser being. She hid it well but Alison knew, given she lived with a narcissist, and she could see the signs a mile away.

There was also something so fake about Marks, just that little bit off, that she couldn't quite dismiss her. After a long internal debate, the violinist's name was added back to the list.

She then came to the cellist who'd caught her eye. Natalya Tsvetnenko certainly seemed strong enough physically. Her CV read like a European holiday itinerary but there was no reference to anything in her life beyond music. She fit the loner profile more than any other member of the VPO.

"Your name was on the top of my short list of suspects," Alison told Natalya. "There was you and daylight behind you."

"The *top*? Why?"

"You know, if you don't want to be considered deadly you might want to work on *that* look," Alison said with a snort. "Simply put, I thought you had a danger about you none of the others had."

Natalya's expression flattened out. "But you said I wasn't your main suspect in the end."

"No. No you weren't."

Alison reviewed her catastrophic error.

Two months had passed and her short list had been gradually whittled down to nine women who could be Requiem. It was far too many to tail. She didn't have the time to do it herself in any meaningful way and the Homicide Squad didn't have the resources, even if her boss was agreeable. Which he wouldn't be.

So, Alison was pretty much screwed.

She'd gotten nowhere trying to rule more names out. She'd put the women's VPO website photos up in her bedroom and would lie in bed looking at them each night, hoping to see *something* in the eyes of one that would give her a clue.

Their impassive, professionally posed faces stared back, revealing nothing.

It was frustrating. Maddening. Not to mention, as she often reminded herself, this was all just one theory stacked on another. It could teeter and crash if even one of her assumptions was wrong. God, what if Requiem wasn't even a musician? What if her own bias in that field had seeped out into her work? That disturbing thought gave her more than a few sleepless nights.

To take a break, she started poking into Zebra again, the story of an allegedly corrupt homicide detective assaulting the poor and powerless, and taking bribes. She'd looked into the case on and off over the past few years without success.

New rumours had surfaced. She'd heard there might be security footage kicking around of him stomping a homeless man to death. Possibly a pair of men.

Everyone she'd spoken to so far on the force dismissed it as some bullshit story designed to make an already unpopular department look worse.

That could be true. After all she knew every detective in Homicide, and while most were cocky, arrogant, sexist pigs, she still had a hard time putting any of them in the picture for murder. Stan Polaski, for instance, would find killing unconscionable because he'd have to get off his lazy ass to do it. Greg Keating, meanwhile, would disdain anything that messed up his fine Italian shoes.

Nonetheless she would have found it easier to dismiss entirely if she hadn't kept getting blocked every time she did a bit of digging.

She did, though, finally discover someone who knew someone who might have a copy of that mythical video. She made a few calls and one visit. Her informant told her she must have a death wish, but he didn't actually say no to getting it for her.

She grinned as she left his workplace. She'd try him again in a few days.

Moore was watching Alison through his glass-walled office when she returned to work. He pointed at her and jerked his thumb over his shoulder, a thunderous look on his face. She detoured towards him, wondering who'd died.

He slammed the door shut and pushed some paperwork over the desk.

"Do you know which state has the worst homicide rate in Australia?" he asked abruptly.

She looked at him in confusion and tried to peer at the papers in front of him. He shoved a beefy forearm over it. "Well?"

"Um, here? Gangland killing capital is Victoria."

His face twisted. "No, it's flaming well not us. The Northern Territory. Six times higher than the national average. They got problems with family violence you wouldn't believe. Two-thirds of all homicides up there are domestic related."

"Uh, okay." Alison stared at him.

"A mate of mine's up there now. He's been put in charge of getting those stats down. He sent me an email last month looking for recruits Australia-wide. He's desperate and the problem is that no one wants to go to the Top End, even with a bump in pay and bonuses. He wanted to know if I knew of any likely candidates."

Moore pushed the paperwork over. "Congratulations. You've requested a job at the Darwin Major Crime Squad," he said.

"I rang Doug half an hour ago and he was over the bloody moon to hear you love sticking your nose into gang crap. Says he has a Hells Angels organised crime problem giving him an ulcer, just for starters. I gave you a glowing reference. You're outta here in four weeks. Best of all you can take that bad-tempered bitch of a mother with you."

"You can't force me to move interstate," Alison protested. "What the hell is this, Barry? My record's impeccable. What's going on?"

"Your mutt I've been looking after all these years is, what, fifteen?" he said, squinting at her. He leaned back in his chair. "You know, no one would even blink if it ended up in doggy heaven before breakfast tomorrow."

"What?" Alison gasped.

"I know some people who'd make sure you had a permanent accident as well. And, I'm seriously thinking of withdrawing your visitor privileges, too, if you kick up about this. My wife and kid will be off limits to you at my home or on the phone for the rest of your damn life."

"You can't! Susan won't put up with that!"

He laughed. "We both know your sister has the backbone of a jellyfish. So, yes, I can and will. Don't think whining to her about any of this will achieve jack. She won't believe you. So bottom line is this: just keep your mouth shut, stop digging into things that don't concern you, and sign on the dotted line right here for a long and happy life. The deal is non-negotiable."

His tone was calm, his bloated face neutral, but his eyes were burning—furious and intense. She could practically feel the waves of hatred. There was something genuinely creepy, though, about the way he looked right through her. And that was the moment Alison realised two things:

Barry Moore was Zebra.

And her sister had married a sociopath.

With her jaw clenched, she reached for the page and signed.

Alison lay in bed that night sorting through a mess of emotions. She'd tried to call Susan, but her sister wasn't answering. Or she'd been told not to.

Her mind shifted to Charlotte. She loved her dog more than life itself. Alison had begged her mother to take allergy meds when she'd first returned to Melbourne with Charlotte so the red heeler could stay with them. Her mother had refused, saying it would conflict with her medicine.

Now she had this insane hostage situation.

She'd have to find an animal-boarding service or something while she worked out what to do next. Because, come hell or high water, she'd find a way to avoid that transfer.

She knew she'd hate living in Darwin almost as much as her mother would. It was hot, isolated, parodied by the rest of Australia as some bad Crocodile

Dundee throwback, and the nearby towns had reputations for terrible social problems.

She had no desire to *work* in the Top End, either. Where was the challenge in a place like that for a homicide detective? It sounded like most murders would be solved by asking the next of kin where they'd been on the night of the killing.

She'd left Traffic in the first place to stretch herself. The day she'd cracked one of Victoria's biggest chop-shop car rackets by simply following a bunch of hotted-up Holdens and Fords that seemed out of place in a poor suburb, she'd discovered the thrill of piecing together puzzles. It dawned on her for the first time that she was good at this. Really good. She knew right then that she wanted to get her teeth into serious crime-solving.

So she'd done the hard yards at the Field Investigation Course and the School of Investigation detective training module, studying her ass off to finish top in the class—only to discover upon starting at the Homicide Squad who its new boss was.

Moore had tossed her straight onto cold cases with a jubilant smirk, proving he'd never forgiven her for her teenage insults. Oh, how he'd loved slamming the door in her face when she'd immediately protested.

And now the bastard was screwing her over again.

Worse, he was doing it when she was so close to one of the biggest breakthroughs in Australian criminal history: She was nine names away from unmasking Australia's top assassin.

Just nine names.

And he wanted to send her to bloody Darwin.

She lay in bed that night examining the musicians' faces. Her eyes fell and lingered, as they often did, on the cellist. The one who oozed confidence. The one who'd given her a sneer just for being in the mix with Marks's adoring fans.

She had long, straight black hair that fell to halfway down her back. Deep, dark eyes that just seemed to stare *into* her.

How would *she* have handled her boss? Alison could easily imagine the cellist picking him up by the scruff of the neck and hurling him out a window. Not even saying a word.

She smiled and rolled over. She needed her rest, now more than ever. She technically only had four more weeks left on Homicide, so she had to get cracking on a way to save her career.

Her last thought before she went to sleep was to wonder exactly where the Bear and Clover Hotel was. And whether Viktor Raven still drank there.

"I'm curious," Alison asked Natalya, now she had the opportunity to find out, "if you had a boss who threatened to force you to transfer to Darwin, what would you do?"

Natalya's jaw tightened. "He wouldn't dare."

"What if he did dare though? What would you do?"

Natalya merely smiled, a glittery, cold smile that promised every imaginable form of pain. "Darwin is the sweaty armpit of Australia," she said, enunciating each word. "He would come to rapidly regret it."

"Right," Alison said. "Well, that's one plan. I went a different way."

"Oh?"

"In a minute. I'm getting off track," Alison said. "So I had nine VPO shortlisted suspects and I needed just one. The problem is that just over three weeks ago, after I investigated a curious warehouse fire, I wound up with two, and picked the wrong one."

"How curious," Natalya said, leaning forward. "So tell me: Who was she?"

Alison looked embarrassed. "I'm betting if I tell you that you'll wish you didn't know."

Natalya studied her intently. "That is a bet you'd certainly lose."

CHAPTER 22

Alison placed the article on the warehouse fire from the *Herald Sun* into her files. Wish lanterns? That was inventive even for her assassin. It seemed like Requiem was upping her game lately, putting even more thought into her killings as the months ticked over.

Her phone rang.

"Detective Ryan, Homicide."

"Oh good, it's you," dulcet tones purred down the phone. "We met at the VPO's launch. My name is Amanda Marks. I'm *quite* sure you know who I am. I was wondering, if it's not too forward of me, could you tell me some more about yourself? Inquiring minds really want to know."

"Um, what?" Alison asked in astonishment. "Whose inquiring minds?"

"Well, just little old me, really. You are, after all, quite fascinating."

Alison stared at the phone in disbelief. So fascinating she hadn't heard from Marks in three months since that season opener?

"I am?"

"Oh yes, dear, you definitely are. Here, let me give you my Facebook details. I really think we should chat more. AmandaMarksTheViolinist. Do you have that? All one word. And you are?"

"Not on Facebook."

"Any social media?"

"Sorry."

"Oh. How positively eighties. That's disappointing. Well then, sign up to Facebook and get back to me at once. All right? Good! Bye, dear."

The phone went dead.

Well. That wasn't weird in the slightest. She frowned. Had she been wrong in dismissing Marks as only a remote chance of being Requiem?

Alison's gaze returned to her desk and the newspaper article. Wish lanterns. The poetry in them was inherently beautiful. Amanda Marks thought herself to be beautiful, too. In fact she prized beauty. Was that really just a coincidence?

Her eye fell to the last part of the paper's story. The warehouse had a weird smell they couldn't place.

She phoned the Herb Circle. Her mother loved the vanilla candles they sold, so Alison was something of a regular. Its owner, Janine, might be a little loopy on crystals and mystical things to most people, but Alison thought she had the warmest personality of anyone she'd ever met. And if there was one thing Janine knew, it was aromas.

Janine agreed to come with her on her fact-finding mission, and she nervously chatted with Alison the entire ride over.

She understood. Crime scenes wigged out most people.

Alison parked at the abandoned industrial estate and pointed to the burnt-out shell of a building. They made their way carefully inside and Janine shivered.

"So much bad energy here," she told Alison. She swept her eyes around the area. "What happened?"

"A wish lantern was used." Alison glanced about, unsurprised but still disappointed not to see any police tape up. Another homicide crime scene abandoned as not relevant to the masses. Moore and his boys were really outdoing themselves this year with their indifference.

"But the smell is..." Janine faded out. "Petrol obviously—on the walls, I think, as well as the floor, yes, there and there—but also...benzoin resin. From incense sticks. And quite a number of them. Given the strength of the smell after all this time, perhaps half a dozen? Eight, tops?"

"Benzoin resin? What does it mean? Any significance?"

"A lot of my clientele like it for its purification properties," Janine said and shivered again. "I would say in the presence of such evil, it's quite fitting."

"Such evil? The killer?"

Janine stared at her. "The horrible man who died. Didn't you see the story in the paper? He kidnapped and hurt a little girl. I, for one, am glad he's off the streets. I'll be honest: I hope you don't try too hard to find his killer."

And there it was. Again. Alison sighed. What would it take for people to care?

"How easy is it to find benzoin incense sticks?" she asked.

"Pretty easy." Janine looked up suddenly. "A cleansing ritual."

"Huh?"

"If there was a wish lantern, the burning incense sticks would have showered down and lit the fire. It would be like falling stars. Like a cleansing. Hence the purification. It would have been quite beautiful except for...well, the rest."

"This killer is pretty poetic," Alison admitted. "Always has been." She looked sharply at Janine. "Please don't repeat that to anyone."

"I won't. On one condition?"

"What?"

"Get me out of here!"

Alison was about to get back in her car when she saw a hint of movement behind one of the industrial bins.

"Who's there?" she called.

Nothing.

"Please let's go," Janine said urgently, getting in the passenger seat. "I have two kids. Please."

"One sec."

She walked across to a nearby building and glanced through the vandalised windows. A young kid with a wild mop of dark, wiry hair looked up guiltily and hid something behind his back. Given the still-dripping paint from the tag on the wall beside him, it didn't take much effort to work out what he'd been up to. She'd seen this tag all over the place, including on the wall of the place that had gone up in smoke.

"Here kid," she said, and pulled $10 out of her pocket. "I just need some answers."

"Who are you?"

"The lady with ten bucks."

"Whaddya want to know?"

"About the night of the fire. See anything?"

"Maybe."

"Hear anything."

"A bit."

"Care to share." She waved the note. "No questions asked about how your tag is all over this place." She reached slowly into her wallet, his eyes following her movement suspiciously.

"I won't bite," she added, showing him her police badge. "But I can arrest you for graffiti. Carrot or the stick," she added waving the money. "You decide."

He studied her for a moment, then folded his arms defensively. "We was sniffing," he admitted. "Not many of us out here nowadays. All the fires gettin' lit. We wasn't gettin' left alone."

"How many of you were there the night of the fire?"

"Me an' two mates."

"So the three of you were sniffing petrol together; then what?"

"Saw a dark shadow go by. Wearing black. It stopped close to me, facing towards me, but he was all in shadow. Then I heard the music."

"Music?"

"Guy had a silver music player. Turned it on. I could see him adjustin' it, like he wanted the right volume or whatever before he put the thingies in his ears. And that's when I heard music. Then he put the ear bits in."

"Most people put earphones in and *then* adjust the volume," Alison said. "Are you sure?"

He shrugged. "Yeah. He seemed a bit, like, I dunno, that was just the way he does his thing."

"Right. How could you hear music so faint? Earpieces aren't loud."

"It was a *real* quiet night. No cars out here. Only sound for miles. Me mates were already down for the count so it was just me holdin' my breath, listenin', tryin' not to be seen in the shadows. I was behind that wall. Only, like, five feet away."

Alison looked at the low wall of crumbling bricks. At night, if there was no other light source, someone could easily hide in the corner, unnoticed, with a clear line of sight of the other building.

"Did you recognise the song?"

"Nah—it's some dead white guy stuff. Ya know, violins and shit."

"You mean classical?"

"Huh?"

Alison pulled out her MP3 player and found a classical piece. She hit play.

"Yeah," he said, eyes lighting with recognition. "Yeah. That kinda thing. And then he left."

"Just drove off?"

"Well wailed off."

Alison frowned. "Wailed?"

"On his bike."

"He had a motorbike," she repeated. "Did it sound powerful or..."

"Fuck yeah. Thing had *teeth*."

"How do you know it was a guy?"

He shrugged. "Ain't they all? He was in shadow though. And tall."

"How tall?"

He shook his head. "Do I look like I have a fuckin' ruler? Taller than you an' me, okay. We done?"

She nodded. He snatched the bill from her.

"Can I get a name?" Alison asked.

He nodded towards his tag.

She glanced at it and saw "Snake." When she turned back he was bolting for another building.

She headed back to the car, mind whirring. So Requiem liked classical music. She'd been right. *Holy hell, she'd been right!* All the pieces were starting to fit. And now she had the biggest clue of all.

As soon as she got back to work, Alison hit the database, cross-checking VPO members with owners of registered motorcycles. Her biggest surprise was just how many professional musicians had them. And how many women, too! Eighteen was a ridiculously high number.

She cross-matched them with her short list of suspects and put a line through all those without motorcycles.

Only four names were left. She had narrowed the killer of dozens of gangland assassinations across Melbourne to only four names.

Amanda Marks (Violin)

Bella Oakley (Clarinet)

Justine Chen (Viola)

Alex Tilsen (Percussion)

She immediately scratched out Chen. If the woman was over five-foot tall it'd be a miracle. Marks, Oakley and Tilsen she'd seen at various VPO events and all three were taller than Alison.

It was odd how surprised she was to find that the cellist wasn't on her list. Tsvetnenko's eyes, so dangerous and cool, had seemed capable of anything. And when it came to height—she definitely had it to spare. And then there was the power…

She changed directories and looked up whether Tsvetnenko held a motorcycle licence—now or ever. She stared at the results, almost disappointed. No. Just a car licence. Nothing else. She tapped a few more buttons.

Not so much a ticket for speeding.

Alison gave a disappointed scowl and scratched "Natalya Tsvetnenko" from her suspect list.

Her eyes returned to the final three. How interesting the timing that one of this trio had called her out of the blue when she had. Suspicious wasn't the half of it.

So now she had a top suspect. She grinned, logged onto the web, and threw herself into setting up her first Facebook page.

Amanda Marks was nothing if not persistent. Over the next two weeks since Alison had created her Facebook page, the violinist had begun to call and message her at random times, sometimes quite late at night. It was clear the woman was hellbent on learning about every facet of Alison's life. She grilled her relentlessly.

Each time Alison had messaged her back to ask why, Marks airily dismissed the question with, "Later."

Then one day she received the note: "Enough of the small talk, darling, come and have lunch with me and we'll talk properly."

Small talk? That's what she called it? Marks could show the Gestapo a thing or two about interrogations.

They'd met for lunch at some small French bistro, La Pierre, where Marks insisted on trying to order in French. She did it smoothly and confidently, her perfect, plump lips arching into a superior smile.

The pained wincing of the waiter told Alison how well she'd actually done at his language.

Alison had been using their chats so far to drill down through Marks's layers of vacuousness and frippery to try and find the real woman. She was curious as to Marks's worldviews on anything other than her own greatness.

How *does* an assassin think, anyway?

She'd been unsuccessful. If Alison thought her own mother was a narcissist, Marks was the gold medallist. Every single conversation, no matter the topic, she turned back to herself. Alison had tested this repeatedly. It had become almost a game.

By the time Marks had turned a grim news story about hostage-taking in South Africa into a discussion about a concert she'd performed in Johannesburg once, Alison was very sure that she was being toyed with by a master.

Did Marks do this for some sort of sick kicks? Alison felt like a small animal being batted around a few times by a predator before it bites its head off. She probably found Alison amusing in that sense.

Alison wished it was mutual.

Over their luncheon, during Marks's unpronounceable French salad dish and Alison's plain croissant, she learned more about the eccentric violinist than she'd actually wanted to know. A documentary on television had sparked the discussion.

"Bondage," Marks exclaimed, "should be more mainstream, not hidden away like a dirty little secret."

"Bondage," Alison repeated, mid-bite. "Um, why?"

"Pain is delicious when delivered well," Marks said and studied her in such a way that Alison shifted nervously in her chair. "It helps that I'm well versed in knots," she added. "I think I'd be good at it."

Alison had stared at her food for a good two minutes, trying to swallow. Either Marks was propositioning her for some kinky times, or she was letting her know who she really was. She had a good knowledge of knots? *Come on.* It was amazing how many times Requiem had expertly hogtied a person.

"I don't think I'd like pain," Alison said, finally forcing the pastry down her throat and reaching for her serviette.

Marks had smirked and patted her hand. "Well, of course you wouldn't," she said and laughed lightly. "Isn't that the point?"

"The point?"

"It's about flipping the experience. It's not *pain* if you're loving it. It becomes pleasure."

Alison looked at her sideways as she wiped her mouth. "I think the idea is that it's still a little painful. That's the *actual* point. Otherwise it's not bondage. Or so I hear."

Marks waved her hand airily. "Who knows? We're just talking. Since you seem so squirmy on the subject of pain, what would *you* like to talk about?"

"Motorcycles," Alison said immediately and returned her serviette to her plate in a scrunched ball. "I'd love to know: Do you own one? I heard a rumour that you do. Something with teeth."

Marks looked delighted. "Well, well, don't you do your research? I knew I was right about you."

CHAPTER 23

"Amanda Marks." Alison watched Natalya closely, and waited for her reaction to the naming of her once top suspect.

Natalya stared at her, disbelief and loathing in a vicious war across her face.

"You must be joking!" she said, outraged. "That woman makes sock fluff look sentient."

"Yeah," Alison agreed glumly. "She really does. Getting to know her doesn't change that impression by the way. The more you dig, the shallower she gets."

"You would put *that creature* in the same league as *Requiem*? The woman is too stupid to even stay *in time*, so how could you suspect her of implementing Victoria's gangland killings and staying under the radar for two and a half decades?"

Alison decided she didn't like the sneering tone and straightened.

"Okay, one, she, unlike you, is an out and proud motorbike owner and I know Requiem rides a motorcycle. You aren't a registered owner or licensed to ride one, but I'll bet if we look in your garage right now we'd find a hotted-up motorbike."

Natalya said nothing but looked a little disconcerted by Alison's level of information.

"Shall we check?" Alison asked softly, "Your garage? Right now?"

Natalya gave her a sour look and abruptly shook her head.

"*Wise.* Two, Marks also made contact with me out of the blue. The timing was really weird. She called me 'quite fascinating.' Fascinating? Me? All of it raised about a hundred red flags.

"Oh, and three, she's also a narcissist who lives in her own fantasy world about her legendary status. Anything's possible with that degree of self-delusion."

Natalya stared at her. "She has the mental capacity of a cockroach."

"Yeah, well, hindsight is 20-20 and all that. Look, she was all over me like a rash, pumping me on my life and my former career, like she was looking for dirt on me or my routines or something, and the timing was super whiffy. And then we had this one lunch that still makes me shudder."

Natalya looked appalled. "An entire meal spent with her? You must take your work very seriously indeed. So what did she want with you? Did she ever explain?"

Alison gave a rueful laugh. "Yeah, two days ago she finally coughed up her reasons. You should have seen the look on my face when I got to the truth."

Alison finished work and headed for the parking garage. As she came out of the elevator and turned towards the yellow section, she saw a familiar figure waiting near the lift doors.

Amanda Marks. Her step faltered. Alison had never told the woman where she parked for work. She certainly hadn't told her that she was driving in today, not catching the train. It was enough to set off every alarm bell in her head and Alison was on instant alert.

"Amanda," she said slowly and looked around. No witnesses. No cameras. Just cars and more cars. She wiped her sweaty hands down her pants, and gripped her keys tight.

"I was in the neighbourhood," Amanda said cheerfully, straightening, "and I realised time was galloping away and I hadn't gotten to the point."

"How did you find me?"

"I have been tracking you," Marks said with an unrepentant shrug. "I activated an app on your phone that you haven't been using." At Alison's confused look, she added, "When you went to the bathroom at La Pierre last week. It was just after you'd downloaded that mobile Facebook app I suggested, so you were all nicely logged in for me. You don't mind, do you, darling? It'll make it so much easier if we're working together."

"Track...wait, what? Working together?"

"Yes, you've been auditioning for a job, whether you know it or not. Well done—you're hired. Oh, don't worry—you can still play with your dead bodies all day, but when you're not doing that, I need someone well-informed to head up my official Facebook fan page. I have auditioned many of my other fans over the past six months but you are by far the most suitable.

"You see, the rest of my public isn't sufficiently musically informed to the standard that I require. That's important. My social media presence is a reflection of who I am. I need my image to be protected and enhanced, but only by someone who knows one end of a violin from another.

"So far you have passed every test—you spell well in your Facebook messages, you deal with awkward topics without temper, and project patience and decorum. You are not gifted in the art of fashion, I admit. This is unfortunate as you would, after all, be representing me, so I do need you to address that area promptly. I could help with a shopping expedition if you like. Say…Saturday morning?"

Alison blinked at her.

Marks looked at her in concern. "I know you're overcome by the wonderful opportunity, so I'll let it pass that you haven't said, 'Oh, thank you, Amanda' yet."

She gave Alison an amused smile but there was a coolness in her eyes at her lack of immediate, enthusiastic response.

"Do you accept?" Marks asked. "What am I saying? Of course you do! We violinists must stick together, right darling?"

Alison swallowed.

"*Did* you accept?" Natalya demanded.

"Well, it was tempting," Alison deadpanned.

Natalya's face froze in an appalled sneer. "You're not serious."

Alison suppressed a smile. Of course she hadn't accepted.

"I think I'm going to be sick," Natalya muttered.

"This is what makes a gangland murderer sick? *This?*"

Natalya gave her a sour look. "Don't call me that."

"You're *still* going to deny it?"

"Assassins are *professionals*. Murderers and serial killers are just amateurs with mummy issues or no self-control. Never confuse the two groups—the only thing they have in common is the bodies."

"So you prefer to be called an assassin?"

"I prefer to be called by my name." Natalya regarded her then tapped her fingers impatiently. "Now, enough games: Who put the hit on you? And how did you find out?"

Alison studied her for a few beats. "Okay," she said, and inhaled. She folded her hands in her lap and braced herself. "I've known from the first day. And I knew because I ordered the hit myself."

CHAPTER 24

Natalya's face became ashen. Her mouth opened and closed a few times before she finally spoke.

"You're insane," she ground out. "Tell me you didn't put a hit on yourself just to avoid a transfer to Darwin?"

"That was one factor that sped up my need to find Requiem quickly. Another is Moore threatened my life, Charlotte, and my access to my family. That was enraging. Then I realised he can't force me to go anywhere if I've just solved the biggest case in Victoria Police history. He would want me around for the glory, so he couldn't do anything to me if I was suddenly the toast of the hour—in fact it would look bad for him if he couldn't keep me on his team. So I decided to back myself," Alison explained.

Natalya was still staring at her.

"Look, it wasn't as nuts as it sounds. It wasn't even a rash decision. I'd been thinking about it for ages, how easy it would be to flush out my mystery assassin if I just had the courage. How simply it could be done. Who I could approach to get to Requiem.

"But I had no real reason to go ahead until Barry did what he did. And something inside just snapped. I thought about how everyone just pushes me around, and I keep taking it.

"So, I had a new look at my unorthodox idea. I broke it all down, what I had to do, like a plan of attack. I knew I had three weeks to flush out Requiem where I was safe from being killed before the deadline expired, and then a week to arrest her before I was forced to leave for Darwin. I had a nine-name list of suspects at that point, but no way of narrowing them down on my own in such a condensed time frame."

"That was an exceedingly stupid plan."

"Was it? Because I flushed Requiem out *and* I'm still alive aren't I?"

"Only by the grace of god. Even then, you're testing me sorely. This is beyond crazy."

"No, crazy is suddenly finding two members of the VPO who are on your initial suspect list appearing in your life within days of ordering a hit on yourself. *That's* weird."

"True," Natalya agreed grudgingly. "So how did you manage to book a hit if you didn't have a clue who Requiem was?"

"How does anyone else do it? Me, I tracked down Viktor Raven and, for a small fee, he agreed to be the middleman and use his contacts to order the hit. I wound up getting an encrypted email message from your associate. In it were a lot of questions about why I wanted it done and I didn't want to answer so I paid double the next day to make the questions go away. I was actually surprised they did."

"How on earth could someone like you afford a Requiem hit?"

"Ever heard of Bunny Leighton?"

"The socialite?" Natalya asked. "Died in a car crash?"

"Yeah. She wasn't just a socialite. She was the Face of Emirates in Australia. She married my dad and she was pretty nice, actually. Like, she always made sure Hailey got tickets to the Birdcage at the Cup each year because she knew how much my niece loved the horses. Bunny's friends at Emirates still send them to us every year."

"So that explains it: You two amidst the gliteratti set."

"I don't usually go—but how could I pass up the opportunity to see the VPO's string section doing a Russian program? Especially since I had a few questions to ask its cellist about why she was suddenly ignoring me." Alison folded her arms.

Natalya's eyebrow rose. "I'm sure you have a theory as to why, now."

Alison ignored that. "So Bunny, who was quite wealthy, died; then a few years later, Dad did, too. My sister and I both got sizeable inheritances from Dad's estate. Mum called it 'whore money' and made it clear that if either of us spent a cent of it in her presence she'd be most displeased.

"I was in a pretty bad place back then and couldn't care less about money. So I left it in the bank and didn't know what to do with it until this came up."

"You blew your inheritance on a hit on yourself?" Natalya asked, incredulously.

"No. I *invested* it. In my career. It would either pay off or not, but I was sick of having my dreams taken off me. I was determined to prove to all those assholes who'd dismissed me that I'm actually good at this. To hell I was going to lose everything I'd built for a second time."

"How is that not insane?"

"It was a gamble, sure. But you take risks all the time."

"This wasn't some sensible risk. You would have DIED, Alison. For what? A job!"

"So? I'd hardly have packed out the church," Alison said dryly. "I'll tell you a secret: it's easy for someone with nothing to lose to risk it all."

"I was wrong: You're not insane, you're suicidal."

"No! I truly believed I could find Requiem before the three weeks were up. All I needed was someone out of the ordinary appearing suddenly in my life, someone on my short list. High risk, high payoff. Of course I knew what would happen if it didn't work. But I saw it as a calculated roll of the dice."

"You're just..." Natalya threw her hands up. "Do you have any idea what Requiem's success rate is? One hundred percent! And your insane gamble didn't pay off, did it? You had Amanda Marks as your suspect! With that mistake you *should* be dead right now."

"Yes," Alison admitted, still annoyed she'd stuffed up so badly. "I should be. So about that—why aren't I?"

There was a long silence as Alison studied the emotions flitting across Natalya's face.

"I suppose you should ask Requiem that, not me."

Alison saw no deception in the use of the third person this time. Natalya actually seemed defeated by the question.

"You don't even know, do you?" Alison asked her quietly.

Natalya gave her an irritated look and then glanced away. "Did Lola know that you'd booked the hit on yourself?"

"Why would Lola know?" Alison asked, baffled. Her brain whirred, joining dots furiously. "Wait, *she* was who I contacted for this? She's your associate? Oh my God—that cruel witch works for you? Or is it vice versa?"

"It hardly matters any more. That relationship has now been severed."

The room temperature shifted, and Alison sensed so much pain in those few words. "I'm sorry," she said, wondering what had happened.

"Don't be. Some relationships go for too long. And some should end before they start because they're that toxic and lopsided."

Alison thought back to the woman she'd seen. Arranged like a goddess. Directing her thug. What was his name? Gunther. How did he even fit into anything?

"Why does Lola need her own bodyguard if she manages the mighty Requiem?"

Natalya gave a hollow laugh.

"Lola has far bigger concerns than just Requiem. Requiem was just a toy to amuse herself with. Her real enterprise was the empire she inherited from her husband when he died."

Alison stared at her, startled at how much Natalya had revealed.

"Empire?" she asked, her heart suddenly thudding. "Um, what's Lola's surname?" she asked, trying not to sound too keen.

"Why?"

"You know why," Alison said. "I have a professional interest in understanding Melbourne's underworld."

"And you also want to know how deep the wounds go? Whether I'd sell her out?"

Natalya looked as though she was contemplating exactly how many wolves she should toss Lola to.

"Lola goes by the surname Kozlovsky when it suits her," Natalya finally said. "Sweetman, as well. But she was Tsvetnenko for a little while, too. Only two years. But they were an educational two years for an impressionable teenage girl in her formative years."

Alison's mouth dropped open at such nuggets of information. Natalya was throwing Lola to *all* the wolves. Then the name recognition hit her.

"Oh! Kozlovsky? As in *Dimitri*?" she said. "Are you shitting me? She inherited his...wait...*Lola* is now the boss of Fleet Crew? Your, what, ex-stepmother?"

"I do not *shit* anyone," Natalya said, turning the word over distastefully. "But essentially, yes."

Alison considered how to word her next question tactfully.

"You two've obviously had a falling out. And now you've shared some information that isn't commonly known. Does this mean you're getting out of this business? Retiring maybe?" She didn't bother to disguise the hopefulness.

"No," Natalya said. "I love being a cellist."

Alison rolled her eyes. "From your *other* job."

"You can't unlearn what you know or unsee what is seen. How could I retire?"

"Just stop," Alison said. "Go cold turkey. Walk away."

"I had thought of a holiday," Natalya said, examining her nails as though the idea had just struck her. "Reassessing certain things, such as priorities and choices made.

"It's funny how I find myself wondering at my motivations of late, for a lot of things. How much of it was Lola pulling strings, and how much of it was my own decisions?"

She dragged her gaze over Alison. "Everything used to be so cut and dried. And now I find my life more in a state of flux."

"Is that why I'm still alive?"

Natalya didn't answer.

"Will you help me then?" Alison asked suddenly. "To bring down Lola? An assassin is small beer compared to a crime family boss. Look, we have a witness protection scheme..."

"No," Natalya said. "Never. I'll not be caged. And assassins are never 'small beer.' Even the dial-a-thug, cut-price ones are still dangerous. Listen to me on that. Never ever dismiss one."

"I didn't mean it like that. I meant I could shift focus if I had a different target. You wouldn't be hunted. She would—as the bigger target."

"No," Natalya said again.

"What about informally? No one would ever know if little hints and tips just happened to come my way," she suggested hopefully.

"So busy with thoughts on my career," Natalya noted. "Let me offer *you* some free advice on yours. It would be wise not to mention putting hits on yourself to your superiors. Your psychiatric assessment would be ordered within the hour, your dismissal on unfit medical grounds within the day. No one in the police force would see the creative side to your insanity. I'm not entirely sure I do, either, and I have a very flexible view on what counts as creative."

Alison stopped cold. She hadn't thought about it like that. Okay, it did sound a *little* nuts. Even if she wasn't. She absolutely wasn't. Yes, she'd gambled big. So what? Go hard, or go home, isn't that what they said?

Natalya shook her head. "Sometimes I wonder where you sprang from, if that was actually news to you. As for my plans, it's no lie to say they are to focus on music for the foreseeable future. I need distance. What you do or don't do regarding Lola or Requiem or anyone else you scrape up from Victoria's underbelly is your concern, not mine."

Alison studied her, seeing only sincerity. Was Requiem announcing her retirement plans? She was about to ask when Natalya spoke first.

"I do need one favour," she said. "In the spirit of our little frank and honest truce." Natalya's eyes were half-lidded.

"What?"

Natalya rose and left the room, returning a few moments later. She held an exotic plant which she placed gently in front of Alison.

"My pride and joy," she said touching one leaf tenderly. "An African violet. I need it looked after while I'm away. I'd collect it later."

"You want me to plant-sit for you, *while* I'm also pursuing you?"

Natalya's lips twitched. "It doesn't like water on the leaves, just water here," she said, pointing to the soil. "Keep it dust-free, too. That's important."

Alison stared at her, mystified by this turn of conversation. "This is kind of nuts."

"So is putting a hit on yourself. I must be in good company. Well?" She indicated the plant and waited.

"God. Okay, okay. Shit, I'll mind your plant while I hunt you down," Alison muttered.

"Good," Natalya said, sounding pleased. "Normally Lola would do this, but I suspect she's going to have her hands full soon." She offered a wicked smile.

Alison turned the plant slowly around, admiring how immaculate it was, then suddenly grinned as a ridiculous thought came to mind.

"What?" Natalya asked suspiciously.

"I just think it's funny: Friends plant-sit. So your request makes us friends, in spite of everything, and as unlikely as that sounds."

Natalya scowled. "It does no such thing."

"And you like me," Alison added, just for the fireworks. She was starting to notice how much Natalya squirmed at the mere mention of emotions. It was curious.

"No." Natalya pointed to her sternly. "And stop that." She twirled her finger at Alison.

"You like me or you would have killed me," Alison suggested with an innocent air.

Natalya looked faintly pained. "Don't make me regret that choice."

Alison tried not to react to the first actual, undiluted admission of who Natalya really was. They'd been dancing artfully around it all morning, but with enough vagaries to drive a bus through it.

She realised Natalya was looking irritated at herself for the lapse.

"I already knew," Alison said quietly. "Of course I did. But I meant it when I said I'm not really here. I never was going to do anything with what we discussed today regarding Requiem. But since we're officially naming the elephant in the room, could you just tell me one thing?"

"Wha-T?" Natalya said, hammering the T like a nail gun.

"Why do you do it?" Alison asked. "Is it for justice? I don't believe it's for the money."

"The high fee is just to keep the riff-raff at bay. The scum who want their wives dead and so on."

"Then why?"

"It's about a power so immense it fills your entire soul," Natalya said. "There's something to be said for the satisfaction in holding up a mirror to these bottom feeders and seeing it in their eyes, the recognition of a life lived badly. As you said earlier, Requiem has her own sense of justice. She kills because it's right. Because she excels at it. And, most importantly, because Lola wishes it."

Alison inhaled. "Have you ever killed an innocent?"

"There have been other no-questions-asked jobs in the early days, before we realised the danger of them. Who can say whether those targets were innocents or not? Requiem prefers to think they were all guilty."

"But now? Only the worst of the worst die, right?" Alison pressed. "That's why you send a message? It's not just for the gang bosses, is it? You do it so they feel afraid and ashamed for what they've done?"

Natalya studied her for a moment. "I wouldn't deify Requiem as some righteous vigilante," she warned. "She's not worthy of the elevation. She's her own creature, black of heart. Yes, she is magnificent, unfettered and free, and that can be intoxicating. But get close to her core and she is cold. She feels nothing. Not love. Not friendship. Not anything at all. Remember that."

"I have an alternative theory," Alison said. "I think Requiem feels so much that she blocks it all out by putting on a mask and becoming this assassin who makes the pain of feeling all that go away."

Natalya gave a short laugh. "I wouldn't try to psychoanalyse her motives. Understand this: She's a lethal, wild beast, straining at the leash. Let her loose, and I promise she will take your jugular and feel *nothing*. Nothing but disdain."

"I don't believe you," Alison said. "You don't feel *nothing*; you can't! You saved Hailey when you didn't have to. You stopped me from putting my hand in the cone snail tank just now. And you didn't kill me the day you were supposed to. I think Requiem feels more than she lets on. She feels *something*."

"You're very wrong. She's a conduit, little more. As I told you earlier, sometimes Requiem lets the fleas go. And speaking of going, I think, now, it's time you left. I have things to do."

It was like the shutters had gone down and the air changed to ice.

"Sure," Alison muttered. "But you're right, I have a manhunt to organise so, yeah, I should go. I'm assuming you didn't poison Charlotte with that steak?"

Natalya gave her head a minute shake.

Alison whistled, and the red heeler came bounding up.

"My furry traitor. You're anyone's for a nice steak, aren't you girl," she told her dog, but her voice was light. Alison glanced back at Natalya and remembered something. "Can you tell me one thing before I go?"

She reached into her back pocket and pulled out a photo. She'd found it when she'd first sneaked into Natalya's home. She'd poked her head inside a few doors to get the lay of the land and found this stuck to a corkboard in Natalya's anal-retentively neat home-office.

It was part of an entire series of surveillance photos, timestamped and ordered, showing Alison going about her day. Photos of her getting the newspaper, arriving at work, leaving work, hanging up the washing, taking the groceries from her car.

Underneath it had been a similar series of photos, these showing Viktor Raven at various destinations, too. His name had been crossed out in a red slash.

Natalya shot her an indignant glare.

"It's the only thing I took," Ryan said hastily. "And the only room I looked in," she lied. "Just tell me: How often?" she asked, holding it up.

Natalya studied it. "Every second day. Sometimes daily."

"I see." Alison rammed the picture back in her pocket. She stared sourly at her. "Jesus. All these damn years! I've wasted my whole life. Even more than I thought."

She wiped her eyes angrily. "Fuck."

"Yes, you have wasted your life," Natalya agreed, not unkindly. "So do something with that photo. Go, eat life, and be the woman you can be."

Natalya paused. "Do you know how rare it is to surprise me? Yet you did. Completely," she said, as though she still couldn't quite believe it. "You are nothing like the woman I thought you were the first day I saw you."

"You're everything that I hoped you weren't," Alison said. "And a few things I hoped you were." She considered her for a moment. "Can you remember something while you're off dodging the police and finding yourself? Everyone in this world is capable of loving and being loved. Including you."

"If you think that, then you don't know me at all. And you never did."

Alison sought the truth in her steady gaze.

"No," Natalya said. "Stop that. Stop trying to filter me through your mainstream prism of empathy and emotions. There's a reason I'm not like anyone you've ever met. It's because I'm not. All I ever desire and feel is *power*—that's it. When I play, when I hunt, when I fuck. There is nothing else inside me. For the last time, I don't do love."

"Sure," Alison said and picked up the African violet. "Whatever."

"Thanks for that." Natalya nodded at the plant.

Alison firmed her shoulders. "You're welcome. Oh, and you get an hour's head start. Next time we meet I *will* arrest you. I expect I'll see you very soon."

"I like a woman who dreams big," Natalya retorted.

"It's not a dream," Alison warned. "Don't underestimate me. I promise you, that's a dangerous mistake."

"Good."

"What?"

"That confidence in yourself. You always needed it. Now, can *you* remember something when you're famous as the detective who couldn't catch Requiem? Find some time for your real passion. You're too good to throw away your music."

She said it in an offhand tone but Alison was overwhelmed. Natalya thought she had talent.

She studied the beautiful, maddening, aloof woman in front of her. A bloodless killer capable of producing profound, exquisite, passionate music. The same woman who said she only felt emotion when her fingers were on a cello.

"I'll miss you, Natalya," Alison said, before she could stop herself. She looked away in embarrassment. Well, that sure as hell cut her "I'm dangerous" speech to shreds.

She abruptly turned, unwilling to see any mockery on the face of a woman she'd come to care about in spite of herself.

Alison called Charlotte to heel and, as she strode across those perfectly manicured lawns to the security gate, head held high, she felt Natalya's intense gaze tracking her.

She wondered, as she tapped in the gate code and heard the heavy metallic click, whether she was a fool to let the assassin slip through her fingers. Would this be her only chance to get her?

She glanced down at the precious bounty she held. No. This wouldn't be the end. The African violet was a promise there would be more.

Alison smiled.

Until later.

Chapter 25

When Alison got home, she headed straight to her mother's bedroom. She stood at the doorway and studied Elsie for a few moments. She looked older than her years, and the grey streaks in her hair were more pronounced than she remembered. Her mother noticed her and glared at the scrutiny. Her ample chest rose and fell in indignation. "What?" Elsie barked.

"We need to talk," Alison said quietly but firmly. She walked to the worn chair beside her mother's bed and sat. The green chair was decades old, wearing badly along the seams, but her mother had refused to have it reupholstered. If it was sent for repair it might come back in worse condition, she would argue.

Because change was like that—an opportunity for life to ruin things. Apparently.

It's why the lounge room wall was still adorned with ugly, faded, striped, 1950s green and silver wallpaper that sorely needed replacing. On one wall were three painted plaster ducks. Alison had spent the better part of thirty-four years eyeing those loathed, chipped monuments to intransigence.

Her mother wasn't big on change, be it plaster ducks, wallpaper, or attitudes.

"Talk? What about? Emily Ryan, you barge in here, it's not even seven. No tea. No meds. No invitation."

"Mother." It was all Alison said but her tone brooked no debate. It was a tone she'd never dared use before. She clasped her hands in her lap as she considered her words. "I know you miss Dad. But it's time we stopped the charade."

"What charade?" Alison could see suspicion in her mother's grey eyes.

"The pretence that you aren't just keeping me around to punish me. That denying me a real life is just about hurting me because you're unable to hurt him. I'm his proxy."

"What nonsense! I'm *sick*! You're here because you're the only one who can look after me."

"That's not true," Alison said calmly. "We could have used nurses. We had the money. Susan and I wanted to use our inheritance on making life comfortable for you with home help, and moving you somewhere nicer. But you refused to even discuss it."

"Making *you* more comfortable, you mean. And you wanted some stranger in here, all day, doing god know's what, while you just ran off and left me? You just want to abandon your responsibilities—you're just like *him*. You are a wicked child. You always were."

Alison let the insult hang between them for a few moments before replying.

"We both know that's not true. Here's the bottom line: I'm moving out. I need my space. I need Charlotte. And I've decided to stop being afraid.

"It's also long past the time you stopped using me as a personal punching bag. I'm not Dad. He's gone and he's never coming back. You need to stop being so angry about life and so hateful to me. All I ever did was try to help."

"If you had my life, you'd understand how hard it is just existing," Elsie shot back. "And now you're abandoning me? How dare you!"

"How dare *I*?" Alison looked at her in disbelief. She rose and carefully laid the photo she'd taken from Natalya's noticeboard onto her mother's bed. It showed her mother walking and laughing as she headed down the street with her 65-year-old neighbour, Norm Strickland. Elsie didn't even have her walking frame.

"Every other day you go out with him, unassisted, and enjoy your day," Alison said in a low, even tone. "Sometimes daily. And you made me believe you couldn't exist without me. That you were helpless to do anything beyond the bathroom and shower basics. You've been lying to me for years."

There was a stunned silence.

"Spying on me now?" Elsie hissed.

"No, not me. And stop dodging the subject. You pretended to be virtually immobile for years just so you could use me as some dog to kick around." Her fingers curled tightly around the chair's armrests.

Elsie's expression shifted from outraged to defensive.

"You don't understand. You've never known what it's like losing someone you thought your future was with and it all got ripped away."

"I *do* know what it's like. Melissa was…" Alison stopped, feeling her heart about to beat out of her chest. She swallowed. "…was more than just my roommate. I left my life with her, and my music, for you."

Her mother gave her a sour look.

"No," Alison said, before she objected, "I know you needed me then and I don't resent that."

Elsie snorted derisively.

"Yes, I was devastated but I knew that you needed me," Alison said. "But what I do resent with a fury that you will never understand was that I wasted fourteen years of my life after that. For what? To be a whipping boy."

"You engaged in illicit relations with that Sydney woman?" Elsie asked, a sneer plastered on her features. "That's disgusting."

Alison closed her eyes briefly. When she reopened them, she allowed some of her fury to show.

"You don't get to play the high moral ground with me, Mum. You just don't. You can drop the act. I'm leaving now. I've wasted too much time on someone who couldn't care less about my happiness. It's time to have something more than this mockery of life."

She stood.

"You'll fail." Her mother said it flatly. Cold and mean, and her tone hardened to bite deep as it always did. "You need me. I'm your security blanket. You're nothing without me. People will see that about you. You won't make friends because you find new people hard to talk to. I know this about you.

"So you'll end up alone and wishing you hadn't abandoned me. Oh, I know exactly where this is going, because I'm your mother, Emily. I know you well. I know you better than you know yourself."

Alison had heard these words before. Just before she'd left for Sydney, in fact. She hadn't failed then, no matter what her mother said. She'd had her opportunity taken from her and that was a big difference.

She straightened.

"I won't fail," she replied with certainty. "And even if I do have some bad days, I'll pick myself up, dust myself off and move on. You, however, will have the reminder of what you did to me for the rest of your life. You will always know you failed as a mother and as a human being."

"How dare you!" Elsie spat at her. She gave her a sideways look, wreathed with disgust. "Running off to be with some *woman*, I suppose?"

"If that's where life takes me," Alison said with a calmness she had not expected to feel. "But there's nothing disgusting about love. People who *deliberately* ruin lives? That's truly disgusting."

She gave her mother a pitying look. "Have a good life. If you want me in it, you can apologise and I'll consider it. If not, I'm more than okay with that. I need to be around people who aren't angry, bitter, and afraid." She smiled. "People like me."

Alison suddenly realised it was true. As she turned to leave, her mother's face betrayed her internal panic.

"What's gotten into you?" she asked sitting up straighter. "You can't leave. I raised you better than to be disloyal. And come back here when I'm talking to you."

"You've got two good legs, apparently," Alison threw over her shoulder as she left. "Why don't you come and talk to *me*?"

Alison tuned out the indignant bellows still emanating from her mother's room as she made her way past the lounge and headed for her bedroom. She paused, taking a long, dispassionate look at her surroundings.

The smell of medication merged with the decay of ageing and the antiseptic bite of cleaning products. There was more to it, though. The lounge was a monument to bitterness and rigidity in every frayed, worn surface her mother refused to change.

Alison knew in her heart she no longer belonged in this room, this home, this life.

Her eye fell on those awful plaster ducks she was sure even her mother didn't like. They were like a permanent mockery of everything she'd endured in this house.

Carefully, she unlatched them from the wall, leaving behind duck-shaped dust silhouettes on the old wallpaper. She contemplated them for a moment, then hurled them to the floor.

The violent noise of the shattering crash filled the house. She ignored the predictable, furious eruption from down the hall and smiled.

"What have you destroyed now, clumsy child!"

Just my stasis, Alison thought.

Because life was finally getting interesting.

Alison began to pack. It was kind of sad how few things she owned. It was as though some part of her brain always knew this life was not for her—temporary and not worth her time or effort.

She sat on her bed, noting its ever-present sag. She'd never liked her bed or this room. She studied it, with its old-lady roses wallpaper and regal trinkets, like a shrine to 1950s England where her mother had grown up. Alison had been denied a right to even her own identity in this room.

She reached under her bed and pulled out her dusty violin case. Her fingers tingled in anticipation and she paused in surprise. Well. That was unexpected.

When she was done packing, she glanced at her phone. It had been over an hour. She had promised Natalya at least that much of a head start. She opened an email. It would take very little to get a warrant underway for Natalya's arrest, now Alison had absolute proof.

When the police had surged into the motorhome on Melbourne Cup day, at one point they'd taken Natalya aside to interview her. Alison had used the opportunity to ask one of the officers to take a photo with his phone of the knots on the hogtied Gunther and email it to her.

He had.

The knots were identical to the seven Requiem hogtied victim cases. Of course they matched—she'd not had a minute's doubt from the second Natalya had burst in and thrown Gunther across the room, her face cold, eyes dead. But this was actual proof.

Not that she'd shared it with anyone.

She could now, though, and she knew Barry, despite being a bullying bastard, would not deny it. He might skate lines if there was doubt, but with actual evidence, he always did the safest, smartest thing to protect his own hide.

She composed an email to him, attaching Natalya's headshot and a short summary of her crimes, and wrote an outline of the proof she had. She stopped, went back up to the name field, and added the Chief Commissioner's name.

Even if Barry slept through the email, she knew the head of Victoria Police would be all over it. Not every day one gets the chance to collar a renowned gangland assassin. Bottom line was that someone very soon would be ordered to get moving on paperwork for warrants and police alerts to airlines.

Alison could even narrow it down for them. Her phone also contained a snap of Natalya's airline e-ticket print-out that she'd seen on her desk when she'd snooped around her home-office earlier in the morning.

QF 438, leaving Melbourne at noon today. It was flying to Paris via Sydney and Dubai. So they had two chances to stop her in Australia alone.

Her thumb wavered above the send button. She wouldn't be doing her job if she didn't do this. Natalya, well, Requiem, had killed thirty-four people—and those were just the ones she knew about.

All scum, her brain whispered. Like Ken Lee. The world was a far better place for women and children without that flesh peddler selling them like dogs. Not to mention Busch. Collins. Beattie. All criminals who put countless innocent lives at risk.

Not the point, Alison reminded herself. Requiem was a *killer*.

It was the right thing to do.

Although, her brain whispered, *she's not going to hurt anyone now.*

Requiem had sworn off killing for the immediate future, so arresting her wouldn't prevent any crimes. All Natalya wanted to do was play cello, make music and rethink her life. Alison had seen the truth of it in her eyes.

If Natalya returned to Melbourne, well, that would be different. But right now, what was the point? Where was the harm in letting her go—for now? Alison could catch her when she returned for her damned plant.

She glanced at it, now sitting on her bedside table.

Besides, hadn't she told Natalya she wasn't going to use anything from her visit? She was never there? The plane ticket photo was a breach of that.

Her thumb trembled.

CHAPTER 26

Alison had known Barry Moore almost her entire life. He'd gone to her high school where he'd excelled at rugby league, disrupting class, dating her sister, and little else.

She couldn't remember a visit to Susan's place that didn't involve his puffer-fish face somewhere in the background, offering a running commentary on society's failings.

In the three years she'd spent butting heads with him at work, he'd tried to make her feel grateful to even be allowed to do cold cases. He'd now threatened her with actively destroying everything she loved. Barry Moore made her stomach drop every time she saw him. He always had.

And in the blink of an eye he was gone.

A few days after Natalya's A380-800 had jetted off for Paris—with its full complement of passengers due to a certain email not being sent—Alison was driving across town, radio blaring. She thrummed her fingers impatiently on the steering wheel as her thoughts went where they always did.

She hadn't yet figured out how to escape that Darwin move, but she had thought of little else. The problem was she'd never had a Plan B. She'd just assumed when she'd started out that she'd either have claimed the scalp of an infamous assassin, or died trying. The idea that Alison would flush her out and then just let her go obviously hadn't been on her list of hypothetical outcomes.

In recent days she'd been toying with the idea of calling Barry's bluff and telling Darwin she wasn't interested. But what if he wasn't bluffing about hurting her? God knows he had the connections.

She'd already tried and failed to tank the Skype job interview with the Darwin chief earlier in the week and the man had just grunted something about "the more bodies on deck the better" and "Barry's reference is good enough for me."

Some high standards then.

Meanwhile Alison had found a temporary boarding kennel for Charlotte out of the bastard's reach.

Susan hadn't even asked why. Her sister had minded Alison's dog for a decade and a half and didn't want to know why Alison had urgently rushed over one morning to rehome the pet in a kennel. Susan wasn't stupid but denial ran deep. It was telling.

She was just pulling up at a traffic light, when the radio news came on.

"Victoria Police is investigating a video that was posted on several news sites today allegedly showing a senior homicide detective involved in the death of two elderly homeless brothers, and the abuse of their dog. A police media spokesman said they were looking into the authenticity of the footage which was sent to several media outlets and IBAC, the independent anti-corruption commission in Victoria. It was marked 'Zebra.' Sources say it appears to have been shot from the loading dock of an inner-city hotel, which has not been named."

Alison almost drove into the truck in front of her.

She pulled over, turned off the engine and grabbed her phone, looking up the video. It wasn't a long search. It was all over YouTube and had been picked up by news services worldwide. It contained grainy security footage vision of Moore stomping in the head of a homeless man, smashing his dog in the ribs with his boots and then turning on a second man. One website didn't mince words, splashing Moore's name and job title all over the video, with the words: "Is this Victoria Police's finest? ARREST THIS ANIMAL!"

She phoned the office immediately.

"He's not in," Lisa, Barry's secretary, reported. "Haven't seen him since the video aired. I tried calling him at home but his wife says he's disappeared. Gone when she came back from picking up their kid from some soccer thing yesterday afternoon. Bags gone, too. Not looking good that we'll see him anytime soon."

So Moore had slunk away, disgraced.

Alison called Susan, who answered with a suspicious "Hello?"

"It's me."

"Thank God. I thought you were more media. They've been camped out for ages already, and ringing all hours."

"Christ! Why didn't you call?"

She didn't answer.

"Susan?"

"I thought you'd say 'I told you so.' I just…I didn't want to hear it. I know Barry's a creep, okay? I've known it since a week after we married, but it's humiliating seeing this everywhere. And everyone's acting like I should have known what he did. How could I? And the last thing I needed was you giving me crap, too."

"I never would have rubbed it in, come on!"

"Even so, I'd know you were thinking it. I've had Mum on the phone all morning, raging about what the neighbours will think. She *does* remember she doesn't actually like her neighbours, right?"

Alison laughed. "Well, I don't know about that," she said, thinking about her mother's outings with Mr Strickland. "I don't suppose you know where your husband ran off to?"

"Like I told those investigators, hell if I know," Susan sniffed. "Does that make me a terrible wife?"

"A normal one, probably," Alison said with a small snort. She paused. "Is Hailey okay?"

"She will be. I know it sounds weird but I get the impression that she's glad he's gone. She was always like that whenever he went off fishing with his mates, like she was hoping he wouldn't hurry home. Oh hell—that's probably where he is right now. At the old fishing shack! Want the address?"

So much for solidarity with her husband.

"Sure," Alison said. "I'll pass it along to whoever our new boss is, because I'm sure Barry's about half a second away from being fired and having everything in the book thrown at him. They'll want to screw over the asshole who makes every cop look bad. Because, Jesus, who the hell kicks old homeless people to death? And that poor dog!"

There was a hiss of breath and Alison reviewed what she'd just said. Her sister had *married* that man.

"Oh," she muttered. "Sorry, Susie."

"Me, too. Shit, Emily. That *total bastard*."

As it turned out, Barry Moore wasn't quickly caught, but a warrant was issued for his arrest, which quieted the worst of the fury from politicians and social media desk jockeys.

A new broom was lined up to sweep through the Homicide Squad. Alison had seen more men in suits in the past week than she had at a politician's funeral. They swept in and out, talking an impressive array of buzzwords, mouthing slogans about stopping the rot, cleaning up embedded corruption, and getting the department back on track.

The Premier suddenly discovered he wanted something done about entrenched organised crime and the "disturbing gangland situation" which had been "left to fester on Moore's watch."

Well, that was a new one. *Now* the people cared about gangs?

Alison's department had been summoned to a meeting—a so-called "frank exchange of ideas" with the Premier's minders and the Victoria Police Chief Commissioner. It was also a chance to meet the new head of Homicide.

Alison sat at the back of the room, not hugely interested, knowing that when this topic and Moore's public disgrace had faded off the front page, so, too, would any appetite to fix the underworld problem.

Besides, as the lecturing and hectoring droned on, she found she was more interested in Facebook. Or to be specific, a curious new post.

She'd received an email alert on her way into the meeting. A Facebook user calling themselves "Harry Partch," from Paris, had tagged her in a link. The picture next to the name showed female hands holding a bow against a cello.

She could virtually picture Natalya's mocking voice, saying, "Who else would get your attention?"

She'd clicked the user's photo which brought up a Facebook page that was now deleted.

What the hell?

"You investigate these homicides—only barely—but don't even ask the right questions. Are the killers affiliated with a gang? Which crime family? Why were the victims killed—was it gang related or otherwise?" The Chief Commissioner was thundering across the room.

"These are the questions we should be asking. Where do these people live? Who do they associate with? Do any of you people even know? Do you get how this looks for us? Do any of you care? Do you have the first clue?"

Alison went back to the original Facebook email alert and clicked on the hyperlink she'd been sent. It brought up a Google+ page which, again, had the user name "Harry Partch." The link led to a photo post. Chocolate. She peered closer at her phone. With fudge centres? They looked like Whitestars brand, her favourites. How the hell did Natalya know about that?

There were no captions, nothing else on the photo at all. Just gooey, gorgeous choc fudge.

"I'm sorry, Detective, are we keeping you from something?"

Alison almost dropped her phone. The police chief's voice was suddenly no longer thundering and the room was eerily quiet. All eyes were on her. She flushed and looked around. "Sorry," she said. "I was pursuing a lead. What did you want to know?"

A tall man with greying hair and sharp eyes leaned forward. The new Homicide Squad boss. Burns. He'd been flown in from Sydney and had a formidable reputation. Oh, and scuttlebutt had it that if you mocked his name, you would be flayed alive.

His first name was Frank. So, not a *M*A*S*H* fan, then.

He leaned forward and with deceptive softness said: "The Commissioner wants to know what, if anything, Homicide knows about the crime families, because it seems to him that you're all incompetent. I would appreciate it if someone could answer his request and prove him incorrect."

His tone dared her to say just one wrong thing.

Alison licked her lips anxiously as she considered her answers. "Which crime family? I have a complete timeline on all of them, dating back to 1998 when the wars started. Chronologies and family trees on each prominent member and basics on the rest. Do you want names of spouses and mistresses as well? Only the enforcers and standover men whose crimes relate to Homicide? Or all of the members, whose crimes cover all departments?"

Burns blinked once in surprise. And then a small, intrigued glint entered his eyes.

"I've been looking into this for the past two years," Alison added by way of explanation when no one spoke. "Um, i-in my own time."

The rest of the Homicide Squad stared at her and their eyes widened with disbelief as she then launched into detailed answers on every question for the next hour. She knew these people inside and out and didn't need any notes, which was good, because she hadn't brought any. With every answer, she could see the shadowy faces of the men and women who had become her life for two years.

At the end of the session, when the rest of her squad packed up and left the meeting room, Detective Senior Sergeant Burns came over.

"Where *have* you been hiding?" he asked. "Especially given that your detailed knowledge of the families runs rings around the rest of those clowns propping up your department. And it's better intel than anything in the official files I've read."

"I've been doing cold cases."

"Why?" he asked suspiciously. "What did you do to get sidelined?"

Alison folded her arms. "You're asking me why a disgraced and corrupt Homicide Squad Chief would sideline the only member of his team who knows all about the gangland families? Seriously?"

Burns gave a sharp bark of laughter. "Good answer. Right, come with me. What's your name again?"

"Ryan."

"Right, Ryan. The Premier and Police Chief Commissioner want to talk to you about a special little project they have in mind."

A month later Alison found herself sitting at a new desk which had a gleaming sign on it. *(Det) Alison Ryan, Head of Gangland Operations Unit.*

She even had her own team of three. Okay, one was an office assistant. But still.

Yeah, it was funny how life worked out sometimes.

CHAPTER 27

"Harry Partch" was not one for chatting. Or posting often. Or saying much of anything.

All Partch had done so far was post that one fudgey photo on Google+.

She wondered why Natalya had not put it up on Facebook since she'd clearly, briefly, had an account.

She downloaded the photo, saved it and zoomed in, wondering if there was some sort of code hidden in the pixels.

Nope. Nothing.

She went back to the Google account only to find the fudge photo had now been deleted. What on earth? Was this some sort of weird "thinking of you" from Natalya?

Pfft. As if that would happen.

She did an internet search and, for want of a better idea, looked up "hidden things in photos" and discovered that pictures could contain something called metadata. This could store information about the photo, such as who took it, where, when, and the camera used. It was used for copyright, apparently.

She also discovered that this metadata detail was stripped out of any photos loaded on Facebook. But, crucially, it was retained on Google+. So— that had to mean something, right? Was the Facebook post just a way to anonymously get her attention in the first place since she knew Alison had a Facebook page? Like a wave?

Heart racing, Alison followed the instructions to open the fudge photo's properties and find the metadata.

She saw a list appear:

```
Source: Simon Monaghan
Location: 190 Sunshine Rd, Footscray, Victoria
Date taken: November 25.
```

The date was set in the future. Two days' time. And the named person was no photographer; she recognised him as a brutal thug who worked for the gaming criminal Carlo Trioli.

She tapped the address into her mapping screen which brought up a dubious-looking warehouse.

So Natalya had just given her a place and time to find a man who was one of Melbourne's most lethal, wanted enforcers. How useful.

And given Natalya had since deleted the source photo from Google+, she'd removed the paper trail back to her. In fact, had Alison shown the downloaded copy of it to anyone, she couldn't even prove she hadn't changed the metadata herself.

It was so clever. A little, isolated clue bomb made for one.

Two days later, on page twenty-nine of the *Herald Sun*, the paper announced the arrest of gangland killer, Simon Monaghan, on seven charges. It was a small story, with only a few lines about some of his victims—all criminals— and a court date. But it was the first win for the GOU.

Four days later Alison discovered Harry Partch had posted a photo of a scenic bistro in Paris. The metadata in this one contained enough details to arrest Santos's most prolific enforcer, as well as two of High Street's top drug makers.

The men couldn't have looked more stunned as they were led away.

That arrest was reported on page seventeen and included a photo of the killer. She heard through the grapevine that his capture had caused unease among all four crime families, who wondered how he'd been found.

After three months had passed, over a dozen leading criminal identities from the underworld had been arrested. Half had come thanks to Natalya. The rest were due to Alison's own efforts and research.

At month six, she snagged the first big shark, Santos—thanks to Natalya. Then almost immediately, Alison accidentally found Trioli by being in the right place at the right time and recognising, then following, his mistress.

Those arrests were reported on pages six and seven. The story included a quote from Detective Burns praising the hard work of the GOU. A newspaper editorial echoed his praise, speculating on what Santos's arrest would do to the crystal meth trade in the state and the profound impact it might have on all parts of society.

Kinda cool, Alison grinned.

She looked up from the paper to see Detective Stan Polaski studying her, his eyes flicking to the headlines. "Nice," he grunted, waving at the paper. "Tired of everyone thinking we're bent or stupid."

He returned to his sports results.

Her eyebrow lifted. It was the first non-sarcastic thing he'd ever said to her.

She went back to work. She couldn't help but notice Fleet Crew members were never targeted in Natalya's tip-offs. Her loyalty for Lola clearly ran deeper than Natalya believed.

At least, that's what Alison thought until she saw the next post.

A photo of sweets from a store in London. Natalya was in England now?

And sweets? Sweetman? Lola!

This one came with a future date and an address. For the first time in months, it even included a time. 5am.

Alison knew this arrest would be the one that made all the difference. A woman with movie goddess looks, charged with running the most prolific, illegal gun-manufacturing operation in Australia? The salivating media would be all over it. The public would finally take notice. It would be national news. Possibly international.

She jotted down the date in her diary and sent Burns a warning of what was about to transpire in their backyard.

He shot her back an email. "I'll let D know what we're in for. If this is as big as it sounds, we'll call in everyone. Good work. Again. Your informant network is certainly amazing."

Network. Riiight.

She smiled. D was the Premier. And Burns, she'd decided, was officially an okay boss. He'd snapped the other detectives into line more than once when they'd muttered jealous crap about her under their breath.

In the old days, her former boss would have been leading the insults.

Operation Frontline took place just before dawn in West Melbourne. Alison had picked her spot carefully, asking to set up position away from Burns and the other team members. She was in an unmarked police car half a block away, remaining out of the fray but with an excellent view of members of the elite Special Operations Group as they swirled around the targeted warehouse complex Lola was supposed to be in, taking up position.

Alison explained to her boss why she'd chosen to hang back. "I want to see it go down widescreen. Forest perspective," she added. "Not the trees."

"Your choice," Burns had replied. "Media's due in at six, so be expected to front a press conference a little after that. Stay by the radio."

The men and women took position. Almost all areas of Victoria Police had been called in. Members of the dog squad headed to the rear with a SWAT team.

The flash grenades smashed through the windows exactly at five and the splintering sound of doors being pushed off their hinges by handheld ramming tools shattered the silence.

Special Operations Group members, dressed all in black, with helmets and goggles, ran in, armed with M4 Carbines, shouting "POLICE."

It should be all done in under ten minutes. She listened to the action crackling across her police radio. At the three-minute mark, Fleet Crew members started to emerge, hauled out with little struggle, straight into reinforced police vans.

At five minutes, a small female figure was docilely led away by one towering SWAT team officer. Alison frowned. The woman wasn't even cuffed yet. She picked up binoculars to check her suspicions and reached for her car radio when she spotted one of her colleagues loitering nearby.

"Polaski. The Asian woman who just came from the west door, get extra bodies on her."

"Pull the other one, Ryan—she's a midget. Looks barely old enough to vote."

"Listen, that's Sonja Kim, Ken Lee's former enforcer. She's deadly and she WILL try to escape. She's playing you right now with that weak act."

"POLASKI," Burns broke into the feed. "Put more men on her. And get that suspect cuffed ASAP. What the hell's going on over there?"

"Yes, boss."

She wanted to roll her eyes as Polaski's bulky form ran forward. His detective ID badge, worn around the neck on a lanyard, slapped him in the face when he stopped too quickly in front of the suspect. A flash out of the corner of her eye made her turn.

The metal door to a small, run-down building on an adjacent block they'd dismissed as empty opened. A figure stepped out and walked quickly in Alison's direction, turning to look over his or her shoulder every ten paces.

Alison watched closely and had to admire the elegance in the stride. Elegance? Around here?

The shape passed under a street light before turning into a small alley. Crap. She grabbed her radio handset. "Sweetman's loose, heading north into the alley, uh…" She tapped a map on her phone. "Taylors Lane. I'm closest. In pursuit. Send backup."

Her car's radio came alive with squawks from multiple team leaders. She bolted after Lola.

Alison lengthened her stride and turned into the alley. The figure wasn't far, and wasn't walking fast. Which made sense—the quickest way to attract attention with half of Victoria Police swarming your neighbourhood is to run.

Lola glanced over her shoulder, spotted Alison, and then suddenly sprinted, zig-zagging away down another street. Alison turned, too, and saw Lola was halfway up a fence. Shit. Alison took an almighty leap, relieved when she made contact with flesh not air, and brought the mob boss to the ground.

She wriggled until she was sitting on Lola's waist, pinning her down. It was only then she realised she had no weapon; no cuffs. She never arrested people in the raids. Why would she, when the state's best of the best were brought in to do the job? Her status was that of observer only.

She could hold her off until her backup arrived. It probably wouldn't be too hard. She had an expert knowledge of chokeholds and Lola had to be especially weak now, after her pale, thin arms had spent so long in double casts.

Blue, accusing eyes stared up at Alison.

"YOU! What the hell are you doing here?"

"I thought I'd subdue a suspect wanted for running an underworld gang family and ordering multiple crimes committed in its name. You have the right to remain silent," Alison said. "I must inform you that you do not have to say or do anything but anything you say or do may be given in evidence. Do you understand that?"

"You're a cop?" Lola spat, her sheen of confidence dissolving into shock. "You? You are kidding me."

Alison stared evenly at her. "You may communicate with or attempt to communicate with a friend or a relative to inform that person of your whereabouts. You may communicate with or attempt to communicate with a legal practitioner."

"Does Requiem know?" she asked. "Her trembling leaf? All this time? Oh my God. She loves a dirty little cop!"

Alison faltered. "Loves?"

Lola laughed gaily. "Oh, you didn't know? Well, doesn't that make it more delicious?"

"Requiem doesn't do love."

"I've no doubt she said that. But the sure sign she likes you is in the fact that she hasn't tossed you down on the nearest surface and shown you all your failings in vivid, naked detail. She thinks I don't know what she gets up to but I hear things. She lives for power plays in all their forms."

Alison blushed, remembering how Requiem had once tried to do exactly that.

"Oh," Lola smirked. "She *did* do that? Well, well. Maybe I was wrong after all. So tell me: Did you like it? Did you want more?" Her voice was so mocking. Alison was taken aback at how much she sounded like Requiem.

She shot Lola a furious glare. "She did no such thing. Now do you understand your rights as I have explained them to you?"

Alison was suddenly flipped over with a strength she'd never have thought Lola possessed. She wound up on her stomach, her face being pressed into the dirt. She struggled but Lola's entire length pinned her down and the angular woman had a good six inches on Alison.

"I understand perfectly," Lola purred, wrenching Alison's arm behind her back in a vicious hold. She leaned forward and whispered into her ear: "In fact I believe I understand everything now. For instance I understand that you most likely love my Requiem or you would have arrested her long ago. And I understand that she didn't give you what you wanted. Maybe just gave you a taste, hmm? And then she left you for her one true love. Her music."

Lola's hand stroked against her cheek as she jerked Alison's arm higher up her back with her other hand. Alison cried out.

"I understand you would love to be with her and she won't give you that," Lola said seductively. "Oh, she is charismatic, isn't she, my Req? She's delicious to watch when she kills, too. She's like a raw, vicious, predatory panther, all power and sinew. A dark angel, come to steal your soul. And she is ruthless. She's my greatest creation. She told you she doesn't do love? She believes it. I taught her to believe it."

Alison flinched.

"But I wonder if that's true?" Lola asked conversationally. "I normally don't dirty my hands but it might be worth it to snap your neck and send her a photo to see what she says. A little payback for daring to lay her hands on me."

Alison couldn't see her face but her voice left her in no doubt she meant it. The pain shooting up her arm was unbearable and she couldn't believe the mistake she'd made in underestimating Lola.

She should have realised a mob boss would have been trained to kill at some point. Alison looked around for her backup. Where the hell was it? Did Polaski hate her this much to risk her life? The whole point of the raid had been to get Sweetman. Where was everyone?

She heard a series of gunshots, and they both paused.

"My, my," Lola muttered. "It seems not all of Fleet is going quietly. Perhaps there could be some unfortunate loss of life on the constabulary side?"

Alison's arm was suddenly released, but the bliss was momentary, then both Lola's hands wrapped themselves around her head, preparing to snap her neck. Alison jerked her hips, kicked and wriggled wildly.

"Don't bother," Lola said. "My dear, late husband trained me too well. Time for night-night."

The hands tightened and tears slipped out of the corner of Alison's eyes from the exertion of trying to throw her off her.

Suddenly Lola's entire weight was gone, as if wrenched off her by some giant, unseen force.

Alison gasped and lifted her face out of the dirt, turning in time to see Requiem slapping Lola so viciously her nose broke and her body was slammed to the ground. Blood gushed down Lola's astonished face.

Requiem turned to look at Alison, her face thunderous. "Are you alive at least?" she asked.

Alison coughed and nodded.

"Well, that makes one of you," Requiem said and turned back to Lola. "I appear to have gotten over my reluctance to hurt you." She flexed her fist. "Which is convenient."

She pulled a small wire from her pocket and uncoiled it.

Lola's eyebrow arched in surprise, as she wiped blood away in irritation. "You wouldn't."

Requiem ignored her. She straightened it.

"No!" Alison pleaded. "The police are on their way. She'll be arrested."

"She will escape. Or talk herself out of a prison sentence. Everyone loves Lola," Requiem sneered. "This is a permanent solution."

Alison, now kneeling, reached up to grab her arm. "Don't. She's not worth it. You haven't killed in months. Don't start that again. Not because of me."

"Ohhh, isn't this lovely?" Lola laughed, getting up gingerly. "A lovers' tiff?"

Requiem turned, took one menacing step towards her, and punched her again. The crunch of fist on jaw was sickening. Lola grunted in pain, falling back to her knees.

"Give me the cable," Alison demanded.

"What? Why?"

"I'll do it. If she's going to die because you've made up your mind, I'll do it. The net result will be the same but you won't slip backwards."

"That's absurd."

"Is it? No more absurd than you falling off the wagon over someone like her. She doesn't deserve it."

Lola laughed again. "Can you two hear yourselves?"

Alison ignored her. "Don't you see, it's the same principle? If she ends up dead either way then why do you care? It's the same!"

"It's not the same at all. You kill once, it stains. You don't go back from that. You're an innocent."

"I'm a cop—hardly an innocent. I look at dead bodies all day long."

"But you've never caused a death. Trust me, the first time will haunt you forever."

"Like it did you?"

There was a silence.

"I got over it," Natalya finally said.

"And so will I." She reached for the cable, and Natalya slapped her hand away, hard.

"No. I won't let you."

"And I won't let you," Alison said.

"I know—don't kill me at all!" Lola piped up cheerfully. "Everyone wins."

"Shut up," Natalya hissed. "You don't get a vote."

"A vote?" Lola mocked. "Since when is assassination a democracy? It's a dictatorship. Or are you so cunt struck you can't even see what she's doing to you? She's trying to rip the teeth out of a tiger. She is making you weak."

"I made you strong. Don't listen to her. Get far away from this sly little thing. Look at her, playing you. She has no intention of hurting me—I can see it in her eyes. She'd crack if she even tried to kill a beetle. She wants to *control* you, Requiem. She has you so messed up you can't even see straight."

Natalya studied her former stepmother, then leaned over her. "I see perfectly straight. I know a manipulator when I see one. I know what ugly is, too. You are both."

She leapt astride Lola's waist and her hands shot forward, wrapping the cable twice around Lola's neck. She snapped the ends out straight and hard. Lola's eyes bulged and a choked cry died in her throat.

"NO!" Alison shouted and bounded forward, pushing Requiem off the prostate woman. With Requiem's hands at Lola's neck, she had nothing to stop herself from sliding to one side.

Alison immediately took her place astride Lola to prevent Requiem returning to the position. Her hands trembled for a moment before coming to rest on the cable. She neither removed it nor tightened it. She just stared, biting her lip.

"Kill her, don't kill her? Make up your fucking minds," came a mocking voice from behind them. "Because this shit's getting boring."

All eyes swung to see Sonja Kim sauntering towards them. The bruising on her face and arms looked like she'd put up a fight with someone. Or several someones. Her hand was spinning a kunai throwing knife with such skill that Alison knew none of them would have any chance if she decided to use it. The question was: Who she would kill?

"Finally!" Lola said with glee. "My lovely new lapdog proves her worth at last. Take them out," she ordered. "And start with her." She pointed at Alison. "I want Requiem to see what happens when she allows emotion to get in the way of duty."

Sonja studied the blade of her knife, running a thumb along its flat surface and then turned to eye the three women.

"No," she said casually.

"What? I said KILL THEM!"

"No. I'm no one's little lapdog. You should treat me with respect."

Lola slumped. "Disloyalty is apparently catching."

Requiem laughed. "Just not your day, is it?"

"You have no cause to laugh, dear. Love has made you weak," Lola taunted. "Look at the three of you. Sickest love triangle in history."

Alison and Natalya's eyes met at the words and Lola used the moment to reach into her pocket.

She was not fast enough.

A knife flashed past them and embedded itself with a sickening thud into Lola's neck pinning her to the ground. Blood gushed from her throat. A startled look was fixed on Lola's face. The woman gave a gasp, before her eyes glazed over and her hand limply dropped. A gun slid out of her pocket.

Alison leapt off Lola and turned to Sonja, who had dropped to the ground.

"Thank you," Alison said sincerely.

"I didn't do it for you." Sonja scowled.

Natalya lowered herself to her haunches, the act of making herself smaller before Sonja an unexpected show of gratitude. She did not offer words.

"She treated me like crap," Sonja told her. "Not like Mr Lee at all."

"But you had to know she was a scorpion," Natalya said. "Why would you join her, knowing her nature?"

"I thought I'd get to understand."

"Understand what?"

"It doesn't matter now."

"Perhaps it does."

Sonja looked down. "I wanted to know how you turned out the way you did. I wanted to be you for a little while. Wear your skin. See for myself."

"Ah. What did you learn?"

"Nothing. All it did was make me hate everything. Hate myself. Hate feeling things. Hate everything that she told me to hate."

"So you learned after all."

Sonja nodded slowly, then winced and her hand went to her waist.

Natalya frowned and wrenched up the other woman's black jacket and shirt. Blood covered her stomach.

"A farewell gift I got," Sonja explained. "They're down a few cops now."

Alison paled. "You killed cops?"

"Maybe." Sonja shot her a glare and then looked at Natalya. "Why is *she* here? Again? With you?"

"This is my raid," Alison said. "I'm a detective."

Sonja's laugh was brittle. "Fuck." She winced again. "Did you know that?" She looked at Natalya.

"Yes."

Sonja gave her a mutinous look. "Then you're a fucking traitor."

"Lola doesn't deserve my loyalty. Or yours."

Sonja stared at her in confusion then winced again, clutching her stomach. Instantly her fingers were coated in blood.

"Hey," Alison said, "you're a mess. We need to get you to a hospital."

"Fuck off," Sonja said. "Your cop mates will kill me on sight. They're just mad I showed up how bad they are at catching one little girl. I led them on crazy chase. Bled all over half the alleys on the far side. They're chasing their own tails now."

"They'll get here soon enough," Alison said. "Come on, let me help. I can make sure they don't hurt you."

Sonja ignored her and her eyes flicked to Natalya.

"Do you love her? That's it? That's why you sell us all out? For some pussy cop? Or cop pussy?"

"I don't love," Natalya said quietly. "You know that. I've told you that. And anyone who has any sense at all knows to stay the hell away from me." Her gaze drifted to Alison's. Message clear.

"So I have no sense," Sonja laughed bitterly. She groaned again.

"We have to call an ambulance," Alison said, rising. "If it gets here in time…"

"It won't," Natalya said softly. She pointed to the amount of blood pooling on the ground under Sonja.

Alison started. *Oh hell.*

"So this it?" Sonja asked, eyes begging for the truth.

"Yes. This time it's over, Sonja."

Sonja exhaled and nodded. She flicked her eyes to Alison. "You're one lucky bitch."

"This isn't anything to do with her," Natalya said firmly. "It never was."

"No lies," Sonja protested.

"I have never lied to you. I don't love. It's a wasted emotion on me."

"Fuck," Sonja whispered. "Fuck me, this hurts so bad."

Alison wasn't entirely sure whether she was talking about her heart or her bloodied side.

"I know," Natalya said. She reached up to the other assassin's face and stroked it with two gloved fingers. "You've been strong; I'm proud of you. It'll be over soon."

"Make sure you tell them I almost killed you," Sonja said weakly. "You tell them that. I went down protecting that Lola bitch and I almost took you with me."

"I will."

"You're still a liar, Natalya Tsvetnenko. A big liar. I can see your soul from here."

"Hmm." Natalya gave a half-hearted disagreeing grumble.

"Natalya?" Sonja whispered, her face rapidly losing colour.

"Yes?"

"Call me Nabi now?"

"Close your eyes, little Nabi."

The distinct whumping of a helicopter sounded somewhere overhead, and a police siren began to get closer. Natalya didn't so much as flinch, her entire being focused on Sonja.

Sonja kept her eyes open, locking them on the brown ones hovering above her. "You're beautiful and you walk around like the whole world owes you a living. You look at the rest of us like we're nothing. You looked at me like that, that night. I hated you. From my whole heart. I hate that you can make me feel this way. I *hate* you. So, so much."

"I know," Natalya said gently, watching her with hooded eyes.

"And I love you." Sonja's eyes bored into her. "Always."

"I know," Natalya repeated and stroked the sweat-matted hair out of her eyes, watching her intently. She slid her other arm around her shoulders, holding her up. "Rest now, Nabi."

Sonja's breathing slowed, and finally stopped, her empty, brown eyes staring up into Natalya's. It was the moment the second-most lethal assassin in Australia died, cradled in the arms of the nation's deadliest.

Tear tracks were streaked down Sonja's dusty cheeks.

Natalya eased Sonja's body to the ground and sat back on her haunches and then stood.

"I have to go."

Alison observed the switch in personality. Like a light going off. "Just like that?" She squatted and checked Kim's pulse, just to be sure. She shifted and did the same to Lola, before rising.

"I don't think it would be believable for me to be accidentally found twice in the company of a crime family boss. One of your colleagues might get certain ideas and arrest me. Unless…" she slid her eyes over Alison and arched an eyebrow, "you plan to?"

"That depends. Why are you in Melbourne and not on tour?"

"And miss the downfall of the great Lola Sweetman? Why do you think I picked the date I did? I'm between engagements. I've just finished depping for the London Philharmonic for the past two months and I'm booked to fly to Prague this afternoon. Moscow's Symphony Orchestra wants me to start there tomorrow."

"So you're not resuming old habits?"

"I have no inclinations to do so. It's like no longer drinking coffee. Truthfully, I'm not entirely sure it agrees with me anymore."

Alison studied the sincerity on her face and exhaled. "Then no, I don't plan to arrest you. This time." Her eyes came to rest on Lola and she shook her head. "I'm sorry, by the way," she said and nodded at her.

"You live in her world…this happens."

"Even so. She was someone you cared about."

"It's complicated," Natalya said. "She betrayed me. She tried to take away my talent to punish me. She wanted to shoot me…" She lifted her hands then shook her head. "To destroy my music."

"Oh my god!" Alison looked at her in horror. "How could she? Your hands are who you are!"

Natalya didn't respond, her eyes closing for a few beats, but Alison could see the agreement there.

"That's not love," Alison added softly.

"No." Natalya looked disturbed. "Lola doesn't do love, either—unless it's love for herself." She shifted uncomfortably.

"About what she said," Natalya muttered, "Lola was trying to get under your skin. It's a skill. She tests you like a predator seeking weaknesses in a fence. She batters away until she hits her mark. But she was wrong. I wasn't lying to Sonja."

"Yeah." Alison's heart died a little. Of course she knew. Intellectually. Besides, it was madness to harbour any other thoughts: a killer and her target? It was a bad punchline. And given what she had planned in under an hour's time at the press conference, Natalya was right. It was for the best.

"You're different," Natalya suddenly said. "More confidence. It suits you. You needed it."

"And you needed compassion. You showed that to Sonja today."

"Not that it mattered."

"It did."

"Don't do that."

"What?"

"Layer my actions with extra meaning. Don't be like Sonja. You know who I really am. See how it ends, caring for me?" She gestured at Sonja.

Their gazes locked.

"And now you have to go," Alison said.

Natalya didn't say anything, but her eyes tracked their surroundings, as though mapping possible escape options. She picked up the wire she'd used on Lola and wiped it clean, dropping it next to her body. She looked pointedly at Alison. The message was clear: if anyone asked about the marks at Lola's neck, blame Sonja.

Alison nodded. She studied the assassin. About to run. Alison wondered if she'd ever see her again.

"Please, for the love of God, Natalya, no more bodies. Can you do that?"

Natalya didn't answer, because clearly it would be too easy to put Alison's mind at rest. Her gaze returned to Alison's and she smiled, the slow-curling genuine one the public never got to see.

Alison was taken aback. How could she be this beautiful and yet so damned dangerous? Her stomach did a pleasant flop and she wanted to bang her head against a wall. It was painful how much she felt for a woman like this. She'd thought their time apart would have deadened any residue of emotion, especially now she had all the facts.

It hadn't.

She tried to look away but instead she was pulled into brown eyes that studied her far too intently. Alison desperately tried to pull on her professional mask.

She must have failed.

"Oh," was all Natalya said at what Alison was trying so hard to hide.

Alison's cheeks flamed. She stepped back and growled. "Get out of here before I arrest your ass," she grumbled, folding her arms.

Natalya gave an amused snort and then pivoted away, the dirt crunching beneath her feet.

Footsteps could be heard at the other end of the twisting alley and Alison waited for Natalya to make her escape before turning towards the sounds.

"Over here!" she called out. "Two suspects. Both deceased."

Detective Polaski rounded a bend and puffed into view. "Finally," he grunted. He leaned over, hands on his knees, and panted to catch his breath.

"Where the hell have you been?" she demanded. "I called for backup fifteen minutes ago!"

"We, ah, thought you said Bailey's Lane—that's six blocks over on the other side." He pointed in the opposite direction and reached for his radio and called in their location. Then he stared at the scene before him.

"Holy fuck. Is that Sweetman and her bitch enforcer? That wiry little shit shot up two of the elite SOG."

"That's them," Alison agreed.

"What happened here?" he asked.

"No idea. This is what I found. They obviously had some sort of disagreement. So...will the cops live?"

"They're fine. Their egos are a bit battered. Like mine."

"Huh?"

He shifted from foot to foot then checked behind him. Satisfied he was alone, he said: "Ah, shit, look, we're not like him. Moore. I know what you must think of us and, hell, yeah, okay, fair call. I swear we didn't know what he was like. We all had you pinned as some crappy, wannabe detective who only got the job because you were Moore's sister-in-law. He told us that's what the score was and we believed him."

"Right," Alison said. "Well, he's gone now. Does that mean your asshole attitudes have too?"

Polaski tried to look indignant but then gave her a snort. "Yeah, okay, I deserve that. Turns out we were fed wrong intel by someone we trusted, so we may have fucked up a bit concerning you. Not gonna happen again."

A bit? He thought he and his colleagues sneering at and excluding her for three straight years was just a "bit" of a fuck-up? And he thought it was fine for the whole team to act that way as long as his boss said it was okay? Her shock was then completely overshadowed by his next comment.

"So, anyway, wanna beer later, when this is all wrapped up?"

Alison shoved her hands in her pocket as she considered the unexpected request. He seemed genuine and his ears were red with embarrassment over even asking.

"Me and the boys," he added hastily. "I gotta wife ya know. And Moore said you didn't ah...you know...swing that way anyway. Shit, this is coming out bad. Anyway, want a drink with the boys tonight? To celebrate? Because we arrested a dozen or so Fleet assholes today. And hell if Homicide doesn't look kick-ass for the first time in years. The boys and I aren't stupid: we know we have you to thank."

Alison debated her options. She'd seen what bearing a grudge had done to her mother. Frankly, the high road wasn't all it was cracked up to be.

"Okay. Yeah. But not beer. That stuff tastes like koala piss."

Polaski grinned. "Sure, whatever you want." He tilted his head and smirked. "You drink a lot of koala piss then?"

She laughed in spite of herself. The sound of thundering boots caught up with them and a number of elite squad officers fanned out around the area.

The commander of the unit stood to attention in front of Ryan and Polaski. "Were there any others?" he barked. "Or just these deceased persons?"

Alison shook her head. "Just these two."

"I see an extra set of footprints," he said, pointing to Natalya's prints in the dirt. He eyed her questioningly.

"Yeah," she said. "They were there before we got here. Old prints."

"Okay," he nodded and tapped his ear piece. "Area secure. We need two body bags."

"Who are you, anyway?" he asked turning back to her.

"I'm Ryan, the head of GOU."

"*You're* the GOU boss?" the man asked, eyes widening in disbelief. He looked her up and down dismissively.

"Well deserved, too," Polaski interjected. He gave the man a warning glare. "Your team brought down that crime family today thanks to Ryan's work."

"That so?" he asked, and his expression shifted a little. "Well done then, ma'am."

"Thanks," Alison said, then injected a sharpness into her voice. "And it's *Detective.*"

The next day the Melbourne Herald Sun ran its first front page story on the gangland crime families in almost a year.

CRIME CLAN QUEEN, LETHAL LOLA, KILLED

By Police Reporter Martin Saxon

The best-kept secret in Victoria's underworld gangs has been uncovered at last. The leader for the past twenty-four years of gun-running gang, Fleet Crew, has finally been revealed to be founder Dimitri Kozlowsky's widow, Lola Gloria Sweetman.

The charismatic slain crime family matriarch, 59, has been dubbed Lethal Lola.

Sweetman was killed, possibly by her own associate, during a pre-dawn warehouse police raid yesterday, which netted thirteen Fleet Crew members. Sweetman's bodyguard, Sonja Kim, also died, succumbing to gunshot wounds at the scene after attempting to escape police.

Sweetman was believed responsible for the hour-long kidnapping on Melbourne Cup day of Detective Alison Ryan, 34, and her 13-year-old niece, Hailey Moore.

As we reported last November, the renowned Victorian Philharmonic Orchestra cellist, Natalya Tsvetnenko, was hailed a hero for freeing them after stumbling across the crime scene and using what Hailey described as "epic martial arts moves".

Tsvetnenko, 41, who is touring Europe with the London Philharmonic Orchestra, was unavailable for comment on the arrest.

Gunther Emil Muller, 39, co-accused in the kidnapping, was arrested at Flemington Racecourse on

Melbourne Cup Day but died while in custody, stabbed by a fellow inmate.

Fleet Crew's other members arrested during yesterday's raid face various charges, mainly involving illegal weapons.

Victorian Premier Douglas Warren held a press conference yesterday announcing the raid a success and calling the arrests the biggest breakthrough of the Gangland Operations Unit (GOU) since it was set up. The unit is headed by Detective Ryan, the Homicide Squad's most experienced Melbourne underworld expert.

"Detective Ryan has been building a case against these criminals for two-and-a-half years," Premier Warren said. "Her work has been remarkable and we look forward to more arrests from her team in the efforts to eradicate this blight on our state's reputation."

Detective Ryan spoke at a press conference yesterday following the raid, revealing the GOU is also tracking an underworld female assassin known as Requiem.

Requiem has been dubbed across social media as the "karmic killer" due to the method of the victims' deaths. Detective Ryan said the assassin would usually match her punishment to the victim's crimes.

"Moonlight Society boss Ken Lee, who trafficked under-aged girls from South-East Asia to brothels around Australia, was electrocuted via his genitals," she said as an example.

"Jason Collins, a meth lab cook linked to the High Street gang, died from fumes after his protective coveralls were perforated a thousand times.

"Uli Busch, the reclusive billionaire German pesticide manufacturer, died of suspected cone snail poisoning. His lungs were paralysed in a similar way to that experienced by farming victims of his now-banned fertiliser, StartGrow.

"Requiem is a killer who made sure her criminal victims got the message. This has made it easier to work out which crimes had her fingerprints over them. We are still seeking her, but our information suggests she has most likely fled the country.

"But while Requiem constantly remains on our radar, the more immediate issue is the four crime families taking the lives of our fellow Victorians unchecked," Detective Ryan added. "Premier Warren said earlier this will no longer be tolerated. The Gangland Operations Unit stands ready and will hunt these lawless clans wherever they're hiding and shut them down—permanently."

Ryan told the media she had no comment to make on the globally trending hashtags #saverequiem and #karmickillerforthewin.

A Victims of Crime's spokeswoman, Miranda Oakley, said she understood why members of the public sympathised with Requiem getting rid of the "dregs of society" especially when "we feel the police have done little to stop these gang warlords in the past three decades."

"She's a hero to many of us," Mrs Oakley said. "I cheered so hard when I heard how Ken Lee died. My kids and all their friends have been retweeting #saverequiem all day. I hope Requiem's exile is somewhere nice."

In other news, former Homicide Squad Chief Barry Moore is still missing, believed to be in hiding. He was stood down on November 6 last year and a warrant issued for his arrest after a video labelled "Zebra" was made public. It allegedly shows Moore caught on a camera committing brutal acts of violence and murder on two homeless brothers and their dog. IBAC investigations are continuing.

Detective Senior Sergeant Frank Burns, 55, now heads up the Homicide Squad. Recruited from the New South Wales Police Force, he says no stone will be left unturned in tracking down his predecessor.

CHAPTER 28

Alison returned home to her one-bedroom apartment and kicked off her shoes. It had been five months since the day Lola died and the world had erupted over news of Requiem. She was exhausted. Ever since the last spate of arrests, things had been busier than usual. And now the media had noticed her and had some weird fascination with writing profiles on her.

Oh, how her mother was loving that. Mrs Elsie Ryan, proud mother of Victoria's much-feted GOU chief, apparently "always knew" that her daughter was destined for greatness someday.

If only they knew. Alison and her mother did not speak at all now, despite her lies to the media. Alison had no interest in a relationship with a woman who wasn't even sorry for treating her like dirt. The fabrications and crap Elsie told her friends about the reason for their rift beggared belief.

Alison opened the fridge and pulled out a bottle of water. When she closed the door, she glanced at her lounge only to bite back a yelp.

Natalya was arranged in a chair, regarding her, fingers templed.

"You could just knock, you know," Alison complained, trying to calm her thundering heart. "Like an ordinary person."

"But I'm not an ordinary person. And you didn't knock at my home, either."

Alison had to give her that. "True. Want a drink?"

"Do you have vodka?"

Alison shook her head.

"Infidel," Natalya said. She folded her hands in her lap. "Never mind then."

Alison sank into the armchair opposite, and twisted the cap off her water bottle. "How'd your tour of Europe go?"

"Better than expected, as I received no visits from local constabulary waving Interpol documents under my nose. Also, no unexpected stops at

Melbourne International Airport on either of my departures. Now why was that I wonder?"

"It's a mystery," Alison said evenly.

"I did enjoy the online coverage of your career exploits while I was away. Congratulations are in order. It's about time more women got ahead in bastard-dominated industries. Speaking of which, where, oh where, has your noxious brother-in-law hidden himself?"

"That's another mystery. But I imagine he has you to thank for sending the disc to IBAC? And leaking it to the media?"

Natalya studied her nails. "It was only gathering dust with me," she said. "It would have been a pity to waste it when his only skill seemed to be making your lives miserable."

Alison frowned. "Lives? Plural? You mean my sister, too? Being married to him?"

"I imagine anyone in his orbit would suffer," Natalya said.

She was parsing her words carefully. Too carefully.

"Anyone?" Alison repeated slowly. "Is there something you're not telling me? I mean…are you hinting about…Hailey? I mean I know he yells a lot but is it…something more?"

"I think it's advisable he's no longer in anyone's lives," Natalya said neutrally. "And that includes your niece."

Alison eyed her pensively. "Maybe I should have a talk to Hailey?"

"A wise precaution."

The two women regarded each other for a few moments. The glass and chrome clock on the wall behind them ticked loudly. Alison fidgeted.

"God, sorry, this is depressing. Trust Barry Moore to ruin any conversation. Let me put some music on."

She rose, went to her stereo, and crouched in front of it. As she flipped through her CDs, she said: "I enjoyed Harry Partch's posts. How did you know I liked all the things in the photos you posted? Like the Whitestars chocolate fudge?"

"I may know an insider with excellent intel."

"Uh huh. Is she cute and thirteen, with a big mouth?"

"I never reveal my sources."

"Right. That's what I thought. So why did you help me with the gangs? Aren't these your colleagues that you're tossing to the piranhas?" She selected a CD, hit play and returned to her armchair as the sounds of Rodrigo's *Concierto de Aranjuez* began.

"They're nothing to me anymore," Natalya said with a sneer. "Just the bottom feeders who paid Lola to have me do their bidding."

"You're still helping the police, though."

"No, I'm helping *you* while destroying Lola's empire and anyone she might have dealt with. And I've also been systematically removing from the equation every enforcer who might be a threat to me if they ever work out who the leak is. You've got them all, by the way."

"So you're finally retired then?" Alison asked, cringing inwardly at the amount of hope leaking from her voice.

"I'm not sure if one can retire from certain professions," Natalya said, casually brushing her pants with the back of her fingers. "But let's just say it's been twelve months since my last 'coffee.'"

"Do you miss…um, coffee?"

Natalya regarded her. "Yes."

Disappointment flooded Alison. Well, what had she expected?

"Alison," Natalya said sternly, "don't ask questions you don't want to know the answers to."

Good point. She licked her lips anxiously. "Okay. Why are you here then?"

"My current tour is over. And I wanted to check in on my *Saintapaulia ionantha*."

Alison blinked at her.

"The African violet." She pointed to the plant on the coffee table between them. "Just how many of my possessions are you tending, that you couldn't work out what I meant?" Natalya drawled.

"Oh right," Alison said, slumping a little at hearing the reason for Natalya's visit. "Your plant," she repeated. "Well, I didn't kill it, as you can see."

"I noticed. I'm rather impressed."

Alison didn't reply. Her gaze took in Natalya's entirely black outfit of tailored, linen pants and a button-down shirt. The buckled, polished midnight ankle boots were especially arresting. Assassin chic? Was Natalya having some sort of a joke?

Neither spoke for a few moments but Natalya's brown eyes held an amused glint.

"Why are we listening to *Concierto de Aranjuez?*" Natalya asked, tilting her head. "Not that I'm complaining. It's beautiful. Languid."

"I'm in a Spanish mood," Alison said with a grin. "I've always wanted to go there and this piece is a shout-out to all things Spanish."

"Why Spain?"

Alison's eyes fluttered closed as blissful thoughts took over. "It's so bright and colourful. The vibrant music. The gorgeous food. Oh my God, the *food!*" Her eyes flew open. "I swoon at the sight of paella. I was always so frustrated because Mum hates it. I'd have it every day if I could."

"Then I will think of you when I'm eating a paella in a few weeks' time," Natalya said with a slow smile. "I'm depping for another orchestra soon and we're doing Spain, Greece, and France, among other stops. One food destination after another."

"My taste buds are so ridiculously jealous right now." Alison leaned forward. "So why are you here? You didn't seriously come back here for a proof-of-life check on your plant, did you?"

"My visit's not entirely plant related," Natalya conceded. "I've been offered a permanent job with the Vienna Philharmonic in a few months' time. It's where I've wanted to play since I studied in Austria. It's a permanent move. I needed to collect my things in storage and tie up any loose ends."

"So...you came to say goodbye?" Alison asked hesitantly.

"Actually, I was in the neighbourhood."

Alison regarded her sceptically. "Sure. And do I want to know how you even know where my neighbourhood is these days? I'm unlisted for security reasons."

Natalya ignored that as though finding the address of the top cop cracking down on gangs was a small thing. "And I was exceptionally curious as to why I read about a master assassin named Requiem in the paper but there were no further names. Why did you reveal her if you had no plan to arrest her?"

"I only needed her to have the desired effect."

"Which was?"

"Strategy. I needed a charismatic figure to get everyone talking about the underworld families again. I had thought Lola would be that person but when she died I knew I needed someone else.

"A brilliant female assassin with a poetic justice hook would be sensational news. And it worked. I have been drip-feeding the details of a different Requiem killing every six weeks. Her exploits are single-handedly keeping media and public interest in the gangs at an all-time high.

"That means ongoing funding for my unit, better resources for raids, and political support from the highest level."

"So Requiem's your modern-day bogeyman." Natalya's eyebrows lifted.

"Or hero," Alison said dryly, "if all those hashtags are anything to go by."

Natalya snorted. "Social media is a shallow cave where all the carcasses of humanity go to be buried."

"It's a very useful cave at times." Alison attempted her most innocent look.

Natalya's eyes narrowed. "Tell me you haven't been hash-tagging 'SaveRequiem' like all those other imbeciles?"

"Don't be ridiculous. Do you know what my job title is? I'd never post that," Alison said archly. She paused and added sheepishly. "I just came up with the tag, let Hailey loose with it, and got her to pass it on to all her friends at school. It caught on like wildfire."

Natalya stared at her in shock and Alison laughed.

"Look, I don't actually *want* Requiem caught, obviously," Alison added. "It would mess up my strategy. As a concept, she's far more useful floating around in people's imaginations. But if, by some outside chance, you did actually get yourself arrested, you already have widespread public support in place. That would mean a far better outcome on sentencing."

"How devious," Natalya muttered. "I may have underestimated you. Again."

"You and everyone else."

Natalya shook her head. "You *say* that but I see you've finally acquired some edge. You wouldn't fly under anyone's radar these days. Congratulations: You finally reek of cop. I'd spot you a mile off now."

Alison smiled. "Thank you."

"That wasn't a compliment."

"It was to me. I actually fit somewhere. It's unexpected. Nice."

"Is fitting in really so important?"

"Not to everyone. Not even hugely so for me. But I was always on the outside, like looking at the world through frosted glass. I felt so disconnected. I hated it, not being part of anything, not belonging. Now I do and, yeah, it feels a little bit better."

"Sometimes fitting in isn't an option. Society can't make everyone conform into its neat boxes. I don't belong; I never will."

"You conform to the rules of music. Why not conform to the rules of society?" Alison asked curiously.

"You really have to ask? I'm the wrong shape, Alison. Where society expects smooth, I'm sharp. It wants docile and compliant; I fight authority and I loathe leashes. I never will be one of you. Sometimes the view through the glass just stays frosted."

Alison hadn't expected anything less. She nodded.

Natalya reached into her pocket. "Since I'm in the neighbourhood, I came to give you my piece of musical perfection. I even composed it myself. In fact it's everything I am."

She placed a USB thumb drive between them, and a fleeting smile twitched at the very corners of her mouth.

"What's so funny?" Alison asked.

"You'll understand when you play it."

Alison reached for the thumb drive but Natalya's hand came forward to stop her.

"Later."

Alison's gaze shifted and she caught a shape behind Natalya, leaning against the wall.

"Why is your cello here?"

"You think I would leave my 1849 Charles Adolphe Maucotel in a hotel room?"

"Oh right. Of course not." Alison studied the case with interest. "You're staying in a hotel?"

"My home is on the market now. As I said, I'm tying up all my loose ends."

"Oh."

This really was a permanent move. An unexpected sadness flooded Alison, and she pushed it down. It was absurd, given who Natalya was. Not to mention how little Alison meant to her. In fact, she doubted Natalya had given her much thought these past months beyond her being a plant caretaker.

"So, can I see it?" Alison asked, after a few moments.

"You want to look at my cello?"

"No, I want to look at *you* with your cello. The first time I ever noticed you was when you were holding it. I thought you were exceptional. Well, you and the oboist."

"*Please*, oboists." Natalya snorted. "Just show ponies. They're almost as bad as violinists."

She went to her cello case, pulled the instrument out, and spun it gently until it faced the room.

Alison admired the beauty of it in Natalya's hands. Her reverence for it. The power this instrument had—the only thing that could move her. The only way she showed emotions. At that thought, she reached for the remote control and turned off the Spanish music.

"Play something for me."

Natalya looked at her in surprise but, instead of arguing, simply reached for a straight-backed chair in the adjacent kitchenette area and carried it to where Alison sat.

She positioned the seat facing her, and then settled herself on it. "What do you wish to hear, my liege?" she asked, eyes mocking.

"You," Alison said. "Play what you're feeling."

An unsettled look crossed Natalya's face.

"You *do* feel," Alison said softly. "Deeply. Even if it's only with that in your hands. So show me. I want to understand, since you'll never tell me."

All playfulness was gone from Natalya's face as she considered the request. Then she closed her eyes, lifted her bow and began to play.

A low, drawn-out, guttural moan filled the small room, a gravelly dirge, like a weeping, old woman at a grave site. The hairs on the back of Alison's arms stood up as Natalya's lithe fingers moved across the strings and her left bow arm slashed fiercely.

Alison was chilled by the mourning sounds. The song was listless and broken. It soon picked up pace and now there was bite to it, too, an iron will behind it, like an angry fist shaking at the heavens. Tears in a storm.

Finally she recognised the composition. Contemporary. Surprisingly so. She wouldn't have thought Natalya would know this piece. So, a *Game of Thrones* fan? She probably shouldn't be shocked. She eventually placed the name.

The Rains of Castamere. A song about a castle broken by war, defeated, crumbling, where the rain falls and no one is left alive to witness it. Defeat snatched from the jaws of the strongest, most dominant forces on earth.

Did the castle mean Natalya? She felt weak? No longer powerful? Or was it to do with losing her place in the world, feeling stateless and purposeless with Lola gone as her driving force?

Whatever it meant to her, it sounded like Natalya's painful requiem.

A tear unexpectedly slid from the corner of Natalya's eye and made its way down her cheek.

Alison rose, padded silently over to her, and lifted her finger to stop the salt water's progress. Natalya's eyes flew open in shock, as though she'd forgotten she wasn't alone.

She stopped playing instantly, laying down her cello and then scrambled backwards until Alison's hand dropped.

"What are you doing?" Natalya demanded harshly.

"Emotion is *not* weakness," Alison said. "It's strength."

"You sound like my father," she retorted, her voice hoarse.

"Your father? What was he like?"

Natalya stared at her intently as though debating answering so personal a question. "A military man. Originally from Russia."

"Ah." Alison's smile willed her to reveal more. "He's still alive?"

"No, he died not long after Lola did. For obvious reasons, it wasn't advisable to attend the funeral. I wasn't sure of the GOU's intentions." Her accusing gaze pinned Alison. "You'd only just revealed Requiem's existence to the world."

Alison swallowed back a sympathetic response that she knew wouldn't be welcomed. She wondered if this was one of the loose ends that had drawn her home. Attending her father's grave. Sorting out his estate. Natalya's pain was evident in the way she bit off the ends of the words.

"What was he like?" Alison asked tentatively. "I'm guessing, given his background, he was tough?"

"Only externally. Somehow, his heart always saw the good in people. He couldn't even begin to grasp what Lola was up to. How she was manipulating everyone around her for her own ends. He saw this harsh, brutal world through a sentimental gaze and prayed to his God that I would follow his path. It was a flawed strategy. To lay yourself bare is the worst kind of vulnerability. And I don't…"

"Do that. I know," Alison said, biting back her disappointment. "I know."

"I was going to say I don't know how."

"Oh, Natalya."

"Don't," she snapped. "Don't look at me like that. What have you done to me? What is this?"

"*This* is emotion."

"I don't like it. It's *chaos*," she said and straightened, eyes icy and cool. "Lola was right."

"Lola was *not* right. On not one single thing has that wicked woman ever been right."

"She's not wicked."

"Oh?"

"She's…*Lola*."

"Ah," Alison said, understanding. Lola's empty, harsh view of the world represented safety for Natalya. "Well, a person might find it overwhelming and chaotic to rub shoulders with the unwashed masses who wear their messy emotions on their sleeves, but it's *living*. Don't be afraid of that. There's nothing to fear."

"I don't fear anything," Natalya said coldly.

"Good, because I'm going to kiss you now and it's going to be okay. You don't need to freak out because you're not prepared. You don't need to do anything. Just feel."

"I don't…" Natalya began and faded out.

Alison didn't know if she was going to say, "I don't kiss" or "I don't know how." Part of her didn't want to know. Both were painful in their own way. She leaned in slowly, giving Natalya plenty of warning.

At the moment before contact, Natalya wrenched her head to one side, a fire flashing in her eyes. And just like that, it was like Requiem had entered the room. Natalya's protector. A shiver slithered down Alison's spine.

"You want me," Natalya taunted softly, leaning in. "Lola wasn't wrong about how you feel, either."

"Is it so one-sided?"

"How many times do I have to tell you? I would destroy you. We're a terrible idea. It would destroy your career if we were discovered. It would destroy my music, you trying to cage me."

"Cage you? What on earth?"

"You would cage an animal of prey. They die inside cages."

"I would never do that."

Natalya gave a sharp laugh. "Your mundane suburban life is a cage. Don't you even see that? You would dull my edge."

"You didn't answer my question. Is it so one-sided?"

"That's what you want to know?" Natalya taunted. She scraped her fingernails lightly down the side of Alison's face. "You have to believe I care too, or this, this feeling you have for someone like me feels self-destructive and pathetic."

"I don't…"

"Yes," Natalya said. "You do. You're afraid of what you feel. So you want to tame me. I can't be tamed. You want to love me. I don't do love. But you're desperate to try. Because if you can only squeeze me into a little box, change me, *then* you can exhale because you'll have cloaked me in the veneer of normal. Well, I don't do normal."

"But you…" Alison protested, "you've already changed."

"Alison," Natalya breathed against her ear softly, "you must understand by now that I'm not deserving of your feelings. I don't feel as you do."

Alison shook her head adamantly.

"Alison, I *kill*." The word was stark. It was the first time she'd ever said it plainly, uncouched by clever metaphors or sly innuendo.

Looking into the eyes inches from her, Alison said unwaveringly: "I know."

Natalya's lips thinned into a line. "Not all of them are innocents," she said harshly. "Requiem might think they're all guilty. I know that's a lie. I *did* kill innocents."

"I know."

"You know and yet you still want me?" Natalya hissed. "Do you know how that sounds?"

"Yes," Alison gasped out, anguish rising in her chest. "Of course I fucking know how it sounds. You think I want to love someone who does what you do? Or did? You think I would *choose* this? Emotions aren't rational."

Natalya's eyes narrowed. Alison sighed. It was clear she thought she was being judged. Natalya didn't understand what this felt like at all.

It was absurd, wishing for a thing she knew she could never have and shouldn't want. It was insanity what she was asking for and they both knew it. Forbidden. So very, disturbingly wrong. Besides, Natalya was moving overseas. This was the end for them. There could be no future in it.

And yet, still she wanted.

"But I don't care," Alison finally admitted, tears pricking her eyes.

"Alison," Natalya said, and gripped her biceps, "Don't you get it? I'm allergic to picket fences."

Her gaze was intense, filled with fear and fury. Alison met it evenly.

"Don't make Sonja's mistake," she continued and there was an edge of pleading that was all Natalya. "She looked up to me and followed me straight into Hell. It was such a damned waste."

"I'm not Sonja," Alison argued. "And I'm not stupid. I know all the reasons this is wrong." She reached out, her fingers trailing up to Natalya's neck. "Stay anyway?" she asked quietly. "It doesn't have to be about anything. No strings attached. A farewell. I'll show you some of the things you've been missing."

Natalya laughed, breaking the tension. "My little mouse, showing *me* the ways of the human body."

"No," Alison corrected gently. "I could show you what it feels like to make love. I think you might enjoy that."

"No. I don't think I would."

Alison boldly placed her palm on Natalya's breast, pressing against the nipple, rubbing. "Are you sure?" she asked, voice teasing.

"That's not for me," Natalya said firmly. "You know that."

"You're missing so much." She dropped her hand.

"Perhaps. But I'm Lola's monster with all that it entails. I'm too old to change now."

"I hate her," Alison said, feeling a burst of rage.

Natalya paused and sighed. "Me, too."

"You also love her. I saw the way you looked when she mocked you at the Melbourne Cup. She clawed at your heart. My mother did that to me; I know how that feels. Lola did it just for fun. She actually laughed in your face at your anguish."

"Yes, she did." The pain in Natalya's voice was almost palpable.

Alison lowered her voice until it was barely audible. "You also loved her as a woman."

There was a sharp intake of breath.

"I saw that, too," Alison whispered. "It gave me such hope. All those times you said you didn't do love, yet…there was Lola. The way you looked at her."

"She's the exception to every rule. She's *why* the rule exists. Why I don't think of love now."

"You and your rules. I thought we agreed they don't apply to you."

"Except for the immutable ones that can't be denied. Laws so set in stone they can't be overlooked. Lola is my zero, Alison. There will always be a part of me who cracks when I think of her. And a part of me who wishes I could try and overcome her hold over me—for other reasons." She looked slowly up at Alison. "But I can't."

"Oh."

"But despite that, we could never have been. For all our similarities, the differences would destroy us. You know that. I know you do."

Alison's gaze raked over Natalya's body. "God, it's insane. I still want you."

"I can't be who you want me to be."

"That's not fair. I've never asked you to change."

"Every time you look at me, your eyes implore me not to be who I am. You don't even know how much emotion you leak."

Alison wanted to deny it. Nothing came out.

"Just one night then," Alison whispered, appalled she sounded so beseeching. "To…to say goodbye. Since we'll never meet again."

Natalya glanced away, her gaze travelling around Alison's apartment as she appeared to consider the request. Her expression was inscrutable when it settled back on Alison. "You want to know that badly? What it would be like? With me?"

More than anything, Alison wanted to shout. She didn't answer immediately. The blush that rose up her cheeks answered for her.

Natalya's fingers slid under her chin tilting her jaw up.

"Is that what you really want?" Natalya repeated, her gaze direct. Her lips curled. "There are no safe words when you're with me. Do you understand?"

"Y-yes." Alison's voice was barely a whisper.

"Be careful what you wish for, little mouse." Her expression openly mocked her now. It was gentle but it was there. Alison resented the hell out of it.

"I'm not a damned mouse," Alison said with heat. "Not anymore. Can't you see? I'm not that naïve woman you first met. Can't you see *me*?"

Natalya shifted forward until she was inside her space, then took another three steps, forcing Alison back until she was pressed against the wall.

"Oh, I *see*," she said. Natalya's smile was dangerous. "Now then, last chance to change your mind and not have me be the one you compare all your future lovers to."

Alison inhaled sharply. "Do you have to be so arrogant?" she asked. "God, Natalya, don't you ever feel anything without a bloody cello in your hands?"

"No," Natalya replied, the backs of her fingers playing with a stray strand of Alison's hair. "That's weak. But I don't object to giving you a farewell fuck to remember."

Her eyes glittered and Alison's stomach did a helpless flop and dropped through the floor.

Natalya slowly plucked every button from Alison's clothing and slid her outer layer off her. Then she added Alison's lacy white bra to the pile on the floor.

Alison's breathing hitched as Natalya's fingertips mapped the newly revealed skin, leaving goose bumps in their wake. When those tantalising fingers tracked across her erect nipples, Alison's knees almost lost cohesion.

Natalya smiled knowingly and stepped back to study her.

It wasn't supposed to be this way. In Alison's fevered fantasies, she had some modicum of power. This was, this was...*oh god*. This was *nothing* like she'd imagined.

"On the table," Natalya ordered. She indicated a small round wooden table in the open-area kitchenette behind them.

Alison shifted onto it, her bare legs dangling. She leaned back, supported by her arms, topless, and wondered what Natalya would do next.

Natalya returned to the couch, which faced the table, and sat regally. She slowly undid her plait and combed her hair out with her fingers. Then, hair fanned and smoothed out, she sat back and raked her gaze over Alison.

"You know it's hard to touch you from all the way over there," Alison said.

"Yes," Natalya purred. "It is."

Their eyes locked and Alison's heart beat picked up. She swallowed.

"Now then, let's begin," Natalya said.

"Begin?"

"Panties off."

Alison caught her bottom lip with her teeth. She slipped her white panties down her legs until they dropped to the floor.

"Excellent. Let me see you."

Alison spread her thighs a little, and caught sight of the moisture already gleaming at the tops of her legs. She was so ready it was embarrassing.

Natalya's dark gaze contemplated her. "Touch yourself."

"Aren't you going to take off your clothes?" Alison asked uncertainly. "I mean I can't just perform…"

"Don't go inside. I'll tell you when."

Natalya smiled—the one with the sensuous edge that promised all manner of dark and naughty deeds. *Oh dear God.*

Alison nervously ran her fingers over herself, combing her neatly groomed hair and then rubbed her clit. She noted the slight colour in Natalya's cheeks now; the flare of her nostrils, the shift in the way she sat.

"You like having me at a disadvantage," Alison murmured. "Is this what turns you on? Power over me?" She arched into her touch now, and fiery tendrils began to spread out from her sex.

"Go inside," Natalya responded, ignoring her question. "Fuck yourself for me."

Alison parted her labia and slid two fingers inside. She leaned back against one arm as she spread her legs wider and set up a rhythm with her other hand. She tilted her head back and closed her eyes.

In her mind's eye she could still see Natalya's intense expression, memorising every detail, missing nothing. Alison's nipples hardened and she withdrew her fingers to slip across her breasts, leaving slippery, slick trails.

Her eyes fluttered open. She gasped.

Natalya was now standing two feet from her, face implacable, but her *eyes.* Her eyes were dark with desire.

Natalya smirked and lowered herself to her knees before her. Alison could barely breathe from the sight in front of her.

"Oh Alison," Natalya said, as she leaned in, her face so close to her sex that Alison could feel the dusting of her breath against fine hairs. "You think you even understand power? Let me show you power."

She lay her hands against the tops of Alison's thighs and pushed them wide apart until the strain burned up her inner thighs.

Natalya gazed for long moments at the intimate sight uncovered. Her warm hands shifted up and down along the thighs, massaging and pushing at the same time, urging them even wider.

Pain and pleasure warred with each other and Alison's arousal built as she stared down at the sight of Natalya bowed before her. It was a deceptive sight. Coiled power and danger radiated from her.

"You like this, don't you," Natalya taunted. "*Me* on my knees before you?"

Alison shook her head, her eyes wide.

"Oh yes," Natalya lowered her voice. "I think you like this very much. Control is intoxicating. And here you have the most powerful person you've ever met, on her knees before you, about to do your bidding. You're a mess, aren't you? And I haven't even touched your *cunt*."

A shudder ran up Alison at her words. *Jesus.* Natalya blew against Alison's folds and she couldn't silence a moan.

"You want me to taste you," Natalya told her. "You want my tongue plundering you. You want me owning you. Fucking you until you can't walk. You'd like that, wouldn't you?"

Alison's clit twitched and she groaned again. Natalya's half smile told her she'd seen it, too.

"What if I didn't," Natalya asked. "What if I didn't touch you at all? Didn't taste you? What if I went back to sitting over there and watched you come undone in front of me. And I just sat there and did nothing. Nothing but watch."

"Oh god," Alison moaned. "Oh no, no. Please."

"*Please*," Natalya repeated in disdain. "What a tortured word that is. I hear it so often."

Alison stiffened as she realised what context Natalya might hear it in. Natalya studied her reaction.

"Oh yes. You're deciding now if it makes you a monster to be aroused by me."

Her lips came even closer to Alison's intimate flesh. "Does it make you a monster to want me? Is that what you're thinking? Or maybe you're too far gone to care? I wonder which it is?"

"You know how I feel," Alison protested. "I don't think you're a monster. I don't think you're evil. I wouldn't be here if I did."

"No?" Natalya's eyebrow lifted. "But still a part of you is screaming at you in the back of your mind. Demanding to know what the hell you think you're doing here with me."

Alison was startled at the truth of her words. Natalya smiled at her expression.

"But another part of you loves that I'm like no one you've ever met. No one else can have you this close to the edge from just the promise of what I might do to you."

She leaned forward, extended her tongue and just dotted the tip of her clit. Alison's entire body clenched in excitement.

"You see?" Natalya noted dispassionately. "I can possess you with just a word, just a breath."

"Touch me," Alison pleaded. "Touch me or I'll explode."

"You'll explode anyway."

Alison shot her a filthy look and was galled when she laughed.

"What did you expect from me?" she taunted, breathing in deeply. "Vanilla sex? The missionary position? Making *love*?"

"I expect you to stop playing me like your damned cello," Alison bit back. "Stop with the games and *take me*!"

"And what if I said no? What if I just teased you for another hour? Two hours? Four? I have excellent stamina."

"You wouldn't dare," Alison said in a growl so low, so furious that it took her aback. "You wouldn't *god damn dare*."

It was like a light switch flicking off. The mockery in Natalya's eyes was instantly gone. In its place lay hunger, keen and sharp. Natalya narrowed her eyes.

Alison smiled, even as her body tightened with tension.

"Oh, and Natalya?" she drawled, copying the other woman's mocking tone of earlier until Natalya's dark questioning gaze met Alison's, "I didn't ask you to be gentle."

Natalya immediately jerked her thighs even wider apart. Her head ducked down and her tongue slid the length of Alison's lower lips, then shifted higher to punish Alison's clit in rough, demanding strokes.

By the time three of Natalya's fingers plunged inside her, half-moon crescents of her other hand biting into her thigh, Alison had forgotten her own name.

Fear was an interesting concept, Alison thought hazily as she flitted between consciousness and unconsciousness. She was naked. In her own bed, with no clear memory of how she got there. Natalya was still fully dressed, only her boots missing, and presently she was wearing sleek, black gloves.

Alison was nearing her fourth orgasm for the evening, fucking herself without shyness. Alison's soaking fingers slipped in and out and Natalya licked her lips.

She certainly did like to watch.

But right now…right now she apparently also liked to invoke fear.

A part of Alison knew, as the first stroke of leather glove touched her skin, that she should be terrified. Natalya's hand lifted higher and higher before settling on the base of her throat.

Yet Alison's body was unafraid. Her nipples were hard as chalk. Her sex clenched and unclenched. Her breath came in short, sharp gasps as she feverishly stroked herself.

Natalya's gloved fingers circled her throat, so gently as if she were a most delicate thing. Her index finger stroked the flesh, sliding up and down the vulnerable skin, the threat clearly implied.

"Are you getting off on this?" Alison asked, shivering under the flitting touch of leather. "Playing games? Control and desire?"

"You think this is about me?" Natalya's burning gaze shifted to meet Alison's. "This is about you. It's your fantasy I'm providing. *This* is what you like about me. How dangerous I am. How your mind plays over all the things I'm capable of. That's what excites you most. I know. It's in your eyes. In the way you tremble when I touch you like this."

Alison shook her head, wanting to deny it, even as Natalya's left hand stopped playing and suddenly pressed into her flesh.

Natalya's thumb pushed into the side of Alison's neck along with two fingers on the other side of her larynx. Then the thumb and index finger began to squeeze.

Fear blasted through her. Alison's carotid artery pushed back against the rigid fingers as it fought to supply her brain with vital blood. She became light-headed as the pressure increased. Natalya leaned over her, her face filling her entire range of vision, and studied her coolly. "It's not my danger that thrills you?" Natalya repeated. "Are you so certain?"

Alison gasped, and her slick hand stilled between her legs. She lifted it hastily to her throat to pull Natalya's hands away. Instead Natalya shook her head abruptly.

"No," Natalya said. "Stopping now will defeat the object of the game. It's all about trust and danger."

Alison understood then. She'd heard of such things—blood chokes. Best orgasms ever—supposedly. She searched Natalya's eyes, hoping to find something that said she knew what she was doing. That this was not some sick excuse to kill the woman who'd been threatening her all over the news. That would be poetic justice, all right. Fucking to death the cop who loved her.

Natalya's hot breath shifted the hairs on her cheek. Alison stared helplessly up. Her hand had already decided. She slid it back down her body and rubbed herself tentatively. Her nerve endings lit up with the heightened sensation.

"Good girl," Natalya said. "And you'll thank me in a minute."

Alison had been near the edge before, and it wasn't long before the tremors began to take over. Her thighs began to lock and shake.

She remembered Natalya's mocking warning: *There are no safe words with me.* Her fear returned but before she could panic, the pressure eased at her throat. Suddenly a rush of blood flooded through her.

Her back arched.

"That's it," Natalya husked, running her lips across her ear. "Come for me. *Now.*"

Alison crashed over with a strangled sound. Then she was floating. The sensation was nothing she'd ever experienced before—a high that left her dizzy and in a haze.

She lay, panting and sated in a dreamy state staring at her ceiling, trying to catch her breath.

Once she'd recovered, she slid her eyes across to the woman lying beside her, looking well pleased with her efforts.

"It's you."

"What is?" Natalya asked.

"It's not your danger," she said. "It's none of that. That's the window dressing. The kick-ass package you come in." Her gaze met Natalya's, willing her to believe her. "But it's you I love."

A strange expression flashed across Natalya's face. Alison inhaled deeply and then rolled to her right side to study her properly.

Natalya was still immaculately dressed. It was so infuriatingly uneven.

"Kiss me," Alison demanded, suddenly anxious to redress the balance.

"No," Natalya said. "I don't..." She faded out. "I never kiss."

Alison pushed herself up into the sitting position, feeling a telltale tug between her legs that told her she'd been fucked to hell and back in the most satisfying of ways.

But still it wasn't enough.

"Take off your clothes then," she said. "Because this is my turn."

There was an almost insolent pause in the way Natalya stared. Alison swallowed, afraid of how shitty and used she'd feel if Natalya just laughed at her and left. She almost saw those words forming on Natalya's lips: That she didn't do *that*.

No. Alison couldn't bear to hear it. Not after everything they'd just done, or the fifty ways Natalya had reshaped the definition of what pleasure meant for her.

"Please," Alison tried again, softer. "I'd really like to see you, too."

Natalya didn't comment but she rose from the bed and shed her clothes without preamble. She folded each item neatly and placed it on a chair. She was left in black boyshorts and a sports bra. Then she returned to the bed.

Alison avidly studied her. "You've had a busy life," she said trailing fingers over the nicks and scars she found.

Natalya looked down at herself. "It's been diverting," she agreed.

Alison slipped her fingers into her long black tresses. She was struck by the effect of it out of its trademark plait. So beautiful. Natalya was breathtaking. A woman in her prime. Muscled, powerful. So strong. She was an apex predator. And she was Alison's for the taking.

She shivered.

Well, she had hopes at least.

"Take off your bra," Alison ordered, her shaking voice undermining the command.

Natalya paused but turned away and slid the sports bra over her head. She turned back slowly, prolonging the reveal until the last moment. Then she held it up and let it drop to the floor. Like a challenge.

She waited for a reaction.

Alison let her gaze roam the sensuous curves unveiled. Her breasts were larger than she'd guessed, but they suited her frame and the broadness of her shoulders. Then she took in a delightful sight. Natalya's nipples were rock hard.

"Your panties. Off," Alison croaked.

Natalya ignored this and instead reached down and pulled aside the crotch of her boyshorts, exposing a dark thatch of hair.

Alison held her breath at the sight of wetness glimmering in the light. The realisation she'd caused that was heady.

"I want to taste you," Alison said. "Make you come so hard you lose control."

"One does not mean the other," Natalya warned softly. "I do not lose control."

She widened her legs but then said: "You can look but not touch."

"What? No!"

"Yes," Natalya said. "But I'll give you a taste."

"Oh come on! That's not fair."

"No," Natalya agreed with a smirk, sliding off her boyshorts. "But you'll do it anyway."

"What makes you so sure?" Alison asked, glaring.

"Because you're dying to watch me touch myself," Natalya taunted. "And nothing on earth could make you leave this bed right now."

Alison flushed dark red. "You don't know anything," she muttered.

Natalya's smug look said Alison wasn't convincing.

With eyes fixed on her, Natalya slid her fingers inside herself and began to rock gently. She made small, faint sounds as she buried herself in the task.

She lifted up a little, giving Alison a better view.

"Oh my God," Alison groaned. "Jesus, Natalya."

The base of Natalya's hand pressed against her clit and her breathing changed. Her eyes began to close.

"What are you thinking about?" Alison demanded. "Right now?"

"The way you looked at me," Natalya whispered, "when I was inside you, when you were mine."

"I still am," Alison said as Natalya's fingers reach feverish pace. "All yours."

"I know."

Vulnerability flashed across Natalya's face and in that moment she spasmed, trembled, and tilted her head back briefly.

Natalya sat up and offered her hand to Alison.

"A taste."

Alison huffed out a breath.

"Only if you want," Natalya said with a shrug.

Alison wished she had the willpower to refuse. Instead she greedily devoured the fingers and discovered the unique flavour that was Natalya. It was not at all what she'd expected. Gentle, sweet, with the faintest edge of piquancy.

Natalya looked like an overfed cat, well pleased with its bowl of cream. She might not have lost control but she'd enjoyed herself—that much was clear.

Alison bit into the fingers mischievously.

Natalya's hand retracted swiftly and she gave her a playful swat. "Since when do mice have such sharp teeth?" she demanded archly.

"Since when do cats *not* let mice play with them?" Alison retorted. "Come on. I want to get my hands on you. *All* of you."

Natalya didn't speak immediately but it was like a shutter had gone down. When she did speak, her tone was flat.

"You know I am returning to Europe for good this time. I won't be back."

Whatever she'd expected her to say, that wasn't it. Alison felt deflated.

"I know."

"This was all there ever could be." The words were more forceful than needed and Alison gave her an indignant look.

Natalya glanced at her folded clothing on the chair, and Alison's heart sank. Over already.

Natalya rose from the bed. The play of her muscles made her look like some lethal yet stunning goddess. A goddess Alison would like to worship a few more times, or a few more decades.

"Why did *she* have to be you?" Alison muttered, not intending to speak aloud. "It's not fair."

"She had to be someone, Alison. There is no force of power on earth—no warlord, drug baron, gang leader or arms dealer—who can stay in business for long without an enforcer at their side."

"There's a depressing thought. I still wish things were different."

"You'll be fine," Natalya said. "Look at you. I told you to eat life. You sat down at the banquet table and ate ten courses. You've shown them all."

"I don't care about *them*. It's you. I'll never forget you."

"Of course you won't." Natalya smiled not unkindly. "How could you?" She leaned forward and her fingers trailed Alison's cheek for a brief moment. It was the most tender thing she'd done to her all night. "Try, though, because I can't change."

Alison's heart lurched again. She knew that. But still, it hurt.

"It's funny," Natalya added, as she slid her underwear on. "People look at you and see the flaws—the small handful of chipped pieces you have because you never bother to hide them.

"They look at me and see only the confidence, the mask. They never see the thousands of pieces shattered on the floor."

Alison stared at her in surprise.

"Underneath we are the perfect opposites of what we appear," Natalya mused. "I'm broken; you're solid. So seek out someone else who is solid; someone who can love you back and be what you need."

She slid on her pants and tightened the belt.

"Did you never feel anything for me?"

Alison definitely didn't mean to ask that. It was embarrassingly needy. They'd already set the rules for this evening. This wasn't even on the cards.

"Haven't you been listening?" Natalya asked archly, pulling on the rest of her clothes. "I've told you so many times, in so many ways. You already know the answer."

She fixed her long hair into a ponytail with a sharp jerk and moved into the lounge to pack up her cello.

Yeah, Natalya had, so many times: *I don't do love.*

Alison padded out to say goodbye. Natalya paused at the door, cello case in hand. No words. They just held gazes and then she turned and was gone.

The soft click of the apartment door echoed around the room.

Alison's eye fell to the USB drive on the coffee table. She pulled out her laptop, plugged the stick in, and hit play.

The source of Natalya's amusement became immediately clear. Alison listened to the track for its entirety, then opened her calculator app, tapping in the length of the song, converting it to seconds.

Of course.

She closed her laptop and stared at it, her mood darkening. She removed the USB drive and flung it against the wall.

Natalya had given her a track with nothing on it but silence. 1935 seconds of silence, to be exact. Arvo Pärt's birthday. So, silence remained perfection for her—because no human could ever mess that up.

The absence of emotion was perfection to Natalya.

Didn't that just say it all? Natalya really didn't care.

Well, she'd just have to do what the great Requiem had suggested and get on with life. She knew how to now, ironically, thanks to the woman who'd just let her down somewhat gently. Alison was stronger than she ever had been. Confident. She even walked taller.

But still, her heart ached and futile tears sprang to her eyes.

Moving on with life without Natalya? Love or not, how does anyone ever forget someone like *that?*

She smiled in spite of herself through the shimmer of tears.

What a stupid bloody question.

EPILOGUE

The crowd at the experimental music club grew hushed as the spotlight fell. Alison stepped out onto the stage, biting her lip anxiously and hit play on her CD player. The low murmur of didgeridoos began, and she placed her violin under her chin, closed her eyes and started to play.

She was instantly *there*. This piece always reminded her of colours. Empty blue skies that stretched endlessly. Streaks of red of the desert earth. Orange of the rock outcrops. Green of spiky spinifex grasses after the wet season.

The movement shifted. There was the pang of loss and broken dreams of the elders. Her violin soared across the high notes as it reached its crescendo. She opened her eyes and her gaze shifted, as it always did, to the back, right corner.

Sometimes, just once or twice, she could have sworn she'd seen a shadow. The figure of someone who should not have been there. Of course it was illogical Natalya would be in Australia at all when the GOU and the Homicide Squad had been closing in on every last member of the gangs. But sometimes Alison wondered if it was her she'd seen. Watching her. Or watching over her—like some hard-ass avenging angel.

She almost laughed at her overactive imagination. Natalya was in Europe. Permanently. Fulfilling her lifelong Vienna Philharmonic Orchestra dream. Alison had read they were touring Spain and Italy now. Getting rave reviews— not that she was surprised.

After her performance, and a few rousing claps from the small crowd, Alison packed away her violin, musing on how life had changed in recent years.

It had taken eighteen months of running the GOU but it was pretty much all over. Alison and her team had decimated the Victorian crime gangs. Oh, they weren't *all* gone, she knew, but their backs had been broken.

The last of the worst of them had been some sneaky little cockroach called Saliya "Sal" Govi who'd filled the vacuum at Fleet Crew after Lola was killed. The special ops team had picked him up in a raid just that morning.

Alison was ready for a change. Truthfully, she was ready for a lot of things. She'd tried to do what she'd promised herself. Tried to go out and live life. Tried dating and getting out of her comfort zone. She'd partied, wined, dined, danced, played the violin, had drinks with the boys from work who were still essentially assholes, but at least not to her anymore. She'd done everything else in between. Everything she thought she was supposed to do.

It had been eye-opening in some ways, but empty in others.

The truth was, no one had come even close. The shadow Natalya cast was unparalleled. Of course the maddening woman was right: They could never be a thing. But still.

She wanted.

Alison hadn't heard from Natalya since the day they'd been intimate a little over a year ago.

A six-figure sum had lobbed mysteriously into her bank account marked only "Refund" and that had been that. She'd checked the date and was relieved the payment had been made before their "farewell fuck." That would have been too much to take. She was no one's paid lay.

Alison knew what she really was at the end of the day: A loose end. Something to be neatened, tied up.

Nonetheless, every day Alison carefully watered and tended Natalya's African violet and thought about what she would never have.

It was futile, actually, caring for someone who'd left her with 1935 seconds of silence to sum herself up. A brilliant, deadly creature who loved empty, silent perfection, and felt nothing.

She sighed and gathered her things, heading for the exit.

"Great work tonight," the barman called out to her.

Lou. He was nice. Kept trying to set her up with his sister.

She gave him a wave and a smile and stepped outside only to find it was raining softly.

God, that brought back memories.

She pulled her jacket's collar up and ran for her car. She watched for puddles as she ran, so she didn't see the shadow standing by her vehicle until it suddenly moved.

She bit back a gasp and assumed an aggressive posture.

"I wouldn't try it on," she growled. "I'm a cop."

"Easy little mouse," came a low drawl. "I'm well aware of your unappealing occupation. It's me."

God how she had missed that voice.

"Natalya?"

The shadow took a step forward, angling itself so Alison could see its features in the street lamp.

Natalya came into sharp relief and smiled unexpectedly, sucking all the oxygen out of Alison's lungs. Her treacherous, thudding heart set up a painful beat.

"You were wonderful tonight. And last night."

Alison blinked at her. "You watched me play?"

Natalya's lip curled instead of answering.

"Are you back in Melbourne?" Alison asked. "For good, I mean?"

"No. Just for a little while. I thought about something while I was overseas. Something I might ask."

"Oh?"

"I was wondering if you'd consider trying the world's best paella. I've found a place that has no rival."

Alison's mouth fell open.

"You want me to…go to Europe with you?"

"If you're done savaging the gang of four, that is. And my informants tell me you are."

Alison was startled she knew that; very few did. Then she remembered Natalya knew far more about the gangs than any police taskforce would uncover in a lifetime of investigating. Natalya had literally grown up with them.

"Why are you asking?"

"I've spent the past year picking apart all the many ways music made sense to me and all the ways that I exist in this world. Whether I can do one effectively without the other. Do you know what I learned?"

Alison shook her head.

Natalya's voice softened as she regarded her. "That there is something to be said for having someone, just once, look at you with love in their eyes."

"You care about love now?" Alison eyed her sceptically. "Since when? Why now?"

"Something happened two years ago that changed everything. It altered the way I thought about things. And certain people. Those events were the beginning. That night, a year later, that you and I said goodbye was the middle. Now, here I stand, at the end."

"What happened two years ago?" Alison asked. "I mean apart from me unmasking you at the Melbourne Cup."

"You don't want to ask that."

A sick sensation rose in Alison's guts when she remembered the "other" things Natalya had done with her life. Things it would be a very bad idea to ask about.

"Yes," Natalya said coolly. "That's why. But even so, one event changed everything, as I'm only now fully beginning to appreciate."

Two Years Ago
Two days after the Melbourne Cup

Natalya adjusted her gloves and studied her handiwork. With a long, casual stride, she walked slowly around the figure in the Newman Pig Farm feed trough. He was naked, covered in mud, trussed and gagged, his eyes bulging with fear.

"You made me miss my flight," she chided, voice low and unimpressed. "I should have been halfway to Paris by now. But no, I had to detour to fix a situation that I realised sorely needed my skills to rectify.

He tried to speak, but the gag got in the way.

She raised a bucket and poured more mud in the trough.

"Now, Mr Moore. Or is it Zebra? You have been a wicked man. I understand that you have been hurting your little girl. And that is intolerable.

"You have also made life miserable for that little girl's mother. She is a husk of the woman you married. Also intolerable. A big brute of a man like you, picking on a woman and a child? Where is your shame?

"You also treated your sister-in-law cruelly. I hear you think she's a dyke who doesn't deserve opportunities at work because that would be nepotism, and you don't feel her colleagues would like her getting her chance to shine. You also planned to exile her.

"Let me tell you what all of that is: homophobic, Neanderthal, misogynistic bullying. Of course these are only the crimes against your family. What about the wider world? What about how you got your nickname?

She arched her eyebrow. "You beat to death a dog. Kicked in the heads of two homeless men. You are the worst kind of individual. And, yes, I am aware of the irony. An assassin calling *you* the worst. But at least *I'm* about delivering justice—it's hard to fathom what you stand for."

He shook his head vigorously.

"Doubts? I thought you might have a few. The thing about working for a crime family or four is you get to know where all the dirt is buried." She reached into her coat and held up a CD.

"Security footage from the back alley at the Hyatt, where you killed. There's also a highlights reel of various other illegal acts gathered over the years. Accepting bribes to drop people's charges was especially crude. But spending the money on prostitutes instead of the people in your life you're supposed to love? Well, that's just sad.

"I've known this CD exists for years. So has everyone else in my circles. This should tell you how bad you are as a cop that almost every criminal in town has a copy of it and no one has ever had a NEED to blackmail you with it. Because you are *that* corrupt, *that* lazy. Even the lowest filth see you as one of them. I suspect IBAC will find this to be fascinating viewing. Maybe the media will, too? Yes?"

She slid the disc back into her pocket. She studied him. "Look at you. Not only making me late, but making me monologue. That never happens."

She prodded his pudgy face with her gloved index finger. "Your daughter has more spirit in her pinky than you have in your whole body. It impresses me that in spite of her gene pool she still has that spark.

"Your sister-in-law has more goodness, decency and innocence in her than either of us will ever see in our lifetimes.

"You picked the wrong people to mistreat this time. Because anyone who mistreats Hailey Moore or Alison Ryan or the ones they love insults me. And no one *ever* insults Requiem. They are under my protection. As such, I intend to make sure that in my absence you can *never* hurt them ever again.

"Ah. I see that surprises you. You think an assassin can't find people worthy of admiration? It's impossible *not* to like them. Which makes your actions even more unfathomable.

"Now don't fret, your family won't be unduly worried about your welfare. I've taken care of everything. I packed your bags and other travel essentials for you while you were settling into these new accommodations a few hours ago. You'll find your luggage weighted at the bottom of the Yarra. Your body, meanwhile, will never be found. You probably don't want to know how indiscriminate and thorough hungry pigs are.

"Now then, deep breath, because I assure you, it will be your last…"

She clamped his head in a vice-like grip, pushing it into the mud and animal faecal matter. She smothered his face in the muck impassively, as the revolting body of the cruellest of men twitched and savagely jerked. Then, finally, Detective Barry Moore suffocated, quite literally, with his snout in the trough.

She glanced around, wondering how often the farmer got to this far-flung end of his vast farm. His main troughs were a great distance away, much closer to the road. Several pigs trundled past her, snuffling, nuzzling at the body. She smiled. Moore was among his own kind now.

Natalya then turned and walked back to her Ninja. She settled onto the seat, pressed play on Arvo Pärt, and slipped her earbuds in.

She still had to leave this country. Still had to slither past a cop who was determined to hunt her.

Natalya smiled in spite of herself. The little mouse had done what no others ever had.

Surprised her.

Really, she couldn't be more impressed at the woman's creativity in trying to find Requiem. The ballsiness of the woman to buy her own hit. The endearing optimism against astronomically low odds.

Natalya would win in the end, of course. She always did. But this time she actually appreciated the challenge.

She started the engine and then sped off into the dark, as the soul-cleansing strains of *Fratres (String and Percussion)* played on.

As she passed by the old trough, her eyes trailed across the body. A strange, lost feeling flooded her about what it meant that she was even here. Detouring instead of running. Giving the mouse this special parting gift she would never know about.

She pushed the unsavoury thought hurriedly aside. She had a replacement flight to organise. And this, whatever it was, was just a foolish distraction.

Present day

"You want to know why I'm here now?" Natalya said. She studied Alison in the soft rain under the streetlight. This face had become so familiar to her. The innocence of it, the softness. It had more of an edge these days, as it should. She ran a police unit. She brought down organised crime.

But still, there was no hiding its appeal. At least to her.

"It takes time to pull apart your soul," Natalya admitted.

And hadn't that been the painful truth.

"But love?" Alison said sceptically. "You don't do love. You don't do any emotion without a cello in your hands."

"Even if I don't do love, I do *feel*," Natalya countered and stared at her intently, willing her to understand. "*You* make me feel. That's the truth. Besides, this isn't just about me. It's time your musical soul was properly fed in Europe, not left wasting away in the Antipodes. You belong there, away from this underbelly of dirt and crime. Join me."

"As what? Orchestra groupie? Travel companion? Convenient fuck?"

Natalya's nostrils flared at the distasteful question but she supposed she deserved it. She took a step closer. "How about an international tourist of music, off feeding your creative soul? And someone who means something to me."

Alison's uncertainty was clear.

"You realise I'm still a cop?" she asked.

"And I'm a non-practising 'coffee drinker.' I may have even kicked the habit; who can say? But you're far worse than a cop. You're a *violinist*."

Alison rolled her eyes.

"The thing is," Natalya said, turning serious, "I've come to realise certain truths. Some things *are* more valid than zero, for example. Some things matter more than immutable rules. They transcend them."

It wasn't a declaration of love exactly. Maybe she really didn't have that in her; Natalya wasn't sure. Not yet. But this was not nothing to her. Far from it. This was more than she'd ever offered anyone.

"How can I trust you?" Alison asked, her body swaying closer, seemingly without her knowledge. "How can I believe that after all this time, that my feelings suddenly matter to you? That you won't break my heart just because you can? And we both know you could."

"Can't you tell?" Natalya asked her in confusion. "Would I be here otherwise? Can't you see *me*?" she added, repeating back Alison's own words.

A small little frown formed between Alison's eyebrows.

"But won't you destroy me? And I, you? You said that once. You believed it."

"Yes," Natalya said with a sigh. "And I still do. That *will* happen. But not today."

"Not *today*?" Alison peered at her. "If it's inevitable then why risk it? Why even bother?"

"Because I'm Requiem," Natalya snarled. "And if *I* can't take a risk, I may as well be already dead."

She shot Alison her haughtiest smile, the one she used to show her arrogance regarding her place in the world. If she had to believe for both of them, she would.

"Yes," Alison said quietly, "You're Requiem. Are you still, though?"

"Why does it matter?"

"I need to know. Do you still hunt? Do you want to?"

"She's part of me."

"I know that. That wasn't the question."

"Lola's gone," Natalya finally admitted. "Requiem lived for Lola. I don't."

And it was true. She could not definitively rule out this part of herself forever. But the circumstances would have to be extreme to force her to kill again. Alison nodded slowly.

"Aren't you afraid of being caged? Picket fences? Suburban dreariness?"

"Yes." Natalya was terrified, actually.

"But still you want me to come with you?" Incredulity edged Alison's tone.

"Yes." Natalya had thought this through. A European tour was the antithesis of being caged. She could play. She could roam. She could…feel. And she would survive.

Until she didn't. Until Alison wanted the picket fences and mundaneness, and left her.

At that thought she added: "It's a crazy idea, I know. We will implode eventually. But as you once said, what a way to go."

"You aren't really romantic, are you?" Alison studied her, her expression half amused, half pained. "I say 'I love you,' and you give me a farewell fuck and barely break a sweat. But then? Then you turn up to say 'Come to Europe, we'll probably destroy each other, but until then, let's get paella.' So this isn't exactly the greatest pitch of all time."

Her expression was tight with tension. Natalya sighed. She was doing this all wrong. She was terrible at this. She should just walk away with what was left of her dignity.

But still. In the lift of the chin, and the fleck of blue, she could see hope there, too.

"You're right," Natalya admitted. "I've never done this before. It's insanity, given all the things I am and what we are to each other. Hunter and prey. But here I am. This is what I am and you know it: I play. I kill. And I feel."

"What do you feel? At least tell me that," Alison asked.

Natalya hesitated. Every lesson from Lola about hiding weakness came rushing back, attacking her like fleas. She pushed the panic aside and said simply: "I miss you."

Alison absorbed this, then said, "That night we shared? Did you feel then? Did you feel anything for me?"

Natalya hesitated. "This matters to you?"

"It does. I don't even know who fucked me that night. It drives me crazy thinking about it sometimes. Was it you or *Her*?"

"It was both of us. And at the end, it was just me. But we *both* felt. I can't tell you how rare that is. That's what I meant when I said I'd been telling you all along how I felt.

"Do you think I'd entrust my African violet to just anyone? Or show you how I touch myself, because I knew it was your fantasy to watch? Or strip myself bare before for you in every sense?

"I showed you how I felt through music. I shared with you in a way I never have before. I laid my soul before you. Couldn't you see that? Didn't you understand? Don't you know I have done that for no one else in my life?"

Alison didn't speak. She simply stared at her, eyes wide with shock.

"Now here I am, asking you to take a leap of faith with me," Natalya continued. "To take a risk, too. Without you, my music feels lifeless. My soul feels alive when you're near. Besides all the sights we will see, the music we will experience will nourish you forever."

And I need you, she almost admitted. She hoped Alison could see that even if the words didn't form on her lips. Words she had never been able to say before.

The rain on Alison's eyelashes made her blink away the water in her eyes. Natalya couldn't be entirely sure it was just rain.

"I don't know what to believe." Alison said. "I want a relationship of equals. I want all of you, not just the parts you allow me to touch. How do I know you're open to that? I need to believe."

"Believe." Natalya leaned forward, hovered briefly and then her lips brushed against Alison's. It was an erotic sensation, with the promise of so much more. A first for her in so many ways.

Alison responded, wrapping her arms around her, and Natalya deepened the kiss. In that moment she knew immediately why she'd never done this before.

This was intimate. So frighteningly intimate. Part of her wanted to recoil. To run. To tear her flawed, human skin off and disappear and never be seen again. It was more powerful than anything in her existence. It filled her senses. It ripped down her walls, every last one of them she'd painstakingly built for three decades. The sensation ricocheted through her body, leaving her weak.

Natalya did not do weak, her brain protested feebly.

And yet, here she was. She made a sound that was both panic and wonder, then Alison clutched her tighter, reassuring her, pressing their bodies together. She could feel Alison's heartbeat, thudding quickly, and the warmth of her. The solidness.

When they pulled away, Alison was grasping at Natalya's rain-soaked shirt and Natalya was trying desperately to anchor herself.

"Okay," came Alison's small, croaked voice. "I believe."

Relief coursed through her.

"Paella you say?" Alison added, offering a lopsided grin.

"Best in the world," Natalya said, trying to regain her equilibrium. "There's a little place in Santiago de Compostela I found. It translates to The Saints. Where better for musical immortals to dine than with saints?"

Alison smiled up at her. "I'm probably crazy…but yes. Whisk me to your paella heaven."

Natalya inhaled. "Yes?" Delight shattered what was left of her reserves and for the first time in her adult life, she made no effort to hide it. She smiled. Genuinely.

"Hell yeah," Alison repeated, grinning from ear to ear.

"Well, this should be interesting," Natalya said. "You and me. Until the implosion."

"Yep," Alison agreed, rocking back on her heels. "Should be."

Natalya looked down to find soft fingers entwining with hers.

Requiem would have laughed at the gesture. Snatched her hand away. Mocked her.

Their first time together, their only time, Natalya had given of herself to Alison in a way she never had another soul. Alison didn't know the half of that, couldn't know, but it was the truth. She had never shared certain things with anyone. She had certainly never sat at her cello and played her feelings for another person to pick apart.

Now Natalya had come back for this kind and gentle woman, the antithesis of Requiem in so many ways. Natalya had kissed her. She had survived. She wanted more.

She might screw it all up tomorrow, but so help her, she needed more.

Not trusting herself with the imprecision of words, Natalya tightened her grip on the small fingers as rain coursed down the beautiful face in front of her.

With a shocked gasp, she finally understood what all of this meant. What it had meant all along.

Because to say Natalya Tsvetnenko felt nothing was incorrect.

A common misconception about those in her line of work.

Love was not nothing.

REQUIEM FOR IMMORTALS SOUNDTRACK

Requiem's Theme
Fratres (String and Percussion)
by Arvo Pärt

Showering with a Killer
Lacrimosa from Requiem
by Mozart

Alison's Theme
Spiegel im Spiegel
by Arvo Pärt

Chaos Theory
The works of Harry Partch

Natalya Feels
The Symphony No. 6 in B minor, Op. 74, Pathétique
by Tchaikovsky

Alison's Perfect Imperfection
Requiem for Immortality
by Alison Ryan and Koori elders

Natalya's Perfection
1,935 seconds of silence
by Natalya Tsvetnenko

The Seduction of Natalya Tsvetnenko
Concierto de Aranjuez
by Joaquin Rodrigo

Breaching the Walls: Requiem's requiem
The Rains of Castamere (Game of Thrones S2)
by Ramin Djawdi

About Lee Winter

Lee Winter is an award-winning newspaper journalist and in her 27-year career has lived in virtually every state of Australia, covering courts, crime, entertainment, hard news, features and humor writing.

These days she's a sub-editor at a Sunday metro newspaper, lives with her girlfriend of 17 years and has a fascination for shiny new gadgets and trying to understand the bizarre world of US politics.

CONNECT WITH LEE:

Facebook: www.facebook.com/LeeWinterOz

OTHER BOOKS FROM YLVA PUBLISHING

www.ylva-publishing.com

The Red Files

Lee Winter

ISBN: 978-3-95533-330-0
Length: 365 pages (103,000 words)

Ambitious journalist Lauren King is stuck reporting on the vapid LA social scene's gala events while sparring with her rival—icy ex-Washington correspondent Catherine Ayers. Then a curious story unfolds before their eyes, involving a business launch, thirty-four prostitutes, and a pallet of missing pink champagne. Can the warring pair join together to unravel an incredible story?

Collide-O-Scope

(Norfolk Investigation Story – Book #1)

Andrea Bramhall

ISBN: 978-3-95533-573-1
Length: 370 pages (90,000 words)

One unidentified dead body. One tiny fishing village. Forty residents and everyone's a suspect. Where do you start? Newly promoted Detective Sergeant Kate Brannon and Kings Lynn's CID have to answer that question and more as they untangle the web of lies wrapped around the tiny village of Brandale Stiathe Harbour to capture the killer of Connie Wells.

Driving Me Mad

L.T. Smith

ISBN: 978-3-95533-290-7

Length: 348 pages (10,700 words)

After becoming lost on her way to a works convention, Rebecca Gibson stops to ask for help at an isolated house. Progressively, her life becomes more entangled with the mysterious happenings of the house and its inhabitants.

With the help of Clare Davies, can Rebecca solve a mystery that has been haunting a family for over sixty years? Can she put the ghosts and the demons of the past to rest?

Blurred Lines

(Cops and Docs – Book #1)

KD Williamson

ISBN: 978-3-95533-493-2

Length: 283 pages (92,000 words)

Wounded in a police shootout, Detective Kelli McCabe spends weeks in the hospital recovering. Her only entertainment is verbal sparring matches with Dr. Nora Whitmore, the talented and reclusive surgeon. Two very different women living in two different worlds. When the lines between them begin to blur, will they run from the possibilities or embrace the changes they bring to each other's lives?

COMING FROM YLVA PUBLISHING

www.ylva-publishing.com

Four Steps

Wendy Hudson

Alex Ryan lives a simple life. She has her farm in the Scottish countryside, and the self imposed seclusion suits her, until a crime that has haunted her for years, tears through the calm and shatters the fragile peace she'd finally managed to find.

Lori Hunter's greatest love is the mountains. They're her escape from the constant hustle and bustle of everyday life. Growing up was neither traditional nor easy for Lori, but now she's beginning to realise she's settled for both. A dead end relationship and little to look forward to. Her solution when the suffocation sets in? Run for the hills.

A chance encounter in the mountains of the Scottish Highlands leads Alex and Lori into a whirlwind of heartache and a fight for survival as they build a formidable bond that will be tested to its ultimate limits.

The Lavender List

Meg Harrington

After the Second World War, Amelia Maldonado opts to live a quiet life bussing tables at a diner during the day and going out for auditions at night. The one bright spot is her friendship with the charming Laura Wright, a well-heeled woman with a mysterious war-related past.

When Laura shows up outside the diner barely conscious and spitting lousy lies, Amelia takes it upon herself to figure out the truth. From mobsters to spies, Amelia quickly finds herself forced back into a world of shadows she thought she'd escaped long ago and thrust into partnership with the one person she's sure can ruin her—the enigmatic Laura Wright.

Requiem for Immortals
© 2016 by Lee Winter

ISBN: 978-3-95533-710-0

Also available as e-book.

Published by Ylva Publishing, legal entity of Ylva Verlag, e.Kfr.

Ylva Verlag, e.Kfr.
Owner: Astrid Ohletz
Am Kirschgarten 2
65830 Kriftel
Germany

www.ylva-publishing.com

First edition: 2016

Credits
Edited by Jove Belle
Cover Design by Adam Lloyd
Vector Design by Freepik.com

CPSIA information can be obtained
at www.ICGtesting.com
Printed in the USA
LVOW08s0019200317
527767LV00001B/103/P